By W. Michael Gear and Kathleen O'Neal Gear
from Tom Doherty Associates

NORTH AMERICA'S
FORGOTTEN PAST SERIES

People of the Wolf
People of the Fire
People of the Earth
People of the River
People of the Sea
People of the Lakes
People of the Lightning
People of the Silence
People of the Mist
People of the Masks
People of the Owl
People of the Raven
People of the Moon
People of the Nightland
People of the Weeping Eye
People of the Thunder
People of the Longhouse
The Dawn Country
*The Broken Land**

THE ANASAZI MYSTERY
SERIES

The Visitant
The Summoning God
Bone Walker

BY KATHLEEN O'NEAL
GEAR

Thin Moon and Cold Mist
Sand in the Wind
This Widowed Land
It Sleeps in Me
It Wakes in Me
It Dreams in Me

BY W. MICHAEL GEAR

Long Ride Home
Big Horn Legacy
Coyote Summer
The Athena Factor
The Morning River

OTHER TITLES BY
KATHLEEN O'NEAL GEAR
AND W. MICHAEL GEAR

The Betrayal
Dark Inheritance
Raising Abel
Children of the Dawnland

www.Gear-Gear.com

*Forthcoming

PEOPLE *of the* LONGHOUSE

W. MICHAEL GEAR AND KATHLEEN O'NEAL GEAR

TOR®

A TOM DOHERTY ASSOCIATES BOOK
NEW YORK

This is a work of fiction. All of the characters, organizations, and events portrayed in this novel are either products of the authors' imaginations or are used fictitiously.

PEOPLE OF THE LONGHOUSE

Copyright © 2010 by W. Michael Gear and Kathleen O'Neal Gear

All rights reserved.

Maps and illustrations by Ellisa Mitchell

A Tor Book
Published by Tom Doherty Associates, LLC
175 Fifth Avenue
New York, NY 10010

www.tor-forge.com

Tor® is a registered trademark of Tom Doherty Associates, LLC.

ISBN 978-0-7653-5979-7

First Edition: July 2010
First Mass Market Edition: February 2011

Printed in the United States of America

0 9 8 7 6 5 4 3 2 1

To Tim, Maria, Brandon, and Connor O'Neal,
for the sacrifices you made while caring for our mother
in her last difficult years. No one could have been kinder,
or taken better care of her. We know it wasn't easy.
You'll always have a special place in our hearts.

Acknowledgments

We couldn't write the PEOPLE series without the dedication and hard work of our archaeological colleagues, many of whom have spent their lives trying to understand the prehistory of this continent. In writing this book, we relied heavily upon the work of Bruce Trigger, Dean Snow, James Tuck, Elisabeth Tooker, William Ritchie, Christina Rieth, John Hart, Mary Ann Levine, Kenneth Sassaman, Michael Nassaney, and Paul Wallace. We are especially grateful to Dr. David Dye, University of Memphis, for his work on prehistoric war and peace movements in the eastern United States.

In addition, the detailed analysis by Barbara Mann and Jerry Fields with regard to dating the founding of the League was very informative. Their article can be found at www.wampumchronicles.com/signinthesky .html; it contains a thorough discussion of the historical record and Iroquoian oral history, and provides an excellent cultural context for dating the famed eclipse.

Lastly, we would like to offer our sincere thanks to Catherine Crumpler, and the Hot Springs County Counseling Center in Thermopolis, Wyoming, for their help in understanding the psychological responses of children undergoing extreme stress. Those lengthy discussions were not wasted, Catherine. Thanks for sharing your expertise.

B.C.

13,000	10,000	6,000	3,000	1,500

PEOPLE *of the* WOLF
Alaska & Canadian
Northwest

PEOPLE *of the* EARTH
Northern Plains & Basins

PEOPLE *of the* NIGHTLAND
Ontario & New York &
Pennsylvania

PEOPLE *of*
the OWL
Lower
Mississippi
Valley

PEOPLE *of the* SEA
Pacific Coast & Arizona

PEOPLE *of the* RAVEN
Pacific Northwest &
British Columbia

PEOPLE *of the* LIGHTNING
Florida

PEOPLE *of the* FIRE
Central Rockies &
Great Plains

A.D.

| 0 | 200 | 1,000 | 1,100 | 1,300 | 1,400 |

PEOPLE *of the* LAKES
East-Central Woodlands
& Great Lakes

PEOPLE *of the*
WEEPING EYE
Mississippi Valley
& Tennessee

PEOPLE *of the* MASKS
Ontario & Upstate New York

PEOPLE *of the*
THUNDER
Alabama & Mississippi

PEOPLE *of the* RIVER
Mississippi Valley

PEOPLE *of the*
LONGHOUSE
New York
& New England

PEOPLE *of the* SILENCE
Southwest Anasazi

PEOPLE *of the* MOON
Northwest New Mexico
& Southwest Colorado

PEOPLE *of the* MIST
Chesapeake Bay

Skanodario Lake

Canassatego Village ○

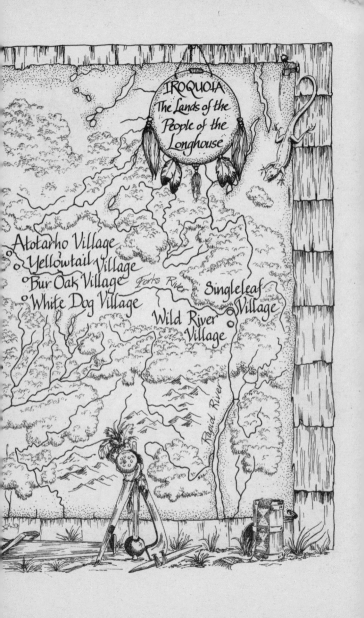

IROQUOIA
The Lands of the
People of the
Longhouse

Atotarho Village
Yellowtail Village
Bur Oak Village
White Dog Village
Singleleaf Village
Wild River Village
Forks River
Rapid River

The Lands of the People of the Dawnland

Forks River

Singleleaf Village

Hawk Moth Village

Bog Willow Village

Wild River Village

Pine Hill Village

IROQUOIA

Rapid River

Quill River

Quill River

Nonfiction Introduction

The origins of Northern Iroquoians is a hotly debated and very complex topic among archaeologists, but generally we agree that the period from roughly AD 1000–1300 demonstrates fluid and shifting alliances, expanding trade networks, and changing settlement patterns. One thing is for certain: Early Iroquoian cultures were remarkably adaptable and diverse.

Most archaeologists divide Iroquoian culture into three periods: The Early Iroquoian period from AD 1000–1300, the Middle Iroquoian period from AD 1300–1350, and Late Iroquoian from AD 1350 to European contact. For the purposes of this introduction, the Early Iroquoian period is particularly important. Not because it was the apogee of the culture—it wasn't—but because something dramatic happened. At around AD 1000, most Iroquoian peoples lived in small fishing villages or farming hamlets, primarily along rivers where they had good fertile soils and easy access to water. Toward the end of this period, they began moving away from watercourses and started building their villages atop easily defensible hilltops. Some were palisaded—for example, the Bates site in Chenango County and the Sackett site near Canandaigua, New York, both of which date to the thirteenth century.

It is also likely that during the Early period Iroquoian

societies changed from being patrilineal and patrilo-cal—meaning they traced descent through the male, and women came to live with their husband's family—to being matrilineal and matrilocal, in which they traced descent through the female and after marriage a man moved in with his wife's family.

During the thirteenth and fourteenth centuries, the size of Iroquois villages began to grow. Archaeologists call this "population aggregation," meaning that more and more people were crowding together within the palisaded walls of villages. We see these expanded long-houses at places like the Furnace Brook and Howlett Hill sites in New York, where archaeologists excavated houses that were 210 and 334 feet long. This Middle Iroquoian period also saw the people becoming in-creasingly dependent upon maize-bean-squash agricul-ture. As in historic times, men probably cleared the fields, built the houses, and hunted, while women were the farmers. They cultivated the soil, planted, tended the fields, harvested and stored the crops. When women began to account for more and more of the food, their lineages also probably became the dominant social av-enue for prestige.

At around AD 1400, the first evidence for individ-ual tribes appears. Differences in pottery styles, burial customs, and types of houses demonstrate divisions be-tween Iroquoian groups. As well, small villages begin to amalgamate with larger ones, forming cohesive so-cial groups, or, we suspect, nations.

AD 1400 is also the time when the Iroquois were building the most impressive longhouses, and many were elaborately fortified. At the Schoff site outside Onondaga, New York, the people constructed a longhouse 400 feet long, 22 feet wide, and nearly as tall. The palisaded settlement may have housed 1,500 to 2,000 people, consisting of many different clans.

As those of you who've read our previous books know, often this type of aggregation is a telltale sign for archaeologists of interpersonal violence. Simply put, people crowd together for defensive purposes. This is also when cannibalism first appears in the Iroquoian archaeological record in the form of cut and cooked human bones.

People of the Longhouse takes place at this critical moment in time.

Why did warfare break out? The fact that the climate had grown cooler and drier certainly contributed to the violence. We know that droughts were more frequent, growing seasons shorter, and food shortages probably more common. As well, larger villages deplete resources at a faster rate. Game populations, nut forests, firewood, and fertile soils would all have played out more quickly, which means they must have had to move their villages more often. Moving may have brought them into conflict with neighbors who needed the food resources just as desperately.

The warfare, we know, was violent.

At the Alhart site in the Oak Orchard Creek drainage in western New York, archaeologists found evidence of burned longhouses and food, and the dismembered remains of seventeen people—most of them male. Historically, it was common practice for women and children to either be killed on site, or taken captive and marched away while the male warriors were tortured and killed. At this site, the fragments of a child's skull were found in one storage pit, and the skull of a woman in another storage pit. As well, fifteen male skulls were found in a storage pit on top of charred corn, and were probably placed there as severed heads, in the flesh. Some of them were burned. Two had suffered blows to the front of the head.

At the Draper site northeast of Toronto, fourteen burials date to this period. One burial, an old man, was missing both arms and his shoulder blades. A chert arrow point was embedded in his right hip bone (the femoral neck). There was also evidence that he had been speared in the chest, and scalped. As well, he had sustained a severe blow to the left side of his head, and showed cut marks from having been dismembered. Dismembering the enemy was historically a method of stopping the soul from taking revenge upon its killers; dismemberment apparently immobilized the angry spirit of the dead.

The Van Oordt site, a late fourteenth- to early fifteenth-century site near Kitchener, Ontario, revealed thirteen burials. One had fragments of three arrow points embedded in his bones. He also showed signs of numerous puncture wounds; which means he was stabbed several times. Then both of his arms were severed, and he was beheaded.

At the Cameron site near Lima, New York, a young male burial was discovered. He'd been burned, and showed signs of having been stabbed and scalped. Afterward, his skull was broken open, probably to extract the brain. The interesting thing here is that this young man was buried in the village cemetery, not in a refuse midden. This may mean that his body was found by his relatives and brought home for proper burial.

As well, artifacts made from human bone are plentiful on Northern Iroquoian sites that date from the late fourteenth through the early sixteenth centuries. For example, two skulls were found at the Parsons site in Toronto. The Parsons site was an elaborately palisaded fifteenth-century village. The two skulls, one male and one female, were found in a trash pit inside the inner palisade. Many other human bone artifacts are found in similar "refuse" situations. Human skull pendants or rattles are found across Ontario and New York at the Moatfield, Winking Bull, Uren, Pound, Crawford Lake, Jarrett-Lahmer, Draper, Keffer, Lawson, Campbell, Clearview, Parsons, Beeton, Roebuck, Lite, Salem, and Glenbrook sites. Often the skulls, or skull fragments, have cut marks made by stone tools that are suggestive of scalping. (As you already know from earlier paragraphs, scalping was not a French custom brought to the New World and adopted by the tribes; it existed long before Europeans arrived.) Such skulls were found at the Draper, Keffer, and Lawson sites. Ground and polished fibulas and femurs (leg bones), as well as arm bones (radii) were used for beads and scraping tools. Pierced mandibles (jaws), and finger and toe bones were used as pendants. Ulnae (arm bones) became awls or daggers, and were also strung as beads. Why is it important to archaeologists that all these artifacts were found in trash middens? Because Iroquoian peoples took very good care of their dead relatives. They had lengthy and beautiful burial rituals to make certain their loved ones reached the Land of the Dead. Since these human remains were not properly cared for, it suggests the bones may have come from less valuable members of society, like enemy captives.

Let's take a few moments to discuss the Iroquoian perspective on captives. By the 1400s, as it was in historic times, warfare and raiding for captives was probably the most important method of gaining prestige in Northern Iroquoian societies. When a person died, the spiritual power of the clan was diminished, especially if that person had been a community leader. The places of missing family members literally remained vacant until they could be "replaced," and their spiritual power—which was embodied in their name—transferred to another person.

Historical records tell us that during the 1600s, the Iroquois dispatched war parties whose sole intent was to bring home captives to replace family members and restore the spiritual strength of the clans. These were called "mourning wars." Clan matrons usually organized the war parties and ordered their warriors to bring them captives suitable for adoption to assuage their grief and restock the village. Once the clan had a suitable replacement, the captive underwent the Requickening Ceremony. In this ritual, the dead person's soul was "raised up" and transferred to the captive, along with his or her name.

This may seem odd to modern readers, but keep the religious context in mind. The Iroquois believed that the souls of those who died violently could not find the Path of Souls in the sky that led to the Land of the Dead. They were excluded from the afterlife and doomed to spend eternity wandering the earth, seeking revenge. However, such souls could find rest if they were transferred—along with their name—to the body of another person. In a very concrete way, the relatives of the dead person were trying to save him.

The souls of men and women killed in battles that were not "raised up" were believed, according to some Seneca traditions, to move into trees. It was these trees with indwelling warrior spirits that the People cut to serve as palisade logs, thereby surrounding the village with Standing Warriors.

Who was fighting? We're fairly sure the warfare was between neighbors, not marauding armies seeking out distant enemies. Why? Archaeologists do craniometric analyses (measurements of skulls) and compare them with other populations to determine their differences or similarities, which indicate probable genetic relationships. In 1998 Dupras and Pratte conducted a detailed study of skulls from the Parsons site and compared them with four other groups, two local (from the nearby Kleinberg and Uxbridge sites) and two more distant groups (Roebuck and Broughton Hill sites in New York). The similarities in the skulls suggest that they came from local populations and probably represented "trophy" heads. Which means they weren't fighting invading strangers—they knew each other.

Iroquoian oral history speaks of this as a particularly brutal time, and clearly the archaeological record supports their stories.

But the violence was also the catalyst for one of the most important events in the history of the world. It led to the rise of a legendary hero, a Peacemaker named Dekanawida, who established the Great Law of Peace and founded the League of the Iroquois—a confederacy of five tribes: the Onondaga, Oneida, Mohawk, Cayuga, and Seneca.

Without the League, the United States would not exist today, nor would our unique understanding of democracy. Concepts like one-person/one-vote or referendum and recall were not European. They were Iroquoian.

And they would prove to be irresistible to the wave of colonists fleeing oppression in Europe.

In 1775, James Adair wrote a book called *History of the American Indian,* in which he described the Iroquoian system of government by saying, "Their whole constitution breathes nothing but liberty . . . [T]here is equality of condition, manners, and privileges. . . ."

Indeed, the system of government espoused by the League was everything that European monarchies were not. The Iroquois refused to put power in the hands of any single person, lest that power be abused. The League sought to maximize individual freedoms and minimize governmental interference in people's lives. The League taught that a system of government should preserve individual rights while striving to ensure the public welfare; it should reward initiative, champion tolerance, and establish inalienable human rights. They accepted as fact that men and women were equal and respected the diversity of peoples, their religions, economic and political ideals, their dreams.

Thomas Jefferson wrote, "There is an error into which most of the speculators on government have fallen, and which the well-known state of society of our Indians ought, before now, to have corrected. In their hypothesis of the origin of government, they suppose it to have commenced in the patriarchial or monarchial form . . . (Indian) leaders influence them by their character alone . . . every man, with them, is perfectly free to follow his own inclinations. But if, in doing this, he violates the rights of another . . . he is punished by the disesteem of society, or . . . if serious, he is tomahawked as a serious enemy."

On the eve of the American Revolution in 1776, English papers began circulating the following account, which was, incidentally, meant to be insulting: "The darling passion of the American is liberty, and that in its fullest extent; nor is it the original natives only to whom this passion is confined; our colonists sent thither seem to have imbibed the same principles."

Indeed, they had.

Gifted writers like Thomas Jefferson and Benjamin Franklin would openly fan the flames of that "passion" for liberty, and set in motion a chain reaction that has yet to end. That passion would become a sweeping wildfire that would race around the globe and shape the very heart of what would, centuries later, become known as the Free World.

Dekanawida, quite simply, changed the course of history.

We can only imagine the terrifying forces that might have hardened his resolve. . . .

PEOPLE *of the*
LONGHOUSE

One

The call still echoed from the depths of the trees.

It made Sky Messenger push onward, down the leaf-strewn trail and into the dark filigree of shadows where glinting eyes watched him from the branches. Night was falling. Soon the owls would lift into the air and vanish like smoke on a windy day, but for now their gazes fixed on the strange old man with the limp.

He cocked his head, listening. The call was growing fainter. Sky Messenger propped his walking stick and continued on down the trail.

He'd first heard the Voice when he'd seen eleven summers. Since that time, the great unrest came upon him every Moon of Falling Leaves. He would be sleeping warmly beneath his hides, his soul walking through springtime meadows with his Ancestors, when suddenly his eyes would jerk open, and he would sit up in bed. It always began as a low keening. When he heard it, he would jump to his feet and dash out into the cold darkness. On and on he would run, as fast as his bad legs would carry him, away from the village and down the forest trails where bears and wolves prowled.

Four nights ago, he'd leaped from his hides, breathing as though slapped awake, and known the caller was close. The hair at the nape of his neck had stood on end. From far out in the trees, the Voice came, clear and crisp, more real than ever before—*Odion . . . Odion.* He'd thrown on his cape, for his old body needed it these days, and rushed outside into the icy woods. It was unlike any human voice he'd ever heard, composed of many notes, like an eerie song. And he knew it, knew the speaker, in the depths of his heart, as he had never known another human being.

Sometimes he pursued the Voice all moon long, looking for it as though it were real. Speaking gently or shouting in desperation, he would limp along the trails like a madman. He used his crooked walking stick to probe beneath fallen logs, or stab into holes in the forest floor where supernatural creatures lived; or he would crouch in the underbrush for days, his eyes wide, sniffing the wind for that otherworldly scent he knew would someday be there. Listening. Always listening for that mysterious voice that called him by name, filling him with wild desires and a vague sweet gladness.

His obsession frightened his children and grandchildren. His clan had begun to say that he was insane, that he was chasing his own afterlife soul that had wandered away into the forest and become lost. None of that mattered. He *knew* he had to find the caller and look him in the eyes.

Sky Messenger stopped to take a breath and looked up into the overarching branches of a hickory tree. He especially enjoyed these rare autumn evenings when he could stand beneath the trees and hear them snapping and cracking as the night cooled.

The Voice faded.

Sky Messenger propped his walking stick and held his breath, listening. In the moonlight, the snow-coated trees had a bluish gleam that seemed to radiate outward into the air, turning it liquid and faintly silver. Deep autumn leaves rustled around his moccasins as he cupped a hand to his mouth and called, "Where are you?"

He searched the forest until he spied movement among the shadows. Concentrating, he thought he saw a black silhouette, standing tall and straight, its arms open to the night sky. Heat flushed his face. Was it real? Was it a . . . a man? Or did it have wings? Black wings that sleeked down its back? Or perhaps the hump was just a bulky Trader's pack?

He slowly moved toward it. He was afraid of falling. His old bones had grown brittle, and he knew that a simple broken arm might kill him. As he sneaked closer, the Voice lowered its arms and turned toward him.

Odion. Are you coming?

For the first time since he'd seen eleven summers he was looking into the dark holes of its eyes. Terror made his hands tremble.

"Th-that was my childhood name. They call me Sky Messenger now."

Hunched over, he limped toward the Forest Spirit, his ancient body aching. Every step was at once a threat and a gesture of love and need. The Voice seemed to sense it. Like all predators, they feared each other. It cocked its head, and its eyes caught the starlight and shimmered as though dusted with quartz crystals.

A fleeting instant later, it dashed out into the trees with twigs cracking in its wake.

"No, wait! Come back!"

Sky Messenger stumbled after it, thrashing wildly through the brush, trying to catch up. He chased it straight into a meadow where the starlight reflected so brilliantly from the snow that the Voice's dark silhouette seemed to be floating above the ground.

"What do you want? Why do you keep calling me? You've been calling me for sixty-five summers."

The creature growled like a cornered wolf, its arms extended as though preparing to take flight.

In a motion as old as predators themselves, Sky Messenger took a step backward, yielding the moment to his opponent, and slowly began to circle around the tree-lined edge of the meadow. He poked at rocks with his walking stick, and sniffed damp tree bark, precisely like the demented old man people claimed him to be. The Spirit kept cocking its head, watching curiously, and after a time it quieted and lowered its arms. But its quartz-dust eyes remained focused on Sky Messenger, charting his methodical progress around the meadow.

It stunned him that the Spirit seemed suspicious and afraid. What could an old man do to harm a Spirit? Then again, maybe it wasn't harm the Spirit feared. Perhaps it was just the way of the chase. Run and feint. Let your prey catch up, then whirl around and snap at it, keep it at bay until the final moment. The final lunge for the throat.

Sky Messenger saw his chance and dashed out into the meadow, heading directly for the Voice . . . and the chase resumed.

Time and again he cornered the creature and tried to force it to answer his questions before it darted away. He stumbled after it in some incomprehensible ancient dance. Was it just a man? Sometimes he thought so. But why would a strong young man let Sky Messenger catch him? The Voice ran until Sky Messenger was right on its heels; then it whirled around snarling. He would never have caught the Voice if it did not wish to be caught. Surely this was some Spirit game.

He halted, breathing hard, and let his gaze drift over the brush and trees.

I'm here, Odion.

He saw it. The Voice stood just ahead, hidden behind a frost-covered dogwood. Its eyes gleamed through the dark weave of branches.

Come. . . . Follow me.

It trotted away, repeatedly looking back over its shoulder, as if to make certain he was still behind; then it disappeared into the forest.

Sky Messenger worked his way down a winding forest trail dappled with snow and frost-rimmed leaves, simultaneously fearing and eager for what he would next see.

"Where are you?" he called. "I've lost you."

From the dark depths of the forest came the call—a long drawn-out wail, his name in the voice of a wolf, howled with chilling effect.

Sky Messenger's bony fingers tightened around the

knob of his walking stick. He was close now. Very close, and he dared not be afraid of what would come. He swallowed hard and limped forward.

On the other side of a birch copse, the trail sloped upward to a high point overlooking a hilly country filled with great stretches of forests and shining creeks.

Odion.

There. On the trail below.

The Voice let him get to within thirty paces, and started slowly walking away.

Through endless towering trees, Sky Messenger followed, step after step, always twenty paces behind, until Elder Brother Sun rose red over the eastern horizon. As the air warmed, an exotic flowery fragrance wafted around him. His nostrils quivered. He took a deep breath, filling his lungs with the otherworldly sweetness, and his old heart began to slam against his ribs. *That scent!*

In the distance, he saw flocks of birds gathered over a bridge, fluttering, waiting. All along the planks of the bridge, mice darted, their furred backs shining in the newborn light. There were other animals, too. A white-tailed doe, and a lean young wolf.

At the sight of the wolf, tears traced warm lines down Sky Messenger's wrinkled cheeks. He had been running from this moment his entire life. He whispered, "Hello, old friend."

The Voice stopped dead in the trail and let him advance to stand at its side. Sky Messenger shivered. He understood now.

He was answering the last call, walking at the side

of the only brother who truly mattered. The brother who had always been there, as unobtrusive as his own shadow, watching over him, fighting at his side on the darkest days.

"You can tell me now," he said, and took a breath to prepare himself. "What is your name?"

The Voice hissed, the sound like a truce being broken by an arrow, and he thought he made out the word *Sonon*.

"Sonon?"

Yes, do you remember me, Odion?

Ancient memories flooded up from behind doors buried deep in his heart, doors Sky Messenger had kept barricaded for sixty-five summers. Behind them monsters still lived and breathed.

He shook his head and stumbled backward. "No. No, I—I can't—!"

Remember, Odion. You must remember now. It's time.

All of the doors he had so carefully guarded vanished, and a sea of ghostly eyes started coming toward him.

Shuddering, Sky Messenger sank down in the trail and squeezed his eyes closed. As the monsters surrounded him, terror swept him back in time to that long-ago day when this journey had truly started. . . .

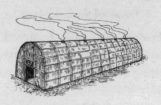

Two

Odion

The patter of rain falling through branches fills the forest and mixes eerily with the laughter of warriors. The sound of children's feet wading through deep autumn leaves is loud.

I dare to glance up. The storm has sucked the color from the trees. The giant oak trunks look black, their branches iron-gray. We are not on a trail, but march through scrubby underbrush. Ahead of me, one boy and four girls walk with their heads down. Some weep softly, but mostly they are as silent as the dead relatives they left behind in their burned villages.

As the enemy warriors herd us up a steep mountain trail, I see a small clearing ahead. Patches of sunlight penetrate the dark clouds and briefly blaze through the brilliant maples and hickory trees. They seem almost too bright. Painful. I squint and force my legs to keep walking until the clouds swallow Elder Brother Sun again.

I am young, eleven summers, and not yet a man. For as long as I can recall, I have feared that this day would come. Warfare rages throughout our country. Many villages have been attacked, and women and children taken as slaves. Now that I am one of them, I feel like a duck hit in the head with a rock—too numb to think.

When we enter the clearing, four white-tailed deer bound away, and I watch them with my heart racing. They are free . . . as I was yesterday.

The girl in line ahead of me stumbles. The warriors curse her as she regains her balance. Her name is Agres. She wears a beautiful white doehide dress. She arrived last night, and carries an infant in her arms. We all assume the baby is her sister.

I stare at the holes in the soles of the infant's moccasins.

My People, the People of the Standing Stone, have a saying: *An infant's life is as the thinness of a maple leaf.* We believe that each person has two souls: a soul that stays with the body forever, and an afterlife soul that travels to the Land of the Dead. Babies are just barely separated from the Spirit world, and vulnerable to being stolen back by unseen ghosts who follow their mothers. The holes tell the ghosts to stay back, that this child's souls have been claimed by the living.

"Agres should throw away those moccasins," I whisper.

If ghosts take the baby's souls, she will be reborn in a new body and won't have to face what lies ahead for the rest of us.

My eight-summers-old sister, Tutelo, tightens her grip on my hand and looks up. "What, Odion? What did you say?"

Tutelo has a pretty oval face with bright brown eyes. A long black braid hangs down the back of her tan dress. Tiny circlets of copper decorate her sleeves and hem.

"Nothing," I answer, and squeeze her small hand. "Don't talk, Tutelo. You know it causes troub—"

One of the Mountain People warriors—the one I have named Broken Teeth because of the jagged yellow teeth that fill his mouth—glares at me. I quickly look away.

Four warriors guard us. Each carries a bow and has a quiver filled with arrows slung over his left shoulder. War clubs and stone knives hang from their belts. Big Man, the one in charge, really scares me. He has a heavily scarred face, and every time he looks back at the line of children, his jaw clenches with hate.

Tutelo whispers, "Where's Mother?"

"Shh."

Tutelo has been asking the same question since midnight. Our mother is War Chief Koracoo. Yesterday morning, Mother led half of our warriors into the forests to scout for the enemy. Father, her deputy, was in charge of defending our village. The attack came at dusk; it was swift and brutal. The People of the Mountain brought three times as many warriors to the fight. Yellowtail Village didn't have a chance.

I remember little of it . . . Father dragging us out of our beds and ordering us to run . . . longhouses burning . . . screaming people racing through the firelit darkness . . . dead bodies. Then standing in the forest, clutching Tutelo's hand, stunned, as enemy warriors rounded us up and marched us away as slaves. I must have more memories—somewhere inside me—but I cannot find them.

I don't know if Mother and Father are alive, but I keep praying they are. If they survived, they are tracking us, coming for us.

Big Man holds up a hand. We all stop, and out in the

forest I hear people moving. I search the shadows and see them weaving among the smoke-colored trunks. One warrior emerges, shoving three girls in front of him. All are beautiful, and have seen perhaps twelve or thirteen summers. The new warrior forces them to join our group.

No one speaks. We just stare at each other in fear and disbelief. The same thing happened last night. That's when Agres and her sister arrived. Big Man has made four stops so far. The red quill patterns on the new girls' capes mark them as Flint People. Was their village also attacked?

Mother says the warfare must stop. She hates it. Father calls her a "peacemaker," and it always sounds like an insult.

Big Man studies the girls carefully, walking around them several times before he nods and hands over a heavy hide sack to the man who brought the girls. The man shakes it, smiles, and disappears into the trees like mist vanishing on a warm day.

They did not say a word. Have they made this kind of exchange so often they do not need to speak?

Big Man lifts his hand again, and we march, heading east through the sun-dappled forest.

"Where's Mother?"

"Stop asking, Tutelo!"

Tears fill my sister's eyes, but she knows better than to cry out loud. We have each taken a beating for crying. Instead, Tutelo clutches my hand in a death grip and sobs without a sound. My souls shrivel.

I lean down to whisper, "She's coming, Tutelo, but we have to stop talking about it, or the bad men will hear us.

You don't want them to know Mother's coming, do you? If they know she's coming, they will ambush her. We must be quiet."

Tutelo looks up with big, tear-filled eyes. In sudden understanding, she whispers, "All right."

As we march deeper into the trees, the scents of rotting wood and damp autumn leaves fill the air. I take a deep breath and let it out slowly.

I keep praying that Big Man told us the truth: We will all be adopted into new families. We will have lots to eat, and though the work will be hard, our new families will come to love us. In time, Big Man says, we will forget our Standing Stone families and be happy in the Mountain People's villages. I will become a great hunter, and Tutelo will marry a good man and give the nation healthy sons and daughters.

Usually, that's how it works. I have seen many children, taken in warfare, brought to Yellowtail Village and adopted into families. Each is miserable at first, but within a few summers he or she seems genuinely happy. I myself was captured in a war raid. Father says I had seen six or seven moons. He pulled me from the burning wreckage of a long-house and carried me home to Yellowtail Village. I know no other home, and I love my adopted parents with all my heart. Mother says that no people can create an empire, they must *become* one, and the best way to do that is to adopt conquered peoples into Standing Stone families and educate them as their own children, without distinction.

Unfortunately, I am beginning to think that Big Man's promises of happiness are worthless.

These are not ordinary warriors. Even I can see that.

They wear no clan sashes, and have no visible tattoos. In fact, I can spot places where they have cut off tattoos, or obliterated them. They never call each other by name, which makes me think they are afraid that one of us will later speak that name in the wrong company.

Broken Teeth trots toward Agres and her sister. All morning long his eyes have sought out Agres, and I do not like the way he looks at her. Agres wears beautiful polished copper earspools, and shell bracelets that click when she walks. She turns away and tries not to notice Broken Teeth's attention. Instead, she occupies herself with caring for her infant sister. The hungry baby mews constantly. Though Agres keeps placing a wet twist of hide in the infant's mouth to suck on, the baby just spits it out, wails, and tugs at Agres' long hair with frantic hands. None of us has had anything to eat, and water only eases the cramps for so long.

As we walk, the endless mountains pass by. In the afternoon, we enter a stand of enormous oaks. Big Man forces us to climb over bare exposed rock. Stones are the bones of Great Grandmother Earth, and like the bones of animals, they are alive. They deserve to be treated with respect. I try to walk gently.

I push Tutelo in front of me where I can watch her. Just ahead of her walks Wrass. He has also seen eleven summers, but he's four moons older than I am—maybe the oldest boy here—and he's brave. My father says that Wrass is destined to be a great warrior. Tall for his age, he has a face like an eagle's, with sharp dark eyes and a hooked nose. Wrass can track better and shoot farther than any other boy in our village. I have always been jealous of Wrass.

As the war chief's only son, much is expected of me, but I have always been afraid. I am the boy who runs when the bear approaches. The boy who hurries home when darkness falls. And I've never been very good with a bow. Not like Wrass, who can shoot a bird out of the sky at fifty paces. For the first time in my life, I am grateful for his skills. My deepest hope is that he is waiting his chance to grab a war club and start a fight that will allow a few of us to escape.

When he turns his head, and I see his profile, my hopes evaporate.

Wrass looks as lost and terrified as the rest of us. Every time one of the warriors glares at him, Wrass starts shaking.

Sunlight pierces the rain clouds and slants across the forest, casting geometric patterns upon the rocks. I let my head fall forward to stare at them, and my shoulder-length black hair hangs over the front of my buckskin shirt. Some of the children have capes, but Tutelo and I scrambled from our beds so fast we didn't have the chance to grab ours. Last night, when Big Man let us sleep for two hands of time, I curled my body around Tutelo to keep her warm, and dreamed of Mother leading a war party into the camp and killing Big Man and all of his warriors.

If I live to see one thousand summers, that dream will still be the best of my life.

Big Man leads us off the rocks and down a steep trail into a small clearing where he calls, "Make the children sit down."

Two warriors trot down the line swinging war clubs, forcing us to drop to the damp oak leaves. Tutelo tucks her hand into mine. Her fingers are icy cold. I lift them to blow on them, and she shivers at the sudden warmth.

"We're going to be all right. Just be quiet, Tutelo."

"Where's . . . ?" She stops herself from asking, and I clutch her hand and nod.

Only when I start looking around do I see that this small clearing has been used before. Holes have been scooped out of the leaves, as though many children slept here and covered themselves with the leaves for warmth. Fragments of a broken clay cup scatter the ground to my left. Beneath a fallen log, I see the top half of a girl's cornhusk doll.

Has Big Man brought other captive children here? Why?

Big Man gathers his warriors around him, and they whisper to each other, but I can't make out any of their words.

I look at the leaves, and my thoughts turn to those other children. I swear I can smell their last moments here. Fear sweat drifts on the air, and I pick up the faint coppery odor of blood. *What happened to you?*

Wrass seems to smell these things, as well. He lifts his hooked nose, scents the wind, and his mouth tightens.

Tutelo bites her lip, looks back and forth between us, and asks, "Where's Mother?"

The words are like spear thrusts to my belly. "Coming," I whisper. "She's coming."

"When?"

"Soon. She and Father are tracking us. It will take some time."

Tutelo heaves a deep sigh and leans her head against my shoulder.

At the head of the group, the three new girls start talking to each other.

Big Man says, "Quiet."

One of the girls says a last word to her friend, and Big Man shouts, "I said, *quiet!*"

Two of the girls sit as if frozen, staring wide-eyed at him, but the talkative girl says, "I just wanted to finish—"

Big Man stalks toward her, and the expression on his face makes my blood go cold. The blow is swift and fierce. The girl shrieks and topples backward. When she rolls onto her side, blood pours from her mouth and spatters the bright autumn leaves.

Big Man glares at the rest of us. "Do you understand now? See what happens if you make me angry? If you do not obey me instantly? Be *quiet!*"

The only sounds are the wind through the trees and the soft sobbing of the baby.

We seem to sit forever, staring at each other, staring at our captors. I am certain that every child is thinking the same thing I am: *Someone is coming for us. That's why we're here. This is a meeting place. Who is coming?*

In less than one hand of time, nine strangers appear. They are like ghosts floating out of the forest. One is a boy about my age. Seven of them are lean, hungry men with mean eyes. The tallest man moves like a gangly stork and carries a heavy hide pack slung over his shoulder. The last person is a woman. She is old, maybe forty summers. Graying black hair hangs in greasy twists around her wrinkled face, and her eyes . . . her eyes are black bottomless pits. She seems to have no souls. Her toothless mouth is puckered and hard, and her nose resembles a sun-withered plum. When she speaks it is as though sandstone boulders are rubbing together. Each word is a scratchy blow: "Get them up. Let me look at them."

"Get up," Big Man orders. "All of you. Stand up. The great Gannajero wants to see you."

We stand. All of us are trembling. I have never heard of Gannajero, but it terrifies me that Big Man does not care if I know her name. It is as though he believes she is so powerful nothing can harm her.

Gannajero drags over the boy who came with her, shoves him into our group, then slowly walks down the line, scowling at each of us. When she looks at me, my legs go weak. Evil lives in her eyes. I can feel it coiling around my heart, squeezing the life from it. I can't breathe. When she moves on to the next child, I stagger and lock my knees to keep standing.

Wrass tries to be brave. He has his jaw clenched and stares back at her without blinking. This makes Gannajero smile at him. It is not a pleasant smile, but a promise of pain to come.

Crows squawk, and Gannajero looks up to watch them soar through the sky. It is a small flock, ten or twelve jet-black birds. In a hoarse voice, she cries, "*Caw! Caw, caw!*" The crows seem startled. As though curious, many of them cock their heads and begin to circle above her, angling their wings, watching, *thocking* inquisitively to each other.

Gannajero's mouth opens in a toothless smile, and she says, "Are any of you children related?"

The oldest of the three Flint girls answers, "We are sisters."

Agres says, "So are we."

I hesitate, not sure whether I should give her this information. Before I can respond, Tutelo says, "We are brother and sister."

Gannajero turns to Big Man and points at Agres. "Why did you bring that one? What use do I have for an infant?"

Big Man gestures awkwardly. "The girl refused to leave it. I thought it was easier to let her keep it for a while."

Agres' face goes white. She clutches her sister more tightly to her chest. Her gaze darts from Big Man to Gannajero. The terrible truth is dawning, but she doesn't believe it yet.

None of us do.

Gannajero walks back toward her warriors. As she passes Big Man, she says, "The baby is yours. I will take the others. Kotin, pay him."

The gangly warrior unslings his heavy pack, walks forward, and hands it to Big Man.

Big Man places the pack on the ground. When he opens it, awed whispers filter through the gathering. The pack is filled with exquisite strings of pearls, pounded sheets of copper, etched shell gorgets, and many things I cannot see. Enough wealth to ransom a village. Big Man chuckles and begins tossing shell gorgets and pendants to each of his friends. They grin and laugh. Broken Teeth does a little dance of joy.

Wrass glances at me, silently asking if I understand this. I shake my head.

I do not understand. Child slaves are not worth so much. A few strings of shell beads for each of us would be enough.

"I'll meet you again next moon. But not here," Gannajero says to Big Man. "I'll send a messenger to tell you where."

"Fine."

Gannajero turns to her warriors. "Bring all of them except the baby."

She trudges away into the forest, and her warriors circle us like a pack of hungry dogs. The tall gangly man, Kotin, holds out his hands to Agres. "Be a good girl. Give me the child."

Agres bursts into tears. "No. She's just a baby!"

"I don't have time to play games. Give her to me."

Agres starts to back away, and this enrages Kotin. He lunges for Agres, grabs her arm, and flings her to the ground. She loses hold of her sister, and the baby bounces into the leaves, shrieking. Agres madly crawls for her sister, but before she can reach her, Kotin brutally kicks Agres in the ribs and sends her sprawling.

"My father is a chief! He's going to kill you!" Agres shouts.

Kotin picks up the bundled baby and tosses it to Big Man. "Gannajero said this was yours."

Big Man catches it. "What am I going to do with it?"

Kotin shrugs, glances at the wailing child, and says, "The rest of you. Follow me."

I grip Tutelo's hand and walk. The world is blurry.

"Get up," one of the warriors says to Agres.

She struggles to rise, but can't. She's crying too hard. "My father—" She chokes on the word. "He'll find you!"

"Yes, yes, I can't wait to meet him." The man acts as though he has heard these same words from hundreds of children. He drags Agres to her feet and forces her into line just ahead of Tutelo. She is clutching her ribs and groaning as though they are broken.

As Agres passes Big Man, she lunges, grabs the baby, and runs into the forest. Spontaneous cheers rise from the children. We are all praying she escapes. If she can do it . . .

Gannajero shouts, "Kotin, teach a lesson!"

Kotin unslings his bow and nocks an arrow. He takes his time sighting down the shaft.

Agres is still running when the arrow pierces her back. She careens forward, trying to keep hold of her sister, but it is too difficult. Blood is drenching her dress, pulsing in time to her heartbeat. She has only enough strength to gently place the baby on the ground, then stagger over to an oak trunk and lean against it.

Big Man and his warriors don't even seem to notice. They split up and trot away in different directions. No one looks back.

"Little fool," Gannajero says, and glares at the rest of us. "Look and learn. If you run, you die."

Gannajero tramps away. Her warriors force us to march up the trail behind her, but I keep looking back. For an eternity, Agres stands there. Finally, she sinks to her knees and collapses into the leaves without a sound.

For another finger of time, I hear the baby crying.

We turn onto a new trail and head down into a grove of pines. My heart is beating in my ears, slamming against my skull, growing louder and louder, until a stunned ringing shakes me.

Crows circle overhead, and I hear magpies in the distance. In a few days, there will be nothing left of Agres or her sister. Their bones will be picked clean, then covered by leaves, and finally melt into the forest floor. No one will know what happened to them.

I can't stop myself from wondering when the same thing is going to happen to Tutelo and me.

Our People believe that the dead must be buried properly or their afterlife soul cannot reach the Land of the Dead. Instead, it becomes a homeless ghost, wandering the forests alone, forever.

Don't think about it. Don't.

It's raining. I look up. Misty veils drift down from dark clouds. The forest begins to hiss, and the bright autumn leaves bob as they are patted by the drops.

Walk. Just keep walking.

Three

As the campfires of the dead flashed between the clouds, they cast a dusty radiance over the rain-drenched forest, silvering the dark oaks and elms that covered the mountains. The muddy trail was awash. In the indigo shadows cast by the wind-touched branches, the water seemed to rise and fall like waves.

Sonon took a deep breath, allowing the pungent fragrances of earth and bark to seep into his exhausted body; then he twined his hands in the girl's long black hair and continued dragging her through the mud. His arms and back ached from the labor. In the constant downpour, he kept losing his hold.

As he walked, he softly sang, *"The crow comes, the crow comes, pity the little children, beat the drum. . . ."*

With each step, he heard the beating of the crow's wings in his head. It was always there. A soft rhythmic pushing of air, as though she lived right behind his eyes, saw his world, knew his most precious dreams. He'd heard her wings since he'd seen six summers. Sometimes, especially at night, he felt her darkness pressing against his eyes like icy hands, trying to shove her way out of his skull.

"*. . . beat the drum, grab the young, and run, run, run.*"

He stopped to catch his breath and take a new grip. His gaze lowered to the girl's perfect oval face. In the flashes of lightning, her copper earspools blazed. He studied her turned-up nose and the unnatural angle of her gaping mouth. Her dark eyes were half-open, staring blankly at the mist that encircled the treetops. Mud coated her white doehide dress, making it cling to her body like a second skin, highlighting the contours of her young breasts and hips. He wiped his drenched face on his sleeve and let out a shaky breath.

It had been raining hard since nightfall, soaking the brittle forest and turning the paths into creeks. Fortunately, the runoff would cover his trail. As always, Sky Woman, the grandmother of human beings, had seen his honor, and chosen to protect him from his enemies—but it made his task much harder. Most of the day, he had carried her in his arms. Now, he could only manage to drag her.

"No," he whispered, and squeezed his eyes closed for several long moments. "We are almost home. I owe her more than this."

Despite his fatigue, he steadied his muscles and bent to slip his arms beneath her to carry her again. It wasn't much farther. He could do this. He lifted her and slogged on down the trail, drowning in the sensation of her stone-cold body pressed tightly against his. Her long hair draped his left arm and stuck wetly to his thigh. Every step he took, those dark strands stroked him, and he longed to weep.

For a time, he just listened to the clicking of her shell bracelets and tried to fight back the memories.

A short while after she'd fallen, he'd gone to her. She'd stared up at him. The silent pleading in her dark eyes had left him trembling.

Blessed Creator, how many times had girls gazed at him like that? How many times had he knelt in their blood and lifted their wounded bodies into his arms? He was a warrior and supposed to be hardened to such things . . . but he doubted he ever would be.

Lightning flashed, and Thunderers dove right over his head. He gasped, and in the sudden glare of brilliantly lit oaks, he felt somehow unreal . . . more like a ghost walking through the Land of the Dead than through lands belonging to the People of the Standing Stone.

As the Thunderers cracked and soared away, a gust of wind rattled the branches. Showers of wet leaves cascaded down around him. Sonon shivered. Already, the nights were colder. It would not be long now until Hatho, the Frost Spirit, came again to live among humans. Hatho was an old man in white who carried a large club that he used to strike against the trees, to make them creak and crack as the icy winds of winter descended upon the world.

Gathering his strength, Sonon forced himself to breathe.

The night scents smelled incredibly clear to him. The tang of damp oaks mixed sweetly with the fragrances of the nearby Forks River and the earthiness of the thunderstorm that seemed to have no end.

Ahead, through the dense tangle of trees, he glimpsed the shell midden used by the People of the Hills. The midden—a trash mound three times the height of a man—marked their territorial border. In a few paces, he would be out of Standing Stone country.

Just the thought filled him with hope. He forced his shaking legs to move faster. The girl's body rocked in his arms.

"Just a little longer," he murmured to her.

Repeated flashes of lightning turned the shell midden into a wildly twinkling hill.

As he started up the steep slope, he stumbled, almost dropped her, and clutched her to his broad chest. "Careful," he hissed, more to himself than to her. "Careful now. We are almost there."

With his sandals skidding and clattering on the wet shells, he carried her to the top of the mound and gently lowered her body. The view from up here was gorgeous. Whitecaps glistened down the length of the wide Forks River, and for as far as he could see, lightning slashed the stormy sky.

"You're home," he said, and bent to stroke her face. Her skin felt cold and clammy.

Sonon straightened. For a few brief instants, he did not hear the rain or the wind through the branches. His souls were filled with a terrible silence. Each person, before he crossed the bridge to the afterlife, had to discover what he was running from and why. This moment—this exact moment—was the heartbeat of his own search. The terror that had stalked him all his life.

"The crow comes, the crow comes, beat the drum,

hide the young, and run, run, run," he sang as he tried to focus his eyes. A dark fluttering filled his head. The iron-gray night was suddenly broken and shimmering, as though each instant was nothing more than a shattered glimpse of death.

Desperation tingled his veins.

He lifted his face to the storm. . . . The rain washed her blood from his hands. . . . The roar of Thunderers drowned his agonized cries.

When he could breathe again, he choked out the words, "One f-final task."

He grabbed the leather cord of his gorget and lifted his precious conch shell pendant from around his neck. The False Face image carved into the shell stared up at him with hollow eyes. Holding it in both hands, he breathed his soul into it, then placed it upon her chest, right over the protruding shaft of the arrow. As he straightened, the old, tarnished, copper beads that encircled the collar of his cape clicked together.

"When I reach the bridge to the afterlife, remember me," he whispered.

He watched the cascades of falling leaves that showered the forest while he thought about death: hers and his own. There was a bridge that spanned a black abyss of nothingness, and each soul had to cross it to reach the afterlife. Standing on this side of the bridge were all the animals a man had known in his life. Those he had helped defended him and gave him the time to cross the bridge. Those he had hurt chased him, trying to make him fall into the abyss, where his soul would float in black emptiness for eternity. On the opposite side of the bridge—if a man was going to make it—he saw all the people he'd ever loved, waiting for him. A man who was not going to make it across saw nothing.

Sonon knew, for he had stood upon the bridge many times and seen across the border of death to what lay beyond. That emptiness still lived in his dreams, calling to him in a lover's voice, luring him to step onto the planks. Someday he would freely walk into those open arms and never return. He longed for that black peace with all his heart.

Cold wind rustled the trees around him, and leaves pirouetted through the air.

He sucked several deep breaths into his lungs and forced his trembling legs down the midden slope toward the trail that led east.

Four

Gonda pulled his elkhide cape more tightly around his muscular shoulders. Sunlight penetrated the forest in bars and streaks of fallow gold, but there was no warmth to it. He was a slender man with a round face and heavy brow. He had seen twenty-six summers pass, but this morning he felt older than the forests. As he knelt to examine a washed-out track in the trail, his short black hair fell forward.

"What are you?" he whispered. "Nothing?"

The scuff mark was frost-rimmed and skimmed with ice. It could have been made by anything—a deer, a man, even a raccoon. He vented a frustrated breath and rose to his feet.

Buttonbush thickets crowded the spaces between the towering sycamores and shorter sassafras trees. Birds perched among the branches, plucking at the few shriveled fruits that clung to the leafless red stalks. A riot of sparrow and wren songs filled the air.

He expelled a breath and propped his fists on his hips.

At dawn, he'd found dim marks at the edges of the flooded trail, as though a man had been dragging a heavy pack through the water and, occasionally, the pack had scooped up mud. But the marks had vanished over one hand of time ago. In desperation, both of them had kept pushing onward up the same trail, hoping to spot more sign, but so far they'd seen nothing certain.

After two days, this was the most promising trail they'd found—if it was a trail—and every instant they delayed, every moment they spent discussing what they should do next, their enemy was getting farther and farther away.

Gonda glanced at his former wife, Koracoo. She stood five paces behind him, examining something on the forest floor. He kept praying she would look up and meet his gaze, perhaps smile at him, anything to keep him going. She did not.

They had been married for twelve summers—until two days ago when she'd set his belongings outside the charred husk of their longhouse and told him to go home to his own clan.

He stepped off the trail and continued his search through the trees.

Blessed gods, couldn't she see that his own guilt was strangling him? Even if they found their children alive and well, he would never forgive himself. The images of burning longhouses and dead friends would remain open wounds on his souls for as long as he lived.

Gonda stopped, seeing a curious shape just beneath the overhanging branches of a bush. He bent over, frowned at it, and called, "Koracoo? You'd better come look at this."

She lifted her head. At twenty-seven summers,

Koracoo was unusually tall for a woman, twelve hands. She'd chopped her black hair short in mourning. It created a jagged frame for her beautiful face. Since the destruction of their village, her large dark eyes maintained an almost perpetually somber expression. Over her knee-length war shirt, she wore a red cape. In the middle of the cape, the blue painting of a buffalo defiantly stared out. "Are you sure?"

"I've been a warrior for thirteen summers, Koracoo. Don't you think I know how to recognize a man's track?"

As Koracoo walked toward him, sunlight gilded the copper inlay in her war club, giving it an edge of flame. It had a name, that club: *CorpseEye*. His own nameless club was made of fire-hardened oak. Hers was a wood no one had ever seen before, dark, dense, and old. Legend said that CorpseEye had once belonged to Sky Woman herself. Strange images were carved on the shaft: antlered wolves, winged tortoises, and prancing buffalo. A red quartzite cobble was tied to the top of the club, making it a very deadly weapon—one Koracoo wielded with great expertise. She constantly polished CorpseEye with walnut oil, as her father had done, and his father before him, and his before him, back into the obscure mists of time.

Koracoo stopped beside him. "Show me."

Gonda held the brush aside for her.

As she knelt to scrutinize the frost-rimmed track, the lines around her eyes deepened.

He watched her. More than anything, he longed to touch her, to lie in her arms and talk about his mistakes until he could bear them. He was the father of her children. Between them was the unbreakable bond of two people who had seen their children stolen away to a fate neither of them dared imagine. Only in her arms would he ever find comfort.

But as the days passed, it seemed less and less likely. On the rare occasions when she looked at him now, it was with the eyes of a cold, impatient stranger.

Koracoo said, "He wore finely woven cornhusk sandals. A wealthy man. A man of status."

"Yes. Let's go. We're wasting precious time."

"I need to study this a little longer." She kept her eyes on the sandal print.

Gonda grumbled under his breath. Every tendon in his body was stretched taut, telling him to leave, to keep searching. But she was war chief, and he was deputy. She made the decisions.

He scowled at the track. The herringbone pattern of the sandal weave was distinctive, woven by the Hills People. There were five kinds of People south of Skanodario Lake: Flint People, the People of the Landing, People of the Mountain, People of the Hills, and their own tribe of Standing Stone People. The People of the Hills had the most warriors and the largest villages. They were—despite what the Standing Stone People wished to believe—the greatest power in the land.

Koracoo said, "He was a Hills warrior."

"Yes. Probably a big, heavy man, because his feet sank deeply into the mud."

Her eyes narrowed in thought before she replied, "Or he was carrying a heavy load."

"Maybe."

Koracoo stood, and her gaze moved to the shell midden partially visible through the tangle of tree trunks. The mound glittered with frost. Canassatego Village, a Hills People village, had used the same trash site for ten summers; it was huge, covered with freshwater mussel shells, broken pottery, ashes from their fires, and other refuse.

"His toes pointed toward the midden," Koracoo observed.

"Yes. So?"

"Let's see if he came here alone, or met someone. You go left of the trail. I'll go right." When she turned to look at him to make sure he understood, his heartbeat stilled. Her eyes were as black and translucent as obsidian, and cut just as keenly. "I'll meet you at the midden." Koracoo stepped away.

Gonda went left. It took another half-hand of time before they reached the base of the mound. It stood three times the height of a man. As Elder Brother Sun climbed higher into the sky, the layer of ice began to melt, leaving the wet shells glistening like river rocks.

"Another track," Koracoo called, and pointed at the ground.

Gonda worked his way over to her and stared down at the place where the man's sandals had skidded off the shells, heaping them into small piles.

There were several more such piles all the way up the midden slope. At this time of the morning, each cast a shadow. "He was careful until he got here; then he started rushing. See where he slipped?"

"Yes."

"Stay here," she ordered. "I'll see if there is anything on top of the midden."

"Koracoo, please, let me do it. You will be a perfect target standing alone at the top. There may be enemy warriors watching from the trees. I am more expendable than you are."

"Stay here." She started up the slope.

Gonda kept his gaze on her. She was moving slowly, climbing, studying, climbing. Since the attack on Yellowtail Village and the loss of their children, he panicked whenever she was out of his sight.

She's all right. Leave it be.

They had faced so many hardships together. Behind them were burned villages, friends long dead, and young dreams smothered beyond all recall. He knew her better than she knew herself . . . and she him. Why couldn't she forgive him?

His practiced warrior's gaze moved over the forest, searching for odd colors or shapes—anything that would reveal a hidden enemy—then darted back to Koracoo. She was almost to the mound top.

In the sky above her, twenty or more ravens soared, their wings flashing in the sunlight. Such large flocks were a common sight these days. Whenever people went to war, they did not go alone. Carrion eaters followed them, waiting their turns to feast.

"There's a body up here," Koracoo called.

Gonda's eyes widened. He glanced at the ravens again. He should have known. "A body? That must be what he was dragging. Male or female? Can you tell?"

Koracoo walked to the edge of the mound and gestured for him to come to her, but added, "Don't disturb the tracks."

Gonda veered wide and hurried up the opposite side of the slope. Long before he reached the top, he could smell the stench of rotting human flesh. Then he saw the girl lying on her back. The birds had pecked out her eyes and devoured most of the flesh of her face. Worse, wolves had been at her belly. Ropes of half-chewed intestines snaked across the shells. The broken shaft of an arrow protruded from her chest.

Gonda gestured to the arrow. "He was a good shot. That's straight through the heart."

"Or he was close." Koracoo swung CorpseEye up and rested the club on her shoulder. The red quartzite cobble glinted. "Her clothing marks her as one of the Hills People, and look at her jewelry."

"Yes, I see."

Shell bracelets encircled the gnawed wrists, and beautiful copper earspools decorated the girl's lobes. An elaborately carved conch shell pendant lay a short distance away. It was gorgeous: A False Face with a long bent nose, slanted mouth, and hollow eyes stared up from the shell. The False Face Spirits who inhabited such masks could cure illness. Had the dead girl been ill? The leather thong had probably been chewed through by the wolves and the pendant dragged off.

Gonda walked closer and searched the area around the mangled corpse for any clues that might reveal her killer. The longer he studied the body, the more unease he felt.

Koracoo clenched her fist around CorpseEye. "She is not one of our children."

"No. Do you think we're on the wrong trail?"

"It's possible, but many villages have been attacked in the past few days. She may have been herded into a group of captives that included our children."

"Child slavery is an ugly part of warfare, but it—"

"This was not warfare," Koracoo said.

"What do you mean?"

Koracoo used CorpseEye to point. "If she'd been killed by enemy warriors they would have taken that magnificent jewelry."

Gonda looked at the copper earspools again. Even now, though he'd have to pull them through rotting flesh, they'd be worth a fortune in trade. "I didn't think of that."

Koracoo walked around the other side of the body. "And no enemy warrior would have carried her up here to the top of this mound. He would have left her where she fell. Who would go to the effort of carrying a dead girl to the top of a trash mound?"

"A man who wanted to make a point."

Koracoo straightened. She had an oval face with full lips and a small narrow nose. "What point?"

"That she was filth? Or refuse? Perhaps her killer hated her."

Koracoo thoughtfully gazed out at the Forks River. "Or perhaps he loved her. The view from up here is beautiful. I can see halfway across the Hills People country." She studied the body again and softly said, "All we know with fair certainty is that she was carried up here by one of her own people."

Gonda used the toe of his moccasin to smooth out a ridge of shells. "Should we keep following this trail? Or go back and start over at Yellowtail Village?"

Koracoo tensed. "This is still the best trail we've found. The only trail. I say we follow it wherever it leads."

He exhaled a breath and nodded. "I agree. Which direction should we go? Do we follow him to the west? Or do we backtrack him to the east and hope we find the place the girl was killed? If we find him, he may be able to answer all of our questions."

"If he chooses to, which I doubt."

"There are ways to 'encourage' his cooperation."

Koracoo shook her head. "That will take even more time and may be fruitless."

Gonda flapped his arms against his sides. "Then I say we backtrack him. If we can find where the girl was killed, it may answer just as many of our questions."

Koracoo didn't respond, and he knew what she must be thinking. At this very moment their clan elders would be salvaging what they could from the charred remains of Yellowtail Village, burying the dead, and trying to decide what to take with them. Though the elders had sanctioned their search for the missing children, they expected Koracoo and Gonda to be home soon, to help defend the survivors as they marched to Bur Oak Village, a Standing Stone village five days away.

"What do you think we should do?" he asked. "We haven't much time."

Her gaze drifted over the crimson-hued forest before

she said, "We backtrack him. If the trail goes cold, or it becomes clear it has nothing to do with our lost children, we will go home."

"Agreed."

Koracoo headed down the midden trail, and Gonda turned to look at the False Face pendant. He walked over, picked it up, and tucked it into his belt pouch.

As he trotted to catch up with Koracoo, melting ice began to drip out of the trees and shower the forest floor. Gonda flipped up the hood of his buckskin cape and shivered.

The morning was warming up, releasing the brittle scents of autumn, and he wanted to enjoy it for as long as he could. He had known Koracoo his entire life. While they could not track in the darkness, for the next few days there would be no real rest. From dawn until dusk, they would be searching the ground and brush. They would eat and drink on the run. At night, they would take turns sleeping. One of them would always be standing guard.

The faces of Tutelo and Odion smiled at him from his memories, and he had to fight back the cry that rose in his throat.

Deep inside him, a voice kept repeating, *My fault. All my fault.*

He focused his eyes on Koracoo's back and tried to think only of her.

Five

Gonda had not had a sip of water all day. Since dawn he had been moving, walking up and down the twisting mountain trails, searching for any sign that a man carrying a girl had passed this way. Now, in late afternoon, he was desperately thirsty. But it did not matter. Off and on all day, they had found sign: a broken branch along the trail, a fragment of white doehide caught on brush, partial tracks, drag marks. This *was* the trail of the man who had carried the girl to the midden. The problem was that they still did not know if this trail had anything to do with the missing Yellowtail Village children. For all they knew, they could be wasting their time while Odion, Tutelo, and Wrass were being sold from one Trader to another. It would not be long until the children's trail went stone cold.

Gonda studied the trees. The damp chestnut limbs stood starkly against the sunlight. Here and there fallen nuts dotted the ground. He reached down, picked up several, and tucked them into his belt pouch, for later when . . .

A strange sound whispered through the forest.

Almost . . . eerie. He heard Koracoo coming up the

trail and held up a hand to stop her. She went deathly silent, listening, as he was.

The sound came again. Leaves rustled, but not with the wind.

Gonda pulled an arrow from the quiver on his back and nocked it in his bow; then he used it to point in the direction of the sound.

A soft hiss told Gonda that Koracoo, too, had nocked an arrow in her bow. After another five heartbeats, Koracoo eased up beside him. Her dark eyes were intent, focused on the source of the sound in the forest ahead.

They stood in silence, both studying the lay of the land, searching for hidden foes. He led the way, warily heading toward the sound.

In another thirty paces, they walked into a small clearing fringed by gigantic oaks. Gonda's eyes narrowed. Someone had been here, recently. The deep autumn leaves that blanketed the grass had been scooped into odd shapes, as though many people had shoved them aside to sit down, perhaps to build fires.

"What is this?" Koracoo whispered.

He shook his head uncertainly.

Sunset painted the forest, glittering from the tallest pines like a fine paint made of ground amber. A luminous wall of Cloud People crowded the sky to the north.

"Smell anything?" he asked.

Koracoo flared her nostrils and shook her head. "No."

Gonda nodded. There was no smell of smoke. If someone had camped here, he would have built a fire to warm himself and cook his food. As warriors, they'd raided and burned enough villages to know how long it took for the stench to fade.

A tingle climbed Gonda's spine. None of this made sense. He needed a few moments to think, and motioned for Koracoo to take cover. She stepped behind a tree trunk two paces away.

Gonda hid behind one of the many lichen-covered boulders that thrust up across the mountains.

Sunset had just begun to purple the western horizon, and the eagle shadows that played in the trees had a vaguely lavender hue. Otherwise, the only movement was the faint breeze through the branches.

The sound . . . leaves moving.

His gut knotted.

Blessed gods, what is that?

Anxious, almost to the point of carelessness, Gonda clenched his bow so hard his fingertips went white. He forced himself to think. They'd been tracking the man all day and had seen none of the refuse that inevitably marked the trails of warriors. It was as though the man had simply grabbed the dead girl and headed toward the shell midden without stopping. Why would anyone do that? Had he known the girl? A relative would have taken her home and buried her properly, so that her afterlife soul could find its way to the Land of the Dead. Or . . . had he been afraid to take her home? Would his village have punished him?

Koracoo hissed to get his attention and used her nocked arrow to point at something beneath a fallen log.

His gaze searched the area until he saw what appeared to be part of a child's toy, a cornhusk doll.

"Koracoo, you circle north; I'll veer south."

She nodded and slipped into the forest shadows.

Gonda carefully stepped off the trail and started moving through the deep leaves. His moccasins crackled softly. Every two steps he halted to listen. As Cloud People drifted across the face of Elder Brother Sun, shadows darkened the trees, then vanished as the amber gleam again flooded the forest.

He swerved around a small outcrop of granite boulders . . . heard again a whisper of leaves moving . . . and forced himself to look at the clearing. To *see*. If there was someone out there, he should be able to make out an odd color, or shape, perhaps a glimpse of clothing. He saw nothing but strange dips and humps in the leafbed.

Across the meadow, Koracoo's shadow slipped through the trees, cautiously approaching the clearing from the north.

Gonda let his gaze drift around the forest. Were there warriors hiding out there, just waiting for someone, anyone, to come to the sound? Was this a clever trap?

Koracoo signaled for him to stop.

He rubbed his mouth with the back of his hand while he waited. He hadn't heard whatever it was that had spooked her.

Koracoo took two more steps through the trees on the north end of the clearing. Then she said, "Gonda? Come here. This may be where the girl died."

Gonda trotted to meet her. For a time, they did not speak; they just looked at the blood that soaked the oak trunk.

"How old do you think that blood is?"

Koracoo slung her bow and knelt. "Two days. Three, maybe. You can see where the mice have been chewing at the soaked bark."

She began slowly pulling away the leaves at the base of the tree. When she neared the ground level, the leaves were stuck together with old blood. She gently lifted the clumps and set them aside, looking for more.

"A sandal track." She tapped it with her finger.

Gonda moved forward and bent to examine it. "A big man. Heavy. Or perhaps he'd already lifted the girl into his arms when this track was made."

"Yes." Koracoo's dark brows pinched over her small nose. She scowled at the track for several moments. "Don't you think it's odd that he's wearing sandals? It's late autumn. He should be wearing moccasins."

"Maybe he's an idiot?"

"Or maybe sandals are all he has, but . . ."

Koracoo tilted her head, and Gonda saw that she was listening again—listening as though their lives depended upon it. He held his breath.

In a clipped voice, Koracoo said, "Do you hear it?"

A few paces away, the leaves whispered.

Gonda braced himself. "Yes."

Hope swelled fit to burst his chest. They both straightened, and their eyes focused on the leaves. They fluttered. "You go," he said. "I'll cover you with my bow."

Koracoo moved forward on cat feet. The leaves continued to flutter as if from shallow rhythmic puffs of air. Breathing? His heart tightened.

Koracoo crouched down, brushed away leaves, then

stopped. In an agonized voice, she said, "Oh, no," and reached both hands deep into the leaves to pull out a tightly wrapped bundle.

"What is it?" Gonda rushed forward.

"It's a baby." Koracoo slumped to the ground and cradled the child in her left arm while she frantically pulled the blanket from its face with her right hand.

Gonda kept glancing up at the forest, his bow still drawn. When he looked down again, a small pale face, framed with black hair, shone within the blanket. The child's dark eyes were slitted, the lids fluttering as though it was just barely alive. "It's a miracle that child didn't freeze to death. The Forest Spirits must have protected it."

"If we don't act quickly, the Forest Spirits' efforts will have been for naught."

Koracoo rested the baby in her lap, jerked her cape over her head, and pulled open the laces of her war shirt. For a brief moment, he glimpsed her breasts, and it comforted him.

"What are you doing?" he asked.

"Warming her." Koracoo peeled off the child's soiled sack—revealing that it was a girl—and tossed the sack into the leaves; then she tucked the baby down the front of her war shirt. "Blessed gods, she's freezing."

"Koracoo . . . we can't take her with us. You know that, don't you?"

"If I stand up, can you slip my cape over my head and tie it beneath the baby?"

Gonda slung his bow and picked up Koracoo's cape. "Yes, but—"

"I'm aware of the problem, Gonda." Carefully holding the child against her, she got to her feet.

Gonda slipped her cape over her head and then pulled the ends up and tied them around Koracoo's waist to form a kind of sling for the baby inside her brown shirt.

"Tighter," Koracoo said. "If I have to fight, I want to be able to use my hands to swing my club."

Gonda complied, retying the ends as tightly as he could. "If you understand the problem, why are you—?"

"We have to find the nearest village. Fast. This child needs food and shelter. Her afterlife soul is already out wandering the forest."

Gonda peered at the soiled sack. "The red-and-black spirals mark her as one of the People of the Hills, probably Hawk Clan. If that doesn't slap some sense into you, I don't know what will."

"The nearest Hills village is Atotarho Village."

Among the Hills People, when a chief died, his clan matron, in consultation with the other women of the clan, selected the new chief, and he was given the name of the deceased man. The new chief was then "raised up" and the dead chief, thereby, "resuscitated." If the new chief proved unworthy of his position, he could be "dehorned," and his name taken away. Villages always took the name of their chief, and Chief Atotarho was no friend of theirs.

Gonda said, "Atotarho is an evil sorcerer. We can't go there. None of us, including the baby, will survive."

The Hills People were their sworn enemies. In fact—though he couldn't be sure—there may have been Atotarho warriors with the Mountain warriors who had attacked Yellowtail Village. The Hills and Mountain Peoples were allies and often combined forces to assault Standing Stone villages.

"We don't have a choice, Gonda."

"Of course we have a choice. She's not one of our people. We can leave her here."

The expression on Koracoo's face went straight to his heart. Granted, she had just lost her children in a raid and didn't know if they were alive or dead, but the way she clutched the baby against her made no sense. They could *not* take it with them.

"I can't leave her to die," she said sternly. "Let's go."

Koracoo started to walk past him, and he grabbed her arm in a hard grip. "No! If you and I are captured or killed, *our* children may be lost forever. Leave the baby here!"

Koracoo shook off his grip and glared at him, but he saw bone-deep pain in her eyes. "Very well. We'll split up. You keep following this trail. As soon as I've found a safe place where the baby will be cared for, I'll catch up with you."

He shook his head as though he hadn't heard right. "I'm not going to let you walk into a Hills village alone. If they kill you on sight, I'll never forgive myself." He held out his arms. "Give me the child. I'll take it away and you won't even have to watch."

The baby mewed, barely audible, and Koracoo's expression turned to stone. "Gonda, you can either keep following this trail, or come with me. Either way, we're losing the light."

Gonda exhaled hard. Arguing more would be futile.

He threw up his hands in frustration, and said, "I'll go with you, but you're insane."

"Fine. You lead."

He checked the sunlight, nocked his bow again, and headed west. The deep leaves made it impossible to walk quietly. Even though wet, they shished and crackled beneath his moccasins. Behind him, he could hear Koracoo speaking gently to the child, telling it not to be afraid, that everything was going to be all right—which he seriously doubted.

Over his shoulder he said, "And you'd better hide CorpseEye somewhere. Everyone knows that club and wants it. They'll steal it for sure."

"I will."

He'd taken another ten steps when he came to a deep pile of leaves. He kicked his way through them, launching several wet clumps high into the air . . . and stopped dead in the trail. Hot blood surged through his veins, and he suddenly felt light-headed.

In a shaking voice, he said, "Koracoo?"

"What?"

He aimed his bow at the bare patch of ground. "Look."

It had been raining that day. Dozens of small feet had sunken into the mud and the imprints had been preserved when the ground had frozen. Later, leaves had blown over the top.

Gonda whispered, "It is . . . isn't it?"

Koracoo came up beside him, saw the tracks, and sucked in a sudden breath. For the first time in days, she looked directly at him, and their gazes locked. He saw panic in her eyes to match his own. For a few brief instants they shared their fear and grief, and he could finally get a full breath into his lungs.

Koracoo knelt, brushed at the leaves, and scrutinized the tracks. "Don't get your hopes up. It's definitely the trail of a group of children, but we have no way of knowing whether they are our children or not."

"Nonetheless, we should follow this trail now. Surely you know that. Forget the baby!"

Koracoo hesitated. Her eyes clung to the small moccasin prints in the mud. Then the baby let out a soft cry, and she squeezed her eyes closed.

"You know I'm right," he said. "Our children are worth more. I wish we didn't have to make a choice, but we do."

In the tawny halo of the light, her beautiful tormented face seemed to be carved of amber. After five more heartbeats, she finally opened her eyes and rose to her feet.

"No, Gonda. I'm taking the child to Atotarho Village, but I'll be back here by dawn tomorrow. I'll catch up with you."

She slogged through the deep leaves and started up the trail.

Gonda stood for several moments staring at the tracks with his heart bursting in his chest. He could see his children's faces, hear their voices calling out to him, *"Father, where are you? You're coming for us, aren't you?"*

The pain in his chest was suffocating.

He opened and closed his fists. When he could stand it no longer, he tore his gaze away from their trail and stumbled backward, breathing hard.

It took another ten heartbeats before he could order his legs to trot after Koracoo.

Six

Odion

A baby cries.

I lift my hands and cover my ears. The wail seems to seep through my skin and drifts on the pine-sharp winds that swirl old leaves up into the oak boughs before blowing them away through the chill golden afternoon. Why can't I get the cries of Agres' sister out of my heart?

Tutelo sleeps in the dead grass beside me. I keep glancing at her. Worrying. We are all shaky from the days of marching without food. We have rarely been on a trail. Usually we march through trackless forest, meadows, or over rocks, which has made the travel even more exhausting. Today our guards ordered Tutelo and me to climb through trees, then across an outcrop of eroding granite where stunted saplings grew as thickly as river reeds. It took two hands of time. I don't know where the other children were at the time. Gannajero has assigned each of us a guard during the day. The guard can take us wherever he wishes if he arrives at dusk in the prearranged location. Often, the men carry us on their backs so they can travel faster.

I look around.

The camp is large. Many warriors have come to see Gannajero. But these men did not bring children to sell.

They came to gamble. Fifteen men sit around a small fire, playing the stone game. There are three teams, each composed of five players. The gangly warrior, Kotin, holds a round wooden bowl. Six plum pits clack inside the dish. The pits are gaming pieces, ground to an oval shape, then burned black on one side and painted white on the other. He shakes the bowl and tosses the stones across an elk hide spread over the cold ground. Whoops and cheers go up from his friends, and howls of dismay from the strangers. Kotin throws his head back and laughs as he pulls in the glittering pile of stone knives, hide scrapers, and copper jewelry. The new warriors grumble and cast evil looks at Gannajero's team.

The wealth being won and lost stuns me, and I wonder if they are not wagering on more than tangles of necklaces and stone tools.

My eyes move to where the old woman sits alone in the middle of the clearing. Her head is back. She stares up at a flock of crows drifting on the wind currents above her. Her breath frosts as she speaks to the birds and makes strange signs in the air with a black feather. Is Gannajero performing some evil magical ritual? Or just praying for the crows to bring her team good luck?

When we made camp two hands of time ago, she pulled aside the three Flint girls and forced them to put on beautiful doeskin dresses. Then she carefully combed and braided their hair. The elaborate red-and-yellow porcupine quillwork on their dresses flashes when they move. The girls kneel together twenty paces from the game, whispering.

I am the only Yellowtail child awake. I roll to my back and

study the bare oak branches. The farther east we go, the fewer leaves there are, and the colder the nights become.

I am feverish and sick to my stomach all the time. I think it's the baby. Her cries are often so loud I cannot hear anything else. I swear her soul is inside me. I have glimpsed it, flitting behind my eyes like blue falling stars.

Her soul is flying. I feel it. It is the flight of the alone to the *Alone.*

At the game, Gannajero's men leap to their feet and shake their fists. Kotin has lost, and passes the bowl to the next team.

The baby shrieks inside me. I glance around, terrified.

"Stop crying!" I whisper. "Please, stop crying."

I must have spoken too loudly. The other boy, who sleeps to my right, rolls over and stares at me. His brow furrows. He appears to be my age: eleven or twelve summers. He has a starved face—all the bones stick out—and hollow brown eyes. His flat nose and big ears make him resemble a bat. He is lucky, for he wears a heavy moosehide cape with the fur turned inside for warmth.

I whisper, "What's your name?"

I just barely hear him say, "Hehaka."

"I am Odion."

Wrass wakes and looks at us, then glances around to make sure our guards are both paying attention to the game before he crawls over to me. His beaked nose glows orange in the firelight. Dirty black hair frames his narrow face. His mouth is moving. He's trying to tell me something.

"I can't hear you, Wrass." The baby's cries drown out his words.

He crawls closer, cups a hand to my ear, and I feel his warm breath, but I hear nothing.

"I'm sorry, Wrass. I can't hear right now."

Hehaka mouths, *What's wrong with him?*

Wrass pushes back slightly, blinks at me, and looks around again, studying the guards. Both men are smiling at the game.

Wrass turns my head to look at my right ear, then my left, and he frowns. Very slowly, his mouth forms the words, *We . . .* then a word I don't understand *. . . run.*

I shake my head. "We can't run! There are too many of them. They will just hunt us down and kill us, like they did Agres."

Wrass clenches his jaw. He looks desperate. He tries again, very slowly. *We . . . need . . . plan.*

Plan. Not run. *We need a plan.*

I prop myself up on one elbow and whisper, "Tell me what you're thinking."

Wrass stretches out beside me in the grass with his back to Hehaka. He clearly doesn't trust him. Hehaka gets the message and crawls away. Wrass waits until he's gone before he says, ". . . don't like him. He . . . Gannajero."

He came with Gannajero?

I can tell Wrass is terrified, but courage shines behind the terror. Faintly, I hear him say, "We . . . can't . . . too long, or we won't . . . find . . . way home."

I try to make myself fill in the words I can't hear: We can't wait too long, or we won't be able to find our way home?

I nod. "We should try to—"

Wrass suddenly jerks to look at the fire, and I see the

men rising. The winners slap each other on the backs. The losers scowl and walk away.

Out in the clearing, Gannajero rises. Her hunched back makes her resemble a buffalo walking on its hind legs. She goes over to the three girls, and as she leans over them, her greasy twists of graying hair sway in their faces. She uses the black feather to stab at their chests. The girls nod.

The winning team of five men circle the girls like a pack of starving wolves, and smile. One of the girls is shaking badly.

The team leader—a skinny man wearing a black shirt—hands over the heavy bag of his winnings. Gannajero takes it, gestures to the girls, and walks away to examine her payment.

The three Flint girls rise as though they've been told to and huddle together.

One of the girls starts crying when she is dragged from the group. The man does not even try to hide his brutality. He slaps the girl, forces her to walk to a tree, and undress. When she is standing naked in the firelight, he shoves her against the trunk. He pulls up his warshirt, spits on his hard penis, and thrusts himself inside her. She screams. Her mouth is wide, her pretty face twisted in shock. She tries to fight, and two warriors grab her arms and pin them. The last two men pick out their own girls.

My gaze jerks back to Wrass. His jaw is clenched so hard his head is trembling. Rage lights his dark eyes. His fists are working, opening and closing as though gripping imaginary war clubs.

The other two Flint girls are thrown to the ground, and the men fall upon them. One flails her arms and tries to kick her attacker, but he slaps her into submission. The other girl lies limply, as though dead.

When the man who has the girl against the tree finishes, he pulls away and another man takes his place.

Wrass' expression suddenly slackens, as though in understanding.

And then I understand, too.

Gannajero is a Trader. But she Trades in things men would be killed for in their own villages. These are children, not women. To couple with a girl before she exits the Women's House is considered the most insidious of crimes. Only incest with a child is worse. If a man forced a girl to couple with him in any village in the country, he would be hunted down and murdered.

But here in the wilderness, they simply have to pay enough.

Hehaka glances at the men, then crawls back over. As though my ears have opened up, I clearly hear him say, "Sometimes the men want boys. You should be ready. They're going to hurt you."

"Tonight?" Wrass asks.

Hehaka shrugs. "I don't know. Maybe."

There is a tornado building inside Wrass. I see it spinning, forming. His dark eyes have a wet savage glitter. He seems to sense my agony. He says, "Hehaka is just guessing. How could he know that?"

Hehaka crawls closer and whispers, "I know. Believe me. There are a few men who keep coming back just for me."

The pride in his voice shakes me to the bones.

"What do they make you do?" Wrass asks.

"Sometimes they just want to lie with me. Other times,

they burn me with sticks, or they tie me up and cut my flesh with stone knives. See these scars?" He pulls up his sleeves, and Wrass and I gape at the white lines that criss-cross his tanned skin. I swear there are hundreds of them, small and thin. Some appear to be punctures.

Wrass licks his lips nervously. "Gods! What's the matter with you? Why don't you run away?"

Hehaka pulls his sleeves down. "I've run away many times. The old woman always finds me and brings me back. Once, about four moons ago, I tried to kill myself." He turns so that we can see the scar that slashes his neck. "I took a chert flake and ripped open the big artery in my throat."

I shrink away from Hehaka, but Wrass leans closer for a good look. "Why didn't you die? You should have bled to death in a few hundred heartbeats."

"Yes, but she's a witch. She stopped my bleeding with a wave of her hand; then she turned herself into a crow and flew out into the forest. She found my wandering afterlife soul and shoved it back in my body. She won't let me die."

I start swallowing convulsively. A thin wail is leaching up through my lungs. . . .

Tutelo's cold hand snakes through the grass and grasps mine. I did not know until this moment that she was awake. I feel as if my insides are melting. I whisper, "I'm right here, Tutelo."

"Odion? I—I'm afraid."

I squeeze her hand. "Try to sleep. We need to rest as much as we can, so we're strong enough to fight them when Mother and Father get here to rescue us."

Hehaka snickers at this, and Wrass grabs him by the hair and punches him solidly in the mouth.

Hehaka shrieks and scrambles away. Our guards turn. In a bored voice, Ugly says, "Why did you strike Hehaka?"

Wrass mumbles, "I don't like him."

"You want me to hit you?" Ugly waves his war club.

"No."

"Then stop causing me trouble, boy!"

Wrass lowers his gaze and seems to be staring submissively at his moccasins. Ugly turns away to gleefully watch what's happening to the Flint girls, and Wrass whispers, "When I have the chance, he's the first one I'm going to kill. Then I—"

A hoarse roar goes up, and we both spin around. Two of the gamblers have gotten into a fight over the girl by the tree. They circle each other with their knives held low, grinning and calling insults.

"She's mine, Hodigo! You told me I could have her after you were finished!"

"Yes, but I'm not finished, you worthless cur! Wait your turn!"

Hodigo lunges with such swiftness his opponent has no time to evade the blade; it sinks deep in the man's belly. Hodigo whoops in victory and dances back.

Gannajero says, "*Stop it!* No fighting. You know the rules!" She rushes toward them as fast as her old legs will carry her. The feather is clenched in her right hand.

"You stabbed me!" The man wipes at the dark blood that drenches his hide shirt. "Blessed Spirits, you punctured a gut!"

Hodigo laughs, and shouts, "Your heart is next, Cattara!" and charges forward for the kill.

"Guards!" Gannajero shouts.

Kotin tackles Hodigo and wrestles him to the ground, growling in fury. "Stimon? Grab his legs!" Another warrior rushes over and throws his body over Hodigo's flailing legs, holding them.

Hodigo's wounded opponent sits down hard in the frozen grass. His friends gather around him, speculating on his wound. They keep giving Hodigo murderous glances.

"This is just beginning," Wrass whispers. "Look at that blood. He's going to die for sure, and his friends will have to avenge his death."

I say, "Good. So long as they leave us alone, I—"

Gannajero throws her head back and lets out a blood-curdling shriek that silences every person in camp. She spreads her arms like a huge bird and hops around in a bizarre dance that resembles Crow hunting mice in a field. As she dances closer to Hodigo and Kotin, men scatter, shoving each other backward to get away.

She stops beside Hodigo with her arms still out. Her black eyes shine and flicker as she cocks her head, looking at him first through one eye, then the other, like a curious bird. Then, with agonizing slowness, she lowers the black feather in her hand toward Hodigo.

Hodigo goes pale when Gannajero leans over him. "What are you going to do with that, old woman?" he shouts, and tries to fight his way free. "Get away from me!"

In an eerie singsong voice, Gannajero chants, "You broke the rules. Hodigo broke the rules."

"You crazy old witch! Let me go!"

She jerks Hodigo's shirt away from his chest and uses

the shiny black feather to paint a series of interweaving lines on his flesh. "Hodigo, Hodigo, empty soul, wants the girl, can't let go."

When Hodigo laughs, Gannajero uses the quill to stab a hole in his chest. He lets out a sharp cry of surprise. Blood wells. Gannajero dips the quill in the blood and continues drawing designs while she sings softly. The men standing around seem fascinated. They must be very afraid of her, or else they would jump her, grab their friend, and leave. Instead, they mutter ominously to each other and watch with huge dark eyes.

Gannajero removes a small black bag from her belt pouch. As she tugs open the laces, she says, "You're safe now," and sprinkles a white powder over the bloody designs, then drags out what looks like a freshly dug root. "Open his mouth."

Kotin cranks open Hodigo's jaws, and Gannajero shoves the root so far down his throat, he has no choice but to swallow it.

Hodigo's face contorts, and he spits in Gannajero's face and chuckles, "You can't scare me! I am Hodigo, the greatest warrior among the Mountain People!"

Gannajero smiles as she wipes off his spittle on her cape.

Within moments, Hodigo starts to pant and writhe. Finally he screams as though being eaten alive by wolves. All of his friends back away.

When Gannajero tucks the bag into her belt pouch and rises, Hodigo lets out one last bellow and goes limp.

"There, there," she gently says. "No more bad dreams."

She grins at his friends and walks away. None of them try to stop her.

Holding the bloody feather to her breast as though she cherishes it, she walks out into the meadow to stare up at the sky. The afternoon is shading toward evening. Long shadows fill the forest. She pets the feather while she whispers to herself, or perhaps to the feather.

Kotin releases Hodigo and calls, "All right, get up, Hodigo." He pauses. "I said, get up, you worthless . . ."

The man doesn't move. Wrass and I stand up to see better. Our guards do not seem to care. They are all breathlessly watching Hodigo.

"What's happening?" I ask Wrass, who is taller than me.

He shakes his head. "I don't know. He's just lying there."

Hodigo's friends bravely move in closer. One man crouches and places a hand to Hodigo's throat. "Blessed Spirits," he says softly. "He has no heartbeat. Is he breathing?" He quickly places his ear over the bloody designs on Hodigo's chest and listens. "I don't . . . I don't believe it! He's *dead.*"

Gannajero chuckles, and my legs go weak.

Tutelo looks from Wrass, to the guards, and back to me, and sobs, "Odion? What happened to that man?"

I cannot look at her.

The other girl in our group silently rolls to her back. I do not even know her name. She is the quiet one. The child no one seems to notice. Short and skinny, with irregularly cut mourning-hair, she has a face like a chipmunk's: round, with small dark eyes, and two front teeth that stick out slightly. She hasn't spoken a word to anyone . . . until now.

"Don't be s-scared. It wasn't the feather," she stutters. "Sh-she probably used helleb-bore. If you gather the roots this time of year, it—it's deadly."

We all turn to look at her. The attention seems to unnerve Chipmunk. She curls onto her side again and turns her back to us. She's shaking all over.

As I am. My legs feel like boiled grass stems. I sink to the ground and put my arm around my little sister. She hugs me tightly.

"It's all right, Odion," Tutelo whispers. "Mother and Father are coming. They're coming."

Seven

The northern sentry cried, "Two people on the north-eastern trail!"

Sindak climbed to a higher branch in the maple tree where he stood guard over the western trails. Glorious swaths of orange, red, and yellow leaves dappled the mountains. He scanned the winding stretches of trail he could see—even in the soft lavender gleam of dusk they seemed to glow. But he saw no travelers. Not that it mattered. He would know who they were soon enough.

He sighed and leaned against the massive tree trunk. A tall, muscular young man, he had seen nineteen summers. His beaked nose protruded far beyond his deeply sunken brown eyes. Shoulder-length black hair blew around his lean face. Few women found him attractive, which was one of the reasons his wife, Puksu, had recently divorced him. There were other reasons of course, not the least being that she despised him. He had committed two crimes in her eyes: He hadn't yet gained acclaim as a warrior, and they'd been married for two summers without a child. Gratefully, he no longer had to listen to her endless complaining.

His gaze drifted back to the broad plaza of Atotarho Village. Arranged in a rough oval around the plaza were four longhouses, four smaller clan houses, and a prisoners' house. The magnificent longhouses—the biggest ever built in the history of their people—were constructed of pole frames and covered with elm bark. The Wolf Clan longhouse was amazing; it stretched over eight hundred hand-lengths long and forty wide. The others were shorter, two or three hundred hands long, but still stunning, especially when viewed from Sindak's height. The arched roofs were almost level with his position, soaring over fifty hands high. Each clan was headed by a matron, and each longhouse was inhabited by the male and female descendants of one woman—around whom many legends revolved—and her maternal female descendants. When a man married, he moved to his wife's longhouse.

Since the People of the Hills traced descent through the females, a child belonged to his mother's clan and owed obedience to its clan elders. Women also owned the fields and houses. That's why women decided when to go to war. Everything at risk belonged to them. Men owned little more than their own clothing and weapons. It meant that men had fewer responsibilities, which freed them to fight, hunt . . .

A shouted curse rang out.

Sindak squinted at the council meeting where over five hundred people had gathered. The village matrons sat in a broad circle around the chief, discussing what should be done next. Chief Atotarho had just returned from a Trading voyage where his party had been attacked.

During the fighting, his ten-summers-old daughter had been taken prisoner. War Chief Nesi had tried to track the enemy warriors, but had lost their trail in the rain. Atotarho had been hoping to trade freshwater pearls for food—but had failed.

Everyone was hungry.

The matrons said that the past one hundred summers had been unusually cold and dry. Sindak knew only that the corn, beans, squash, and sunflowers rarely matured. He gazed down at the six women pounding corn in the plaza. They used a hollowed-out log as a mortar, threw in handfuls of dried corn, then beat it to a fine powder with a heavy wooden pestle, about twelve hands long. The rhythmic *thunk-thunk* echoed. A short distance away two women stood roasting the corn that would be ground in the mortars. They roasted whole ears over an open trench filled with glowing coals. Y-shaped sticks stood at either end of the trench; then ears were hung from a pole placed in the crotches of the sticks and roasted until completely parched, whereupon the women shelled the kernels into a bark barrel and stored it until needed in the mortars. This time of year, there should be two hundred women pounding and roasting corn—not six.

The harvest had been very poor. Meager harvests made people hunt harder, but after so many summers, the animals were mostly hunted out. The simple truth was that they were all growing desperate. Winter was almost upon them, and they had little food to stave off the cold. When people couldn't feed their children, they had to take what they needed from nearby villages.

Stealing had become a way of life. When it failed, warfare broke out. Battles had been raging, off and on, for more than one hundred summers, but it had gotten particularly violent in the past twenty summers. That's why a forty-hand-tall palisade of upright logs enclosed the village.

Sindak watched the people milling around inside the palisade. During the autumn most people spent every moment until total darkness down along rivers where the fields were, collecting the last green-corn cobs or picking late squash blossoms—but everyone knew this council meeting was critical.

Sindak climbed to a higher branch, where he could see better. Two of the clan matrons—both white-haired and skinny—waved their arms. Chief Atotarho, who had seen fifty-two summers, sat with his head down and his eyes closed, as though he could bear no more of this. He'd braided rattlesnake skins into his gray-streaked black hair, then coiled it into a bun at the base of his head and secured it with a tortoiseshell comb. The style gave his narrow face a starved look. On this cool day, he wore a smoked deerhide cape over his shoulders. Red paintings covered the golden hide, mostly images of men in battle, for he had once, a long time ago, been a great warrior. But now, the cape covered a crooked and misshapen body. Every summer, he seemed to grow thinner. The village Healers said he had the joint stiffening disease. His enemies, however, said Atotarho was a powerful sorcerer, a witch, and his evil deeds had come back to haunt him.

As evening settled over the land in a smoky veil,

long purple shadows spread through the forest, filling in the hollows of Atotarho's gaunt face. He had lost his only son in a raid seven summers ago; now his daughter was gone—probably being held hostage, maybe being tortured or worse. Atotarho must be frantic to get his daughter back.

Old Tila—matron of the Wolf Clan—leaped to her feet and shook her fist at Atotarho. More shouts rang out.

Sindak would love to be down there listening to the arguments, but his duty today was to keep watch on the western trails. Three other guards watched the northern, southern, and eastern trails. The boredom was excruciating. He often caught himself wishing Standing Stone warriors would attack just for the relief it would offer.

Kelek—matron of the Bear Clan—shouted at Atotarho, and the chief dropped his face into his hands as though totally defeated. His False Face pendant fell from his cape and swung in the dim light.

It was strange to see it around the neck of a man. Ordinarily the sacred pendant was passed from clan matron to clan matron, but Atotarho's only sister had died as a child. Since his mother had no daughter to give it to, the clan had bestowed it upon Atotarho when he became chief.

Sindak stared at it in awe. The pendant was ancient and chronicled the most sacred story of all: the great battle between human beings and Horned Serpent. At the dawn of creation, Horned Serpent had crawled out of Skanodario Lake and attacked the People. His poisonous breath, like a black cloud, swept over the land, killing almost everyone.

In terror, the People had cried out to the Great Spirit, and he sent Thunder to help them. A vicious battle ensued, and Thunder threw the greatest lightning bolt ever seen. The flash was so bright many of the People were instantly blinded. Then the concussion struck. The mountains shook, and the stars broke loose from the skies. As they came hurtling down, they hissed right over the People. Thousands slammed into Great Grandmother Earth. The ferocious blasts and scorching heat caused raging forest fires. The biggest star fell right into the lake on top of Horned Serpent. There was a massive explosion of steam and—as Horned Serpent thrashed his enormous tail in pain—gigantic waves coursed down the river valleys and surged over the hills in a series of colossal floods that drowned most of the People. Of the entire tribe, only five families remained—the five families who would become the Peoples that today lived south of Skanodario Lake.

Sindak propped his hand on his belted war club and checked the western trails again, ensuring they were still empty. He looked toward Forks River, where a group of young women were bathing. Several splashed around in the water. Another group sat on the darkening shore, naked, combing each other's hair while they dressed.

He smiled, letting erotic thoughts run through his mind. He . . .

"Are you watching the trails, or a woman?" a voice called from below.

Sindak looked down. His friend, Towa, stood below with another warrior named Pova. At twenty, Towa had waist-length black hair and a face women swooned over: oval, with a straight nose, perfect smile, and serious eyes. Unfortunately, Towa didn't see very well, which meant he couldn't hit a longhouse with an arrow at ten paces. But he was especially skilled at war strategy, which was probably why they were best friends. They balanced each other's weaknesses. Towa had recently been wounded in battle and still wore his left arm in a sling.

"I must be watching the trails. We haven't been attacked, have we?" he called back.

"No, but it's only a matter of time. The matrons voted."

"We're going to war to get the chief's daughter back?"

"We are. Our elders do not believe we have the luxury of doing nothing. They say we must act quickly or the Standing Stone People will view our lack of response as a sign of weakness and attack us. That's why I'm here. War Chief Nesi wants to see you. Pova will take your place as western sentry."

"And do a better job," Pova added.

Sindak grinned and scrambled down the tree, using the branches like a ladder. When he leaped off the last branch and landed in front of Towa, a burst of autumn leaves puffed up.

Pova chuckled at Sindak and climbed up to take the sentry position.

"Have I been chosen for the war party?"

Towa said, "You have."

"What about you?"

He yanked a thumb toward his wound and looked miserable. "Nesi told me I can't fight until the wind stops whistling through the hole in my shoulder."

"Well, don't worry. I'll kill two Standing Stone warriors in your honor."

Towa gave him an askance look. "Without me along to watch your back, I fear you may not even make it past our border. Be careful and don't think too much. It always ruins your aim."

"Thinking is for old women. I'll take a good fight over a peace council any day."

Towa walked beside him as Sindak headed back toward the plaza along the leaf-strewn trail. Fragrant autumn winds gusted through the trees, swirling leaves like tiny tornadoes. One careened along the trail in front of them.

"This war party is foolish, Sindak. If you can get out of it, do it."

"Why? I need all the chances to prove my valor I can get. No one is ever going to marry me again if my reputation as a warrior doesn't improve."

"Maybe. But you and I both know that Atotarho's daughter is probably dead, which means many of our warriors are about to die for no reason. Including you."

"But the Standing Stone elders would be idiots to kill Zateri. They could demand a huge ransom of corn for her and get it."

Towa gave him a somber look. "That would make things worse. If we emptied our food storehouses to buy Zateri back, we'd just have to raid someone else to replenish them. Besides, there's nothing the Standing Stone People need. Their harvests were good this year. That's the problem. Their storehouses are overflowing with food, and everyone wants it." Towa exhaled hard.

Sindak shrugged. "We need it. Our people are hungry."

"Yes, I know. We also need their hunting grounds, fishing lakes, nut forests, and especially their agricultural fields. As our numbers grow each year, our harvests get worse. To survive, we must take what they have. Where does it end? With all of us dead?"

Sindak frowned and kicked his way through a particularly high pile of leaves that blocked the trail. He didn't like thinking. Towa was the thinker. Fortunately for the Hills People, they had the greatest number of warriors in the land. They could take what they wanted, and did. No one liked warfare, but if it kept the Hills People alive, it was necessary. Throwing away lives on a futile mission, however, seemed folly.

"I have worse news yet," Towa said. "Because the council was divided on this issue, they only authorized Nesi to take twenty warriors on the war party."

"Twenty?" Sindak stopped in the middle of the trail. "That's idiotic."

"I told you. Get out of it if you can."

Sindak could suddenly envision his death, and he didn't like the looks of it. He started walking again. "I can't. I don't want to spend the rest of my life making excuses for why I didn't die with honor."

"You'd rather be in somebody's stomach than look cowardly?"

"Absolutely."

Two little boys ran up the trail. They veered wide around an ancient maple that fluttered crimson leaves down upon them and laughed as they raced by. Towa smiled and turned to watch them as they splashed their way through a pile of leaves. Two summers ago, Towa had lost his children and wife to a fever. He never talked about it, but sometimes Sindak could still see the pain in his eyes. "Blessed Ancestors, I don't—"

A shout rang through the trees: *"Two Standing Stone warriors coming!"*

They looked toward the northern sentry position, but they could just barely see him amid the dark hickory branches.

"The two travelers are Standing Stone warriors?" Towa's bushy black brows lowered. "Are they imbeciles? We'll slaughter them."

Sindak broke into a run. "Maybe they bring news about Zateri?"

By the time they reached the palisade, fifty Hills warriors were already assembled outside the main gate with arrows nocked in their bows. War Chief Nesi stood in front. A square-jawed bear of a man, his black headband held his chopped-off hair in place. Of medium height, he was all muscle. Ridges of white scars covered his face. Rather than a bow, he carried a massive stone-headed war club in his fist.

The two Standing Stone warriors came up the trail with their hands in the air. The woman was a tall, hard-eyed beauty. Her short hair was jagged, cut in mourning, and she had a sun-bronzed oval face with large dark eyes. She wore her red cape oddly tied over her belly.

"Blessed gods," Towa said, "I think that's Koracoo."

"It can't be," Sindak said disdainfully. "She's too smart to do something like this."

The woman called, "We come in peace!"

Sindak frowned at the man. His face, once handsome, looked much older than his jet-black hair would suggest. Battle walks did that, left telltale signs. Wrinkles etched lines across his forehead and cut deeply at the corners of his eyes.

"I think that's Koracoo's deputy, Gonda."

"Her husband? You may be right. I saw him once, five summers ago on my first raid."

Every eye in the village focused on the Standing Stone warriors. The matrons whispered behind their hands and made the sign against evil to protect them from any Spirits that may have walked the forest trails with the enemy.

Koracoo stopped short. "We must speak with Chief Atotarho."

Nesi stepped into the path in front of her, blocking her way just outside the palisade. "What message do you carry, War Chief Koracoo?"

Conversation burst out across the village. Everyone knew her name. In the past two summers since she had been elected war chief, she had killed many of their warriors.

Koracoo fearlessly walked up to stare him in the eye. "My words are for the chief's ears."

Towa leaned sideways to whisper, "She's smart. We can't kill her until we know."

Sindak's gaze went over Koracoo. She wore a red cape painted with the image of a blue buffalo. Her full lips were pressed into a tight white line, and her eyes promised death a hundred times over. She seemed to have something hidden in her tied cape.

Chief Atotarho lifted a hand. "Nesi, it's all right. Bring her to me."

A path opened through the crowd, and Nesi gestured for Koracoo to walk it. As she did, Gonda started to follow her.

Nesi thrust out his club to block Gonda's path. "Just her."

"I am her deputy. I *never* leave her side."

Nesi raised his club as though to strike, and ordered, "You will do as I say, warrior. Or I will club you senseless."

Sindak had to give Gonda credit; he didn't flinch. He stood his ground and growled, "Get out of my way!"

Atotarho called, "Nesi, let them both approach!"

Nesi glowered at Gonda, but stood aside and allowed him to follow his wife.

Sindak whispered, "She's magnificent, isn't she?"

"Hmm?" Towa said absently. He was staring at Gonda. "Who?"

"Koracoo. She's stunning. Though I've heard Nesi say she's timid, and that's why she doesn't go looking for fights to prove her valor. Do you think she's timid?"

Since Koracoo had become war chief, her village

rarely fought, and then only when attacked. That fact had led many Hills warriors to assume she was weak.

Towa replied, "For a timid woman, she's slaughtered a lot of our best warriors. It's far more likely that she picks her battles carefully."

Sindak grunted. Given the choice, he'd rush in with his bow singing and contemplate the repercussions later—an attitude that had gotten him into more than one impossible situation and earned him more than his share of ridicule. "You think much as she does, Towa. Someday, if you ever learn to aim, you may make—"

Koracoo stopped less than two paces from the chief and said, "Chief Atotarho, I have brought a child that needs your help."

Atotarho glanced at her belly. "What child?"

Gonda untied Koracoo's cape while Koracoo kept her hands on the bulge in her war shirt. When she gently reached beneath her war shirt and pulled out the naked baby, astonished cries rose from the spectators. People surged forward to look, pushing Towa and Sindak closer.

Atotarho asked, "Who does the child belong to?"

"We don't know, Chief. We've been tracking the war party that stole our children after the Yellowtail Village attack. Along the way, we found this baby, alive, but not well. Her soul is loose. She needs food and shelter immediately."

"Why should I care? She's not from this village."

"Perhaps not, but she is one of the People of the Hills. The blanket she was wrapped in bore your distinctive spiral designs."

Atotarho's eyes narrowed suspiciously. "Where is the blanket? Let me see it."

"It was soiled. We left it. But I have no cause to lie to you. She is a Hills child. In one of your villages, someone must be desperate to find her."

Koracoo extended her arms, holding out the baby. Several of the women in the crowd looked hard at the child, but none came forward to take it.

Koracoo said, "Chief, once you notify the other Hills villages that the baby is here, I'm sure her grateful family will arrive and shower you with gifts. Even if her parents are dead, her clan will want her back. Will you deny them the right?"

A pretty young woman, perhaps sixteen summers, shoved through the crowd and asked, "What color were the spirals on her blankets?"

"Red and black."

The woman turned to Atotarho. "Chief, those are Hawk Clan designs. I am Hawk Clan. If you will allow it, my family will take her until her family arrives."

Atotarho looked annoyed, but he flicked his hand at her, and she scurried forward, took the baby from Koracoo's arms, and hurried away toward the Hawk Clan longhouse.

Atotarho stood stiffly. "I understand little of this, War Chief Koracoo. Please tell me more of your story. Yellowtail Village was attacked?"

Koracoo exchanged a look with Gonda before she replied, "We assumed that perhaps some of your warriors were on the raid."

"No. I was on a trading expedition to the Flint lands.

I took sixty of our warriors with me and left the rest here to protect the village while we were away. When did this happen?"

"Five days ago."

Atotarho scanned Koracoo's face, then Gonda's, as though he feared trickery. "When did you find the baby?"

"Just this afternoon. We also think we found the trail of the warriors who stole our children, which means we need to resume our search as soon as possible."

"Your children? You mean your own children? Not just Yellowtail children?"

"My son and daughter were among those captured," Koracoo explained.

Sindak leaned over to whisper to Towa, "Zateri was also stolen five days ago. Is there a connection?"

"How could there be?"

Atotarho said, "War Chief Koracoo, do I have your oath that none of your warriors were involved in the attack on my trading party?"

She frowned. "Your trading party was attacked? I know nothing of it. Half of our warriors were killed when we were attacked, and I ordered the other half to guard our village survivors while they cared for the dead and collected their few belongings. I assure you, Yellowtail Village has sent no war parties into Hills country."

Atotarho's cape flapped in the wind as he considered her words. In a fearful voice, he said, "Were there other children taken?"

"Yes, several. Though I can't say they were all taken by the same war party."

Atotarho shivered suddenly, as though the thin lance of the forest night had pierced his cape. He stepped closer to Koracoo. His misshapen body crackled as he moved, and his face had taken on an almost skeletal appearance. "I pray it is not so . . . but I fear we may have a common enemy."

"Who?"

He backed away, saying, "I need to discuss this with our matrons before I tell you more." He lifted a hand to Nesi. "War Chief? Take them to the prisoners' house until I know the matrons' wishes."

"No!" Gonda shouted. "We need to get back on the trail immediately."

"Quiet," Koracoo ordered softly.

Eight

Nesi pointed his war club. "You four: Sindak, Towa, Ober, and Akio, take these warriors to the prisoners' house and set up alternating watches." Nesi looked toward the eastern side of the village, where the prisoners' house nestled against the high palisade wall. On the catwalk near the top, warriors stood guard. Then his gaze scanned the crowd. People had started to grumble. Several had picked up rocks. "And hurry, before anyone takes a notion to avenge his dead relatives."

"Yes, War Chief." Sindak gestured for Koracoo and Gonda to start walking. Gonda gave him a hostile look, but walked.

Sindak let Ober and Towa escort the Standing Stone warriors, while he and Akio brought up the rear.

Villagers coalesced into a small mob and followed them.

"This could be unpleasant," Akio whispered. He had seen just sixteen summers and spent most of his time lounging around his family's longhouse, which was why he was pudgy and perpetually out of breath. "Our village lost many warriors in that battle with the Standing Stone people last moon."

"Last moon's battle was not with Yellowtail Village," Sindak pointed out. "White Dog Village—"

"It won't matter to the families that lost loved ones. For them a Standing Stone warrior is a Standing Stone warrior."

Akio was right. Sindak kept turning around and noticed that Koracoo, too, was carefully observing the crowd. Her shoulder muscles had gone tight under her red cape.

Akio said, "I wonder where she stowed CorpseEye?"

"Her legendary war club? I had forgotten all about it."

"It must be somewhere close. She wouldn't leave Yellowtail Village without it. It's supposed to have great Spirit Power." His fat florid face reddened with excitement. "And it's worth a fortune."

"You're a greedy boy, Akio." Actually, it was a good idea. If they could find it and deliver it to Nesi, he would reward them handsomely. "Tomorrow morning, if they are still captives, I'll help you hunt."

Akio smiled. "I'll be ready. Maybe we should ask Towa to help, too?"

"I don't think so. He doesn't believe in Spirit Power."

"He believes in wealth, doesn't he?" Akio gave him a sideways look. When Sindak didn't respond immediately, Akio added, "And not believing in Spirit Power is dangerous. Someday a Spirit is going to sneak up on him and suck his souls out through his ears."

Sindak shrugged. "It will be interesting to see if he notices."

As they approached the prisoners' house, one old

woman shouted, "Standing Stone filth," and threw a rock at Koracoo. It struck her in the shoulder. Koracoo swung around to glare at the woman just as another rock whistled past, thumped off the house, and bounced across the ground.

"Hurry," Towa said. "Let's get them inside."

The prisoners' house stretched forty hands long and twenty wide. The walls were not of bark construction, but sturdy oak planks reinforced with cross-poles.

Ober pulled back the heavy door—hung on leather hinges—and said, "Quickly, before we have to put down a riot."

Koracoo and Gonda disappeared into the darkness. Ober closed the door and dropped the plank across it to lock it.

A boy picked up another rock and grunted as he hurled it as hard as he could. It cracked against the house. "You killed my brother!" he cried, and broke into tears. "My only brother! I hope you die!"

Ober shouted, "Get out of here! All of you. Go home. You can call insults tomorrow!"

No one paid attention to him.

Several knots of people formed. They stood around grumbling, shouting insults, and casting hateful glances at the prisoners' house. Stones continued to thump the walls.

Towa turned to Sindak. "I think you and I should take first watch."

Sindak nodded, and they took up guard positions on either side of the door.

Ober scanned the remaining people, then walked

over to Towa and softly asked, "Can you do this, Towa? You're still injured. What if trouble breaks out?"

Towa smiled. "Don't worry. I'll be all right. I'll shout for help and hold them off until you get here."

Ober stared hard into his eyes, silently judging Towa's strength and ability. "Very well. Akio and I will sleep with the Wolf Clan tonight." He aimed his war club at Tila's longhouse. It was a massive structure, the largest in the village, and as night deepened, it loomed like a huge dark monster. "We'll be no more than twenty paces away if you need us."

"Thank you, my friend."

Ober and Akio walked away. Several members of the crowd cursed them for protecting the prisoners, knowing all the while the men had been ordered to do so.

"Filthy Standing Stone beasts!" an old woman screamed and hurled a pot at the prisoners' house. It shattered against the planks, and sherds cartwheeled across the ground. "I'll kill you myself before you leave here!"

"I'll help her!" A muscular warrior named Tadu shouted, and hurled another stone. It whacked against the house and clattered down among the broken potsherds.

Sindak, about to comment on the situation, turned to Towa . . . and saw something. A momentary flash of light, like the flare of a hidden lightning bolt. It frosted the wooden roof of the prisoners' house. He blinked.

"What are you looking at?" Towa asked.

"There's a storm coming. I just saw lightning."

"What lightning? There isn't a cloud in the sky."

"How would you know? You have the vision of a mole. It was right there." He pointed.

Beyond the palisade wall, a gigantic maple stood, its scarlet leaves like drops of blood against the bruised evening sky. In that moment, Sindak would have sworn the great tree had eyes. Eyes fixed right on him.

Sindak glanced at the warriors who stood guard on the catwalk. They held their weapons in tight fists, staring out at the coming night as though they sensed it, too. Many had their jaws clenched.

"Don't you feel that, Towa?"

"Feel what?"

"That eerie sensation, as though there's something out there, something not human. And it's waiting to pounce on us."

"Like a bear?"

"No, not like a bear, like one of the Faces of the Forest, or a Stone Giant. Maybe even a Flying Head." A prickle climbed Sindak's spine. Flying Heads were terrifying creatures. They had no bodies, just long trailing hair, and huge bear paws for hands, which they used to capture and eat anything they wished, including humans.

Towa laughed. "Lightning? Flying Heads? You are very inventive, my friend."

Sindak grinned, but he couldn't shake the feeling that something, or someone, was watching him with glistening inhuman eyes.

Nine

Sonon perched on a high branch, hidden by the red maple's thick trunk. Less than twenty paces from Atotarho Village, he had a good view.

They'd found the baby he'd covered with leaves.

Moving carefully lest the sentries on the catwalk see him, he folded his arms beneath his cape and hugged himself. Odd. He could not feel the child's afterlife soul moving through the trees around the village. He'd been hoping to see her again. It hurt that he did not, but perhaps that was good. The girl's soul might be staying very close to its body, which would make it easier for a Healer to find it and tie it to the child's flesh again.

Only the faintest whisper of wings broke the silence as an owl sailed over the treetops and, somewhere in the distance, a wolf yipped. Both creatures were out on their nightly hunts, looking forward to finding and killing prey to fill their bellies with warm blood.

Sonon wiped his sweating hands on his cape. Men needed blood as much as wolves. At the edges of appearance and disappearance there was always blood.

He studied the warriors who walked the palisade catwalk. He could see their heads bobbing along as though disembodied. All around them, the endless eyes of night were opening, but the guards saw only the shadows cast by the soft glow of the evening. The *communion* of the night was lost to them.

Sonon rubbed his eyes. The communion was all he had. The hunter became the hunted. Perceiver the perceived. The endless eyes stared into eternity, and it stared back.

Sonon patiently waited until the darkness grew too deep for the sentries to glimpse him; then he carefully descended the maple, silently dropping from branch to branch. The wet leaves squished when he dropped to the ground.

Grandmother Moon would awaken soon. He needed to get away before she flooded the forest with light. Slipping behind an elm tree, he faded back into the striped forest shadows and melted into the blackness.

Ten

"Atotarho looked frightened," Gonda said. "And I don't think he's the type that frightens easily. What do you think scared him?"

The odor of mildew pervaded the dark prisoners' house, and insects skittered across the floor, or perhaps they were mice. Gonda couldn't be certain. If he was lucky, they were mice, and one would scurry close enough that he could catch it and twist its head off to ease his hunger.

"Whatever it was, he didn't want his People to overhear him talking about it."

Koracoo sat on the floor with her back against the wall. In the moonlight that penetrated around the door, he could make out the shape of her body. No one but Gonda would realize how desperately worried she was. He could see it in the tension in her shoulders and in the way her jaw was set slightly to the left.

"Was he worried about alarming his warriors?" Gonda asked skeptically.

"My gut tells me he didn't feel he could trust them with the knowledge."

"Perhaps it's just his war chief he doesn't trust. I didn't like him, either."

Wind gusted outside and breathed through the wall behind him, chilling his back. He wrapped his cape more tightly around his shoulders.

Fatigue numbed him, and long ago he'd learned that sleep was essential to survival. Death walked at every warrior's shoulder, waiting for him to drop his guard so that it could dull his wits and slow his reactions. Less than a blink was enough.

"You have to get some rest," he said.

"I need to think for a time."

Gonda stretched out on his side and closed his eyes. He tried to concentrate on the sensation of breathing, of air rushing in and out of his lungs. It distracted him from thinking about tomorrow. If all went well, they would return to the murder site, pick up the children's trail, and track them down. If all did not go well . . .

We're prisoners. Why did I agree to come here when our own children are in danger?

He clenched his teeth to hold back the tidal wave of emotion that overwhelmed him. He'd been trying to take each moment as it came, trying not to see ahead. It did no good to imagine what was happening to Odion and Tutelo. The images only sapped his strength, leaving him quivering and useless.

Koracoo must be enduring the same agony, and perhaps with even more intensity than he did.

Gonda opened his eyes. "Tomorrow. We'll pick up the trail, and it will lead us right to them."

Koracoo did not answer. She stared at the square of moonlight that outlined the door. Occasionally, shadows crossed in front of it, and the house momentarily went black.

Gonda added, "They can't be that far ahead of us. The tracks were only one day old, and it looked like the warriors were herding eight or nine children. That many captives slow men down."

Koracoo leaned her head back against the wall and looked at the roof. Tiny points of light sparkled. Holes. If it rained, by morning they would be drenched.

"Koracoo, what will we do if Atotarho does not release us in the morning? Have you considered that? It would be a great boon for him to capture War Chief Koracoo and her deputy." He paused, watching her. "We *must* get back on the children's trail as soon as possible."

He waited.

Her silence was like an enormous black bubble swelling in Gonda's chest, cutting off his air. It was an accusation: *This is all your fault. The destruction of our village. The loss of our children. The deaths of hundreds.*

He tried to calm himself by taking deep, even breaths.

"Please, Koracoo," he begged. "Talk to me. I can't bear your silence."

She exhaled softly and turned to look at him. Her eyes reflected the moonlight like perfectly still ponds. "Gonda, I will talk strategy with you. You are my deputy. But I will not discuss our children. If I do, you will *not* feel better. Do you understand?"

He jerked a nod. "Then let's talk strategy. If they do not release us tomorrow, I've been thinking we may be able to gather more warriors to help us. Atotarho said there are many people who have lost children. If we can recruit a large-enough force—"

"More warriors mean arguments, politics, and intrigue. You and I are enough."

Koracoo shifted her back against the wall and laced her hands over one drawn-up knee. Her short moon-lit hair shimmered with her movements. "Besides, Atotarho is going to release us. He must."

"What makes you think that?"

"Something in his voice. He wants us out there on the trail. I do not know why, but it's important to him."

"His daughter?"

She took a breath and let it out. "He may think she is with the others."

She had carefully avoided saying, *with our children.*

Gonda proceeded cautiously. "What would make him think that? They were all taken at different times by different warriors."

"Hope often draws connections where there are none. Perhaps he—"

The hissing of warriors' voices silenced her. Her gaze riveted on the door.

Outside, a warrior said, "He's coming this way."

"No, he's not. He's just out for a walk. Probably worried about his daughter."

"He is so coming here! Why would he—"

The warriors hushed. Feet shuffled, and shadows passed back and forth, blotting out the silver gleam that rimmed the door.

"Open the door," Chief Atotarho ordered.

"Yes, my chief."

Wood clattered as the locking plank was lifted and the door swung open.

Gonda studied the five men standing outside. Atotarho carried a small oil lamp. Behind him, moonlight streamed across the village, turning the longhouses into enormous black walls. A few dogs trotted through the night, their tails wagging. Ordinary village sounds echoed: people snoring, children crying, a few coughs.

Koracoo softly said, "Chief? How may we assist you?"

Atotarho moved painfully, rocking and swaying as he entered the house with his lamp. To the warriors, he said, "Close the door behind me."

"But . . . my chief, you can't go in alone. There are two of them. What if they attack you?"

"I will risk it. Close the door."

The warriors hissed to each other, but obeyed.

As the door swung closed, the lamplight seemed to grow brighter, reflecting from the plank walls like gigantic amber wings. Atotarho wore a beautiful black ritual cape covered with circlets of bone cut from human skulls. When the lamplight touched them, they flashed. A halo of gray-streaked black hair braided with rattlesnake skins encircled his bony face. "War Chief Koracoo, Deputy Gonda, I must speak with you in confidence. Is that possible between us?"

Their people had been at war for decades. It was a fair question.

Koracoo rose to her feet. "You have my oath, Chief. Whatever we say here remains between us."

Gonda got to his feet and stood beside her. "You have my oath, as well."

Atotarho came forward with great difficulty. "Forgive me; I cannot stand for long. I need to sit down." He lowered himself to sit upon the cold dirt floor and placed his oil lamp in front of him. "Please, join me." He gestured to the floor, and Gonda noticed that his fingertips were tattooed with snake eyes, and he wore bracelets of human finger bones. "This will not be an easy conversation for any of us."

Gonda and Koracoo sat down.

Koracoo asked, "What is it you wish to discuss?"

He didn't seem to hear. His gaze was locked on the lamp. The fragrance of walnut oil perfumed the air. Finally, he whispered, "Stories have been traveling the trails for several moons, but only I believed them. She has been gone for many summers—perhaps as long as twenty, though no one can be sure. She's very cunning."

Koracoo seemed to stop breathing. "Who?"

Atotarho bowed his head. "Have you heard the name Gannajero?"

Gonda felt like the earth had been kicked out from under him. More legend than human, hideous stories swirled about Gannajero. She was a Trader who specialized in child slaves. Evil incarnate. A beast in the form of an old woman.

Koracoo softly answered, "Yes. I've heard of her."

Atotarho continued. "Rumors say that she has returned to our country. Many villages are missing children. I have been . . . so afraid . . ." He rubbed a hand over his face.

"That your daughter was with her?"

He seemed to be trying to control his voice. "Yes. All day, every day, I pray to the gods to let my Zateri die if she is with Gannajero. I would prefer it. Anything would be b-better. . . ."

Koracoo gave him a few moments to continue. When it was clear he could not, she said, "I understand."

Atotarho's mouth trembled. "No, I do not think you do. You are too young. When she was last here, you were not even a woman yet, were you?"

"I had seen only seven summers, but I recall hearing my family whisper about Gannajero, and it was with great dread."

Atotarho extended his hands to the lamp as if to warm them. His misshapen knuckles resembled knotted twigs. "When I had seen five summers, my older brother and sister were captured in a raid. My sister was killed, but my brother was sold to an old man among the Flint People. I heard many summers later that my brother was utterly mad. His nightmares used to wake the entire village. Sometimes he screamed all night long. He eventually killed the old man, slit his throat, and ran away into the forest. No one ever saw him again."

"Our people, also, have lost many children in such raids."

Gonda looked from Atotarho to Koracoo, watching their expressions. Neither trusted the other, and Gonda wondered what Atotarho might be telling them if they did.

Gonda asked, "What makes you think Gannajero is

behind these recent kidnappings? They could be ordinary raids for women and children. In that case, the children are all well and being adopted into families as we speak."

"I pray that is so, but if Gannajero *is* behind these kidnappings, our children are not well." The chief's eyes narrowed against some inner pain. "My daughter was studying to become a Healer. She knows Spirit plants and how to make poultices. I pray it is enough to allow her to survive Gannajero's torments."

In a deadly earnest voice, Koracoo said, "If Gannajero harms any of our children, I *will* find her. I promise you that."

"Perhaps, but many have tried before you. No one has ever been able to track her. Her trail just seems to disappear. It is said that she has many *hanehwa* at her command, and they help her mislead her pursuers."

Hanehwa were human skins that had been flayed whole by a witch and served as guards. These skin beings never slept. They warned witches of a pursuer by giving three shouts.

Atotarho opened his mouth to continue, then hesitated.

"Go on."

He looked at Koracoo with shining eyes. "The men she travels with are evil, mostly outcast warriors who enjoy getting rich off the suffering of children. If the children are lucky, they do not live long. Two or three moons, perhaps."

It took all of Gonda's strength to keep his thoughts from straying to Odion and Tutelo.

The lamp flickered when Gonda abruptly leaned forward. "Let's talk about how she accomplishes all this. How do men know where to meet her? To bring her the children?"

Atotarho shook his head. "No one is sure. The last time she was in our country, we thought we understood how she worked. She usually arrived moons before she actually began buying children. The time allowed her to set up her contacts, prepare her trails and meeting places, assemble her men. She—"

"Then . . ." Gonda's belly knotted. "She may not have just arrived here. She may have been here for moons?"

"It's possible. Though I suspect not. We almost caught her last time. She knows she must use great care."

Trancelike, Koracoo sat perfectly still, but she said, "Please, go on with what you were saying. You said that twenty summers ago, you thought you understood how she worked. How?"

"We kept watch on her meeting places. She hired men to leave children's toys at specific locations. For example, if she would be at that location to purchase children in five days, the hired men left five toys. Each day that passed, one toy would disappear, until the final day when the man cut the last toy in half, indicating that she would be there that day."

Koracoo straightened. It was a subtle movement. Gonda doubted the chief even noticed, but Gonda understood. Koracoo was remembering the clearing where they'd found the baby. The cornhusk doll had been torn in half.

A coincidence. Our children were taken by Mountain People warriors. . . .

"It would help me"—Koracoo's voice was slow and precise—"if you told me everything you know about Gannajero. Who is she? Where is she from? I know only old stories that make her sound more like a Spirit than a human being."

A gust of wind penetrated around the door, and the golden lamplight cast their shadows like leaping animals upon the walls.

Atotarho clasped his hands in his lap. "I don't know much. No one does. They say she was born among the Flint or Hills Peoples. Her grandmother was supposedly a clan elder, a powerful woman. But during a raid when Gannajero was eight, she was stolen and sold into slavery to the Mountain People. Then sold again, and again. She was apparently a violent child. Several times, she was beaten almost to death by her owners."

"And now she does the same thing to other children?" The hatred in Gonda's voice made Atotarho and Koracoo turn. "What sort of men would help her? How does she find them?"

"I wish I knew. Twenty summers ago, we thought they were all outcasts, men who had no families or villages. Then we discovered one of her men among our own. He was my sister's son, Jonil. A man of status and reputation. He'd been sending her information about planned raids, then capturing enemy children and selling them to her."

Gonda clenched his fists. Warfare provided opportunities for greedy men that were not available in times of peace. Since many slaves were taken during attacks, it was easy to siphon off a few and sell them to men who no longer saw them as human. War did that. It turned people into *things.* It gave men an opportunity to vent their rage and hatred in perverted ways that their home villages would never have allowed.

"Why?" Gonda blurted. "Why did he do it?"

Atotarho bowed his head, and the shadows of his eyelashes darkened his cheeks. "She rewards her servants well. When we searched Jonil's place in the longhouse, we found unbelievable riches—exotic trade goods like obsidian and buffalo wool from the far west. Conch shells from the southern ocean. An entire basket of pounded copper sheets covered with strings of pearls and magnificently etched shell gorgets."

Koracoo sat quietly for a time, thinking, before she said, "That means it will be difficult to buy the children back."

"Virtually impossible. She profits enormously from her captives. With all the stealing and raiding going on, there are too many evil men with great wealth."

Koracoo toyed with the hem of her cape, smoothing it between her fingers. Gonda frowned. Had she been hoping they could simply buy the children back and be on their way? Where had she planned to get the wealth? They were carrying almost nothing with them—just their capes, canteens, small belt pouches, and a few weapons.

"But . . ." Atotarho broke the silence. "If my daughter is being held captive with your children, I will give you whatever I have to get all of them back."

Koracoo held his gaze, judging the truthfulness of his words. Atotarho looked her straight in the eyes without blinking. Finally, Koracoo asked, "Why would you buy our children? We are your enemies."

"If you are willing to risk your lives to save my daughter, you are not my enemy."

Gonda sat stunned. The night had gone utterly quiet. The guards must be holding their breaths, listening. Very softly Koracoo asked, "Why haven't you already mounted a search party and sent them out with this same offer? Surely you can trust your own handpicked warriors more than you can us."

Atotarho looked over his shoulder, glanced at the door behind him, and whispered, "No. The attack on my trading party was well organized, and they went straight for my beautiful daughter." His knobby hand clenched to a fist. "As there was many summers ago, I fear there is a traitor here. So, you see, I would rather trust an enemy who shares my interests . . . than a friend who may not."

Koracoo's gaze roamed the firelit shadows for thirty heartbeats—long enough that Atotarho began to fidget. When she looked back, she said, "Tell me more about your trading mission. It's autumn. Many villages have had poor harvests. Raiders are on every trail, Chief, stealing what they can. Especially stealing women and children to replace the family members they've lost. Why would you risk going out at such a time? What were you trading for?"

His long face slackened, making his eyes seem larger. "Ocean pearls and salted seafood. Why?"

"Just curious," Koracoo answered calmly, then added, "We will need to discuss your offer."

"I understand." The chief groaned as he rose to his feet, and the circlets of skull that covered his cape flashed. "I'll leave you the lamp; it will provide a little warmth until the oil runs out." The effort of rising seemed to have cost him all of his strength.

He stood panting for a time before he said, "Many of my people believe I am the human False Face prophesied in our legends. The Spirit-Man who will save the world. It has never been an easy title to bear. Especially now when I cannot even save my own daughter." Without making a sound, he turned and started for the door. "Let me know your decision as soon as you've made it, and I—"

"One last thing."

He turned. "Yes?"

"What assurances do we have that you will keep your part of this bargain? Gannajero will not believe me if I tell her you will pay her later."

Atotarho braced his hand against the door to steady himself. "I will send a man with you who can verify my offer. Now sleep for as long as you can. If you choose to accept, the next few days will not be pleasant for you." He pounded on the door. "Guards? I'm ready to leave."

The door opened, and he stepped into the night.

Gonda watched him walk away with his personal guards. The remaining guards whispered to each other, then turned to stare in at Koracoo and Gonda.

Koracoo asked, "How much did you hear, Sindak?"

The shorter man replied, "Not nearly enough, War Chief."

The door swung closed. After the locking plank fell into place, Koracoo said, "I feel the same way."

"As do I," Gonda whispered.

An excited conversation erupted outside.

Sindak hissed, "By the Spirits, I would hate to be the warrior he sends with Koracoo. He'll be asking for a stiletto between the ribs."

"She won't kill him. She can't. He's her lifeline to saving her own children. Besides, that would be the least of my worries."

"What do you mean?"

"I mean, I'd be far more afraid of what Atotarho would do to me if I failed to bring his daughter home safe and sound."

"Oh," Sindak said. "That is terrifying. I've always worried that someday my own people would turn me into a feast."

Gonda looked at Koracoo. She hadn't moved. "Are you all right?"

"As well as I can be after a discussion about Gannajero."

"Forget about her. Our children were captured by Mountain warriors. Not Gannajero. She died long ago." He grunted. "If she ever actually lived."

For a long time, Koracoo stared at the lamp's flame, as though deep in thought; then she stretched out on her side.

Gonda curled up on the other side of the lamp. The faint warmth was a balm on his face.

The warriors continued talking outside.

Sindak asked, "Have you ever heard of Gannajero?"

"She's a myth."

"How do you know? We hadn't even been born the last time she was in this country."

"True. But if she's as bad as Atotarho said, there would be many stories about her evil deeds."

"Maybe there are stories, but we haven't heard her name because our people are forbidden to speak it—as we are forbidden to speak the names of outcasts."

There was a pause, then Sindak said, "Well, one thing is for certain—if she exists, someone needs to kill her."

"Yes, she . . ." His voice went too low to hear.

A breath of wind penetrated around the door, fluttering the lamp's flame and filling the house with the scent of mildew.

"Gannajero. The crow," Koracoo whispered.

"What?"

"Gannajero the crow. Black. Black as coal. It was a song we sang as children. My father used to threaten me when I was bad, tell me that he was going to sell me to Gannajero."

Gonda opened one eye to stare at her. "Your father was a stiff-necked old villain. I never liked him."

After a long pause, Koracoo said, "Not many did."

Eleven

As she slid deeper into sleep, the dream swept over Koracoo. . . .

She led her war party up the trail toward Yellowtail Village at a dead run. Ahead, a gaudy orange halo gleamed against the velvet darkness. Veils of snow gusted by. The pines and oaks drooped mournfully beneath the weight, creaking and groaning in the wind. And in the depths of the trees, she saw the silver-silk flash of people moving. Quiet. Deathly quiet. As though they feared being seen.

Heartbeats behind them, enemy warriors filed out of the darkness, clutching bags or bows, smiling as they trotted right for Koracoo's war party.

"Mountain People!" she cried, and her fatigued warriors charged out to meet them. The sounds of clubs striking flesh, grunts, and shrieks tore the night.

Koracoo leaped upon the closest man. . . .

Her hands jerked. She woke and glimpsed the plank walls of the prisoners' house, smelled the sweet walnut oil in the lamp.

A dream . . . just a dream.

But when her eyes fell closed again, the fragrance of the oil became the pungent odor of smoke, and blind terror stalked her as she again charged headlong up the trail with her heart beating in her throat. The sound of one man's feet pounded behind her.

"Koracoo! This is foolish!" her deputy, Deru, called. "We should stay with our war party!"

As she rounded a bend in the trail, he caught up with her. He was a big, muscular man with massive shoulders. He gripped his war club in a tight fist.

"Go back, Deru!" she yelled as two Mountain warriors leaped onto the trail in front of her. Koracoo danced in with CorpseEye. She slammed the first man in the face, and spun to catch the second man behind the knees. When he hit the ground, she was on top of him, hammering his brains out. Her warriors flooded around her, shrieking war cries as they charged for home.

And ran straight into a group of enemy warriors herding freshly captured women and children before them. All of the children were crying, and several of the women clutched babies in their arms.

"Those are my children!" a man cried.

Another yelled, "That's my wife!"

The sharp cracking of war clubs filled the night. Women and children scattered. Koracoo waded in with her war club swinging. In the darkness, she couldn't tell the identities of the children who ran past, but she kept searching, searching for her own family. Asleep, dead, or reborn in another body, she would know her children. She knew the way they moved. Even in darkness she would recognize them, wouldn't she?

A mother with four children rushed down the trail toward her, one little boy gripping the woman's torn dress and sobbing. As the boy ran closer, Koracoo could see his blood-soaked shirt.

Koracoo broke free of the battle and ran hard for the village. Deru was right beside her.

"Gonda must have been overrun."

"Clearly," Deru answered.

How had she so miscalculated the number of warriors he would need to defend the village? She'd missed something. Something critical. He should have been able to hold off a force three times his size.

Gonda, where are you?

Koracoo leaped a fallen log and sprinted for the rear palisade, her heart jamming against her ribs. Enemy warriors still surrounded the burning village. Twenty or more stood laughing near the front gates. Were they totally unafraid? Was there no one left to fight?

Forgive me, Gonda. . . .

Tears of desperation burned her eyes. She reached the wall—found a charred section that had been mostly burned through—and used CorpseEye to bash a hole in it. Then she hit the ground and slithered through on her belly.

When she got to her feet, the air was so thick with smoke she could barely see across the plaza, but the vision stunned her. Every longhouse burned, the flames leaping fifty hands into the sky, and the dead scattered the ground. Cries and screams laced the air. Many people wandered the plaza, turning over bodies, obviously searching for loved ones.

"Koracoo!" Deru scrambled through the hole and stood at her shoulder. "This is dangerous. What do you think you can do here? We should at least wait until our war party catches up before we—"

"I must find out what happened." *And find Gonda and my children.*

Koracoo trotted through the smoke. As she veered around a smoldering section of wall, she caught sight of a little boy crouching in the shadows. Five or six summers, his soot-coated face was streaked with tears. He stared up at Koracoo and clenched his jaw.

"Oh. No." Koracoo headed toward him.

"Koracoo, we don't have time. If we're going to do this, we—"

"I can't just leave him here. He's alone and scared."

She hurried to the boy. Blood clotted his cape. The child stared up at her as she stroked his filthy cheek.

"What's your name?"

"Saga." He fell into a coughing fit. Blood coated his hand when he lowered it.

"Are you hurt, Saga?" Koracoo reached for the cape.

"Not so bad," Saga said. He lifted his arms and allowed Koracoo to look beneath at his chest.

Something in her soul cried out. An arrow must have gone straight through his thin body. Every time Saga inhaled the hole blew bubbles. But the wound was at the very top of his lung. There was a chance . . .

"Deru, there must be a place where the medicine elders have been treating the wounded. We need to find it."

Deru gave her a disbelieving look. That was the first thing the enemy did, kill the elders, but he said, "Yes, War Chief."

"It's . . . it's over there." Saga pointed. "Near the Bear Clan longhouse."

"Deru, you lead. I'll carry Saga."

Deru scanned the smoke as Koracoo slipped her arms beneath Saga and gently lifted him. "Saga, I'm going to carry you over to the medicine elders."

Deru stepped out, leading the way with his war club at the ready.

As they walked, Saga stared up at her with glowing eyes. "I know stories about you. My . . . my mother . . . tells me stories at night." His breathing grew more labored. Koracoo could feel the rattling in her arms. She walked faster.

"Good stories or bad stories?"

Saga smiled. "Good. They're stories about our village heroes. Mother says . . ." He started coughing again, and blood gushed from his mouth. When it was over, he gasped for air.

"Hold on, Saga. We're almost there. The elders will Heal you."

"Do you . . . remember? Remember . . . that fight where fifty Flint warriors had you trapped . . . just you and Gonda . . . and you killed all of them . . . before you escaped? Where did that happen? I'm too . . . tired to remember."

Saga looked up at her with such love and admiration that Koracoo's heart ached. There had only been seven warriors, but Saga didn't need to hear that now. "That was over on the shores of Skanodario Lake."

Saga feebly reached out to touch Koracoo's red cape. He caressed it reverently. "Sometimes . . . when I play with my brother . . . I pretend I'm you."

"Well, I hope you also pretend you have another couple of thousand warriors. I need them. Especially tonight."

Weakly, Saga whispered, "It's all right. You'll win."

A wave of futility went through her. "Someday, when you grow up, I'm going to make you one of my deputies."

Saga's eyes went wide. "I'll be a good . . . deputy."

"I know you will."

Deru was moving quickly, hugging the western palisade wall where the smoke was the thickest. After fifty paces, he stopped and said, "There's someone ahead. I think it's Yanesh. The Speaker for the Women."

The Three Old Women, the clan matrons, announced their decisions through their Speaker. Yanesh was tall and thin, with graying black hair. As Koracoo approached, the woman turned. It was indeed Yanesh. She moved through a sea of wounded people. There had to be hundreds, lying in rows, their faces covered with gray ash from the fires.

Koracoo carried the boy over to where Yanesh stood among the wounded.

"Saga?" Yanesh said. "Put him here. Gently!"

Koracoo eased the boy to the hides spread out over

the ground and said, "Get well, Saga. I'm counting on you."

Saga just smiled and closed his eyes as though the walk had taken all of his strength.

"Yanesh, what happened?" Koracoo asked.

Yanesh expelled a breath. She had a catlike face, a broad nose, and long lashes. She had seen forty summers pass.

"The enemy attacked with overwhelming force, Koracoo."

While Koracoo talked with Yanesh, Deru stood guard, his intent gaze scanning the smoke.

"But I left you with enough warriors to hold off—"

"Gonda split his forces."

She stared at Yanesh as though the woman was mad. "That's not possible. I ordered him to keep all of his warriors inside the palisade. He would never—"

"He disobeyed you." Yanesh's mouth quivered as she clamped her teeth. "The council told him not to, told him to keep fighting, but he sent half our warriors outside, and as soon as they were gone, we were overrun. We didn't have enough warriors left to defend the village."

Koracoo gripped CorpseEye in a hard fist. She didn't believe it. "Where is Gonda?"

Yanesh shook her head. "No one knows. He led the group of warriors who ran outside. We haven't seen him since. He's probably . . ."

Yanesh didn't say it, but Koracoo finished the sentence for her. "He's probably dead."

"Yes, and where were you, War Chief? You were

supposed to be back by nightfall!" Her voice broke, and she sobbed.

Guilt ravaged Koracoo. "We were attacked, Yanesh. The battle was fierce. I lost one-third of my warriors. The rest of us barely got away—"

"Koracoo!" Deru shouted, and leaped forward swinging his war club as four Mountain warriors appeared out of the firelit smoke and charged them.

"Yanesh, get down!"

Koracoo lunged forward. When CorpseEye collided with the enemy's war club, a stinging wave flashed up her arms. . . .

And woke her.

She stared at the roof over her head, where shadows danced in the flickering light of the oil lamp.

Gonda rolled over and stared at her. "Are you all right?"

A terrifying brew of rage and despair was running hot in her veins.

"Koracoo?" Gonda whispered.

She fought down the shout that climbed into her throat, said, "Yes," and closed her eyes.

Twelve

Odion

As Grandmother Moon climbs high into the night sky, a ghostly sparkle filters through the trees and coats the autumn leaves with a liquid silver sheen. The yips of wolves carry on the cold breeze sweeping up the trails, and I have the chilling feeling that the night is filled with wandering forest Spirits. Sometimes I see them, flitting between the trunks like white scraps of cloth.

"I need more corn brew!" a man shouts. "Come over here, boy."

I peer out at the warriors who perch like vultures on logs around the fire, using their teeth to rip hunks of meat from roasted grouse. The fire's orange gleam reflects from their greasy mouths and hands. Hehaka wanders through the gathering, carrying a gourd filled with a brew made from fermented corn, pouring it into cups. I watch him. He moves as though he's done this many times, and I wonder how long he's been a slave.

I think about the corn brew, and my throat aches. I tasted it once. Our people pound corn kernels to mush, then leave it until it turns sour. Finally, they pour off the liquid to create the bitter brew. I don't know how anyone can drink it. It scorched my throat like fire.

Gannajero crouches on the far side of the circle with a clay cup of tea in her hands. All night long, she has been staring into the fire, or talking quietly with her deputy, Kotin. He smiles a lot, and his yellow broken teeth glint in the firelight.

I roll to my side and find Tutelo wide awake, staring at me.

I smooth her hair with my hand. "You should be asleep, little sister."

Tutelo sucks her lower lip for a while, then says, "Where's Grandfather?"

"Grandfather?" I find it curious that she did not ask for Mother.

"Yes. Where is he?"

"Oh, let me see, he's been dead for four summers. Don't you remember singing his afterlife soul to the Land of the Dead in the Sky World?"

Tutelo seems to be trying to remember. "There were new green leaves on the trees. It must have been spring."

"Yes, that's right."

Tutelo slides closer to me and nuzzles her cheek against my shoulder. "When is he coming home?"

"Who?"

"Grandfather."

Icy wind gusts through the forest and creeps spiderlike through my clothing to taunt my skin. I feel slightly sick to my stomach. I look down at her. Has her afterlife soul left her body?

"He can't come home, Tutelo. Someday we will go and find him in the Land of the Dead, but I hope that will not be for a long time."

"I miss him."

"I miss him, too."

Tutelo's teeth flash as she flops onto her side and props her head on her hand. Her brow is furrowed, concentrating very hard on what I will say next. "Sometimes the dead come back, but if he can't, we should go see him."

"I don't want to go to the Land of the Dead. Not yet."

"Can I go by myself?"

My heart aches. Is she serious? Does she want to die? "But what would I do without you? You are my only sister. I need you." I adjust Tutelo's collar, pulling it up around her throat.

"Did you see that man in the forest a little while ago?"

I frown. Two men guard us, and warriors are always walking around in the forest, but she seems to mean something else. "What man?"

"I don't know his name. He just stood out there and stared at us. He picked up one of my copper ornaments." She touched the sleeve of her dress. "I keep losing them."

I glance at the place where the tiny ornaments were sewn. Several are gone, probably torn off by the brush. "Was he one of the warriors?"

Tutelo shakes her head. "No. He wasn't a warrior."

"How do you know?"

"He didn't have any weapons."

My gaze roams the clearing while I consider this. Every man in camp carries a weapon. Quivers bristle with arrows, and belts are heavy-laden with knives, clubs, and human arm-bone stilettos. We are at war. No one can risk being without a weapon.

"He's a human False Face."

"Who is?"

"The man. Can you tell me the story again?"

It takes me a few moments to stop thinking about the man in the forest and understand she's moved on to a new topic. Since the Flint girls were hauled out into the forest, Tutelo has been acting strangely. She found a twig on the ground earlier and has refused to let go of it. She has been clutching it all night long, and this has been a night of desperate nightmares for her. She's awakened me several times, crying; then she twists away from me when I try to touch her. I imagine that in her dreams she is running . . . running with every bit of her strength. But now, suddenly, she is smiling and longing to hear me tell her stories.

"What story?"

"About the human False Face."

"Do you mean the story about the end of the world, or the contest between Hawenniyo, the Master, and Shagodyowehgowah, the Great False Face?"

"Either one."

I take a breath and think about where to begin. The entire story takes too long. "Well . . . the ending is the most interesting part, so I'll start there. In the Beginning Time, the Master was wandering around inspecting creation when he met the Great False Face. The Great False Face was a huge man who lived far west at the edge of the world. The Master and the Great False Face got into an argument about who created and owned the earth. To solve the argument, they decided to have a contest to see who could command the mountains to move. Whoever made the distant mountains come the closest would win. They both sat down with their backs to the mountains. The Great False

Face, Shagodyowehgowah, shook his magical turtle shell rattle—"

"And the mountains moved," Tutelo filled in.

"Yes, but only a finger's width. Then Hawenniyo lifted his hand and called to the mountains in a great roar, and the mountains immediately moved to rest right behind him. The Great False Face, who was impatient to see how far the mountains had moved, spun around very fast and—"

"Smashed his face into the mountain!" Tutelo smiled.

"That's right. He broke his nose and jaw. That's why the Faces today all have bent noses and crooked mouths."

Tutelo giggles happily and buries her face in the folds of my sleeve.

I pat her back, and stare across the clearing. The warriors do not seem to hear us.

"Like the man," Tutelo says. "He has a crooked nose. Maybe we should give him a name, like Shago-niyoh?"

I don't answer for a time. "You think he's a combination of Shagodyowehgowah and Hawenniyo? That would make him very powerful."

"He is very powerful."

Fear moves like a cold wave through me. If she did see something it might be one of the *hanehwa*. Witches flayed human beings whole and used their skins to serve as guards. *Hanehwa* never slept. They warned witches of a stranger's coming by shouting three times. Cautiously, I ask, "So he had a crooked nose. What else did he look like?"

Tutelo softly hums to herself and kicks one foot. "He was very tall and handsome—except for his crooked nose— and he had a shining face and cape."

"You mean they shone in the moonlight?"

She shrugged as though she didn't know.

"Did the man speak to you?"

Tutelo blinks. "Why? Are you afraid of him?"

"A little."

She holds out her twig, and in a frightened whisper asks, "Do you want to hold the club?"

She keeps a tight hold on one end of the twig, but hands up the other end for me to grasp. I wrap my fingers around it.

"Thank you, Tutelo."

It's a war club. I should have known. Mother sleeps with her war club across her chest. Every time I wake in the night and see her holding CorpseEye, I know I am safe.

Tutelo's fingers creep up the twig to touch mine. She sighs.

Did she really see a man? I doubt it. How could a stranger have gotten so close without raising an alarm? He must have been one of Gannajero's warriors but . . .

Odion.

I stiffen. I swear someone whispered my name. I stare around the forest, searching, before I say, "Did you hear that?"

"He's a human False Face." Tutelo's voice is sleepy. She yawns. "If I went to the Land of the Dead, he would stay here with you."

I do not know what to say to this. Our people have a legend that foretells the coming of a half-man half-Spirit False Face. It is prophesied that he will don a cape of white clouds and ride the winds of destruction across the land, wiping evil from the face of Great Grandmother Earth. We have to memorize the story by the time we've seen eight summers.

Tutelo makes a strange hiss, like a snake. It startles me. I stare down at her. As Grandmother Moon continues her journey above the branches, a silver slash paints the middle of Tutelo's pretty face, leaving one eye in darkness and the other glowing like a frosty ball of ice.

She hisses again.

"What are you doing?"

Tutelo presses her forehead against my arm. "He told me I must never cry, or they'll kill me." But with tears in her voice, she says, "Do you know that clouds cry in the voice of the rain?"

A curious numbness spreads through me. These are not her words. Where did she hear them? From one of the other children? I haven't seen her speaking with anyone. We are all so frightened, we've spoken very little, and we are never together during the day. Gannajero sends one or two of us off with different warriors; then we meet again at nightfall. I don't even know the names of most of the captives.

"Rain," she says in a hiss.

And I realize, finally, that the hiss is not a snake sound. It's rain falling through the forest.

"Are you a cloud, Tutelo?"

She nods.

I kiss her forehead. She has found a way to cry without being beaten. I wrap my arms around my sister and hold her tightly.

Thirteen

Sindak spread his feet and yawned. Grandmother Moon stood straight overhead. Their watch was almost over. Akio and Ober should be coming to replace them soon. He let his gaze drift over the silvered darkness that cloaked Atotarho Village. The warriors on the palisade catwalk resembled slender pillars of moonlight. Twenty paces away, a happy dog trotted through the night with a half-chewed packrat dangling from his jaws.

Towa whispered, "Where are Akio and Ober? They should be here by now."

"Akio is probably sound asleep. You know how he is. All he does is eat and sleep."

"Yes, but Ober takes responsibility seriously. And one of them better get here soon, or I'm going to faint from hunger. Do you realize we haven't had supper?"

"Why didn't you tell me you were hungry? When I knew I was going to be on sentry duty today, I stuffed my belt pouch with food." He untied the laces on his pouch and pulled it open.

Towa leaned sideways to look inside. His waist-length black hair swung out like a dark curtain. "What did you bring?"

Sindak pulled out jerked venison, wild rice cakes— hard enough to cause brain injury if thrown—and a chunk of half-rancid bear fat. He tore off a piece of jerky, worked it into a gummy mass, then used his teeth to rip off a hunk of bear fat.

Towa winced. "I can smell that fat from here. It's gone bad. Don't eat that."

"It just smells bad. It tastes fine."

"You're disgusting."

"My wife used to say that."

"Please, do *not* tell me why."

Sindak knelt, picked up a rock, and smashed the rice cake to bits. He scooped up the crumbs and ate them. Around a mouthful, he said, "If you chew these up together, it tastes a little like quality aged pemmican. I discovered that one night on guard duty."

Towa's brows lifted. "You are truly the bravest man I know."

Sindak grinned and handed him a piece of jerky. "Here. Try it. Eat the jerky first."

"No, thanks."

"Then you are not starv—"

Sindak straightened when he saw Akio and Ober emerge from the Wolf Clan longhouse. Ober towered over the pudgy Akio. Both wore knee-length capes and carried war clubs. He could hear them talking softly.

"It's about time," Towa said. "I'm tired."

"How can you even think about sleeping? That story about Gannajero will keep me awake for days. I'm going to go back to my longhouse, wake everyone, and find out what each person knows about her."

"That should make you a hero with your relatives."

"Well, think about this: If Gannajero is bold enough to steal Chief Atotarho's daughter, she is bold enough to steal anyone's."

"I doubt Gannajero knows that Zateri is Atotarho's daughter. She probably doesn't ask who the children are or where they're from."

"Why not? That could be useful information. There could be rewards out for a child's safe return."

"I suspect no reward can rival what she earns from allowing outcasts to mistreat them."

Sindak swallowed and ripped off another chunk of jerky to chew.

Akio and Ober walked up, Akio panting. "Anything interesting happen?" Akio couldn't walk more than twenty paces without panting.

Towa shrugged, and Sindak said, "Have you ever heard the name Gannajero?"

Akio said, "No, who is he?"

"She. She's a Trader who hires men to steal children."

"Sounds like my grandmother." Ober gestured over his shoulder to Kelek's longhouse. "She's always demanding that we bring back more slaves from our raids."

"That's different," Towa insisted. "Everyone takes children as slaves, but we adopt them into our families. Gannajero, apparently, makes money by allowing them to be used abominably by outcasts."

"What? That's impossible! Anyone who would—"

"Wait. I think I've heard of her." Ober's face suddenly slackened. "When I was a boy, my grandmother told me a story about an evil woman Trader. She said there was a Trader who stole children's souls and condemned them to wander the forests forever. Could that be Gannajero?"

"I don't know," Towa said. "What's the rest of the story?"

Ober swung his war club up and rested it on his shoulder. The chert cobble on top shone in the moonlight. "I don't remember much, just that the Trader used a sucking tube—you know, the sort our Healers use to suck evil Spirits from sick people? Anyway, she used a hollow eagle-bone sucking tube to suck out the children's souls; then she sealed them in a pot and hauled them far from their homes before she blew the souls out into the air again."

Sindak shifted his weight to his other foot. "So that the souls could never find their villages or loved ones?"

Ober shuddered with disgust. "I guess so."

"That's inhuman. If a ghost is near its village, it can see its loved ones now and then, eat the dregs left in the cooking pots at night, and maybe even sit around fires with old friends. But if she releases the soul in an unknown territory, it's utterly alone, cast adrift among strangers, perhaps even enemies. That's a fate only truly evil souls deserve."

"Yes, certainly not the souls of innocent children."

Sindak tried to imagine what that would be like. Sometimes, usually after an illness, or a hard knock to the head, the afterlife soul wandered away from the body and couldn't find its way back. Families hired great Healers to go out into the forests, find the lost soul, and bring it back to the body again. If they couldn't, the soul became a homeless wanderer, forever condemned to travel the earth.

Sindak added, "If I ever meet her, I'm going to kill her as fast as I can."

"After what Atotarho said," Towa pointed out, "I don't think that's as easy as it sounds. What makes you think you're smarter than the dozens who have already tried?"

"I'm not smarter. I'm sneakier."

"Thank the Spirits," Akio said. "I was so afraid." He shivered for effect, and Ober chuckled.

Towa said, "This is not a joke, my friends. If Gannajero is behind this, you'd better think twice before crossing her."

"I'm not good at thinking," Sindak responded. "If I have to do it twice, I'll be dead."

Akio and Ober laughed out loud, and they heard stirrings in the prisoners' house. Someone cursed, probably Gonda.

"Shh," Towa said. "War Chief Koracoo and her deputy have to be back on the trail long before dawn."

Ober hooked his thumb toward the house and whispered, "I don't think my clan will allow Atotarho to free them. Two summers ago, she killed my cousin, Roton. CorpseEye bashed his brains out."

Sindak said, "So? You don't look all that brokenhearted."

"Yes, well, he was a worthless worm, but nonetheless, my family has sworn a blood oath against her. I am obligated to kill her."

"Well, don't do it before you get an approval from Chief Atotarho. He might let Koracoo use CorpseEye on your brain." Sindak paused. "Assuming, of course, that she can find it."

Ober's bushy brows drew together over his pug nose. "Does the chief favor her?"

"Maybe. He was here earlier. He spoke with Koracoo for a long time."

"About what?"

Towa answered, "We couldn't hear most of it. Just that our chief fears his daughter is being held by Gannajero, along with the Yellowtail Village children. He has authorized Koracoo to buy his daughter back."

"Really? For how much?"

"He said only that he would be sending a warrior along with Koracoo at dawn, a man who could verify his offer."

Ober's eyes widened. In a worried voice he asked, "Did he say which warrior?"

"No."

"I hope it isn't me," Akio whispered. "I'm afraid of Koracoo. I'll have to sleep with one eye open, which means I'll never get any rest."

"Another brave friend." Ober jabbed him in the ribs with his war club, and Akio danced sideways.

"Hey! Stop that!"

Sindak said, "Atotarho wouldn't pick Akio. Half the time, he'd be puffing like a wounded elk and stumbling around through the brush, lost. Gannajero would hear him coming from a full day's walk away."

Akio grinned. "Spoken by a legendary warrior

destined to wind up with an arrow in the back of his skull. That is, unless someone can finally convince you to turn around and face the enemy."

Ober and Towa roared with laughter, and half the dogs in the village started barking. Two dogs near the Hawk longhouse got into a fight, and a whirlwind of flying fur broke out. The larger dog must have gotten in a good bite, because the smaller one yipped and ran off limping.

Ober said, "Woosh, even the dogs get upset by stories of Sindak's bravery."

Sindak scowled.

Towa said, "All right. Let's get back to the subject. I suspect Koracoo has sworn blood oaths against many, or all, of our families. Any man ordered to accompany her may be getting a death sentence."

"Surely she wouldn't kill the man who could verify the chief's offer?" Ober said.

"Not before he verified it," Sindak replied. "But after? Who knows?"

They stood around staring at each other for thirty heartbeats, and Sindak enjoyed the dismay he'd conjured. Fortunately, with his reputation as a warrior, he didn't have to worry about any of this.

"Maybe he'll send Nesi. Nesi can take care of himself." Akio swiveled around, and his plump face and buck teeth reminded Sindak of a beaver.

"He can't send Nesi. The war chief needs to stay in the village to protect it. Though he might—"

A loud knocking sounded inside the prisoners' house.

Akio's eyes went wide. He hissed, "They're knocking on the door. What do we do? Are we supposed to talk to them if they call out?"

From inside the longhouse, Gonda answered, "Yes, you idiot. Since we can't sleep, we've been talking about your chief's offer."

Towa walked over to the door. "Have you arrived at a decision?"

Koracoo answered, "We have. Please tell Atotarho that we accept his offer."

Towa nodded somberly. "Very well." He turned. "Akio, deliver this message to our chief: War Chief Koracoo has made her decision, and she accepts his offer."

"Yes, Towa." Akio puffed away across the plaza toward the Wolf Clan longhouse with his chubby belly jiggling.

"Do you think the chief will come down here after he knows?" Sindak wondered. "Or will he wait until just before dawn?"

"If it were my daughter out there, I'd want the search party on the trail immediately. Or at least before Ober's relatives find out I'm letting Koracoo go."

"So. We wait?"

Towa gave him a skeptical look. "Would you really want to miss this?"

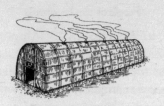

Fourteen

Koracoo stood across from where Gonda knelt warming his hands over the oil lamp. He watched her in the dim light. Her beautiful face and chopped-off hair glowed faintly orange.

"What are you thinking?" he finally asked.

"I was just wondering what I would do in Atotarho's place."

"Well, I can tell you what I'd do. I'd pick a warrior I trusted to deliver my message exactly. This is going to be very delicate. One wrong word could bring disaster."

She folded her arms beneath her red cape, and the hem swayed around her long legs. "The simple solution is to pick someone who fears him."

"You mean a man who is terrified of what Atotarho will do to him if he fails?"

"Of course. Anyone who is afraid of being executed in front of his beloved family will probably do as instructed."

Gonda got to his feet and expelled a breath. "That's why you are war chief. You're pitiless."

Koracoo's expression hardened. "I'm practical. I remember the lessons old Faru taught me."

"Faru, the Healer? What lessons?"

Koracoo hesitated. She toyed with her sleeve, smoothing it. "When I first exited the Women's House, she sat down with me to tell me my duties as a new woman. Her first lesson was about men."

"Really?" The rituals that introduced new women to the world were reserved exclusively for women. It was forbidden for a man to ask anything about them—but since he had the opportunity . . . "What did she say?"

"Faru told me that if I truly wished to unravel the knot in the hearts of men, I had to live their deaths every waking moment."

Gonda frowned at her. "What does it mean?"

"I'm still working it out. But one thing I know: Every time I look at one of my warriors, I live his death. On the fabric of my souls, I see through his eyes as he's captured, tortured, killed. It reminds me of my duty to keep him safe."

"But what does that have to do with unraveling the knot in the hearts of men?"

A faint smile turned her lips. "For most men, the knot is fear. It's what ties their afterlife souls to their bodies; it keeps them alive. Keeps them sane. If you grasp what a man is afraid of, you can either kill him, or save his life."

He thought back to their earlier discussion. No wonder she would choose a man who feared her. If that's what tied his soul to his body, he would follow her orders exactly and come home alive.

A gust of wind penetrated the house, and the lamp's

flame wavered, throwing multiple shadows across the walls and ceiling.

Gonda stared at her. From the first instant he'd fallen in love with her he'd been doing the reverse: He'd been *dying her life*. She had endured so much, lost so many loved ones, and suffered greatly while serving as war chief. For the past thirteen summers, every shimmer of tears in her eyes had been a little death for him.

He said, "What are you afraid of, Koracoo?"

She cocked her head as though she couldn't believe he had asked. "You know my fears."

"A few of them, yes, but I don't know the fear that ties your soul to your body."

Koracoo opened her mouth to respond, but hushed voices erupted outside.

Chief Atotarho's voice ordered, "Open the door, Sindak."

The locking plank thudded as it was lifted, and the door swung open. Grandmother Moon's gleam was so bright Gonda had to squint against it.

Atotarho stepped inside. The circlets of human skull on his black cape shimmered. He appeared wide awake. Perhaps he hadn't slept at all since they'd seen him last.

"I understand that you have decided to accept my offer."

Koracoo replied, "Yes, Chief. And we would like to leave as soon as you can arrange it."

The lines around Atotarho's eyes deepened. He nodded. "I will be sending two men with you. It will take them perhaps a half-hand of time to gather their things."

Koracoo dipped her head. "We'll be ready."

Atotarho stepped outside again, and the door swung closed.

The warriors went silent, as though waiting for the chief to speak.

Atotarho said, "Sindak, Towa, you will both be accompanying War Chief Koracoo and Deputy Gonda. Gather whatever you will need. Then I want Towa to meet me at my longhouse as soon as possible."

The chief's steps softly moved away.

After another twenty heartbeats, Sindak hissed, *Blessed Spirits!* Why us?"

"Oh, stop it. You're not the one he asked to meet him at his longhouse," Towa said. "I wonder what he wants?"

The two other warriors chuckled, and it sounded like men slapping each other on the backs. "Lucky you," someone said. "You have the chance to prove your valor to your chief in a way few men ever have."

"What are you talking about, you imbecile? If we fail, he'll roast us alive and eat us."

"I want your liver," another man said drily.

Sindak replied, "That's not funny, Akio."

Towa said, "Come on. We don't have much time to get ready."

Two men trotted away, and the new guards took up their positions on either side of the door. They continued to chuckle. Akio whispered, *"Gods, I'd hate to be them."*

Koracoo smiled wryly, walked to the wall, and sank down. As she leaned back against it, she closed her eyes, trying to get a few last moments of rest.

Gonda knelt in front of the oil lamp and held his cape open over the flame, letting the heat rise up and warm the inside of the buckskin.

Softly, Koracoo said, "I fear the same thing you do, Gonda—that I will fail to protect my family."

His hands quaked. He lowered his cape and let the warmth seep into his flesh while he squeezed his eyes closed. He tried not to sound like he was strangling when he asked, "Blessed gods, how did you know that was my greatest fear?"

The smiling faces of Odion and Tutelo reared inside him, and he longed to get up and run back to the place where he'd seen the children's moccasin tracks.

Koracoo looked up at him. "The only question that matters now is what does Odion fear? If we know, we may be able to save his life. He—"

"He fears he won't be able to protect Tutelo." Gonda hated to say it. "And he won't. He's not a fighter. We both know that."

Odion feared everything: wolves howling in the distance, unfamiliar sounds in the night. The first time Gonda had taken the boy hunting, Odion had seen six summers. As nightfall descended upon the forests, the boy had started crying, and no matter what Gonda said to comfort him, Odion would not stop. He loved his son with all his heart, but Odion was timid and girlish.

"Fortunately, Wrass is there. That boy is a born warrior."

Koracoo's face tensed. She looked away, and he realized she must have thought his comment was meant as an insult to their son or his upbringing. Because their people traced descent through the female, Koracoo's children belonged to her clan, not his. While a father might be concerned about his children's upbringing, it was none of his business. He was responsible only for bringing up his sister's children.

"Koracoo, I didn't mean to intrude or suggest—"

"No one is born a warrior, Gonda," she said stiffly, and frowned at the flickering oil lamp. "We are made warriors by suffering, anger, and hatred. You fear that your son will never become a warrior. I fear that he will." She squared her shoulders, as though bracing herself for a calamity. "I fear that his training started five days ago."

Fifteen

Sindak waited for Towa just outside the Wolf Clan longhouse. He had a bow and a quiver of arrows slung over his left shoulder, and carried a knife, war club, and two deerbone stilettos tied to his belt. Inside his belt pouch, he'd stuffed as much food as he could. And in the pack he wore on his back, he'd placed his cup, a horn spoon, and boiling bag, as well as an antler tine for resharpening stone tools, a blanket woven of twisted lengths of rabbit hide, and an extra pair of moccasins.

He sighed and looked around Atotarho Village. In Grandmother Moon's glow, the frost-coated walls of the longhouses glittered. It was cold tonight, and getting colder. He longed to be on the trail. When a man was walking, he could keep warm. He rubbed his arms beneath his cape and shivered.

From inside the longhouse, he heard Towa say in a low voice, "Yes, my chief." Then, "Yes, I will."

Towa ducked beneath the curtain that covered the longhouse entry and marched toward him. Sindak frowned. Towa's face had a sober, vaguely lost expression.

Towa passed Sindak, said, "Let's go," and continued on toward the prisoners' house.

Sindak trotted to catch up. "What happened in there? It took a long time."

Towa flipped up the hood of his cape. "The chief just wanted to make sure I understood my duties."

"I assume those are also my duties, so what did he tell you?"

Towa glanced at him. He'd pulled his hair back and braided it. The style made his face look leaner, more dangerous. His unblinking eyes resembled moonlit holes. "We are to find his daughter and bring her back. No matter the cost."

"It would have taken five heartbeats for the chief to tell you that. What else did he say?"

Towa shook his head, indicating that he couldn't repeat a word of it.

"Are you telling me he gave you secret orders?"

Towa looked away.

"But I'm much braver than you and a better warrior. If anybody was going to be trusted with secrets, it should have been me."

Towa glared at him. "I didn't *ask* for this burden. I'd gladly give it to you if I could."

"Burden? What burden?"

Towa focused his gaze on the prisoners' house, where Akio and Ober stood guard on either side of the door. Both friends were watching them with wide, expectant eyes. As Towa and Sindak came closer, they started whispering to each other.

Akio called, "Is the chief coming?"

"No," Towa answered. "You are to release the Standing Stone warriors and open the palisade gates for us."

Suspiciously, Ober said, "On whose authority? Yours?"

"Yes, mine." Grumbling, Towa jerked a magnificent carved gorget from his shirt and let it swing before their eyes.

"Blessed gods," Ober hissed. "The chief gave you his sacred pendant? That means he grants you his authority. Whatever you say comes as if from the chief's own mouth."

Sindak stared openly at the pendant. Very few people had ever seen it up close. It was not a thing for ordinary eyes. He could feel Power pulsing around the hideous False Face, representing Horned Serpent, and the falling stars that filled the background. It was big enough to cover half of a man's chest. Legend said that at the time of the cataclysm, two pendants had been carved by the breath of Horned Serpent. One belonged to the chief. The other to the human False Face who would don a cape of white clouds and ride the winds of destruction across the face of the world.

Sindak whispered, "Put it away, Towa. Our eyes should not look upon such a Powerful thing."

Towa tucked it back into his shirt and gestured to the door. "Open the door to the prisoners' house, Ober. In the meantime, Akio, tell the guards on the catwalk that the chief has ordered the palisade gate to be opened."

"Yes, Towa." Akio waddled up to the palisade gate and shouted, "Bostum? The chief has ordered that the gate be opened so that War Chief Koracoo and her party may leave."

"What?" Bostum shouted back. "You're just a fat boy, Akio. I'm not going to listen to you. Where's Nesi? I want to hear it from him."

Akio turned back to Towa, obviously thinking Towa would bring out the pendant again. Instead, Towa said, "Go and fetch Nesi. The fewer people who know about the gorget the better."

"I'm going." Akio hurried across the plaza and ducked into the Hawk Clan longhouse.

As Ober lifted the locking plank and swung open the door to the prisoners' house, Sindak waited beside Towa. His friend was breathing hard, as though the weight of the pendant resting on his chest was suffocating him.

Sindak whispered, "How's your belly?"

Towa gave him an askance look. "Why would you want to know?"

"Not even a hint of weasels thrashing around in there, trying to get out?"

"Well, small weasels . . ." He halted when War Chief Koracoo and Deputy Gonda walked out and stood quietly in the brilliant moonlight. Koracoo adjusted her cape, then tied her belt more securely around it.

"Towa. Sindak." She looked both of them straight in the eyes. "Are you ready?"

Towa answered, "Yes, War Chief. You should know that Atotarho has instructed us to obey your orders as we would his."

Gonda's heavy brow wrinkled. He glanced suspiciously at Towa, then Sindak, and finally said, "We'll see how long that lasts."

"What do you mean?"

Gonda grimaced as he walked past, heading toward the palisade gate.

Koracoo looked at Towa. Her chopped-off hair fell in uneven lengths around her beautiful face. "As I understand it, Towa, you are the chief's personal representative. You are carrying his sacred gorget, aren't you?"

"I am." Towa shifted uncomfortably.

Koracoo searched his eyes, and Towa must have felt her scrutiny like a blow to the stomach, for he stopped breathing. "Very well. It's after midnight. Let's get as close to the clearing where we found the baby as we can; then we'll eat and try to rest until we have enough light to track."

Without waiting for a response, she led the way to stand beside Gonda in front of the gate.

"They must want to be out of here badly," Sindak said.

"Wouldn't you? They took their lives in their hands when they brought the baby here."

"They must have thought that baby was very important," Sindak commented. "We should have killed them. They're our enemies."

"Well, keep that to yourself. The chief says that in this one instance, they are our allies and we are to treat them as such."

"Until they prove otherwise, you mean."

Towa tightened the laces on his leggings. "Atotarho told me our first duty is to protect Zateri, then ourselves, and finally the other children."

"He gave no orders about protecting Koracoo or Gonda?"

"They can protect themselves, and he knows it."

Sindak turned when Nesi stalked forward with Akio trotting behind him. In the darkness, Nesi looked like a wounded giant. The scars on his face might have been a tangle of white cords.

He marched straight to Towa, placed his hands on his hips, and barked, "Who gave you the authority to tell the guards to open the gate?"

Towa turned so that Koracoo and Gonda could not see the pendant, and drew it out for Nesi. Nesi's face slackened. For several heartbeats, he seemed confused as to what to do about it. Sindak thought Nesi might even be thinking that Towa had stolen the sacred gorget.

Finally, Nesi said, "Why do you have that?"

"The chief is sending us out on a special mission with War Chief Koracoo to find his daughter and bring her home safely."

Nesi's scars twitched. "Why you two? You're the last two warriors I'd choose."

Sindak shrugged expressively, and Towa said, "You should, perhaps, ask the chief."

Anger, or maybe suspicion, flared in Nesi's eyes. He looked up and lifted a hand to Bostum. "Open the gate, Bostum. Let them out, then close it up tight."

"Yes, War Chief."

Nesi glanced hatefully at Koracoo and Gonda, gave Sindak and Towa a final unnerving appraisal, and stalked back toward the Hawk Clan longhouse.

Towa put a hand to his heart and sucked in a fortifying breath. "Blessed Spirits, I thought for a moment he was going to tackle me and rip the gorget from my throat."

"So did I. He seemed very unhappy that we had been chosen for this task."

"Well, he does think we're useless. Maybe he thought the chief would select him. Who knows?"

Sindak pointed to Towa's wounded arm. "I notice that you removed your sling. I assume that's so it's not as obvious that you're useless."

"Exactly."

"You should have left it on. Koracoo and Gonda are going to find out soon enough anyway."

"Thanks. I feel better."

They headed toward the gate. By the time they got there, Bostum had removed the locking plank and pulled the heavy gate open wide enough for one person to pass through. Koracoo went first, followed by Gonda, Towa, and lastly, Sindak.

Only the faint whisper of frozen leaves underfoot filled the night as they walked out into the forest.

They'd gone perhaps fifty paces when Koracoo stopped beside a sassafras tree. Clusters of blue fruit clung to the tree branches.

"What's she doing?" Sindak asked.

Towa shrugged.

Gracefully, Koracoo knelt, reached behind the tree, and pulled CorpseEye from beneath a bed of leaves. The legendary club glowed in the moonlight.

Sindak stared openly and hissed, "There it is. Blessed gods." He fervently hoped that in the days to come, she would not have an excuse to use it on him.

Sixteen

As they marched up the twisting moon-silvered trail, the air was fragrant with the ghosts of long-dead ferns and rushes. Gonda shivered beneath his cape. With each frigid gust of wind, the trees shook moisture down upon them. The drops sprinkled Koracoo's hood and shimmered like white beads upon her shoulders. Black spruces and ankle-deep drifts of moldering leaves lined the mountain path. He slogged his way through them behind Koracoo.

Sindak and Towa brought up the rear. His new allies had been quiet for most of the journey, but had started to whisper to each other. It annoyed Gonda. Even barely adequate warriors knew better. A man on the war trail did not speak. He listened for the sounds of the enemy, or wound up with his throat slit. Either by his enemies, or his friends.

The trail curved around a hillock of rounded boulders. As he silently passed, in the night sky high above, he heard the distinctive, lonely honks of geese.

Gonda looked up, trying to see them, and made out a faint chevron of black dots, headed south. Their calls were melodic, soothing.

Sindak said, "A medicine elder told me that geese mate for life. Do you believe that, Towa? I mean, they probably don't trace descent through the female, right? If women don't rule the goose world, why would males mate for life?"

"Sindak—"

"Old Kelek also told me that the Flint People build platforms in the marshes for them to nest upon. The geese. Not the Flint People. It makes hunting them much easier. We should do that."

"Hunt the Flint People?" Towa asked.

"No, the geese, you moron. We already hunt the Flint People."

Gonda turned and glared at them. They both went silent. They made a strange pair. Towa stood a head taller than Sindak and had broad muscular shoulders. Sindak, on the other hand, was lean and homely. His beaked face and deeply sunken eyes reminded Gonda of a winter-killed hawk that had been drying in the sun for too long. But the youth moved like a warrior. He was agile and catlike, whereas Towa always seemed to be stumbling over something.

Koracoo veered around a wind-piled mound of autumn leaves, and Gonda saw the cornhusk doll clearing. Moonglow sheathed the crooked limbs of the gigantic oaks that fringed the meadow, icing them in white.

"At last," Gonda said. "Let's eat something and get to sleep."

"I agree. Daylight is not far away."

Gonda trudged into the clearing. He unslung his bow and quiver and set them aside; then he knelt and began scooping aside leaves. Koracoo tied CorpseEye to her belt and crouched to help him.

Sindak and Towa stood looking on as though mystified.

Curtly, Gonda said, "I'll build the fire if someone else will gather wood. Like you two."

Sindak scanned the leaf-filled clearing. "Are we camping here? It looks damp. Why don't we get out of the wet leaves?"

Irritated, Gonda said, "Why don't you close your mouth and go collect wood?"

Sindak stiffened. Gonda's tone had obviously offended the youth, but Gonda didn't care. When Sindak and Towa made no move to obey his order, Gonda rose to his feet to be even more unpleasant. . . .

Koracoo said, "Sit down, Gonda."

He clenched his fists, gave her a distasteful glance, and then did as she'd instructed.

Koracoo explained, "Sindak, once we get the fire built, it will be warmer sleeping among the leaves than out in the open. If you and Towa will gather some dry branches, we'll cook something to warm our bellies; then we'll rise before dawn. That means we don't have much time to rest."

Sindak muttered something Gonda couldn't hear, but it sounded mutinous. Gonda glowered, and Sindak took a threatening step toward him.

"Enough," Koracoo ordered in a voice that brooked no disagreement.

Towa quickly grabbed Sindak's arm. To Koracoo, he said, "We will gather wood, War Chief."

As he and Sindak wandered away and started collecting wood, Koracoo watched them. They moved through the oaks, breaking the dry lower branches from the trees, casting glances at Koracoo and Gonda. "They're curious, aren't they?" she asked.

"Curious? I think they're both simpletons. We should send them home before they get us killed."

Koracoo kept her eyes on the young men, studying them. "They are careless. At least Sindak is. I thought for a moment he might try to take you."

"That would have been a fatal error."

"It would also have been your fault. You seem determined to split our party in two. Stop it. We all have to be on the same side."

Anger rose hotly in his veins. In a hushed voice, he said, "They are Hills People, Koracoo. They don't know what *our* side is! They are our enemies. Do you really think they want to help us rescue *our* children?"

Her expression turned to stone. "I am always prepared for the worst, Gonda. But until they demonstrate they are not on our side, I plan to treat them as though they are."

"Well, that's foolish. They probably have secret orders to kill us and our children as soon as they have Zateri."

"They may, indeed." She tucked a lock of windwhipped black hair behind her ear. "But given their inexperience as warriors, I doubt they can accomplish it. And our best defense against treachery is to try and befriend them."

"Befriend them? Are you joking?"

"We will be traveling together for many days, Gonda. Perhaps, moons. It will not help us if you are constantly antagonizing them. I won't tolerate it."

He felt like he was about to explode. To ease some of his tension, Gonda dug into the leaves with a vengeance, scooping armfuls away and piling them to the side. He needed to clear a swath of ground large enough for three people to sleep. One person would always be on guard. Through gritted teeth, he finally said, "I will do as you ask, Koracoo."

"Thank you."

When he'd scooped enough armfuls away to reveal a broad circle of bare earth, his anger had faded. He sank down and slipped his pack from his shoulders.

Koracoo unslung her pack, as well. While she rummaged around inside, pulling out sacks of jerky, cornmeal, and dried onion, Gonda fought the overwhelming sensation of despair that descended over him like a black fog. His heart was beating a slow, dull rhythm against his ribs.

He removed the small stone pot where he kept coals from the morning fire. "By the way," he said, trying to lighten the darkness, "if these are the two best warriors Atotarho has, we need to attack the Hills People immediately. We should be able to conquer the whole nation in a few days."

She smiled faintly. "I'll consider it. After we've found the children."

Gonda removed the stopper from his pot and dumped the coals on the ground, then began carefully selecting the driest leaves he could find and piling them over the coals.

Koracoo's smile faded, and her gaze returned to Sindak and Towa, who were cracking off dead branches while they murmured to each other. She shook her head lightly. "I can't figure it out, but there's more here than is apparent, Gonda."

"What do you mean?"

"I'm not sure yet. I need to think about it for a time. By morning, I'll have pieced it together better."

Koracoo pulled her boiling bag and tripod from her pack. The tripod, three long sticks tied at the top, stood five hands tall. She spread the tripod's legs, then suspended her boiling bag in the center and tied the laces to the top of the tripod.

"I still have a full water bag," Gonda said. He removed it from his belt and handed it to her.

Koracoo loosened the laces, tipped it up, and poured the water into the boiling bag. "That should make enough soup to feed us tonight and tomorrow morning."

As Koracoo started crumbling venison jerky into the boiling bag, Gonda bent down to blow on the leaf-covered coals. The longer he blew, the brighter the glow became until the scent of smoke rose. It took several moments before the leaves caught and flames flickered. Gonda added more dry leaves to keep the small blaze going.

When Sindak and Towa saw the flames, they trotted across the clearing to dump their armloads of wood beside the fire.

"I could eat an entire buffalo," Towa said, and crouched before the fire. "What are we having?"

"Jerky and watery cornmeal gruel with dried onions," Koracoo said.

"Good enough." Towa smiled, trying to be pleasant. "While we were out in the trees, I picked up a good cobble for the boiling bag."

He pulled a rounded stone the size of his fist from his pack and set it at the edge of the flames; then he helpfully began laying twigs over it. As the wood burned, it would heat the rock.

Sindak made no attempt to help. He knelt and glanced uneasily at Gonda and Koracoo. Oddly, that made Gonda feel better. Getting too friendly too fast was the dead giveaway of an assassin.

As the tiny blaze grew to a fire, Koracoo lifted the sack filled with dried onions and poured some into the boiling bag. The sweet fragrance of onions rose.

In anticipation, Towa pulled his wooden cup from his belt pouch and nervously turned it in his hands while he waited.

Sindak's nostrils flared at the aroma. To Towa, he said, "My wife used to make jerky and cornmeal gruel."

Towa looked at him askance. "Puksu cooked?"

"Not often, but occasionally, when she wasn't over at her mother's place in the longhouse cursing me."

"Was it good?"

"Her cursing?"

"The gruel."

"Oh. Sure. Unless she'd poisoned it. I don't think it's

healthy for a wife to know so many Spirit plants. The temptation is too strong."

"As I recall, the study of Spirit plants was something she took up after she married you."

Sindak scratched beneath his chin. "She told me she wanted to become a Healer. I believed her."

Towa chuckled and shook his head.

Gonda sat quietly for several moments before he said, "I hope you two are a whole lot smarter than you look or sound."

The two youths blinked, and Koracoo glared at Gonda with lethal intent.

"Uh . . . ," Gonda said with a shrug. "That was a joke."

"Oh. Ha." Towa smiled politely.

Sindak looked like he wanted to get his hands around Gonda's throat.

Gonda placed more branches on the flames and glanced around the clearing. Fire shadows danced through the massive oak limbs. He watched them for a while; then his gaze returned to Sindak, and he found the youth staring at Koracoo's breasts as she bent to stir the gruel. The neck of her cape had fallen open, revealing a glimpse of her chest. Generally, the youth had dark beady eyes that shifted as though rolling around loose in their sockets, but not now. He'd fixed unblinking on Koracoo's breasts like a starving wolf about to leap upon an unsuspecting rabbit.

"Sindak," Gonda said.

He turned. "What?"

"Life is an uncertain thing. You might want to consider that."

Sindak's brows lifted. A small smile tugged at the corners of his mouth; then he nodded and looked away. He had understood perfectly, but Koracoo did not. She glanced between Gonda and Sindak with a hostile expression on her face.

Gonda explained, "Nothing to worry about. I'm befriending him." He casually watched the sparks flit upward into the night sky. Only the brightest campfires of the dead shone in the wash of moonlight.

"War Chief?" Towa said. "The cobble is probably hot enough. Should I drop it into the boiling bag?"

"Yes, thank you."

Gonda evaded Koracoo's eyes. She still had her evil gaze squarely on him.

Towa rose, pulled two branches from the woodpile, and used them to pick up the hot rock. As he walked around the circle, he tripped, almost dropped the rock down Sindak's collar, and continued to the bag. When he dropped the cobble into the water, an explosion of steam gushed up, and the rich scent of venison filled the air.

They sat in silence for another one hundred heartbeats; then Koracoo said, "Gonda, please fill everyone's cup. Starting with mine." She pulled her cup from her pack and handed it to him.

Gonda dipped it full and handed it back.

"I'm taking first watch." She rose, holding her cup in both hands. "Towa, I'll wake you in two hands of time. You'll take the last watch."

"Yes, War Chief."

Koracoo walked out into the darkness and vanished amid the trees.

As soon as she was gone, desperation returned to taunt Gonda. He ordered, "Towa, give me your cup."

Towa handed it over, and Gonda returned it full. When Sindak started to extend his cup, Gonda said, "This is awkward, isn't it? I mean, when I was a child if anyone had told me I'd be sitting around a war camp joking with two Hills warriors, I'd have kicked him in the groin for being an imbecile. But here I am." He filled Sindak's cup and handed it to him.

Sindak looked down into the gruel as though he suspected Gonda had spat in it. "I'm glad I didn't know you as a child."

"Let's face reality. None of us is going to trust the other for a long time, if ever, so I guess we should just try to make the best of it. What do you say? I agree not to slit your throat in the night, if you agree not to slit mine or Koracoo's."

A gust of wind blew Towa's long black hair around his face. In a slightly confused voice, he said, "Deputy, we are bound by our chief's orders to obey you. We will do whatever you tell us to."

"I take that as a yes. What about you, Sindak?"

Sindak leaned over to sniff his cup, and the nostrils of his beak nose flared. When he looked up at Gonda, suspicion pinched the lines around his eyes. "Are you still married to Koracoo?"

"*What?*"

"Are you still married? She doesn't act like it, but you do. Are you?"

Gonda sat back. "No, she divorced me. Why? Thinking about crawling between her blankets some night?"

"Of course not."

"That's smart, because you'll have a stiletto through your balls before your voice can change. Think how embarrassing that will be."

Sindak took a drink of his gruel and wiped his mouth on his sleeve. "You *are* trying to befriend me. Thanks for the advice."

Gonda dipped his cup full of soup, swallowed it in six big gulps, then glared one last time for good measure and rolled up in his blanket to sleep.

After a few hundred heartbeats, Towa whispered, "I don't think he likes us."

Seventeen

Odion

The fire has died down to a crimson gleam, leaving the woods frosty and smoke-colored, streaked here and there by the last echoes of moonlight.

I've been shivering for over a finger of time. That's when the shouting started. I watch Gannajero through the weave of frozen grass stems. A pile of riches rests on the ground before her: quivers decorated elaborately with porcupine quills . . . etched copper breastplates . . . a shirt covered with elk ivories . . . and many necklaces, stone tools, feather pouches. But she is apparently unhappy. She paces before two Flint warriors, shouting and waving her fists. One is a big crazy-eyed man. He is stocky, and geometric tattoos cover his face. The sides of his head are shaved, leaving a central roach of hair on top. White feathers—war honors—decorate it. Each man holds a Flint girl by the arm. One of the girls weeps inconsolably. The other keeps trying to fight.

"You fools! This isn't enough to buy one of the girls, let alone two! Release them!" Gannajero's wrinkled face has contorted into a hideous long-nosed god mask.

The fighting Flint girl shouts, "Leave my sister alone! Let her go. Take me! Take me!" and repeatedly lunges at the big crazy-eyed man, who smiles and shoves her to the ground . . . over and over.

Her sister just hangs in the thin man's grip like a soaked rabbit-fur doll, sobbing.

I don't know where the other Flint girl is . . . or He-haka. He's gone, too.

"Give them to me, or the girls stay here!" Gannajero yells.

"I'm not giving you my soul!" the crazy-eyed man shouts back. "You can't have it! I've given you everything else I own! "

"Then you can't have the girls." Gannajero folds her arms over her chest.

Kotin and three other men move in, surrounding Gannajero as though to protect her, or perhaps to kill the men with the girls if it becomes necessary. They have war clubs in their fists.

I lift my gaze to the trees. Their faint shadows are like smudges of gray silk in the branches, swaying, flying.

"What's ha-happening, Odion?" Tutelo whispers.

"They're still fighting. Try to sleep."

"I can't sleep!" She weeps softly. "No one could sleep with all the shouting."

I stroke her long hair and hug her. "Then just don't cry. Be a cloud. All right? Remember what Shago-niyoh said. Be a cloud."

Tutelo squeezes her eyes closed and hisses like a snake.

From my right, Wrass murmurs, "The old woman has lost her soul. She's totally insane."

Chipmunk stutters, "M-Maybe she needs one of their souls to p-put in her own body."

"Maybe," I answer. "I just wish she'd kill them and take the girls back. I—"

When Gannajero whirls around and stalks toward us, Wrass yips, "*What*—?"

"Don't move!" Gannajero says. Ten paces away, she spreads her arms like a bird and spins toward us. She is so graceful she might be a crow sailing on wind currents.

We all sit as if carved of wood. There is a rotten blood stench about her. It envelops me as she leans over. Wrass clenches his jaw and stares at her, but I turn away, too afraid to look into her wild black eyes.

A heartbeat later, Wrass lets out an enraged cry, and I jerk around. Gannajero has grabbed his left hand. "Hold him!" she orders our guards.

Ugly and Worm swoop down, pin Wrass to the ground, and hold him as Gannajero drags a hafted quartzite blade from her belt. It glints.

"I'm going to teach you a fine lesson, boy," she says. "You think that someday you will kill one of my men and escape? Watch carefully."

She slams his hand to the frozen ground and saws off the top of his little finger, neatly severing it at the joint. Wrass kicks and writhes, twisting to get away while he screams.

Gannajero picks up the bloody tip of his finger and cradles it in both hands as though it's a great prize. "Yes, yes, watch now."

The guards release Wrass, who sits up, whimpering, and stanches the flow of the blood with his cape.

"Wrass!" I madly crawl over to him and press my hands atop his, trying to place enough pressure on the wound to congeal the blood.

Wrass seems to be in shock. He can't take his eyes from Gannajero as she slowly, deliberately, bird-walks back across the clearing to where her two men hold the Flint girls.

Crazy-Eyes says, "I am not Hodigo, old woman. That doesn't scare me. I have cut a thousand men apart!"

The wind must have caught the coals just right. They flare suddenly, and firelight coats Gannajero's face like a thick amber resin, catching in a searing line along her extended arm. "You're really not afraid?" she asks mildly.

"Of course not!"

Gannajero steps closer, tempting him to run. He stands his ground and grips the Flint girl's arm tighter. He can't run now. The eyes of every man in camp are upon him.

Gannajero smiles as she walks right up to him, then uses the bloody fingertip to paint a zigzagging Spirit line down his sleeve. He flinches, but does not flee. "Oh, yes, look." She turns to his friends and nods. "He is brave."

He throws out his chest and glances at his partner, who holds the other Flint girl. "See? I told you. She's just an ugly old woman."

Gannajero smiles and reaches into her belt pouch. When she pulls out a hollow eagle-bone sucking tube, the man goes rigid. He starts to back away, dragging the girl with him.

Before he can get too far, she orders, "Stop."

As though he's been commanded by his chief, he does it. The Flint girl fights harder—she's kicking his legs and butting her head into his side—but he barely seems to notice. He stares at the sucking tube and swallows hard. As Gannajero walks closer, he says, "Wait."

She stops and cocks her head back and forth in that eerie birdlike manner. "Yes."

"If I let you suck out my afterlife soul, can I have my copper breastplate back?"

Gannajero seems to be considering it. Finally, she nods.

The man grits his teeth and extends his arm. "All right, but hurry. I have plans."

Gannajero slowly tiptoes forward, rubs the fingertip over the tube, consecrating it, then places the tube against his exposed wrist and sucks. Then she suddenly leaps backward.

He staggers and blinks, as though dazed by the experience.

His friend says, "Dinyoteh? Are you all right?"

"Of course, I—I am."

"Did it hurt?"

"Don't be foolish. I don't feel any different at all. If she thinks she has my soul, that's fine. I know she doesn't. Let her suck yours out, too, so we can go."

His friend pales. "But I don't—"

"I'm telling you, Sondakwa, it's all nonsense. Do you really think this ugly old woman can steal souls?"

His friend hesitantly extends his arm, and Gannajero edges forward, places her tube against his flesh, and sucks out his soul.

When she's finished, she pulls a small pot from her belt pouch, removes the wooden stopper, and blows their souls into it. Then she tucks Wrass' fingertip into the pot and stuffs the stopper back in. "All right," she says with a flick of her hand. "Take the girls and go."

Crazy Eyes, Dinyoteh, grabs his breastplate, and he and

his friend drag the two Flint girls away and disappear in the forest. I can hear the girls' screams for a long time.

Wrass is rocking back and forth, holding his bloody hand.

Chipmunk crawls over and says, "Wrass, let me look at it?"

Shaking, he pulls the finger from his wadded cape and extends it. It's still bleeding badly.

Tutelo's eyes go wide.

Chipmunk scrutinizes it and says, "It's a clean cut. We just need to keep the evil Spirits from infecting it. As we walk, I'll find a bear oak, shave one of the old knots, and brew you a tea. It will help."

Tutelo looks from Wrass, to the guards, and back to me, and sobs, "Odion? Let's run away! Hurry. Let's run!"

I glance around at the warriors, and my throat closes up. I lean close to her ear to whisper. "Soon. But not now. *Not now!*"

Eighteen

Just before dawn, Koracoo rolled over, shook Gonda's shoulder, and whispered, "It's time. Let's rise."

Exhausted, shivering with cold, Gonda heaved a sigh and sat up. The frost-coated clearing glittered with the first blue rays of dawn. Beneath the oak trees, ten paces away, the sleeping body of Sindak made a dark hump. The sight surprised Gonda. Sindak must have moved out into the trees in the middle of the night, but Gonda hadn't heard a thing. Towa stood a short distance from where Sindak slept, watching the trail.

As Gonda stumbled to his feet, he whispered, "Will you wake Sindak, or should I?"

"Let's get the fire built and heat up the leftover corn-meal gruel from last night. I suspect with all of our clattering, he will wake himself. Or Towa will wake him."

Gonda reached down, picked up his weapons' belt, and tied it around his waist. It was colder this morning, and he thought he caught the fragrance of snow on the breeze. Cloud People sailed the heavens.

He walked to the fire pit and grabbed a stick from the branch pile they'd collected last night. "The first thing this morning, we should clarify their duties with our new allies."

"I thought you did that last night."

Sheepishly, he said, "Did you hear that?"

"Most of it. You sounded like an idiot."

Gonda glanced over at Sindak. "I was defending your honor, my former wife. And I wasn't the only idiot there. Sindak is impulsive. He's the one most likely to act on instinct without thinking first. He reminds me of me at his age."

Koracoo pushed short black hair behind her ears. "I remember. You were reckless."

"I was young." Gonda used his stick to stir the ashes from last night's fire. It took twenty heartbeats to separate out the warm coals and pile them in the center of the pit. As he began laying twigs over the coals, he softly said, "Did you get any sleep?"

She knelt across the fire pit from him. Her face looked haggard, her dark eyes dull. "Not much. Towa and I stared at each other for most of the night. He's the cautious one."

The sound of their voices woke Sindak. He sat up and stretched, then turned to look at Towa. Towa had worn his deerhide sling while he stood watch to keep his wounded arm from shifting. Towa whispered something to Sindak, who yawned and nodded.

Koracoo's eyes narrowed.

"What's wrong?"

"While I was staring at Towa last night, I had time to think about them."

"About Sindak? Or Towa?" He bent over and blew

on the coals until the twigs caught and flames burst to life. He added more twigs, then lifted the tripod with the boiling bag and moved it closer.

"About Sindak, Towa, and Atotarho," she replied. "I still don't know why he chose these two. They are not physically suited to the task. Because of his injuries, Towa is not a reliable fighter. And they are friends— probably best friends. That means that when Towa gets in trouble—and that will be very soon into the fight— Sindak will forget his responsibilities and concentrate on protecting his friend."

"Leaving you and me to rescue the children." Gonda added a branch to the fire and watched the flames leap around the new tinder. Sparks flitted into the deep blue predawn sky. "If you're right, what are we going to do about it?"

"Plan ahead, prepare for when it happens."

"Then you'd better threaten them thoroughly to start with."

"I plan to."

Gonda pulled two sticks from the woodpile and reached into the boiling bag to remove the cobble, which he placed at the edge of the flames to heat.

Then he turned to watch the two young warriors. Towa winced as he removed his sling, picked up his quiver, and slung it over his shoulder. Sindak was speaking softly to him while he adjusted his weapons' belt. Towa's braid hung down the back of his elkhide cape. Though he had a handsome face, Gonda decided it was slightly feminine. His eyelashes were too long and his chin too pointed. Sindak, on the other hand, kept his right hand propped on the hilt of his belted war club. That told Gonda a good deal about him.

Gonda added two more branches to the fire—enough wood that the flames crackled. When he looked back at Koracoo, he could see the thoughts roiling behind her eyes. They had known each other long enough that they often entertained the same thoughts, and he suspected he knew what was bothering her. "So. What conclusions did you arrive at? How much of Atotarho's story did you decide you believe?"

"Very little."

He frowned at the fire. "I arrived at the same conclusion. That complicates our plan."

"In more ways than one." She used her chin to indicate Sindak and Towa. "How much do you think they know?"

"About Atotarho's plans? Probably nothing. But we need to find out."

"Yes. Just in case this turns into a brawl, we should loose our clubs."

"Don't you think that's a little obvious? They'll think we plan to crush their skulls."

"Depending upon what they do or do not know, we may."

"Now you're talking like a Standing Stone war chief." Gonda untied his club and rested it within reach near the tripod.

As she stood up, Koracoo untied CorpseEye from her belt and propped it on her shoulder.

Towa and Sindak noticed, started murmuring to each other, and loosed their own clubs.

"Are you ready?" Gonda quietly asked.

"Of course."

Nineteen

Sindak swung his club up over his shoulder and whispered, "I don't like this. They look too eager to see us."

"They probably just want to get started on the trail."

"I don't think those are impatient expressions on their faces—they're murderous."

"You're imagining things."

A soft morning breeze whispered through the trees, shaking the branches and swirling brown oak leaves across the clearing. Sindak studied Gonda and Koracoo. Neither looked happy this morning. Both wore their capes hooked back over their weapons' belts, which made it much faster to pull out a stiletto or knife. Sindak's eyes lingered on Koracoo. With her red cape pulled back, he could see her brown war shirt beneath . . . and the curve of her hip and the outline of one long muscular leg. Looking at her affected him like a Spirit plant in his veins. His pulse pounded and his mouth went dry. The only thing that ruined the image was CorpseEye resting on her shoulder.

"If they just want to get on the trail, why did they loose their war clubs?"

"Maybe they heard something in the forest?"

"Maybe they heard us. That would certainly explain why Gonda looks like he swallowed a handful of rabbit droppings."

"Well, don't worry about it. We'll find out soon enough. In the meantime, let's pretend there's nothing wrong."

Sindak readjusted his weapons' belt. His collection of stilettos clacked against his stone knife. "I'm not good at pretenses, Towa."

"Just make the effort, will you?"

"Right up until someone jumps me."

Towa brazenly walked toward the Standing Stone warriors, wading through knee-deep leaves. The colors stirred up by his feet were stunning: brilliant scarlet, pale yellow, and a red so deep and dark it looked purple. As well as a hundred shades of brown. When Gonda saw Towa coming, he stood up . . . and Koracoo walked a short distance away to stand beneath an oak tree.

"I don't like it," Sindak whispered to himself, and followed Towa with his eyes narrowed.

As they entered the clearing by the fire, Towa said, "A pleasant morning to you," and circled around to stand opposite Gonda.

"And to you," Gonda replied. The firelight flickered from his clenched jaw and heavy brow.

Sindak glanced to where Koracoo stood, then gave Gonda a solid appraisal. Their positioning reminded him of a war council, where one warrior was always stationed a few paces from the fire so he could leap forward and commit murder if necessary.

Towa smiled uneasily, knelt, and rested his club across his lap; then he extended his hands to the flames to warm them. "It's frigid this morning."

"Yes, and I fear I smell snow on the wind," Gonda replied. He almost sounded friendly.

Sindak continued to stand, glancing from Gonda to Koracoo. Gonda appeared tense, but Koracoo's face might have been cut from stone. She wore no expression at all.

Sindak and Gonda stared at each other in uncomfortable silence for a time; then Gonda gestured to the fire and said, "Please, sit down, Sindak. Warm yourself."

Sindak waited for Gonda to slowly drop to a crouch before he did the same. He glanced at Gonda's club, which rested near the tripod, within easy reach, and clutched his own more tightly in his hand.

"We didn't have time to talk about the children's trail last night," Towa said. "Is it close?"

Gonda pointed to the northwestern edge of the clearing. "Right over there."

Towa twisted around to look. "Does it head east or west?"

"Due east."

Sindak gazed at Koracoo again. She hadn't moved a muscle. It was unnatural. And he swore CorpseEye was watching him. The red cobble head had two black spots that resembled shining eyes. "Well, we should eat and be on our way."

"Yes, as soon as possible." Gonda reached into his belt pouch, pulled out his wooden cup and a buffalo horn spoon, and set them aside. Then he pulled a stick from the woodpile and proceeded to stir the half-frozen bag of gruel. Ice crystals shished.

Towa and Sindak glanced at each other, drew their cups from their belt pouches, and waited.

After an agonizing amount of silence, Towa leaned sideways to whisper, "Why is Koracoo staring at us like that? She looks like a hunting cougar."

Sindak glanced up. Despite her chopped-off hair, she was tall and beautiful, and dangerous. Threat seemed to ooze from her.

Sindak whispered back, "She's trying to decide whether or not to pounce on us and rip out our throats."

"What makes you think that?"

"I've seen that look before. I was married to Puksu."

Koracoo stepped forward, met each man's gaze, and said, "While the cobble heats up, let's talk about our goals."

Towa blinked. "I assumed we were going to track the children, find them, and rescue them."

"That's the ultimate goal, yes. But we're going to take it one day at a time. No running ahead. No guessing. I want only facts. We've had a lot of strong winds, as well as rain and snow. In many places, the trail will have vanished. Each of us must pay excruciating attention to the ground, or we'll never find the trail again."

Towa gave her a disgruntled look. "We know that. You don't have to explain to us as though we are five-summers-old boys."

Sindak said, "What Towa means, War Chief, is that

we are warriors. So let me assure you that I am an expert tracker, and Towa is a genius with strategy."

Under his breath, Gonda said, "And you're modest, too."

Sindak smiled at him, but it was a promise of death.

Koracoo continued, "Good, Sindak. This is the plan, then: I will lead, and Gonda will bring up the rear. You will walk along paralleling the south side of the trail, and Towa, you will walk on the north side. Today, we stay close together, no more than fifty paces apart. If one person finds an interesting track, call out. The rest of us will work our way over to you. Do you understand?"

Towa squinted. "Of course we understand."

Sindak asked, "But . . . are you sure that's a good idea?"

Koracoo's brows lifted, and the forest seemed to go silent. "I take it that you don't?"

"I mean no disrespect, War Chief. I am just worried that they may suspect they are being followed."

Koracoo shifted CorpseEye to her other shoulder, and Sindak's fist instinctively tightened around his war club.

Koracoo said, "If the children were ordinary slaves, their captors would be herding them to villages to be adopted into new families. The warriors would be moving fast, interested only in getting home as quickly as possible. They wouldn't be paying any attention to their back trail. On the other hand—"

"If their captor is Gannajero, it's prudent to assume the worst," Sindak finished the sentence for her. "Which means she's watching her back trail like a hawk."

Koracoo nodded. "Yes. She can afford no risks. She has been pursued before, many times. She must expect it as a matter of course."

"So she may have scouts watching us even now?" Sindak asked.

"It's possible."

Towa exhaled hard, and his long braid sawed up and down his back. "Then is it wise for us to stay bunched together? If we fan out, they may get one or two of us, but it will be hard to kill us all."

"A lone warrior is far more vulnerable, Towa. If we stay together, we can defend each other. So, for now, we stay together."

Gonda reached over with two sticks, pulled the cobble from the fire, and dropped it into the gruel. Steam gushed up, and the bag boiled furiously for several moments before it settled down.

The delicious aroma of jerky and roasted corn filled the air. Sindak enjoyed it for a moment before asking, "That means, of course, that when she's sure we're following her, she'll attack us."

Koracoo's hard eyes sent a tingle up his spine. "Expect an ambush, Sindak. If we're on Gannajero's trail, it will be there. Maybe not today or tomorrow, but eventually she will take measures to eliminate us. Believe it. Prepare for it."

Sindak held her gaze. There was a strange hypnotic light in her eyes. He wouldn't mind seeing that every day of his life.

Koracoo added, "Just obey my orders, and I promise you that you will live through this."

"We have sworn to obey you, War Chief, and we will," Towa said. "Do you doubt that?"

"No, Towa. I'm just practical. It is one thing to swear it before your chief, but quite another to actually obey an enemy war chief in the midst of battle. But I hope you do. . . ." She lowered CorpseEye to her side and took a new grip on the shaft. "Because I'll kill you myself if you don't."

Wind swept through the forest and blew smoke into Sindak's eyes. He turned his head away for a moment, and it gave him time to consider her threat. Koracoo was right to worry that in the heat of battle he might choose to do what he thought best, regardless of her orders. Because he might. These were Standing Stone People. His enemies. He'd been taught that from birth. Not even his chief's orders could overcome a lifetime of hatred and distrust.

Koracoo seemed to read the tracks of his souls. She walked around the fire and crouched less than three hands from Sindak. He could smell her faint fragrance, a mixture of wood smoke and something spicy, as though she'd washed her cape in water scented with spruce needles. She carefully propped CorpseEye across her lap and said, "Is that true, Sindak? Do you know your duty?"

"I know my duty, War Chief." He smiled.

She smiled back, but it didn't reach her eyes. "Good. Now that we understand each other, let's eat and talk of other things. Please fill your cups."

Gonda filled his cup, then backed away from the boiling bag. Towa came forward next, filled his cup, and went back to kneel in his former position.

Sindak tied his club to his weapons' belt and cautiously rose with his eyes still on Koracoo. Her gaze followed him, unblinking, like a lynx watching prey. He went to the bag to fill his cup, then said, "May I fill yours, War Chief?" He extended a hand.

Koracoo slipped her cup from her belt pouch, rose, and walked around the fire to give it to him. He filled it. When he handed it back, their fingers overlapped. Conflicting emotions danced across her beautiful face: suspicion, desperation, determination. They stood side by side, the contact lasting much longer than he'd intended. By the time she pulled her cup from his clenched hand, blood rushed in his ears.

Koracoo turned away. "Eat as much as you can hold. It's going to be a long day."

Sindak exhaled the breath he'd unwittingly been holding and walked back to crouch beside Towa. He ate without a word, while Towa blew into his cup and studied Koracoo from the corner of his eye. Her cheeks had flushed. Towa gave Sindak an uncomfortable look.

And Gonda was glaring pure death at him. Who would have guessed that a man's face could contort like that?

Sindak drank his gruel with one hand on his war club.

Somewhere out in the trees, a hawk shrieked, and the call carried in the stillness.

Koracoo tilted her head to listen, and Sindak had the feeling that she suspected it might not be a hawk, but a warrior's signal. The hawk called again, and Koracoo relaxed and knelt near Gonda. She propped CorpseEye over her knees and sipped from her cup. Sindak continued listening for a time longer.

After a few more bites, Koracoo said, "Towa, as the chief's representative, I'm hoping you can help me understand some things."

Towa lowered his cup. "What things?"

"Your chief's recent Trading mission seemed foolhardy."

Towa straightened. "Why?"

"Warfare is rampant throughout our country. Why would your chief take his young daughter with him?"

Towa shrugged. "He loves her. I think he just wanted her close. He often took Zateri with him on trips."

While she chewed a bite of jerky, Koracoo looked away from them, methodically surveying the oaks. "I find that strange. But then, I don't believe in coincidence."

"What do you mean?"

"I mean it makes no sense that a chief would risk the life of his daughter for a few bags of pearls and salted seafood. You live in rich lake country. A wise man would have stayed home, eaten lake trout, and worn freshwater pearls until the trails were safer. There must be another reason he undertook the Trade mission."

Sindak could see the hot blood rushing to Towa's face, and he understood it. She was either calling their chief a fool or a liar.

In a surprisingly calm voice, Towa answered, "We have more mouths to feed than you do, War Chief. Our people are hungry. Our harvests were poor this autumn. Any village with food is holding onto it with a granite fist. Atotarho knew that the only way he might be able to acquire more food was if he went himself."

"And he took sixty warriors to make sure the party was safe. Sixty of our *best* warriors," Sindak added.

Gonda looked up. "Best? I thought you two were there?"

Sindak had the overwhelming urge to tear his heart out.

Koracoo swung CorpseEye suggestively, which kept Sindak from carrying out his urge.

She continued, "Atotarho could have hired the finest Traders in the land. He didn't have to go himself."

Dawn's gleam had started to shade the forest, blushing color into the black branches and the autumn leaves that blanketed the ground. As the air warmed, the scents of wet bark and moldering leaf mat grew stronger.

Finally, Towa said, "Perhaps it would help if you understood some things about Chief Atotarho."

Koracoo nodded. "Anything you can tell me will be helpful."

"He was once a great warrior, but about ten summers ago his joints began to stiffen."

"That's why standing is so difficult for him? I thought it might have been a battle injury."

"No. Evil Spirits have crept into his joints. When he could no longer serve as a warrior, he became a Trader, and he was very good at it. He loved Trading. I suspect he didn't think anyone could do a better job. That's why he didn't hire Traders. Ever."

Koracoo continued to eat at a leisurely pace, filling

her buffalo horn spoon, putting it in her mouth, chewing. She appeared to be totally absorbed by her own thoughts.

Gonda, on the other hand, was watching them over the rim of his cup, and his eyes had an alert glitter.

Sindak lifted his cup and angrily sucked down the last few bites; then he grabbed up a handful of leaves, wiped out his cup, and stuffed it back in his belt pouch. Koracoo's questions had him thinking, which he hated. He always got into trouble when he tried to think something out. But . . . there was something amiss here. Even if Atotarho loved to Trade, he knew how dangerous the trails were. Undertaking the expedition was very perilous. First of all, it left the village with sixty fewer warriors, which meant it was more vulnerable to attack. Second, Atotarho could have waited another moon to undertake the journey. They had enough food for a moon, and raiding always died down in the winter, though the snow also grew deeper. What had been so important about the Trading mission that he felt obliged to risk his daughter's life, and the lives of sixty warriors?

Towa set his half-finished cup of soup on the ground, as though no longer hungry, and laced his fingers over one knee. After several moments of hesitation, he said, "Let me see if I understand you, War Chief. Are you suggesting that Atotarho wanted his daughter to be captured?"

"That's the only thing that makes sense to me, Towa."

"He loved her. Why would he do that?"

Koracoo drank the last dregs from her cup, then

turned it upside down on the frosty grass to drain and replied, "I don't know."

"When you spoke with him, did he seem genuinely concerned about his daughter?"

"He did. In fact, he seemed terrified for her safety."

"Then her capture must have been an accident."

Koracoo didn't respond.

Gonda asked, "Where was War Chief Nesi when the girl was taken?"

Towa looked at Sindak. When Sindak shrugged and shook his head, Towa replied, "We were under heavy attack. We were trying to stay alive. I don't know where he was."

"Under heavy attack?" Gonda unlaced his belt pouch and tucked his cup inside. As he tugged the laces tight again, he frowned. "Who were they? How many warriors did they have?"

"I'm not sure." Towa glanced at Sindak again, silently asking if he knew.

Sindak said, "Maybe eighty. Maybe one hundred. Some of them were Mountain People, I think. The rest, I don't know. I didn't recognize the designs they wore. Why?"

Gonda's mouth pursed with disdain. He stood, lifted the boiling bag from the tripod, and walked around the fire to empty the final drops into Towa's cup. "Who was assigned to protect the chief's family?"

"Nesi and a hand-selected group of warriors." He picked up his cup again and took another sip.

Gonda said, "How many hand-selected warriors were in Nesi's group?"

"Five, I think."

"You *think*?" Gonda's brows plunged down over his flat nose. "You're a warrior. You should know."

"Well, I don't," Towa snapped.

Gonda stared down at him through slitted eyes. "Was the chief at the head of the expedition? Or was he walking in the middle, perhaps at the rear?"

"In the middle where he was surrounded by warriors."

"And where were you and Sindak?"

"We were last in line."

"So you didn't really see much of what happened around the chief's family?"

"Well . . . no."

Gonda rolled up the boiling bag and tucked it into his pack. "Did the attack come from the rear?"

"The bulk of the warriors struck the center and stole the chief's daughter, but at least thirty warriors attacked the rear. Both attacks happened simultaneously."

Koracoo gracefully rose to her feet, and Gonda stood up beside her. Instinctively, Sindak gripped his club.

In a low voice, probably meant for Gonda's ears alone, Koracoo said, "It *was* well organized. That's why they were chosen." Then she turned and headed across the clearing toward the place Gonda had indicated earlier, the place where they'd seen the children's tracks.

Gonda started to follow her, but Towa lunged to his feet and caught Gonda's arm as he passed. Gonda stopped and, eye-to-eye, they stared hard at each other.

"What did she mean?" Towa asked.

Gonda glanced at Koracoo, apparently to make sure she couldn't overhear them, then softly replied, "You're here because you were too far away to have played a role in the kidnapping. You are also young fools. You actually believe Atotarho sent you along with us to help rescue his daughter."

"Why else would he have sent us?"

Gonda pulled loose from Towa's grip. "I want you to think long and hard about that."

He walked away, leaving Sindak and Towa standing by the fire.

Sindak propped his hands on his hips and glowered after Gonda. "You should have slit his throat. He's an arrogant fool."

Towa reached up to massage his wounded shoulder. It must have hurt, because he squeezed his eyes closed. In a pained voice, he said, "Gonda is not a fool."

"Of course he is. The chief sent us to help rescue his daughter. Nothing more."

Towa adjusted the strap of his quiver and expelled a breath. "Sindak, how many warriors in Atotarho Village are better, more experienced fighters than we are?"

"What difference does it make? The chief chose us."

"Yes, but why?"

He gestured lamely. "He trusts us."

Towa murmured, "I don't think so. I think he chose us because Chief Atotarho fears there's a traitor in his midst—a very powerful man who has the loyalty of many warriors. But you and I are not among them."

Sindak shifted his weight to his other foot. "What are you talking about?"

Towa smiled and bowed his head as though surprised it had taken him so long to figure it out. "I'm talking about two young fools who are not part of that 'inner circle.' Young fools who still believe what their chief tells them."

"But if Atotarho doesn't trust us, why would he give you his sacred gorget? He wouldn't risk losing that!"

Towa placed his hand over the gorget and looked down. "I don't understand that part yet."

"Even if you and I are the only two warriors Atotarho doesn't suspect of treachery, the gorget is too precious to risk on fools. He *must* trust us."

Towa murmured, "It's possible. But I doubt it," and walked toward where Koracoo and Gonda knelt, scooping leaves from the trail and piling them to the side.

Sindak stood rigidly for a few moments. If there was a traitor, a man who commanded the loyalty of many warriors, the logical choice was Nesi. But Sindak did not believe Nesi capable of such treachery. He'd fought at Nesi's side for five summers and seen only an honorable, if touchy, man striving to protect his people. Why would Nesi betray his chief?

"If not Nesi, then who?"

Sindak heaved a frustrated breath and walked toward Towa.

Twenty

Odion

In the dream, I wake to the sound of Father's hushed voice. . . .

"I'm going," he says. "Who will watch your back? There's no one else—"

"I need you here, Gonda," Mother answers softly. "I want you to be in charge of defending Yellowtail Village."

I sleepily blink at the firelight reflecting from the bark walls of the longhouse. Almost everyone else is asleep. Someone close by is snoring softly, and I hear my little cousin, Ganahan, mewling as Aunt Tawi fusses to get her to nurse. Grandmother Jigonsaseh is muttering softly in her dreams. I smile. These are pleasant sounds, the sounds of early morning in the Bear Clan longhouse.

I yawn and roll to my back. Forty hands above me, tied to the roof poles, ears of corn, whole bean plants, pawpaws, squash, and net bags of puffballs and mushrooms hang. They were picked a moon ago and already have the black coating of soot that protects them from mold and insects. Through the smoke holes, I see a few of the campfires of the dead glittering.

When I inhale a deep breath of the smoky air, I smell corn pudding, and my heart sinks. This is the dish Mother makes for us when she's going away on a war walk. It's my favorite. Made from parched corn mixed with chunks of maple sugar and roasted pumpkin, then boiled in hickory nut milk, it is a special sweet breakfast.

I turn my head to look at Mother and Father. They sit by the fire with their backs to me. While Father stirs the pudding with a wooden spoon, Mother quietly places food in her belt pouch: a bag of venison jerky, another of dried blueberries, two cornmeal biscuits, several dried lichens wrapped in bark. I heave a sigh of relief. She's only going to be gone for the day—just a scouting mission close to the village. If she were going to be gone for longer, she'd be filling her pouch and her warrior's pack. Her quiver of arrows and bow rest atop her red cape at her side. Corpse-Eye, her war club, lies diagonally across them.

Father whispers, "Who are you planning to dispatch as scouts?"

"Coter and Hagnon. They're careful."

Father expels a breath. "Please, reconsider? If we keep all six hundred of our warriors in the village, we can repel any attack that comes. Perhaps we should—"

"We have to know for certain, Gonda. It's the end of harvest. Our people need to be in the fields gathering the last crops from the dead plants, not huddling behind the palisade in fear."

"I know, but—"

"Gonda, if the trader was right, and he really did see Mountain People warriors skulking around our village, they were probably scouts assessing our harvest. If they discover that we had an excellent harvest, they'll be back to take it. We need to capture them and find out who sent them.

There could be a war party out there just waiting for those scouts to report back. I don't want to give them the chance."

Father hesitates for a long time. He stirs the pudding, then in a low disgusted voice, says, "It's probably Yenda, that two-footed piece of filth."

Mother's long black braid saws up and down her back as she nods. "That is my guess, as well. His People are very hungry, and he's a cunning war chief."

"Cunning?" Father scoffs. "He's a cowardly weasel. He's bent on destroying us, and every other member of the Standing Stone nation. The Mountain People would starve us to death if they could. We should kill every one of them."

Mother's mouth tightens into a hard line. "You don't mean that."

"Oh, yes, I do. I want all of the Mountain People dead, as well as all of the Flint, Landing, and Hills Peoples."

Mother's voice is barely audible as she replies, "You've become a warmonger, Gonda."

"Yes, and I wish you were, too. Once all of our enemies are dead, we can live peaceful lives."

Mother draws up a knee and laces her fingers around it. She is very tall for a woman, twelve hands, and I've heard many of her warriors say she's beautiful "in a frightening sort of way." She has an oval face, with full lips and large black eyes. She doesn't say anything, though Father seems to be waiting for her response.

Father irritably tosses another branch on the fire. The wood crackles and spits as the sap burns. He is a medium-sized slender man with a round face and long black hair. The folds of his plain buckskin cape catch the firelight.

Mother softly says, "The Hills People just attacked White

Dog Village. Soon we'll be flooded with starving refugees. Half of our harvest will be gone in less than a moon. Don't you want this to end, Gonda? The warfare must end. Soon. Or we will all be dead."

Father lightly shakes his head. "Instead of worrying about feeding refugees, you should be worried that we're Chief Atotarho's next target."

Atotarho is an evil sorcerer from the People of the Hills. A cannibal who adorns himself with human bones.

Slowly, the images forming in my head begin to take on a horrifying reality. Atotarho could attack tomorrow. Even tonight. This is my greatest fear. I often have nightmares of our village being attacked, Mother and Father killed, and Tutelo and me being marched away as prisoners. Panic rises and overwhelms my heart. It begins to slam against my ribs. *Father is right! We have to kill them first. Before they can attack us!*

"Gonda," Mother says, "try to imagine what it would be like if all of our Peoples were united. If one village had a good harvest and another didn't, we could pool our food, and share it. No child would ever have to be truly hungry again. Not only that, we would be the greatest power in the land. No one could defeat us."

"Don't be ridiculous. We're too different to get along."

"There can be brotherhood in diversity. Brothers can respect each other's differences, even honor them."

Father lets out a low disdainful laugh. "You're a dreamer, Koracoo. We'd never be able to cooperate long enough to discover each other's differences, let alone—"

"We must try, Gonda. It's our only hope."

Father looks unconvinced. He scowls at the fire. "I will

tell you one thing for certain, my wife. I will *never* take food from my own children's mouths to give to my enemy—not even if our elders order me to do it. I want the Hills, Flint, Landing, and especially the Mountain People to starve. And so does everyone else in this village."

Sadness lines Mother's face. She bows her head. Her gaze is faraway, as though she is seeing a peaceful world where everyone has enough to eat, and she knows it can never be. "It's people like you who make our future precarious, Gonda."

He snaps, "And people like you who make *today* precarious. Forget about the future! Start thinking about who we have to kill to keep our People alive for another moon!"

Mother pulls the laces on her belt pouch tight, then slips it around her waist and ties it. "I'm going to take three hundred warriors. We'll be home by dusk. I'll leave you the other three hundred. That should be enough warriors to allow you to hold off any attack Yenda can muster."

Father doesn't answer.

Mother says, "Keep every warrior inside the palisade until I return. Do you understand?"

Father turns to glare at her. "What makes you think I would disobey one of your orders? Have I ever disobeyed you?"

"No, but your tone of voice tells me that this morning you'd like to, just to spite me."

Father opens his mouth to say something hostile, and I rise up in my hides and croak, "Mother? I—I'm scared. Are we going to be attacked?"

Father's mouth purses. He gives me a glance that makes

me long to run away and hide. He says I'm always scared, and that I'll never be of any use as a warrior.

Mother comes over, sits down, and gathers me into her arms. After she kisses my forehead, she says, "Don't be scared, Odion. Here, let's play a game. I want you to try and imagine a world where all of our Peoples are united and there is peace. Can you imagine such a world?"

I lean against her and close my eyes, trying hard. On the fabric of my souls I see people moving about villages, smiling. Dogs and children running happily across plazas. "I want to," I answer. "I don't like being afraid." I cast a glance at Father, who is shaking his head.

Mother strokes my black hair gently. "Someday there will be peace. I promise."

A profound sense of relief washes through me, as if something has opened in my chest and all the fear has drained away. I believe her. Perhaps her way is better? All of the agony, the indecision, the premonitions of disaster fade—vanishing amid the wave of peaceful firelight that now seems to fill the longhouse. The bark walls glitter as sparks float upward toward the smoke holes in the roof. People's faces shine, and now I hear laughter and loving voices as people begin to wake.

All I want is to stay here forever in the warm circle of Mother's arms, dreaming about a time when all the Peoples will be one, and no one will ever be hungry again.

"How do we make peace, Mother?" I whisper so that Father doesn't hear, and look up into her dark eyes.

Mother smiles down at me and whispers back, "We hold our tongues and listen. We open our eyes to the

tears of others. We act out of stillness, not out of anger
or—"

In a low hiss, Father says, "War Chief Koracoo, the
blessed *Peacemaker.*"

There is such loathing in the word that I freeze as
though I've suddenly seen a snake.

Mother lifts her head to look at Father. They glower at
each other.

I want to run away again. Instead, I bury my face in the
folds of leather over Mother's shoulder and just breathe. If
I dream hard enough, I'm sure my soul will find a way to
walk to that peaceful world Mother longs for.

When I close my eyes I can almost . . .

Mother pats my back, says, "I love you, Odion. I'll be
home for supper."

I swallow hard. "Be careful, Mother."

"I will." She kisses my cheek, releases me, and rises to
her feet.

As she goes over and slips on her red cape, Father says,
"If I'm engaged in the middle of a pitched battle when you
return, perhaps you should just trot up to Yenda and tell
him you want to make peace? I'm sure he'll be happy to sit
right down and negotiate like a good boy."

Mother slings her bow and quiver over her left shoulder,
picks up CorpseEye, and walks from the longhouse without a
word.

When she's gone, Father drops his head into his hands
and quietly curses himself: *"When did I turn into such a
fool?"*

As I pull up my deer hide and stare at him over the silken
rim of tan hair, I wonder if he is a fool. Or if he's right that

Mother is the fool for believing that peace is possible between the Peoples who live south of Skanodario Lake.

Father stirs the pudding again, and I let my gaze drift around the longhouse. Along the walls, melon baskets make dark splotches. Before the frost, we dig up melon vines with unripe fruit, and replant them in baskets of sand. During the winter, the melons ripen. They are Healing plants. We keep them for the sick.

Father calls, "Are you still awake, Odion?"

"Yes, Father."

He pulls a half-full ladle of pudding from the pot and blows on it. "Why don't you come over and taste this for me? I think it needs more maple sugar. What do you think?"

I smile, throw off my hides, and run to taste the pudding. Father puts his arm around me and hugs me as he brings the ladle to my lips. . . .

Somewhere in the depths of my souls, I hear warriors moving around a camp, and know I am freezing cold.

I struggle not to wake.

Twenty-one

Two days later, Sindak knew for certain they had lost the trail. He floundered around, weaving back and forth through the falling snow, searching for the slightest hint that even one man had passed this way—let alone an entire war party herding a group of unwieldy children. Blessed Spirits, how had Gannajero managed to so conceal the trail? They had followed a wide swath of tracks until midmorning; then a dozen trails had split off from the main one. They'd gone in every direction, as though men were abandoning the party, heading home to different villages. Gonda had argued vehemently for following one particular trail, and though Sindak had disagreed, Koracoo had ordered that they go with Gonda's choice. Gradually it had narrowed to the width of one man's path, and soon after vanished.

Sindak was not the only one frustrated and discouraged. Koracoo knelt at every snapped twig, picked it up and examined it, then gently placed it back exactly as she'd found it. In the rear, Gonda was down on his hands and knees, crawling with his nose practically touching the snow that filled in the trail; and to Sindak's right, Towa stood beside a snow-rimed mountain laurel, studying it for broken branches, or the smallest fibers left from clothing.

When Towa glanced across the trail and found Sindak staring at him, his brows lifted. Sindak shook his head in answer to the unspoken question: *Have you found anything?*

Towa moved on to a thicket of dogwood.

White veils spun through the chestnuts and basswoods that lined the trail. Already the snow was over Sindak's ankles, and growing deeper by the heartbeat.

Though he knew it was futile, Sindak started wading through the drifts again, searching. He spotted a few hickory nuts and tucked them in his belt pouch.

"I found something!" Gonda shouted. As he brushed at the trail, he called, "Koracoo? Come quickly."

She worked her way back to him, carefully stepping in her own tracks so as not to disturb anything that might be hidden on the trail beneath the snow.

Sindak and Towa also walked toward him.

They all arrived at about the same time and stood in a triangle, looking down at Gonda. His forehead was furrowed, and deep lines engraved the corners of his brown eyes. He had his finger placed below a badly washed-out track.

Koracoo knelt and began brushing away the surrounding snow.

They all crouched and brushed at the thick coating of snow and leaves near the "track." As he scooped away the snow, Sindak grimaced. Hundreds of might-be tracks dotted the frozen soil, but there was nothing that he would even remotely assess as being made by a man. He turned to stare at Towa. Towa shrugged and rose to his feet.

Koracoo spent a long time scrutinizing the indentation Gonda had found. All the while, Gonda watched her with desperation in his eyes, obviously praying that she would say it had been made by a child.

Koracoo expelled a breath, shook her head lightly, and got to her feet. "This is nothing, Gonda. We've lost the trail. We all know it."

"But it's the best track we've found," Gonda objected. "We should break off branches and start sweeping every step of the ground."

Sindak waited. Surely Koracoo knew Gonda's suggestion was folly. They were all exhausted and hungry. It would be far better to make camp and start fresh in the morning after a good night's sleep.

Koracoo looked up at the dim gray sky. Flakes swirled through the air. "We have perhaps a half-hand of light left. Let's stop for the day."

"What!" Gonda exploded. "We can't stop! We have to keep looking! The snow is growing deeper by the moment. By morning, their trail will be completely hidden!"

Koracoo's gaze wandered over the forest and came to rest upon a big pine. The area beneath the thick branches was dry and clear of snow. It was the best place to take shelter for the night.

Gonda seemed to sense her decision. "Koracoo, no. Please, let's keep searching." He gave her an imploring look, begging her to listen to him, to keep going.

Somewhere out in the forest, a turkey gobbled. Koracoo turned toward the sound, and Sindak hoped she'd order him to hunt it for supper.

Instead, she said, "No, Gonda. Let's make camp and fill our bellies with what's left in our packs. We'll start again at dawn tomorrow."

"But, Koracoo, we can still—"

"No, Gonda."

"You're being hasty! Think this through before you—"

"Sindak?" She turned to him. "Could you and Towa start cracking dead branches from the trees and piling them in the dry area beneath that big pine?"

"Yes, War Chief."

Sindak and Towa trotted away from the trail. As they snapped off the lower dead branches from two elm trees, they piled them in the crooks of their left arms and watched the interplay of emotions on Koracoo's and Gonda's faces.

"You're being foolish," Gonda said through gritted teeth. Every muscle in his thin wiry body had contracted and bulged through his cape and leggings. "We should keep searching as long as we have light. Every moment we rest or delay, our children—"

"That's enough, Gonda," she said, trying to keep her voice low. "Come. Let's go over and clean out some of the pine duff for a fire pit."

As she started for the pine, Gonda called, "You blame me, don't you?"

She stopped and turned to face him. "For what?"

"At that last fork in the trail, Sindak wanted to go left,

but I insisted we go right. You would have taken the left fork, wouldn't you?"

Koracoo stared at him, her face still and desolate.

Sindak whispered, "Dear gods, the panic in his voice gives me a stomachache."

Towa's shaggy brows drew together. He whispered back, "If it does that to you, imagine how Koracoo feels. But he's right—your trail was the better choice. If he hadn't argued so vehemently . . ."

Koracoo softly said, "Gonda, I was the one who made the final decision to take the right fork. Not you. If it was the wrong choice, I am to blame. But we will not know that until tomorrow when we go back over our tracks and find the place where we erred."

Gonda shook his fists as though he longed to scream at her to ease his own fears. After four or five heartbeats, he replied, "You don't trust me, do you?"

Exasperated, she threw up her hands, then turned and walked to the pine, where she ducked beneath the overhanging branches and crawled back into the dry shadows.

Gonda trudged through the snow and crawled in behind her. "Koracoo, answer me."

She propped CorpseEye against the trunk, then unslung her pack and quiver, laid them aside, and used both hands to start digging a hole for the fire pit in the pine duff. Even in the dim light, the red cobble head of CorpseEye gleamed like old blood.

When she just kept digging, Gonda reached out and his hand tightened around Koracoo's wrist like shrunken rawhide. "I know what you're thinking. Just say it."

Sindak and Towa both went rigid.

Koracoo lifted her gaze to Gonda. Death lived in those dark eyes.

Gonda released her as though he'd been holding a poisonous serpent, then slumped to the ground breathing hard. "Forgive me. I didn't mean to—"

"You're arrogant, Gonda." Koracoo resumed digging. "It has always been your failing. One of these days, it will cost you—or someone you love—his life."

"You mean *their* lives, don't you? Our children?"

She crawled away and began breaking off the dead branches at the base of the trunk, tossing them into a pile near the fire pit.

Gonda watched her expectantly, then dropped his face into his hands. "This isn't my fault, Koracoo. It's yours. If you weren't always trying to make peace with our enemies, we'd have killed them all long ago. There'd have been no attack on Yellowtail Village."

Her eyes filled with such a deep, aching sadness that Sindak had the insane urge to run over and wrap his arms around her. The fact that she'd kill him stopped him.

He placed another branch on the big bundle in his left arm. "I can't hold another twig, but I'll feel like I'm interrupting a private argument if I go back now."

Towa stepped up beside him with an even larger bundle cradled in his arms. "Don't worry. Our arrival will be a relief to both of them. Let's go."

They trudged down the hill and ducked beneath the pine boughs. As they worked their way back to the scooped-out hollow, neither Koracoo nor Gonda watched them. Sindak and Towa dumped their armloads by the pit, and Sindak looked askance at Gonda. He hadn't moved. He sat with his hands over his face.

"I'll start the fire," Towa said. "Sindak, can you gather some needles and twigs for tinder?"

"Of course."

Sindak went around collecting handfuls of old pine needles and twigs, which he piled beside Towa's right moccasin.

Towa unslung his quiver and set it near Koracoo's; then he arranged the tinder in the pit and removed two fire-sticks from his pack. He placed the punky stick on the ground, took the pointed hardwood stick and set it in its notch—a prepared hole in the punky stick—and began spinning the hardwood between his palms. The air was damp; it took around five hundred heartbeats for the friction to create an orange glow in the punky wood. Towa kept spinning the hardwood stick until the glow expanded and began to crackle; then he dumped it onto the nest of twigs and dry needles and softly blew on them until flames curled up.

Sindak knelt near the woodpile and extended his hands to the faint warmth. From the corner of his eye, he watched Koracoo. All night long he'd had erotic fantasies about her. It was hard to shove them out of his mind as he watched her remove the boiling bag from her pack and tie the long laces to the tripod. Every move she made had a distinctive muscular grace that brought back his dreams with aching clarity. When she finished, she carried the tripod over to the fire and set it up near the blaze. "How much food do you have left in your packs?"

Sindak said, "I have a little dried fish left."

"And I have some venison strips."

"Good. I have some hard cornmeal biscuits, baked with blueberries and sunflower seeds. Let's throw in everything we have, heat the soup, and fill our empty bellies so we can sleep warm."

"Yes, War Chief. Did anyone see a good rock for the bag?"

"I did." Towa rose, ducked beneath the overarching limbs, and went out into the trail to kick loose two small rounded rocks.

"Gonda?" Koracoo said. "What's left in your pack?"

He lowered his hands and looked at her with hollow eyes. "A few bear cracklings."

"Please throw them into the boiling bag."

Gonda unslung his pack and dug around until he found the small hide sack that held his dried food. He upended the sack over the boiling bag and shook out every morsel that remained.

Towa carried the two rocks back, ducked beneath the sheltering branches of the pine, and rolled the rocks into the fire.

"We need water," Koracoo said. She untied the buffalo paunch canteen from her belt and emptied it into the boiling bag. As she pulled the canteen's laces tight again, she said, "You'll each need to add more water from your own water bags."

"I have some left." Sindak emptied his canteen into the bag. The rest would be frozen by morning anyway.

As Gonda tipped his canteen over the bag and water trickled out, he said, "Koracoo, we need to discuss—"

"Tomorrow, Gonda. I'm going to bed. Sindak, please take first watch."

"Yes, War Chief."

"You're not going to eat?" Gonda squinted at her.

"I'm more tired than hungry. I'll eat in the morning."

She crawled over to CorpseEye, gripped her club, and went to the opposite side of the tree trunk, where she rolled up in her cape and propped CorpseEye across her chest.

As darkness fell, snow gusted down the trail and the forest branches clattered together. Towa dropped the two rocks into the boiling bag, and they sat in silence as steam began to rise. The smoky scent of jerked venison filled the air.

"We'll all feel better after we eat," Sindak said. "Hand me your cups and I'll fill them."

Gonda didn't move. He stared at the flames with haunted eyes. Towa handed Gonda's cup to Sindak. Sindak filled it, and Towa set it beside Gonda's moccasin. He didn't seem to care. He kept twisting his hands in his lap.

What a difference. Last night, he was an offensive wolf. Tonight, after losing the trail, he's a trembling ruin of a man.

Sindak stared at him and said, "Give me your cup, Towa."

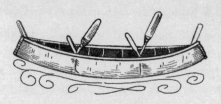

Twenty-two

Towa handed over his cup and went back to staring at Gonda. In the firelight, the muscles of Gonda's jaw quivered.

Sindak crouched down on the opposite side of the fire and filled his own cup. The limbs gave them just enough room to sit up straight. As the wind blew the branches the radiant halo of firelight shifted, casting shadows across their faces and creating strange dark wraiths in the snow that gusted by.

Towa asked, "What did you do, Gonda?"

He lifted his head, and guilt lined his round face. "What do you mean?"

"Koracoo doesn't trust you. Why?"

Anger hardened Gonda's mouth. "That's none of your concern. I—"

"If she does not trust you, how can we? Do you have a weakness we should know about? Forgive me for asking, but in the heat of battle, such knowledge may save my life."

Gonda seemed to be weighing what he should and should not say, and Sindak found that curious. Any other man accused of being weak would have reached for his war club and started swinging. Last night, Gonda would have. But not tonight. He turned away, dug his buffalo horn spoon from his pack, and used it to shovel meat into his mouth. After he'd chewed and swallowed three heaping spoonfuls, he quietly responded, "I made a mistake."

"A mistake?"

"Yes."

"A mistake that led to the destruction of Yellowtail Village and the loss of your children?"

Gonda looked like he wanted to talk about it but didn't have the strength, or perhaps he couldn't figure out how.

Towa said, "I had children once, Gonda. A brave little boy and a sweet, beautiful girl. I lost them both, along with my wife, to a fever two summers ago. I have some idea what you must be feeling."

Gonda's expression softened, but he just continued eating his soup.

Sindak frowned at Towa. He never talked about the loss of his family. Ever. It hurt too much. What was he doing? Trying to create some kind of tie with Gonda?

Gonda swallowed a bite of soup and softly said, "Do you still live the nightmare of their deaths, Towa?"

"Every day."

As Gonda brought up one knee and propped his cup on top of it, he kept his gaze on Towa's somber face. "Then perhaps you can imagine what it would be like to live the nightmare of your children's lives as Gannajero's slaves. Every instant I see my children hurt, or hungry, or being tormented by enemies. Or I fear they are dead and their souls are out wandering alone in the forest, calling out to me, trying to find their way home."

Towa's breath misted in the air. "That must be like having a belly full of obsidian flakes."

The scent of the campfire grew stronger as night deepened and smoke hung in the pine boughs just over their heads.

Sindak said, "They may have just been captured by an ordinary war party, and are being well cared for. No man mistreats a child he plans to adopt into his own family."

Gonda continued spooning soup into his mouth, chewing, swallowing.

Towa gave him some time before he added, "And even if the children are with Gannajero, they're alive. They're too valuable to kill. We *will* find them and bring them home."

Gonda's spoon halted halfway to his mouth. "We may bring them home, Towa, but I'm not sure even our best Healers will be able to cure them."

Out in the forest, frozen trees cracked and snapped beneath the brunt of the icy wind, but Sindak pinned his attention on Gonda's agonized face. Brief, hard flurries of sleet had started to whip by just beyond the pine. Gonda seemed to be watching the veils of snow as they careened down the trail.

Sindak asked, "What was the mistake you made?"

Gonda set his cup down and rubbed his hands over his face. In a voice almost too low to hear, he said, "I disobeyed an order."

Sindak shifted, and the frosty pine needles at his feet crunched. "What order?"

When Gonda didn't answer, Towa said, "When we accompanied Atotarho on the trading expedition, we heard rumors that Mountain People war parties were scouting near Yellowtail Village. You must have heard them, too."

Through a long exhalation Gonda said, "A Trader came through the morning of the attack and told us he'd seen Mountain warriors just a short distance from Yellowtail Village."

"What did you do?"

"The only thing we could. Koracoo took half our warriors out to verify the rumors. They could have been false. She wanted to make certain."

"But you did not go with her?"

Gonda stared absently at the ground. "No. I was in charge of defending the village."

A sleety gust rattled the branches over their heads. Sindak flipped up the hood of his buckskin cape and cradled his warm cup in both hands.

Towa softly asked, "What happened?"

Gonda cast a surreptitious glance at Koracoo, and Sindak had the vague feeling that Gonda hoped she might come to his rescue by answering that question herself. When she did not, he heaved a heavy sigh.

"She ordered me to keep all of my warriors inside the palisade until she returned."

Towa's brow furrowed. "You didn't?"

Gonda took another bite of soup and took his time swallowing it. "Just moments before the attack, two terrified scouts came running into the village, claiming there were over one thousand enemy warriors in the forest."

"One thousand?"

He gritted his teeth. "I panicked. You wanted to know the truth? That's it. When the palisade was on fire in fifty places, and I could see them massing for a final assault, I panicked. Their eyes glinted in the starlight. I led half my warriors outside to create a diversion—"

"You disobeyed *Koracoo's* orders?"

Gonda hung his head. "At the time, it seemed like the right decision."

A cold shiver went down Sindak's spine. Among the People of the Hills the penalty for disobeying your war chief's orders was death. If he had disobeyed Nesi's orders and half the village had been slaughtered as a result, Nesi would have paraded Sindak from longhouse to longhouse and allowed those who had lost family members to take out their vengeance on Sindak's flesh. The pain would have lasted for days.

On the other hand, if Sindak had been in Gonda's position, looking into hundreds of glinting eyes out in the forest, he might have done the same thing— regardless of the consequences. A desperate man facing overwhelming odds had to believe in his Spirit Helpers. Obviously, Gonda's had let him down.

Towa said, "What happened to the warriors you led outside? Were they killed?"

Gonda tightened his grip around his cup to still the tremors in his hands. Barely audible, he answered, "A few of us survived."

Against the firelit background of whirling sleet, Gonda appeared thin and haunted. His round face was worn down to its heavy bones. He couldn't have seen more than twenty-six or twenty-seven summers, but in the short black hair that covered his ears, scattered filaments of silver caught the light.

Sindak said, "Afterward, you didn't have enough warriors inside the palisade to defend the village, did you?"

He shook his head. "We were overrun with stunning swiftness."

Even now, days later, he must still see the tormented faces of his dead friends and relatives. Or was he thinking of his children? Perhaps hearing their last cries?

Sindak said, "So, Koracoo blames you? She thinks that if you'd kept all of your warriors inside the palisade, as she ordered, they might have been able to hold out long enough for her war party to get back and turn the tide of battle?"

Gonda twisted his cup in his hands. "She won't talk to me about it."

Sindak didn't really like Gonda, but he said, "Gonda, if the enemy forces were truly as large as you say, they would have overrun Yellowtail Village anyway."

A faint roar underlay the keening wind. They all tipped their heads to listen to it. It resonated like the thrumming bass note that seems to linger in the air long after the song is finished, more felt in the bones than heard.

Towa asked, "How many warriors did Koracoo have with her?"

"The same number I had—three hundred."

"Well, Gonda, if Koracoo's warriors had returned, they would have suffered the same fate as the men you sent outside. They would have been destroyed. The ending would have been the same."

Gonda shook himself as though trying not to remember. "Don't you understand? I sent one hundred men out to face over one thousand enemy warriors. It was . . . hopeless."

"You were desperate."

Gonda turned disbelieving eyes on Towa. "I gave the order, Towa."

"I'm not trying to anger you, Gonda. It's just that my people believe a war chief should be a good enough judge of character to know when a man isn't suited for great responsibility. Nesi would have never put you in that position."

Sindak shifted slightly to look at Koracoo. He wondered if Towa had not inadvertently hit upon the problem: *Koracoo can't forgive herself for leaving Gonda in charge. Perhaps it isn't Gonda she distrusts. She's lost confidence in herself.*

Gonda hung his head and shook it. "I was perfectly suited. I've done it dozens of times. Koracoo made the right choice in selecting me for the duty. I just . . . I—I . . ."

Towa kept glancing down to where Gonda's hands gripped his cup as though to strangle the life from it.

Gonda smiled weakly. "It's getting late."

"I just have one more question," Towa said. "I don't know you very well, Gonda, but you have a reputation for valor and brilliance in war. In fact, none of our warriors wishes to face you in battle."

Gonda stared at Towa with his jaw clenched.

Towa seemed to be worried about how to phrase it. "Men make mistakes in the heat of battle. Koracoo knows this better than anyone. So, my question is, why doesn't she believe it was a mistake? Earlier, she called you 'arrogant.' Does she think you deliberately defied her orders?"

Gonda's nostrils quivered. "I would very much like to know the answer to that question." He rose unsteadily to his feet, wiped out his cup, and said, "If she ever tells you, let me know." Then he tramped away.

Sindak watched him roll up in his cape and prop his head on his pack. Just before he closed his eyes, he grabbed his war club and dragged it close.

A powerful gust of wind blasted the forest, and a branch broke in the fire. The scattering sparks threaded Towa's handsome face with crimson light. Sindak studied his taut expression.

Quietly, so Gonda could not hear, Sindak said, "I'm surprised he told you as much as he did."

"I'm not. Gonda's been desperate to discuss this with someone. The guilt is eating him alive."

Sindak considered that. His grandmother had once told him to make carelessness his enemy and righteousness his armor, because guilt was like a very dull blade; it could kill, but it took a long time and the pain was excruciating. "I can't wait to hear Koracoo's side of the story."

Towa gave him an askance look. "Hear it? Never, my friend."

"No?"

"Why would she tell you?"

"How many friends does she have out here to talk to?"

Towa's brows lowered. Barely audible, he warned, "You're going to get yourself killed trying to 'befriend' her."

In the shadows on the other side of the tree trunk, he could just make out Koracoo's face. It had a pale gleam. Bluntly chopped-off locks of black hair fell over her cheeks. He thought her eyes might be open. Was she watching them? Trying to hear their discussion?

Towa followed his gaze and softly said, "Even if you 'befriend' her, she won't tell you. She would consider it a sign of weakness."

Sindak drew his knees up and locked his arms around them. "As would I."

"Would you?"

"Of course. Any man who needs to discuss his feelings is a coward."

"That's silly." Towa kicked at the woodpile. "Do you recall when you told me that I thought much as Koracoo did?"

"Yes."

"Well, I don't. But you do. Keep that in mind."

Towa set his empty cup beside the fire pit, rose, and walked over to stretch out near Gonda.

Sindak's gaze returned to Koracoo. He swore she was watching him. Firelight reflected in her open eyes. He just couldn't be certain if she was looking at him, or out into the forest. His gaze drifted to the trees, where wind-thrashed limbs created such a noise an entire war party could be upon them before they heard a whisper of moccasins on the leaf mat. Stealthily, his right hand lowered to the war club tucked into his belt.

Koracoo gave him one last look, then closed her eyes.

Sindak finished his soup and crawled to the edge of the pine boughs to keep watch on the trails.

Twenty-three

Sometime around midnight, a groan woke Koracoo. She rolled to her side and looked at Gonda. He'd been making soft agonized sounds for over a hand of time—fighting the battle again. She had seen him do this same thing for thirteen summers. After every battle, she spent six or seven days refighting it in her dreams. Gonda spent moons.

Her gaze shifted to Sindak. He was no longer sitting beneath the pine where the flames could blind him to the night, but had moved to stand outside, facing east, looking up the trail. The sleet had stopped, leaving the deep blue sky clear. As the icy breeze gusted through the trees, Sindak's buckskin cape billowed around his broad shoulders. Though he clutched his war club, he also carried his slung bow and quiver.

Gonda made a sound like a suppressed scream.

Sindak glanced back over his shoulder, shook his head, and went back to watching the trails.

Koracoo stared out past Sindak to the stars visible just over the treetops. They glittered as though silver flames burned in their hearts. *Where are you, Mother? Are you alive or dead?*

Her mother's half-dead eyes seemed to be branded on her souls—always there, always pleading for help. She'd found Mother lying in the charred remains of their long-house with Koracoo's sister, Tawi, beside her. For the rest of Koracoo's life she would wonder whether or not Tawi had been trying to pull their mother to safety when the burning wall had collapsed on top of them.

Koracoo rested CorpseEye across her chest and put her hands on either side of her head, pressing hard, endeavoring to force some sense into her worry-laced soul. She felt like a sleepwalker, just going through the motions of life, not really here.

"Come on," she hissed. "Wake up. Wake up, blast you."

By now, the Yellowtail Village survivors would have arrived at Bur Oak Village, and rumors would be running wild. They'd blame her for the attack. They'd say that if she'd left Deputy Deru in charge, instead of assigning Gonda, their families would be alive—which was probably true. They'd say she'd depended upon the wrong man, that she'd favored him because he was her husband, and it had cost them everything. . . . Or they'd say she should have never left on the scouting mission the morning of the attack.

She looked at Sindak, Towa, and Gonda. When the fight came, could she depend upon any of them? The only person she was absolutely certain she could depend upon was herself, which meant she would have to be the linchpin of any plan. What would happen if she fell? Which of them would take over and rescue the children?

For twelve summers, she had known the answer to

that question. The fact that she no longer did terrified her. Memories were her greatest enemy. One, from three summers ago, kept replaying over and over. It always started the same way. She saw the forest fire reflected in Gonda's eyes. The rest of their war party had been killed during the first day of fighting. She and Gonda had been running through the burning trees for four days, trying to find a safe way home—but Flint warriors had cornered them in a narrow rocky canyon. When Koracoo had fled there, she hadn't noticed that it dead-ended twenty paces back. They'd scrambled behind a tumbled pile of boulders, and the victory cries of the Flint warriors had been deafening. . . .

"How many are out there?" Gonda had asked as he'd checked the arrows in his quiver. Sweat matted his black hair to his round face, making his nose seem longer.

"I'd guess fifteen or twenty."

"I hate to tell you this, but that's fourteen more than I have arrows for."

"And fifteen more than I have." She'd pulled Corpse-Eye from her belt.

As the warriors clambered through the rocks around them, Gonda had given her a grin. "I've heard the elders talking. You're going to be war chief someday soon. Surely the future war chief of Yellowtail Village can figure a way out of this trap."

Koracoo had laughed. He'd always done that to her—made her laugh in the most dire of circumstances. Five arrows simultaneously battered the rocks around them, showering them with rock chips. They'd both hit the ground and covered their heads.

When she'd dared to look up, she said, "Absolutely. Are you ready?"

He'd given her a surprised look. "What are you going to do?"

"I'm going to climb out of here and start bashing out the brains of any warrior who leaps up to face me."

"That doesn't sound like a very sound strategy to me. There are a lot of arrows flying out there."

"Would you rather wait here? They'll be coming soon."

He'd rolled to his hands and knees. "No, I wouldn't. But before we die, I want you to know that you are everything to me. If we die here—"

"Stop being sentimental. Tell me tomorrow." She'd jumped up and started swinging CorpseEye.

He'd been right behind her. . . .

Koracoo forced the memory away, but not before an incapacitating ache filled her chest.

As though he knew, Gonda whimpered.

Koracoo listened, her heart pounding. He was not a coward, or stupid. But by disobeying her, he had broken her heart and betrayed her trust. She vacillated between longing to beat him to death with her bare fists, and bury her face against his chest and weep until she had no tears left.

For days, she'd secretly endured the same fear that lived in his eyes—the fear that they would never find their children, or that Odion, Tutelo, and Wrass were injured, or being tortured. Worst of all was the knowledge that their children were lying awake at night, praying that she and Gonda were on their trail coming to save them.

Even worse, *even worse,* every time Gonda looked at her, his eyes were reverent with faith in her. And she understood perfectly. Gonda believed that Koracoo would save their children.

As the knot in her belly tightened, she quietly rose and went to stand beside Sindak. He kept his gaze on the trail. She guessed his age at eighteen or nineteen summers. His shoulder-length black hair gleamed in the starlight, and his lean face reminded her of an eagle's, beaked, with sharp brown eyes.

Without looking at her, he said, "My watch is not over. You have another hand of time to sleep, War Chief."

Koracoo studied the faint crystalline haze that filled the air. Amid the swaying branches, elusive winks of stars flashed. "At dawn, we will go back and take the left fork in the trail."

"Very well."

By the glow of the fire, she could see every small line of his face, from temple to jaw, thrown suddenly into shadow. It made him look older, more sure of himself. He turned, and curiosity glinted in his brown eyes.

"What is it, Sindak?"

"I was just wondering, that's all."

"Wondering about what?"

He used his chin to gesture to Gonda. "Why did you bring him on this journey? It's hard on him. And will be harder still if we don't find the children."

"He'll survive."

"Will he? I suspect you can stand whatever life throws at you, Koracoo. I'm not sure he can. Every step we take, I feel like I'm watching him fall apart. One day he's desperate to fight me, the next he barely has the strength to keep hold of his club."

Koracoo's fingers unconsciously moved over Corpse-Eye, caressing the fine dark wood like a lover's skin. Sindak glanced down, noticed, then apprehensively lifted his gaze to her eyes again.

She said, "This journey may be hard on him, Sindak, but it is also his redemption."

"Even if we fail?"

"Especially if we fail. At least Gonda will know that he did everything he could to find them."

"Ah, I see. If you'd left him home, he would always wonder if he could have made a difference?"

"Yes."

Sindak's brows arched, as though surprised by her answer. "Then bringing him was an act of kindness on your part."

"Did you think it was an act of cruelty?"

He shrugged. "I wondered, that's all."

She propped the cobble head of CorpseEye on the ground and leaned against the shaft like a walking stick. Power tingled beneath her fingers. When it grew too uncomfortable, she shifted her grip. It might just be the warmth of the wood against her freezing hands. Then again, CorpseEye could be trying to get her attention, to tell her something. She scanned the trees. The forest appeared calm, and she heard nothing unusual.

Sindak said, "What's wrong?"

"Nothing . . . it's just . . . nothing."

He glanced up the trail. "Your expression suddenly changed, War Chief. You looked worried. Why?"

Koracoo petted CorpseEye. Sindak watched with an intensity she found unsettling. "CorpseEye is old," she said. "And wise. He often hears or sees things I do not. When he does, he tries to get my attention."

"How?"

She gestured uncertainly. "Power flows from Corpse-Eye into my hands. It's a warmth. At times, it's painful."

"Was it painful just now?"

"Don't worry about it, Sindak. I'll search after you've gone to sleep. I'll have lots of time before dawn. That way if it's nothing, I—"

Sindak walked out onto the trail, where the starlight gilded the arrows in his quiver like points of flame. His cape flapped around his long legs. "Let's search now."

Koracoo followed him.

The gusting wind had blown the snow and sleet into drifts and exposed patches of the forest floor. Dark irregular blotches of soil marked the trail.

She said, "It will be far easier to search at dawn."

"You said we would head back to the fork in the trail at dawn."

"We will, unless we find something here." She swung the club up to rest on her right shoulder. "Truly, Sindak, you should get some rest."

"I won't be able to sleep until we know it's nothing."

"All right, we'll head east."

Sindak nodded.

Starlight coated the ground and reflected from the snow with blinding strength. Koracoo concentrated on the places that had been blown clean. They hadn't been able to see those patches earlier in the day.

As she searched, her thoughts strayed to Gannajero. She'd been thinking a lot about her as they'd tried to work out her trail. The mysterious old Trader had survived for forty summers, which meant she was shrewd. She probably kept eight or ten men around her, but no more. A few wary, trained warriors were necessary. They could move fast, and shoot enough arrows to allow Gannajero to escape. More than ten were just loose ends that would need to be disposed of later.

Including herself, Koracoo had four warriors, and three were not fully functional. A draining emotional haze clouded her vision, as well as Gonda's, and Towa had a wounded arm. It took every bit of concentration she had to try to think clearly. At the same time, she had to keep Gonda focused so that he didn't run off on some misguided mission of his own.

That was the other reason she'd brought him. He wouldn't have stayed home. No matter what orders she'd given him, he would have disregarded them and gone searching for their children.

Koracoo walked around a fallen log and saw, behind it, a smooth grassy meadow dotted with boulders. On the far side of the meadow, the mountainside sloped steeply upward. Several trees were down, probably blown over in last moon's storms. Their roots, ripped from the earth, stuck up like dark crooked arms reaching for the heavens.

Koracoo's breath, her heart, and time itself seemed to stop. As if he'd heard something, Sindak looked over at her, then out into the darkness. For a long while only the hissing of her breathing filled the silence.

Then at the meadow's edge, near the blown-down trees, something glimmered.

She cautiously walked toward it. Sindak seemed to understand. He shifted his course to intersect her path.

"What did you see?" he asked.

"I'm not sure yet." A flicker, like a shiny string of polished blue beads had caught the light just right.

As they approached, walking side by side, that twinkle came again, brighter this time, as though a stream of pale blue fire had raced down the length of the object.

Sindak murmured, "I see it."

Koracoo put a hand on his wrist, stilling him. "Let's go carefully now. It could just be a vein of quartz crystals unearthed by the falling trees, but it could be a decoration on a warrior's cape."

As they edged toward the twinkle, Koracoo saw a moose. It skirted the edge of the meadow in the distance, its eyes flashing as it trotted off.

"Stop!" Sindak hissed suddenly and thrust out an arm to block her way. His gaze had fixed on the snow two paces in front of them. "Do you see it?"

"What?" She searched the snow . . . and saw an unnatural shadow, running straight as an arrow's flight to connect with the pale blue line that sparkled at the base of the downed trees.

"It's a trail," Sindak said. "A deep trail. Despite the snow, you can still see the swale left by the passage of many feet."

Koracoo tried to fight down the hope that rose sweet and hot in her breast. "Let's make certain."

She went to stand over the swale. It was wider than it

looked—ten hands across. Starlight glimmered from the frozen edges of the trail like white paint. "Whoever made this path is walking out in the open, going through meadows and probably across bare rock, loosely paralleling the trails."

"That's why we're having such a hard time staying with them. Should I wake the others?"

"No. Let them sleep." She propped her left fist on her hip. "We don't know that this is the children's trail. It could have been made by any stealthy war party."

"But you think it's their trail," he said.

"Yes," Koracoo said. "But we won't know until we can really examine the tracks. Come on. Let's go back. I'll start my watch, and you can rest. At first light, we'll pick up right here."

They walked back to camp, listening to their feet crunching the snow.

When they reached the pine, Sindak stopped and extended his hand to touch CorpseEye, but his fingers halted a hairbreadth away. "Is this all right?"

"You may touch him." Koracoo extended the club.

Sindak touched the cobble head, then gently ran his fingers over the carvings in the wooden shaft. An expression of wonder came over his young face. Could he feel the warm heart that inhabited the club?

Sindak said, "We'd have never found the trail without CorpseEye. At dawn, we'd have headed back to the fork in the trail, and gone the wrong direction."

She smiled faintly. "*If* this is the trail."

Sindak removed his hand and clenched it, as though to hold onto the sensation; then he looked at her.

Something about the softness of his expression touched her . . . and worried her. She'd seen that look before in the eyes of young warriors. Usually it was youths who had seen fifteen or sixteen summers. Sindak was a little old for this, but he knew her less well. At this point, it was just attraction, but if his gaze began to get that worshipful glow, she would have to do something about it. And afterward, he would never look kindly at her again.

"Get some sleep, warrior," she ordered.

"Yes, War Chief."

Sindak ducked low and crawled beneath the pine into the firelight. He pulled his rabbit-fur blanket from his pack and stretched out beside Towa. Towa said something too low to hear. When Sindak answered, Towa smiled.

Their conversation woke Gonda. He grumbled, threw them hateful looks, then flopped to his opposite side and went back to sleep.

Koracoo spread her feet, heaved a sigh, and watched the trail.

Twenty-four

Odion

Gannajero's shrill voice makes me sit bolt upright. Crystalline snowflakes fall from a lavender sky.

Last night was freezing. I barely slept. All night long I lay with my body curled around Tutelo's trying to keep her warm while I listened to the terrifying sounds of the camp. Sobs and cries filled the darkness.

I lift my head. I don't see any of Gannajero's warriors. By now, I have memorized some of their names: Kotin, Hanu, Galan, Tenshu, Waswan, Ojib, Chimon. . . . But several of the gamblers remain rolled in their blankets, snoring. A few wander about unsteadily. Weapons clatter as belts are strapped on and quivers slung over shoulders. I watch two men walk into the forest. A short time later, the scent of urine carries on the wind. Where is she?

"Are you awake?" Wrass says softly.

I roll over. Snow coats the hood of his cape, encircling his narrow beaked face with a white frame. A bandage wraps his little finger. "Yes, I'm awake."

He doesn't look at me. I follow his gaze and see Gannajero. She's hissing at Hehaka and one of the Flint girls. Shaking her fist in their faces. The girl weeps.

"What's happening?"

"They're being punished."

"Why?"

"Hehaka was up all night. He was so tired he stumbled and sloshed corn brew on one of the warriors. I don't know what the girl did."

I sit up and see Gannajero's warriors. They have gathered out in the trees. They already have their packs on, as though ready to march. "Are we leaving?"

"Yes, soon, I think."

"Where are we going? Did you hear them say?"

Wrass shakes his head. "No."

Several of Gannajero's men disperse into the trees. Each walks away alone, heading in a different direction. This makes me frown. While several gamblers are still sleeping, only four warriors remain. Two guard us, and two—Kotin and another man whose name I don't know—stand talking in the trees. "Where are they going?"

"They may be scouting the trail ahead."

"But they walked away in different directions."

"Maybe they're scouting the trails in every direction."

My heart pounds.

Gannajero grabs Hehaka and the Flint girl by the hands and drags them back toward us. She keeps growling at the girl. When she arrives she shoves Hehaka to the ground and grips the girl's shoulders so hard the girl yips.

Tutelo jerks awake in terror and flings her arms around my waist. "Odion, what—"

"You little fool!" Gannajero shouts at the Flint girl. "If you ever try that again, I'll let the man kill you. Do you understand? If it weren't for me, you'd be dead right now."

The girl sinks to her knees and weeps. "Let me die. Please let me die?"

Gannajero kicks her in the chest, and the girl falls backward, making hideous choking sounds. She can't breathe.

For a few terrible instants Gannajero's wild eyes fix on me. She leans forward and says, "After last night, you must be worried about your sister. Hmm?"

I can't find my voice. Terror has killed it.

Wrass says, "Where did the men take the other two Flint girls? Why aren't they back yet?"

Gannajero laughs and walks away.

The girl on the ground writhes, fighting for air.

Wrass crawls over to her. "Sit up. You'll be all right. She just knocked the wind out of you."

Tutelo looks up at me, and tangled black hair falls down her back. "What did that girl do, Odion?"

"I don't know."

Wrass helps the girl to sit up, and she finally manages to suck in air. As she breathes, her tears begin to subside. Except for the puffy red welt on her oval face, she's very pretty, with long eyelashes and a small nose. Long black hair sways around her.

"Are you all right?" Wrass asks.

"Sh-she sold my sisters. To the men who claimed them last night. They're gone!"

"She sold them forever? I thought she was just selling them for the night?"

"No. They're gone. I'll never see them again!"

"You don't know that. The men may take your sisters

home and adopt them into their families," Wrass says gently. "And you are all right. That's all that matters right now. You—"

Tutelo says, "Why didn't she sell you?"

The Flint girl glances at Tutelo and chokes back a sob. "I—I found a rock on the ground and hit the man in the face. It left a gash. He tried to kill me."

Wrass says, "And Gannajero stopped him?"

"Yes. She said I was too v-valuable to die just yet."

From the far side of the group of children, Chipmunk rises on trembling legs. She walks over and squats in front of the Flint girl, then lifts a shaking hand to touch the swollen knot on the side of her face. "What's your name?"

"Baji."

"Where are you from?"

"S-Singleleaf Village."

Chipmunk gently strokes her hair. "I've studied Healing. I'll make a poultice from snapping alder bark. You won't even have a bruise. I promise."

I turn to watch Gannajero. She is packing up camp, collecting huge bags of trade goods—her payment from last night. When she finishes and piles all of her packs in one place, she stalks around camp, shouting curses and kicking sleeping men, forcing them to get up.

Hehaka draws my attention when he rolls to his side and seems to melt into the bed of leaves.

"Tutelo, I need to go speak to Hehaka. Will you be all right?"

She nods and releases me so that I can crawl over to Hehaka. "Are you all right, Hehaka? Are you hurt?"

He looks up at me with agonized eyes. His lean, starved

face has gone pale. "She sucked out my soul," he whispers, and glances around, hoping none of the other children hear. But Wrass does. He turns to gaze at Hehaka. "She sucked it out with that eagle-bone sucking tube and blew it into the little pot that she carries in her pack."

"Why?" Wrass asks.

He squeezes his eyes closed. "She told me that when she kills me, my afterlife soul will never be able to find its way home. I'll be chased through the forests forever by enemy ghosts." Tears leak from the corners of his eyes.

"She's an old fool," I say in anger. "She's not powerful enough to do that. It would take a great shaman, and she's—"

"Shh!" He grabs my arm and shakes me hard. "You mustn't say that. She'll hear!"

"She can't hear me, Hehaka. She's way over on the other side of cam—" As I speak the words, Gannajero turns and stares right at me. Her eyes are like black suns burning me to cinders. My mouth goes dust dry.

"She's a witch!" Hehaka whispers. "She can hear voices from half a day's walk away. I swear she can. I've seen it."

Wrass moves over and crouches beside me, staring down at Hehaka. He holds his wounded hand protectively against his chest. "You've seen it? How long have you been her slave?"

"S-seven summers," Hehaka whispers.

Stunned, I hiss, "Seven?"

Wrass asks, "Why hasn't she sold you? Where do you come from?"

"I don't know." Hehaka shivers and covers his eyes with

his arm so that he can cry unseen. "She won't let me go. I don't know why. She says she'll never sell me."

Wrass clenches his fists and whispers to me, "That doesn't make any sense. She's a Trader. That's what she does: sell children. Why would she keep Hehaka?"

I grip his arm and tilt my head, telling him I want to talk with him alone. Wrass rises. We walk a few paces away. The warriors guarding us straighten. One nocks an arrow in his bow. Another swings his war club suggestively.

I pull Wrass close to hiss, "Do you think she's a witch?"

Wrass swivels around to gaze at Gannajero. "She's evil, that's for sure. Do you think she really sucked out Hehaka's soul?"

I lick my chapped lips, taste blood, and glance again at our guards. They are watching us with half-lidded eyes. One wrong move and they'll kill us, just like they did Agres and her sister. "I don't know. Do you remember when old Pontoc lost his soul? Mother told me that his afterlife soul walked out into the forest and left his body like a moth flying away from a cocoon."

"But Pontoc couldn't talk after his soul left, and Hehaka is still talking."

We both turn to study Hehaka where he lies on the ground, shivering.

I say, "And Pontoc went insane. He started sneaking up on people in the night and trying to strangle them."

We stare at each other. Wrass is probably remembering— as I am—the morning when Pontoc's own relatives dragged him screaming from the longhouse and clubbed him to death. They had to do it to protect their clan. The Standing

Stone People followed the Law of Retribution. Murder placed an absolute obligation upon the kinsmen of the dead man to seek revenge by claiming the life of either the murderer or someone closely related to him. Since they traced descent through the female, the obligation fell particularly upon the murdered person's sisters, mother's brothers, and sisters' sons. If Pontoc had actually managed to kill someone, the victim's family would have had the right to claim the life of anyone else in Pontoc's clan that it wished to be rid of, including the chief or clan matron. No clan could risk that.

"We should keep watch on Hehaka," Wrass said. "If she really does have his soul captured in that pot he'll go insane, and we'll need to protect ourselves."

"Yes, I think—"

My gaze lands on Chipmunk as she moves to kneel beside Hehaka. She speaks softly to him: Hehaka nods, as though whatever she said soothed him. As Chipmunk rises, she takes a deep breath, fixes her gaze on me, and walks forward. Her mourning hair clings to her round face in irregular locks.

Wrass sees her and frowns. "What's she doing?"

"Coming over here."

When she gets close, she bows her head so it's impossible to see her lips move, and whispers, "I can h-help. I know Healing plants."

"What do you mean you can help?" Wrass asks. "You mean you can help heal Hehaka and Baji?"

The girl nervously licks her lips. She's so scared she looks like she might faint. "No, I—I mean if you can get me close, I c-can . . ." She swallows hard, waiting for us to fill in the rest of the sentence.

In a stunning moment of understanding, I say, "Blessed gods, yes."

"What?" Wrass sounds annoyed.

I grab his arm and pull him very close to hiss, "We can fight them. With her help, we can escape!"

He glares at me like I've lost my senses and opens his mouth to say something unpleasant, but before he does, understanding widens his eyes. He stands perfectly still for a moment, staring at me. Then he glances between us, and in a dire voice says, "If we do this, we'll only have one chance. We have to do it right."

I turn to the girl. "What's your name?"

She swallows hard before she stutters, "Z-Zateri."

Twenty-five

"Find anything?" Towa called from the edge of the meadow to Sindak's left.

Tree-covered mountains rolled like storm-heaved waves across the land, rising and falling in breathtaking swaths of autumn color. High above, unmoving Cloud People seemed to be planted in the blue sky.

Sindak lifted his head from where he'd been concentrating on patterns in the frozen leaves. Towa had plaited his long black hair and tucked the braid into the back of his cape. Standing in the snow-frosted grass with two gigantic pines behind him made him seem taller and thinner. As Elder Brother Sun continued his journey to the west, afternoon light streamed between the pine boughs and landed across the meadow like dropped scarves of pure gold.

"No. You?"

Towa shook his head.

Sindak propped his war club on his shoulder and squinted at Koracoo. She was far ahead, walking through a grove of beech trees. He turned around and glimpsed Gonda bent over, searching what appeared to be a rivulet of snow melt.

Sindak called, "I don't understand it. The morning went so well. What happened? Where did we lose it?"

"In that elderberry thicket."

Sindak sighed and propped his hands on his hips. They'd found the trail at dawn, and been able to follow it for a full three hands of time; then it had vanished in the middle of an elderberry thicket. It was as though the children had been lifted straight up off the earth and flown away to the Spirits only knew where. Since the thicket, they'd been floundering, going in circles, finding nothing.

Sindak went back to searching. He carefully stepped through the snow-crusted leaves that lined the shadowed west side of the meadow. There was something here, but he wasn't sure what yet. The afternoon warmth had melted out patches of leaves and grass, but he felt certain he was seeing more than that. Here and there, leaves appeared to have been turned over, as though they'd stuck to the bottom of a moccasin and been flipped as the man passed. Unfortunately, the pattern wasn't regular—as a man's steps would be. He stretched his taut back muscles and stared upward. The shadows cast by the branches kept changing as Elder Brother Sun descended toward the western horizon. Each moment, the meadow looked different.

Towa let out a frustrated breath and walked over to Sindak. "I'm starting to feel like we're chasing our tails. As I suggested at noon, we should return to the thicket and start over."

Sindak's bushy eyebrows drew together. "Koracoo is sure we're on the right trail."

"Yes, but why? We haven't found any sign in over four hands of time."

As they walked, Sindak said, "It's that club of hers."

Suspiciously, Towa said, "CorpseEye?"

"Yes. It's alive."

Towa laughed disdainfully.

Frozen leaves crackled beneath their moccasins as they walked around a boulder and onto a trail that fringed the trees. Deer tracks cut perfect hearts in the mud. Ahead of them, a rocky granite slope two hundred hands across covered the hillside.

Sindak continued, "Laugh all you want, but you know that trail we were on at dawn? CorpseEye found it."

Towa gave him a skeptical look. "Found it?"

"I know you don't believe it, but I swear upon my Ancestors' graves, it's true. Around midnight we were talking when suddenly Koracoo got a worried expression on her face. When I asked her what was wrong, she said that CorpseEye was old and sometimes he saw or heard things that she did not. When he did, he tried to tell her."

"Her club talks?"

"No . . . at least I don't think so." Sindak made an uncertain gesture with his hand. "She says the club grows hot, sometimes painfully hot—and that's what happened to her last night. That's why we started searching in the darkness."

Towa stepped over a pile of deer droppings and followed the path as it curved back out into the frosty meadow. Deer trails twined through the fallen leaves, creating a braided weave of shadows, but there was no sign that humans had passed this way. Especially not a war party with an exhausted group of children. Men might carefully follow in each other's tracks to hide their numbers, but children generally failed. They didn't seem to have the ability to concentrate on the task.

"All right. Let's discuss this," Towa said, sounding very logical. "Did CorpseEye actually lead you to the trail?"

"Well, no, not exactly. I found the trail, but—"

"That's what I thought. You're an excellent tracker."

Sindak scratched the back of his neck with his war club. "Maybe, but that pale blue line of stones that we found at the base of the toppled tree? I think Corpse-Eye led Koracoo to it, and it connected with the trail."

"But the line of stones was natural. It hadn't been placed there by someone. And you told me that you thought the line of stones was in a different place than the blue glimmer you'd seen in the night."

"True, but—"

"Nonsense. It was an accident."

Sindak shrugged. It was generally useless to talk to Towa about supernatural events since he thought they were all wild flights of imagination. "Think what you want, my friend. You didn't touch CorpseEye and feel his Power run up your arm like icy ants."

"Sindak, it's just a very old piece of wood with a red quartzite cobble tied to the top."

"And two black spots for eyes. It watches me, Towa. Really." Sindak stabbed a weed with his war club. No matter what Towa said, he'd *felt* something when he'd touched that club, and he didn't believe in tempting Spirits. "I'm going to do everything I can to make that club like me."

Towa laughed. "You remind me of my cousin."

"Which cousin?"

"The one I despise. Neyot."

"Oh, thanks."

"Neyot once spent three moons trying to make a dog like him, in the hopes that the 'woman of his dreams' would come to agree with her pet."

"Did it work?"

"No. He was always grabbing the animal by the ruff and talking right in its face. The poor frustrated dog had no choice but to chew off his nose. The incident did not impress the woman of his dreams."

Sindak dredged up memories of Neyot's mangled face. The dog had eaten off the flesh and half the bones. "Your cousin is a dull-wit."

"True. But your wits over the past few days haven't been any too sharp, either. Do you really believe you can seduce Koracoo?"

Sindak tipped his head. "I'm not trying to seduce her. It's just very pleasurable to look at her and dream about her. What's the harm in that?"

"What's the harm? I can't believe you said that. You're going to wake up some night with Gonda's war club embedded in your skull. He still loves her."

"Really? He has a curious way of showing it. All he does is whine and shout at her."

The deer trail wound through the meadow and

headed toward the broad granite slope covered with stubby trees. Boulders and broken spalls the size of a longhouse littered the base of the slope. The chances of finding anything up there would be slim. On the other hand, that's exactly where Sindak would have gone if he'd been trying to hide his trail.

Towa massaged his left shoulder. While he'd been sleeping with his sling on, he took it off during the day. Walking with his arm hanging straight down obviously caused him pain.

"I don't know why you don't wear your sling during the day, too. It would be easy to throw it aside if we get into a fight."

"If the pain gets too bad, I will." He gave Sindak an askance look. "And you can't change the subject that easily. Every time you talk to Koracoo I want you to keep the image of a war club embedded in your skull right behind your eyes."

Sindak paused. Finally, he softly said, "I can't help being attracted to her, Towa. What man wouldn't be?"

"Me. But I'm smarter than you."

They walked out of the meadow and into the cold shadows of the boulders beneath the slope. Lichen-covered and streaked with black minerals, many stood four or five times Sindak's height. Every place that a tree could take root, it had; stunted saplings grew in the crevices and curled around the bases of the rocks. In places the saplings grew so thickly, they formed a dark impenetrable wall.

As Sindak began climbing through the detritus, still following the deer trail, the earthy fragrance of soaked granite and moss encircled him. In many places, the deer had leaped over the rocks that cluttered the slope. Sindak had to work his way around them while keeping his gaze on the ground, searching for evidence that humans had passed this way.

From behind him, Towa called, "This is going to take time. We have to move slowly through this kind of jumble. I wish—"

"Towa?" Sindak's breath caught. Something sparkled amid the saplings.

"What?" His moccasins grated on stone as he hurried up the slope. "Did you find something?"

Sindak knelt and pushed aside a clump of saplings to reveal the tiny circlet of copper that had lodged in the grass at the base. It was no bigger than a fingernail.

Towa's eyes narrowed. "Don't move. I'll go fetch Koracoo and Gonda."

While Towa trotted away, calling, "Koracoo? Gonda? Come look at this!" Sindak stared at the copper. It was a small ornament with a hole punched in the top. Among the People of the Hills, children's capes or moccasins were often sewn with such decorations. But who knew when it had been lost here?

While he waited, Sindak searched the surrounding area. The outcrop was wide enough that ten men could have walked abreast up the rocky slope, but if they had, their feet would have disturbed the sand and gravel, shoving it into distinctive man-made lines. He didn't see anything out of the ordinary. But who knew what the rain and melting snow had washed away?

"What is it? What did you find?" Gonda called as he

scrambled up the slope, breathing hard. He looked like a man awaiting a sentence of death. His dark eyes had a wild look, and his round face ran with sweat.

Koracoo and Towa were close behind him but taking their time, trying not to disturb anything.

"A copper ornament," Sindak explained, and shoved aside the saplings again.

Gonda dropped to his knees to study it, then, in a trembling voice, whispered, "Oh," and grabbed the ornament. He squeezed it tightly in his palm, as though he feared it might vanish at any moment.

Koracoo walked up behind him and saw his shaking fist. "What is it?"

Gonda handed it to her.

As she tipped the ornament to get a better look, the copper flashed in the sunlight. Recognition seemed to dawn slowly. "Gonda," she whispered. "The night of the attack, was Tutelo wearing—"

"Her tan doehide dress." Gonda's eyes sparkled with tears. "Yes."

Koracoo's gaze moved from his agonized face to the granite outcrop and the forest of saplings that covered it. Puddles of melted snow filled every hollow. On this windless afternoon, they appeared to be a field of calm, glistening eyes.

"May I have it back?" Gonda extended his hand.

Koracoo seemed confused at first; then she gave him the ornament. He clutched it to his chest.

Koracoo turned to Sindak and Towa. "Spread out. Keep searching. There must be more than this."

Sindak headed up the slope, picking the path through

the saplings that looked the easiest for children to travel. Towa went left, cutting across the outcrop, clearly searching for parallel trails.

When Sindak looked back, he found Gonda still sitting with the copper ornament against his chest, rocking back and forth.

Koracoo was kneeling beside him with a hand on his shoulder, speaking quietly.

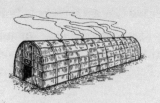

Twenty-six

Sonon crouched on the riverbank, surveying the willows where a collection of bones clung in a tangled embrace, still held together by fragments of cloth and sinew.

The river was not quite dark. As the dove-colored veils of evening settled over the land, the water took on a pewter sheen. If he kept his eyes half-closed, the current seemed to move like a phantom serpent, twisting out of its banks and writhing in the air above, keeping the skeletons suspended between Great Grandmother Earth and the Land of the Dead in the Sky World.

The men had been laughing when they'd killed the girls. He'd arrived too late, at the very end, and had watched from the shadows, unable to understand it.

Like them, he had been a warrior. He had suffered wounds, buried loved ones, and been as brave as his own weaknesses had allowed him to be. He knew only too well the hardships of war and the things men did when they thought no one was looking.

But this . . . this had been monstrous. He suspected the men would have preferred an audience.

As though to remind him of the horror, the bones

rustled. Spots of leaden brilliance ruptured the water's surface, and rings bobbed away. Occasionally he saw a tail flip. Fish. Feeding on the rotting flesh, cleaning the bones.

He rose in silence and walked forward.

Perhaps more clearly than anything else, he knew the meaning of duty.

Duty was all any man really had. After all, life was warfare, a journey across an alien land filled with pain and devastating loneliness. Humans never really understood it until too late; then the clarity of the realization was like a spear thrust to the soul's heart. You woke up. Truly. For the first time.

He waded out into the willows and began collecting the bones. Most he could simply rake ashore, but he had to reach deep to pull out a shoulder blade that had become mired in the mud. When he dragged it up, he found that it was attached to a collarbone. He collected every bone he could, then sank down on the shore beside them. Long black hair clung to the skulls. He smoothed it away from their gnawed faces to stare into their empty eye sockets. He didn't see them in there, but he hoped the girls' souls were still hovering close by. Soon, he would go searching for them and bring them back to their bodies. Then he would take them to a hilltop and leave their bones facing east, looking in the direction of their Flint families. Perhaps they would recognize the way home, and be able to get there.

He exhaled hard.

Out in the trees, shadows wavered.

A symphony of whimpers, creaks, and birdcalls rode the wind, the music of the forest; it serenaded him as he got to his feet and headed out on his nightly hunt.

Twenty-seven

Odion

Tutelo snuggles against me and whispers, "Brother? Do you see him?"

My eyelids flutter, but I do not open them. We marched hard all day. At dark, Gannajero gave us each a single corn-meal biscuit filled with walnuts, the first freshly cooked food we've had, and I was so grateful I gobbled mine down. Right after I brushed the crumbs from my hands and left them in a pile for the birds and mice, I fell asleep. "See what, Tutelo?"

She is being very still, as though trying not to attract the attention of a predator that stands nearby. Her innocent young face with its large eyes and small nose are framed by straight black hair. "Out there, by the fire cherries."

I turn my head to look. There is a big grove of fire cherries twenty paces away. The branches have lost all of their leaves, and in the starlight they look like nothing more than spiky undergrowth. Fog moves along the ground and twines in the canopies of the trees. I don't see anything unusual. Our guards stand ten paces away. The man I call Ugly because of the enormous scar that slashes his face leans against a tree and yawns. His real name is Hanu. He is very tall, maybe eleven hands, and has shoulders like a bear's, broad and meaty. The other guard, Galan, is new. Wrass named him Worm because he is so skinny. Worm has his feet spread and is watching the camp. Gannajero and the rest of her warriors sleep soundly around the fire. While the flames have burned down, the coals blush red when the wind breathes over them. The scent of smoke hangs heavy on the frosty air.

"I don't see anything, Tutelo," I whisper. "Go back to sleep." I roll over.

"No, look, Brother!" she insists, and tugs on my shoulder. "He's right there."

Grudgingly, I roll back over and stare out at the fog. The streamers move like snakes, twining around trunks and slithering over the ground. Beyond the fog, I can make out the dark looming shapes of sycamores. Their spreading branches reach so high they disappear into the mist. My gaze traces down one massive trunk that is wider across than Ugly is tall. Against the black bark, the elusive wink of starlight flashes on metal.

My breathing dies. I do not blink. Just stare.

It moves, a kind of weightless, leisurely drifting that is as noiseless as the passing of a cloud shadow. For a long while, the only sounds in the night are the soft hissing of the breeze in the trees and the wild hammering of my heart.

Starlight catches in the metal, and there is a prolonged glimmer, as though it has stopped and is watching us.

The hair at the nape of my neck prickles.

Suddenly, a flurry of wings batters the fire cherries, and birds shoot away through the fog. Our guards spin around with their war clubs up, ready to strike down whatever they find. They hiss to each other, study the fog, and Ugly stalks toward the cherries.

Gannajero sits up by the fire and stares out at the fire cherries.

Ugly circles the trees, uses his club to poke between branches. When he is satisfied, he walks back over to Worm and shoves him hard enough to make Worm stagger, then says, "You idiot." They both chuckle, and continue talking softly.

My gaze returns to the fire cherries.

There is something almost hypnotic about the stillness. The wind has stopped. The fog seems to have frozen in place. The dark branches resemble hundreds of fingers reaching toward the Sky World.

A brief blue flicker shines near the big sycamore.

I prop myself up on one elbow. Is it a Forest Spirit?

Odion.

I feel the whisper along my bones, a faint creeping sensation like spiderwebs trailed over the skin.

Terrified, I drag Tutelo against me, shielding her from the unknown. In her ear, I hiss, "Don't move."

She obeys.

Very faintly, I hear it again—the unmistakable sound of my name whispered by a man, and the soft scrape of leather against wood.

Then the trees rustle, and I think I see a dark cape billow as a man walks away through the glistening fog.

Tutelo whispers, "It's Shago-niyoh."

The milky stillness of her calm is unnerving.

"D-did he talk to you?" I stammer.

Tutelo tilts her pretty face and stares at me owlishly. "Did you see him?"

I feel like my lungs are starving. I gasp in cold air before I exhale the words, "I'm not sure. Maybe."

Ugly turns our direction and scowls. "Stop talking. Go to sleep. We have to carry you tomorrow, and it's a lot harder to carry someone who's asleep." He aims his war club at us.

We both stretch out on our sides, and I curl my body around Tutelo to keep her warm. She heaves a weary sigh and closes her eyes.

Blood pulses so powerfully in my veins that I feel slightly ill.

Gannajero rises and silently bird-walks across the ground. Her black eyes are huge and, if I didn't know better, I'd say scared. She stops by her warriors and hisses, "What did you see?"

"Nothing."

"What frightened the birds?"

Ugly shrugs. "I don't know. We didn't find anything."

Gannajero's gaze slowly moves over the fire cherries, as though expecting to see something or someone. No one makes a sound. In the darkness, her greasy twists of graying black hair hang about her wrinkled face like black fringes.

Gannajero takes ten silent, measured steps toward the cherries. She's breathing hard. In a hideous gasp, she says, "It's the *Child*."

Ugly frowns. "The children are all accounted for. It can't be—"

"*He's found us.*" Gannajero quickly retreats to stand

between her warriors. Her gaze darts over the forest, as though an ancient evil has risen and is about to swallow them all.

I twist my head to stare back out at the fire cherries. Waiting.

But now there is only fog and forest.

Gannajero wildly glares down at me. "Did you call it?"

"Wh-what? I don't under—"

I sit up and her fist is like a meteor plummeting out of the night. It strikes me squarely in the jaw and knocks me hard to the ground. Tutelo screams. I feel dazed. My head is spinning. I can't seem to sit up. All the other children wake and start talking at once, asking each other questions.

"*Never* call to it!" Gannajero hisses. "Never *speak* to it! Not even if it speaks to you first. Do you understand me?"

I manage to jerk a nod before I roll to my side to spit mouthfuls of blood on the ground. Two teeth roll out. I can feel the gaps in my lower jaw, on the right side.

Gannajero bends over me with blazing eyes. "Tell me you heard me. Don't just nod!"

Before I can speak, she draws back her hand again, and I cover my head, preparing for another blow. But from the corner of my eye, I see Wrass leap up and grab Gannajero's fist as it plunges toward me.

I scream, "No, Wrass, don't!"

Gannajero cries out hoarsely and tries to twist free of his grip. Wrass is hanging on, trying to wrench her arm out of its socket. Her men instantly leap into action. They beat Wrass off Gannajero with their war clubs.

He curls into a ball on the ground, huddling against

the beating. The sound of his grunts and cries wither my soul.

None of us dares to go to his aid. We are all too afraid of getting beaten to death ourselves.

"Enough," Gannajero finally orders, and her guards back away.

Wrass is lying with his arms over his head, whimpering, and rolling as though in great pain.

Gannajero meets each of our gazes, and her wrinkled lips pucker as if she wants to spit upon us. "If any of you dares to touch me ever again, you will all be beaten bloody. Do you understand?"

We nod.

Tutelo crawls over to me and puts a cool hand on my back. "Odion? Odion, are you all right?"

"I . . . I think so."

Gannajero turns to her warriors. "This means we're being followed. He's leading them right to us. Tomorrow, at first light, I want both of you to scout our back trail. And if you see anything, *anything*, return and tell me immediately."

"Yes, Gannajero."

The old woman marches back to the fire and drags Spirit charms from her pack—painted weasel skins, carved buffalo horn sheaths, and what appear to be wolf fangs. She places them in a circle around her and begins singing a song that sounds like a series of growls and yips.

Ugly whispers, "What's she doing?"

Worm shakes his head. "I swear she's madder than a foaming-mouth dog."

I crawl over to Wrass. "Wrass? Wrass! Why did you do that? You should have just let her hit me!"

Wrass is panting, groaning, but he manages to look up at me. Blood coats his entire face like a wash of paint. "We have to protect each other, Odion. No one else is going to protect us."

"But they almost killed you!"

Father was right. Wrass is the warrior. He cannot stand by and watch any of his People hurt.

All of the other children gather around Wrass. Baji is weeping silently, and Hehaka looks like he longs to run away and hide, probably because he knows exactly how Wrass feels. Tutelo has both hands over her mouth, smothering her cries. Only Zateri has the courage to do what's necessary to help Wrass.

"Wrass," Zateri says. "I n-need to touch your head. Is that all right?"

He nods and lowers his hands. The sight almost makes me wretch again. Large patches of Wrass' scalp have been torn loose, revealing the bloody skull beneath. Zateri pulls the scalp back into place and carefully uses her fingers to explore his head, stopping here and there to probe more thoroughly.

"Don't worry," she says to Wrass. "You're going to be all right. They didn't crack your skull, at least not that I can see or feel. But you'll have a bad headache for days." She reaches into her leggings and pulls out a small hide bag. As she loosens the ties, she glances up at the guards. They've returned to talking softly among themselves, smiling. "I gathered these strips of birch bark this morning. Chew on them, Wrass. They will help with the pain." She tucks them in Wrass' hand, but he barely seems to notice.

He just shivers and seems to sink into the grass as though he's melting away.

Then Zateri moves closer to me. Her brown eyes are ablaze as she whispers, "I gathered other things today. Special things. Skunk cabbage root, spoonwood leaves, thorn apple seeds, musquash roots."

My heart pounds. "Keep them hidden. Tomorrow, we'll figure out what to do with them."

She nods and tucks the small bag back into her legging. "Odion?" she says, "Wrass needs to be warm. Let's all sleep curled around him tonight."

"Do as she says," I order, as though I am now in charge. Me. The boy who is always afraid.

Zateri is the first to lie down and press her body against Wrass' back. I lie down behind her and reach my arm over Wrass and Zateri, pulling them both close. One by one, the other children join in, pressing tightly together around Wrass, becoming one big warm animal with many legs and arms.

"Tutelo?" I call.

She is sitting a short distance away, staring out at the fire cherries. Her pretty face is taut with concentration. She must be looking for the Child.

"Tutelo? Are you coming?"

She turns and looks at me. She's sucking on her lower lip, and it makes her face appear misshapen. "He's coming back," she whispers. "I know he is."

I lower my head and rest it on my arm.

I don't know who starts it, but a strange thrum begins. It's like distant thunder, barely heard; then the whispers blend into one low growl as they flash through our group: "*Gannajero says someone is following us. Someone's coming for us. It's my parents! They wouldn't just abandon me! No, our war chief must be searching for us. It's an entire war party. A thousand men!*

Our guards chuckle. They are amused by hope. Perhaps because they've seen it die in the eyes of so many children.

I close my eyes and concentrate.

Beneath all the noise, I can hear Father's voice as he jerks me from my bed: "Odion, take Tutelo. Run as far away as you can and hide. I'll find you, no matter where you are. *I'll find you.*"

Peace fills me. He's coming.

Mother's with him. They'll be here before I wake in the morning. We'll all go home together. We'll help our clan build a new longhouse. We'll be happy. . . .

Twenty-eight

As Gonda slogged through a swampy area on the east side of the pond, hopelessness taunted him. Every time they thought they were on the right path, it vanished. He felt weak and desperate. He didn't know exactly when it had happened, but somewhere in the past few days, he'd lost himself. What remained sickened him— the husk of the man he'd once been. And he was weary enough, disheartened enough, that all he wanted to do was to crawl inside that husk and hide forever.

Koracoo met him as he slogged out of the water and stepped onto dry land. She was less than six hands away, and he felt her nearness like a physical blow.

"Did you find any evidence that they marched through the pond?"

He shook his head. His drenched moccasins squished with his movements. "At first, I thought . . ." He turned to look back across the small pond to the place where he'd thought he'd seen a track. Steep rocky mountains rose on either side of the narrow valley. Towa and Sindak were still searching the trails that led to the pond. "I didn't even find a bent reed. Did you find anything around the edges?"

Her face was drawn and pale, and the bones beneath her tanned skin were too sharp. Her unevenly chopped hair stuck out oddly from too much time in the wind. "No."

He waited for instructions, but Koracoo just hung her head and closed her eyes, as though too tired to think straight.

"Are you all right?"

"Tired. That's all."

Gonda turned away and looked northward to where a wall of bruised clouds massed.

She had never asked him what had happened the night of the attack. She was a pragmatist. She'd found him, made sure he was all right, and led him back to the burning village to attend the emergency council meeting. The few surviving elders had all blamed Gonda for the debacle. Koracoo had carefully questioned them, heard their stories, and helped them plan what to do next. Immediately thereafter, she'd walked to the Bear Clan longhouse, pulled out what few belongings she could find that had belonged to him, and set them outside the door—divorcing him.

Less than one hand of time later, they were on the trail, searching for their children. The shame and grief were still unbearable.

"Gonda, I need your advice. What do you think we should do? I'm out of ideas."

He felt a sudden lightness, as though all the horrors that lived inside him had suddenly dropped away. She needed him. He straightened to his full height. "What's CorpseEye telling you?"

She pulled the club off her shoulder and held it in both hands. "He's gone stone-cold."

The two black spots that dotted the red cobble head of the war club seemed to be looking straight at him, as though to say, *Stop being foolish. You know the way.*

"Perhaps because we're on the right trail," Gonda said.

Koracoo cocked her head doubtfully. "Maybe, but there's so much I don't understand."

"Like what?"

"Why is it that we can track them across bare stone, but not across the ground?"

Softly, Gonda said, "We both know now, don't we? We're not tracking warriors with slaves. Warriors heading home wouldn't take the time to hide their trail this way."

She jerked a nod. "We both know."

Hesitantly, he continued, "There's something I've been thinking about."

"What?"

The sudden arrival of a flock of crows made her look up. The black birds cawed as they playfully dove and soared, their ebony wings flashing in the sunlight.

"I have the feeling we're tracking an orb weaver, Koracoo."

"An orb weaver?" They were spiders that spun spiraling webs.

"Yes. Each night the spider's old web is replaced by a new one, spun in complete darkness by touch alone."

"You mean she travels at night?"

"I mean she's a creature of darkness. She stands in her web at night, but retreats from it during the day. I suspect that all of her spiderlings do the same. She orders her warriors to meet in a certain place at nightfall, but at dawn—"

"They scatter."

Tingling heat flushed his body at the look on her face. She stepped closer to stare him in the eyes. "During the day, they all take different paths to hide their numbers? That would explain some things. It is much easier to track a war party than a single man, especially a skilled warrior taking pains to hide his trail."

"If that's what they're doing, we need a new strategy."

The longer they stood staring at each other, the more powerfully he longed to touch her. Strands of black hair curled over her tanned cheeks, and there was something about the sternness of her expression—as though she were holding herself together by sheer willpower— that built a desperate need in his heart.

"What are you thinking?" Gonda asked.

"I'm wondering if Towa wasn't right to begin with. We should spread out more. Work exactly the opposite of how we've been working. Instead of walking eastward, paralleling what we think is the trail, perhaps we should work perpendicular, cut across the forest from north to south looking for sign."

Emotion rose up to choke him. She was right. Why hadn't he thought of it himself? Gonda lifted a hand to touch her face, but halted, and let it hover awkwardly. If she would only take a step toward him. But she did not, and he clenched his hand into a fist and lowered it to his side.

"Let's try it," he said simply. "It's a good idea."

She held his gaze for far longer than she had since the attack. It was an instant of shared hope and pain, and he cherished it. He engraved her expression on his soul, so that he could pull it up again and again when he thought he could bear no more of the futility of the search.

"Koracoo, I wish that you and I . . ." Tears burned his eyes.

He clenched his jaw and looked away. She hated excessive emotion. She said it weakened everyone who witnessed it. He recalled once on a raid when a man had thrown himself over the body of his dead friend and begun wailing. The grief had spread like a contagion. Within ten heartbeats, every warrior was sobbing or sniffling. Koracoo's response had been to walk straight to the man who'd started it and slap him senseless. Shocked, he'd looked up at her. She'd ordered, "Get up now or you'll be joining your friend in the afterlife."

Gonda blinked away his tears and shot a look at Towa and Sindak. They were carefully examining the bark on an oak tree, as though they'd found something. For the past hand of time, they'd been walking through gigantic oaks. A canopy of laced branches roofed the trails and cast brilliant geometric patterns across the acorn-covered ground.

"All right," he said. "Here's my advice: If we don't find anything here, I think we should split up, send Towa and Sindak back to the place where we lost the trail, and let them cut for sign while you and I continue north and do the same thing."

"When and where will we meet?"

"What about dusk south of Hawk Moth Village? You know the place where the main trail forks?"

They both watched Sindak. He'd climbed up into the oak and seemed to be examining the limbs. Below him, Towa was apparently asking questions—his mouth was moving.

"It's risky. We'll be on the border of Flint People lands. They might kill us just for daring to step into their country."

"We were worried about the same thing with Atotarho. We survived."

Wind blew her short hair around her face, spiking it up more than before. She faintly resembled a startled porcupine. In the old days, he would have told her that, and she'd have laughed. But there was no laughter between them now.

"All right. Let's tell our allies the new plan." Koracoo started back for Towa and Sindak.

Gonda followed her around the edge of the pond and back into the laced shadows cast by the heavy oak boughs. Even the small limbs were as wide across as his shoulders. These ancient giants must have seen hundreds of summers pass.

Sindak jumped down from the tree, and he and Towa watched their approach with narrowed eyes. Towa stood a head taller than Sindak. He'd braided and coiled his long hair into a bun, then pinned it at the back of his head with a rabbit-bone skewer. The style made his handsome oval face appear regal. Sindak, on the other hand, looked shaggy. His shoulder-length hair was disheveled and matted to his forehead by sweat. In the mottled light, his deeply sunken brown eyes resembled dark pits and his hooked nose cast a shadow.

"War Chief," Sindak said. "We found something."

Koracoo picked up her pace. "Show me."

All four of them gathered around the base of the oak, and Sindak put his finger below a fresh scar on the bark. It was a lighter-colored patch, no bigger than a thumb.

Gonda examined it and said, "It might be a scar left by a buck. They sharpen and clean their antlers on the trees—but it's small for an antler rub."

"Or it could have been made by a flicker. They love to bury insects in cracks in the bark," Koracoo added.

"That's what we thought at first," Sindak said. He shoved damp hair away from his homely face and continued, "But if you look at the rest of the tree, you'll see more of them."

Sindak climbed back up into the tree, and Gonda followed him. As they climbed higher, the rich fragrance of wet wood encircled them. Gonda breathed it in—a soothing scent that reminded him of his childhood, when he'd done a great deal of tree climbing.

Sindak stepped out onto the first major branch and bent down to show Gonda another bark scar. This one was even smaller than the first, but clearer. "If you climb higher, you'll find these small scars on almost every branch."

Gonda stared upward into the crooked sunlit limbs. A few old leaves and acorns clung to the highest branches. They swayed in the breeze. "Are the scars always right next to the trunk?"

"Yes."

Sindak was looking at him expectantly, as though the truth should be obvious.

"So," Gonda said, "you think someone climbed up here using the limbs as a ladder?"

Sindak pointed to the place twenty hands above them where the massive limbs of two trees met. "Right there, where the limbs overlap, it looks like the climber stepped from this tree to the next one. And if you'll look over there"—he pointed to a place where the limbs of the next tree overlapped with a tree farther north—"you'll see that he could have moved to yet another tree."

Gonda let his gaze scan the oaks. With careful planning, a man could go a long way climbing from one tree to the next. And if he did it often, he could do it relatively quickly.

"They . . . they're climbing through the trees? Is that why we keep losing the trail?"

Sindak nodded. "It might be. I have noticed that every time we lose it we are surrounded by giant hickories, or oaks, or other big trees with spreading limbs. That's what made me start looking closely at the trunks. I wanted to see if I could spot scars left by feet."

Hope flooded Gonda's veins, and without thinking, he slapped Sindak on the shoulder approvingly. "You are a good tracker, Sindak. Just the way Towa said. Let's tell the others."

They climbed down.

Before they'd even jumped to the ground, Koracoo called, "Well? What did you find?"

Gonda said, "Sindak is right. There are scars all the way up the trunk. Someone has been using the trees, climbing through the branches, moving from tree to tree."

"We can't be certain, of course," Sindak said, "that this is the trail we seek, but it's a trail."

Koracoo's gaze shot upward and darted over the limbs, moving, as the climbers must have, from one heavy limb to another to another. It would have been even easier for children. They were lighter and could have used more of the forest canopy to travel. "This changes everything."

"What do you mean?"

Gonda nodded at her, then said to Towa, "Earlier, Koracoo and I were talking. Koracoo said that instead of paralleling the trails, we should cut across them, moving from north to south, searching for sign. But now that we know they are using the trees—"

Towa interrupted. "Wait. Are you suggesting that the warriors are . . . are each walking different trails? That's why you want to cut for sign from north to south?"

"We think it's possible."

Sindak rubbed a hand over his face as though stunned by the realization. "Of course they are. That's how they do it. If each warrior takes one or two children and picks his own route, he can climb over rocks, wade rivers or ponds, climb through the trees. That's why the sign is so confusing."

Towa seemed to be putting all the pieces together, and not liking what he saw. His expression became a grimace. "If this is true, their trails may be spread out over a vast area of forest. It's going to take forever—"

"That's why no one has ever been able to track

Gannajero." Koracoo was gazing out into the depths of the forest, but thoughts moved behind her dark eyes. "Time. The trails seem to go in different directions. They start and stop, or vanish altogether. It takes so much time to unravel them that people give up."

"If only we had another fifty warriors," Towa said, "we might be able to do it. But without them? I don't know."

Frustration was building. Gonda could feel it in the air. The task suddenly seemed overwhelming. Despair lined Towa's young face, and Sindak looked angry.

Gonda said, "We don't need fifty warriors."

"Why not?" Towa raised his voice. "How can four people accomplish anything? I—"

"Listen to Gonda," Koracoo said. She was watching Gonda, waiting to see what he was doing before she interfered. It was the way they'd always operated. They worked as a team to get their warriors to figure out the problem.

Gonda continued, "You were right in the beginning, Towa. We need to spread out so that we can cover more territory. We'll arrange a place to meet at night; then over supper we'll discuss what each of us has found, and pick which trail to pursue the next morning. We'll follow it until it disappears. When it does, we'll return to cutting north-south again."

"It seems like we're grasping for—"

"Towa." Koracoo put a hand on his shoulder, and he turned to peer into the dark depths of her eyes. He looked faintly mesmerized. "Think this through. If you were arranging such a ruse, how would you do it?"

Towa shook his head as though he had no idea, but after a few moments, he blinked, and said, "Well, I—I suppose I'd tell my warriors to fan out—to get as far from each other as they could—and to pick the most difficult paths through the forest. Both strategies would slow the pursuers down to a crawl and give me more time to get away."

"But . . ." A thoughtful expression lined Sindak's beaked face. "As the day wears on, as each person gets closer to the meeting place, the trails will start to converge."

"Yes." Gonda nodded. "And that's the first thing we should look for. Patterns like that. If we can figure out even the most basic pattern it will cut our search time in half."

Koracoo gazed up into the oak tree to study the interlacing branches again. Sunlight sheathed every twig. "If we assume that this is one of the trails, and they are headed east, there should be other trails to the north and south of this one. We just have to find them."

Cloud People drifted through the sky high above, and their shadows roamed the trees like silent Spirits, plunging them into a suddenly dimmer world. Wind murmured through the branches, rising and falling in an ominous cadence. Gonda waited until the shadows had passed and Elder Brother Sun's gleam again sparkled through the trees.

"All right," Gonda said. "Where are we going to meet?"

Koracoo answered, "The main trail forks just south of Hawk Moth Village. I say we meet there."

Gonda turned to Sindak and Towa. "Do you know where that is?"

"Yes," Sindak said. "We've been there several times, on raids. Frankly, I don't think the Flint People like us very much. If they catch us, they're liable to cut us into tiny pieces and feed us to their dogs."

"The same is true for us. That means we need to stay out of their way," Gonda said.

Koracoo gestured to the oak tree. "Sindak, you found the scars on the tree. Why don't you start with this trail?"

"Yes, War Chief." Sindak grabbed a branch and started climbing up into the oak.

While she watched him, Koracoo said, "The rest of us will spread out along an east-west line and start walking north, cutting for sign. I'll start from here—the base of this tree."

Gonda looked at Towa. The youth still had a skeptical disheartened expression. "Towa, I'm going to trot east for two hundred paces, then cut north. Why don't you trot west for two hundred paces, and cut north. If you find sign, follow it out. If not, don't worry about it—just meet us at dusk south of Hawk Moth Village."

Towa nodded. "I'll be there." He took off at a slow trot, heading west.

Gonda headed east. When he turned to look over his shoulder, he saw Koracoo walking due north into the jade-colored pines, and Sindak maneuvering through the bare oak branches, tracking his prey from tree to tree like an overgrown squirrel.

Twenty-nine

The pattering of acorns falling on the forest floor mixed with the pounding of Towa's heart. Somewhere close by he heard movement. It might be an animal, but he was fairly certain it was a man.

Gently, so he made no sound, he grasped the scrub oak branch blocking his path and eased forward. When he'd stepped by, he returned the branch to its former position and scanned the deep forest shadows. Slippery elms and yellow birches were in the process of crowding out the oaks. As he tiptoed by a birch, he silently broke off a twig and chewed it. The flavor of mint filled his mouth. Birds watched him, their feathers fluffed out for warmth, but few dared to chirp. He lifted his nose and sniffed the air. A curious odor rode the breeze, like days-old blood, and he thought . . .

"Sondakwa?" a man called in a strained voice. "S-Sondakwa! Where are you?" Brush crashed and twigs snapped, as though he'd stumbled.

Towa nocked an arrow in his bow and forced a swallow down his dry throat. The wind gusted, and a wealth of acorns let loose. When they struck the brown leaf mat they made a faint drumlike cadence.

More stumbling . . . then a voice: *"Sondakwa? Is that you?"*

Something swayed ahead. Towa stood perfectly still, watching. The man thrashed through the brush, panting and whimpering. He had a war club in his fist.

Towa drew back his bowstring, just in case, and his shoulder wound ached with fiery intensity.

"Sondakwa, where are you? Stop hiding from me!"

As he came closer, Towa could see the man better. He was big, stocky. Black geometric tattoos covered his face. To create the designs, warriors pricked their flesh with bone awls, then rubbed the tattoos with charcoal to darken them. The sides of his head had been shaved in the manner of the Flint People, leaving a central roach of hair on top. A few limp, soaked feathers decorated the style.

The man staggered and had to grab hold of a birch limb to keep standing. Then he lifted his head, saw Towa, and pinned him with wide, vacant eyes.

Towa blinked. The impact of that gaze struck him like a spectral fist in the dark. His scalp prickled. When his grandfather had been dying, there had been a moment at the very end when Grandfather's eyes had suddenly opened . . . but there was no soul there, no awareness, just a sort of surprised stare. That's what he saw now.

Softly, Towa called, "Who are you?"

The man didn't seem to hear him. He kept holding onto the branch for a few instants longer. Then he swayed on his feet, and slowly toppled facefirst to the ground.

Towa watched him for fifty heartbeats before he

released the tension on his bowstring and gazed out at the trees again. Only a few faint triangles of sunlight managed to pierce the canopy. The rest of the forest was cloaked in shadow. The man had been calling to a friend. Was there someone else out there Towa needed to worry about? He inhaled a breath and let the scent of wet wood fill him, then cautiously walked forward.

Towa stopped two paces away and studied the man's shaven head and the white feathers in his roach. The man didn't seem to be breathing. His war club had bounced from his hand, but it was within easy reach.

Towa slung his bow and tucked his arrow back into his quiver; then he pulled his war club from his belt.

Leaves crackled as he walked to stand over the man. He kicked him in the side. Nothing.

Towa knelt and scooped leaves away from the man's face. His brown eyes were open, and dead. But just to make sure, Towa touched the man's eyeball with his finger. Again . . . nothing. Towa flipped the man's cape up and tugged his pack from his shoulders, then rummaged through it.

Stunned, he pulled out a magnificently etched copper breastplate. Leather cords hung from the corners of the plate, clearly for tying it on. A master artisan had etched the copper with hundreds of miniature False Faces. Some had wide smiling mouths and long noses. Others had hideous, terrifying expressions with enormous eyes.

Towa rested it to the side and continued going through the pack. The breastplate seemed to be the only thing of real value the man owned—along with several bags of food.

"You won't need these anymore," he said softly as he drew open the laces of several small sacks that contained jerked duck, hard acorn meal biscuits, sunflower seeds, walnuts, and hulled beans. Even a bag of what looked like chunks of dried squash.

Towa stuffed all the food into his own pack, then rose to his feet. He didn't know what to do with the copper breastplate. It was too large to carry in his pack. But he certainly wasn't going to leave something so rare and beautiful here to corrode. It was awkward with his wounded shoulder, but he managed to flip up his cape and tie the breastplate on over his chest.

Towa squinted at the man's trail. He could see it clearly in the leaves. It was serpentine, weaving all over the place. He followed it eastward.

Late in the afternoon, Towa reached up, taking sight on the sun and moving his hand, palm width by palm width, to the western horizon. He had less than one hand of time left before he'd have to head straight for the fork in the trail to meet Sindak, Gonda, and Koracoo. He continued following the dead man's trail.

When he entered a thicket of shining willow, he saw two deep knee prints, then another set, and nearby he found grooves in the mud left by frantic fingers. The man had fallen down several times in the thicket, clawed his way back up, and staggered on. Towa kept walking. On the other side, he saw a narrow deer trail lined by holly and headed for it, expecting to see more of the man's tracks there.

Instead, he found another set of tracks. The man's lost friend?

Towa knelt to examine them. The distinctive herringbone weave was made only among the Hills People. He whispered, "A Hills warrior? What are you doing out here, my friend?"

As he rose to his feet, he wondered if one of the other Hills villages had dispatched a war party into Flint lands. If so, this man had gotten separated from his party, because there was only one set of prints.

Or . . . perhaps Atotarho had decided he couldn't trust Koracoo and Gonda?

Towa's thoughts drifted back to his conversation with Koracoo the first night on the trail, when she'd suggested that Atotarho had not sent Towa and Sindak to help rescue the girl, because he'd wanted his daughter to be captured. That idea had been plaguing Towa for days. His hand rose to touch the sacred gorget where it rested beneath his cape. Atotarho had given Towa specific instructions to present the gorget to Gannajero within moments of laying eyes upon her.

But he did not know why. The gorget was valuable, yes, very valuable, but would it be enough to buy back Zateri and the other children?

Towa didn't know.

He backtracked the herringbone trail until it intersected with the dead man's tracks, and his eyes narrowed. Something strange had happened here. The dead man had started running, first one direction, then another, charging about as though being pursued. But the herringbone sandals hadn't moved. He'd been standing still.

A cold shiver climbed Towa's spine.

"Why did you start running? Did you see something that frightened you? Why didn't the man wearing the sandals run?"

Wind clattered in the branches—a thin rattling that reminded Towa of teeth chattering.

He ran his fingers over the copper breastplate beneath his cape and tried to fathom what had happened here. The dead man had been panicked, taking long strides; he'd clearly been running for his life.

Towa turned to stare at the herringbone sandal prints again . . . and decided to follow them.

Twenty paces later, he stumbled over a second dead man. Another Flint warrior, or at least he wore the same hairstyle. The first man's lost friend? Sondakwa? Towa walked closer. He saw no blood. The man hadn't been shot, or clubbed; he just lay sprawled on his back staring emptily up at the storm clouds that filled the afternoon sky. He looked like he'd just fallen down dead in the trail.

Towa glanced around. Birds and squirrels hopped through the trees, unconcerned, but a deep gnawing sense of dread filled him.

"I have the feeling," he whispered uneasily as he stared at the herringbone sandal prints, "that now I know what frightened the first man into running. I wish I had more time to track you, my friend."

But he didn't.

Towa checked the faint shadows, figured the direction, and broke into a trot, heading for the rendezvous place.

Thirty

Rain fell, misty and cold, from a charcoal-colored dusk sky. Sindak's cape and war shirt dripped onto his moccasins as he maneuvered around the hickory trunk, trying to remain hidden. He felt like a hunted animal, running for its life with no hope of escape.

Soft steps pattered the trail behind him. At first, he'd thought the sounds were nothing more than splashes of rain hitting the ground, until one of his pursuers stepped on a twig and snapped it. Now he knew better. The stealth with which they stalked him told him they were warriors.

How many?

Doesn't matter. Even if only one man is following me, he might be the advance scout for an entire war party.

Sindak looked northward. White pines covered the hilltop where he'd taken refuge, but in the distance he could see giant hickories and beech trees thrusting up through the ground mist. He was less than a half-hand of time from the fork in the trail where he was supposed to meet Towa, Koracoo, and Gonda. It was too late to make a mad dash for them, and he wouldn't even if he could. No matter what happened, he would not lead the enemy to his friends.

As the steps came closer, he heard murmuring. One voice? Two? He couldn't be sure. Sindak nervously licked his lips. There wasn't enough light left to effectively use his bow. If they came at him, he'd have no choice but to start swinging his club and pray.

More murmuring, the voice at once sad and reproving, as if the man were speaking to a wayward child.

Sindak closed his eyes to hear better, and it magnified the shishing of the rain and the faint tapping of the man's feet on the trail.

More than one man . . .

The steps of the other two people were almost inaudible. More like wings batting air than moccasins striking earth.

It was almost night. Surely these warriors would return home when they could no longer see.

Sindak didn't move a muscle, but his gaze drifted northward again.

Towa would just be starting to worry. He'd be staring out into the darkness with a frown on his face, probably cursing Sindak for being late. In another hand of time, Towa would stop cursing. No matter what War Chief Koracoo said, he would trot out into the forest to start looking for Sindak, and maybe run right into the arms of Sindak's pursuers. Sindak couldn't let that happen.

He sniffed the rain-scented breeze. It was pine-sharp and cold. Wherever men went, they carried with them the odors of their fires or their sweat, maybe the food they'd spilled on their capes. He didn't smell any of those things.

In the distance, silver light penetrated the storm clouds and shot leaden streaks across the pine-whiskered mountains. Here and there, orange halos of firelight painted the underbellies of the clouds, marking the locations of villages. The glow to the east was probably Hawk Moth Village, but it could be a large war camp. In all likelihood, the men who followed him were from there, warriors sent out to scout the Flint borders.

Very faintly, a voice called, *"Odion?"* Then, again, *"Odion?"*

Sindak's breathing went shallow.

The howls of hunting wolves echoed through the trees as the steps moved, almost silently, up the trail less than fifty paces away. Then he heard a strange rattle. Branches clattering together in the breeze? An odor he knew only too well wafted to him: the stink of rotting flesh.

A shiver climbed Sindak's spine.

To make matters worse, there was only one set of footsteps now. Where were the others? Had they split up? Maybe they'd spotted him and two of the warriors were sneaking around through the trees, hoping to surprise him.

Frantically, he searched every place a warrior might appear. The storm light made the brush and rocks look like crouching beasts. He gripped his war club in both hands.

The steps moved past him, heading up the trail with

catlike grace. Barely there. Just one man, but clearly a man who had lived too long with death to ever be careless.

The man's cape slurred softly over the ground, and Sindak thought he heard weeping—but it might have been the wind through the branches.

Sindak waited for the rest of the war party he was certain would be coming.

The whisper of the man's steps eventually died away.

Sindak boldly chanced looking around the tree, out into the twilit stillness where rain sheeted from the sky and created shining puddles in every hollow. He saw no warriors.

After another quarter-hand of time, Sindak risked stepping from behind the hickory. Darkness had taken hold of the world. He flipped up the hood of his cape, quietly walked out onto the trail, and ran north toward Hawk Moth Village as fast as his legs would carry him.

Thirty-one

While they waited, Gonda, Koracoo, and Towa gathered pine poles and created a makeshift ramada beneath a canoe birch. Covered with a mixture of pine boughs and moss, it was mostly dry underneath.

"Where is Sindak?" Gonda grumbled as he crawled under the ramada and sat down cross-legged.

"I'm sure he's coming." Miserable and wet to the bone, Koracoo sat in the rear hunched over a cup of rainwater. This close to Hawk Moth Village, they couldn't light a fire for warmth or to cook food for fear that they'd be seen.

Gonda said, "I say we forget about him and go to sleep."

"Let's give him a little longer." Koracoo leaned back against the birch trunk.

"He's irresponsible," Gonda said. "He should have been here two hands of time ago."

As soon as he'd said the word *irresponsible,* brief, agonizing images of Yellowtail Village flitted across Koracoo's souls. She forced them away. How strange that she felt nothing now—nothing except a weariness that weighted her limbs like granite and a hunger that made her knees tremble. Even her anger was gone, replaced by a lassitude in which all things seemed vaguely unreal.

She stared out at the growing darkness.

"Something must have happened," Towa replied from her left, where he stood against the shelter pole. "He wouldn't be late unless something had happened."

"You'd better be right. If he wanders in here with no wounds, I'm liable to give him some," Gonda replied.

Towa's mouth quirked, but he obviously knew better than to say anything. He glanced unhappily at Koracoo, who just shook her head lightly and looked away. From the corner of her eyes, she studied Gonda. He restlessly twisted his cup in his hands. His hair and clothing were soaked, and he looked to be on the verge of an enraged fit. Rage was his way of dealing with fear. Perhaps it was the way every warrior dealt with fear, but she pitied him. She saw it now with sudden clarity. She had never pitied him before. He had always been the strength in her heart, and the warmth in her souls. When had he become so weak and frightened? She wondered if maybe Sindak hadn't been right after all, that she shouldn't have brought him along.

No, despite everything, he deserves to search for his own children, to know for certain that he's done all he can to find them. I owe him at least that much.

Gonda took a sip of water and glared out at the rain.

Koracoo refilled her cup from a thin stream that ran off the roof, and took a long drink. When Sindak arrived, if he arrived, they would discuss what each person had found and make their decisions about what to do tomorrow. The rain was going to make things much harder for them. They needed a good plan and as much rest as they could get.

Towa picked up one of the brown twigs that littered the ground and toyed with it, tapping it on his palm. "Maybe he found the trail. Did you think of that? Maybe Sindak found it and followed it for as long as he could before he lost the light."

"I hope so. That's the only thing that will save him from my wrath." Gonda tugged his hood down over his forehead and clutched it beneath his chin. "Since none of us found anything significant today, what are we going to do tomorrow?" he asked belligerently.

Koracoo said, "Towa found fifty tracks, and two dead men, and I found two clumps of rabbit fur on branches."

"The dead men probably had nothing to do with our children, and two clumps of rabbit fur? That's nothing. It could have been left by—"

"I've never seen a rabbit jump ten hands high," she said before he could finish his tirade. "Therefore, I assume they were ripped from a cape. I consider both finds to be significant."

"So are you saying I'm the only one who found nothing?"

She almost shouted at him, but stopped herself. Images fluttered up again, and she saw Yellowtail Village burning, filled with smoke, dying people laid out like firewood. Her children gone. Her husband missing. It had been the worst she could imagine. Running through the flaming longhouses, searching for survivors, the injured quivering, screams, hands plucking at her cape. And when she thought it could get no worse, she'd found her mother burned almost beyond recognition.

The eyes of Gonda's souls must be seeing things equally as bad. Or worse, since he'd fought the battle. Guilt was smothering him—but she could not muster the strength to care.

"Our plan worked, Gonda." Koracoo shifted to bring up her knees and propped her elbows atop them. Her red cape looked black in the storm light. "Both trails appear to parallel the route Sindak found through the trees."

"Both trails? They weren't trails. At best they were—"

"They were trails." She bent over and drew three short lines in the wet dirt, showing the approximate locations of the sign they'd found. The lines were staggered. Towa's trail was far west of Sindak's, and Koracoo's trail was far east.

"It takes a good imagination to see those three dots as parallel trails, my former wife."

For just an instant, utter despair tormented her. She longed to yell that it was because of him that she would never again lie down as a mother and wife with her family's love surrounding her. She would never again be able to look across the longhouse where she was born and gaze into her mother's wise old eyes, or watch her sister cooking supper. Small things. Things she'd taken for granted now meant everything to her.

When grief began to constrict the back of her throat, she said harshly, "They are trails. If you can't see it, it's a good thing you're not in charge."

The words must have affected him like lance thrusts to his heart. His mouth trembled. He shouted, "You mean, *as I was at Yellowtail Village?*"

"Be quiet, you . . . !" She bit back the bitter words and forced herself to take a deep breath.

Towa was watching them with his eyes squinted, as though considering whether or not to run before Koracoo and Gonda brought the entire Flint nation down upon them.

"We're just—we are all exhausted and hungry," Koracoo said. "Let's not argue."

Gonda glowered down into his cup. Black hair stuck to his cheeks, making his round face look starkly triangular. His eyes resembled bottomless holes in the world.

Towa cautiously reached out and tapped the ground beneath the dots. "All three trails seem to head in the same direction, almost due east, toward the tribal home of the People of the Dawnland. I agree that it may be coincidence, but—"

"Even if they do all head east, it means nothing! We didn't find a single track today made by a child. Your 'trails' could have been made at different times by different war parties, scouts, or hunters that have absolutely nothing to do with our lost children!" Gonda declared.

Towa drew back his hand and tucked it beneath his cape. "Yes. True."

On the verge of hopeless fury, Gonda set his cup aside and stared up at the roof.

Calmly, Koracoo said, "We need to focus on the task. If we—"

Feet pounded the trail to the south. Each of them reached for weapons and turned to look at the wind-blown pines. The trail, which ran with water, shone as though coated with molten silver.

"Move," Koracoo said as she pulled CorpseEye from her belt, got to her feet, and slipped out into the rain behind the tree. Gonda and Towa vanished into the mist.

As the Cloud People shifted, a distant flicker of starlight glinted from the eyes of a man on the trail and illuminated a pale face. Koracoo studied him. She hadn't known Sindak long enough to memorize his movements, but she thought it was him. The wind stirred the hem of his cape, swaying it. As he trotted out of the trees and saw the fork in the trail, he grew more careless. His long stride quickened, and his feet splashed in the puddles.

Thirty paces away, Towa stepped from where he'd been hiding in a copse of dogwoods, and Sindak broke into a run. Towa trotted out to meet him. They embraced each other, and a hushed conversation broke out as they headed back toward the ramada.

Koracoo remained hidden behind the tree. The pines whispered in the wind, but she thought she heard something else out there. A voice . . . or distant music. Singing?

Gonda ducked beneath the ramada again and slumped down in his former position. As the two young warriors trotted up, his eyes narrowed. He looked at them like they were the enemy.

Sindak and Towa crawled beneath the ramada, smiling, glad to see each other, and Towa said, "See, I told you he was coming. Where's Koracoo?"

"What took you so long?" Gonda asked.

Sindak unslung his bow and quiver and set them in the rear of the shelter; then he sank to the ground and heaved a sigh. "I was followed," he said. "I had to hide while the warriors passed by."

"Followed? Did they see you?"

"No." Sindak shook his head, and his shoulder-length black hair flung water droplets in every direction.

"How many were there?"

"Three, I think. I was afraid to look when they passed by, but it sounded like the steps of three people."

Towa dipped his own cup beneath the water stream coming off the roof and handed it to Sindak. "Here. You must be thirsty."

Sindak took it with a grateful smile. "I am. Thanks." He emptied the cup in four deep swallows and handed it back to Towa. "Where's Koracoo? I have news."

Koracoo silently stepped from behind the tree and walked back toward the ramada. The rain had lessened a little. Stars glimmered in the distance. When she got to within five paces, she softly called, "What news?"

Sindak swiveled around to look at her. "I found a trail, War Chief. A clear trail. It was made by three people. They kept climbing into the trees, traveled for a ways, then climbed down and walked on the ground before they retreated to the trees again."

Gonda said, "It was probably an earlier trail made by the same three people who followed you."

Sindak sat back at Gonda's harsh tone. "I suppose it might have been."

Koracoo knelt just inside the ramada. Towa and Sindak turned to watch her with expectant eyes. Koracoo reached over to the place where she'd drawn the fragments of trail earlier. "This is where your trail started this morning." She tapped the place. "Show me the one you found today. How did it run? Where did you lose it?"

Sindak bent over the drawing and carefully sketched out what he'd found.

Towa glanced up at her. "Sindak's trail runs parallel to the one you found, Koracoo."

"Yes. It seems so." She squinted at it.

Sindak frowned before asking, "These other lines are trails? You also found trails?"

"We think—"

Gonda interrupted. "Don't be fools. We've lost the trail completely, and we all know it!"

Koracoo didn't even deign to glance at him. She looked at Sindak. "How far east of here did your trail end?"

"About a half-hand of time. But I—I didn't lose it, War Chief. I was still on it when I realized I was being followed and had to hide. After that, it was too dark to search any longer, so I ran directly here."

Koracoo nodded. "You did excellent work today, Sindak. And you, also, Towa. We know a good deal more tonight than we did last night. Tomorrow, we will all fan out and try to follow Sindak's trail. It seems to be the clearest. We—"

"This is a waste of time!" Gonda snarled.

"*I* decide when it's a waste of time, Gonda. Not you."

He flopped onto his side and turned his back to them.

Towa and Sindak went silent. They both stared questioningly at Koracoo. She said, "I will take first watch tonight. The rest of you should get some sleep."

As she rose to her feet, grabbed CorpseEye, and stepped out into the light rain, she heard Sindak ask, "What did you find today, Towa?"

"Two dead Flint warriors, and—"

"What killed them? Certainly not two arrows from your bow. You've never hit two targets in a row in your life."

"See? This is why it's hard to imagine sometimes that you're my best friend."

"Of course I am. So, someone other than you killed them. Who?"

Towa made an airy gesture with his hand. "They may have been killed by a Hills warrior. I'm not sure, but I found about fifty tracks made by a Hills warrior near both of the bodies."

"Really? How do you know he was one of our People?"

"His sandals had our distinctive herringbone weave—"

A cold tingle climbed Koracoo's spine. She whirled around at exactly the same instant that Gonda lurched to sit up. He had a panicked expression on his face. Drenched black hair stuck to his cheeks.

Towa's voice died in his throat. He blinked at them. "What's wrong?"

Gonda said, "Was he a—a big man? Did his tracks sink deeply into the mud?"

"Yes, that's why it was easy to track him . . . at least for a short distance."

Koracoo held Gonda's gaze. "It may be just another Hills warrior."

"Wearing sandals in the winter? I doubt it. He's following us."

As though a dark, cold feeling was forcing him to stand, Towa got up. "Who? Who is following us?"

Koracoo walked back and stepped beneath the ramada to face him. Towa stared at her like a suspicious animal. "The morning after the attack," she explained, "Gonda found a similar track. Made by a big man wearing sandals with a distinctive herringbone weave."

"Where?" Sindak asked.

"Far west of here," she said. "Near Canassatego Village."

"Canassatego Village? That's Hills country. What were you doing there?"

"We were tracking the warriors who attacked our village and captured our children."

Towa stood for a moment, not certain what to say. "I thought you said Mountain warriors attacked Yellowtail Village?"

"Most were." Gonda drew up his knees. "I'm not sure they all were."

In the long silence that followed, Koracoo heard a dog bark in the distance, and then the faint shout of a man. Both came from the direction of Hawk Moth Village. The sculpted curves of Towa's face hardened as he clenched his jaw. For a time, she watched the thoughts churning behind his dark eyes and thought he might stalk away. Finally he said, "Where did the big man's tracks lead?"

Gonda answered, "You know that enormous shell midden—"

"The one that sits on the border between our countries?"

"Yes. The man's tracks led to the top of the midden."

Towa shifted his weight to his other foot. "Why? What was he doing up there?"

"Carrying a body. A dead girl. And one of high status, too, given her jewelry."

Astonished, Sindak said, "She was still wearing jewelry?"

"Yes. Strange, isn't it? Any warrior worth his weapons would have stripped every piece and taken it home with him."

Towa asked, "Why are you telling us this? Do you think the girl was one of Gannajero's captives?"

"No. Gannajero is a Trader. Her warriors would definitely have taken the girl's beautiful copper earspools and shell bracelets. And her shell gorget with the magnificent False Face surrounded by stars—"

"She was wearing a False Face pendant?" Towa asked as though shocked. "With stars?"

Gonda created a circle with his fingers and lowered it to his chest to show them the size. "Yes. A big one. And the False Face had a serpent's eyes and buffalo horns. . . ." He stopped when both Towa and Sindak went rigid. They looked like surprised geese. "What's the matter?"

Koracoo studied them as they whispered to each other. Towa had placed a hand over his heart, as though protecting something hidden beneath his cape.

"Is that Atotarho's gorget you're touching?" she said.

As the storm drifted eastward, starlight broke through the clouds and brightened the night. The rain-slick ground shone with a frosty radiance. Every twig and branch seemed to be coated with a thin layer of silver.

Koracoo said, "Why don't you show it to us, Towa?"

Towa carefully pulled a huge gorget from his shirt and let it rest upon his cape. It covered half his chest.

Gonda leaped to his feet and extended his hand. "Let me see that?"

"No," Towa said. "He ordered me to wear this at all times. It's been in his clan for hundreds of generations. It's been passed down from matron to matron since the creation of the world."

"But it's identical to the one we found at the midden," Gonda charged.

Towa shrugged. "There are supposed to be two. Don't you know our story of the battle between Horned Serpent and Thunder?"

Koracoo leaned her shoulder against the ramada pole, and the wet hem of her cape stuck to her leggings. "It's very similar to our story, isn't it? At the dawn of creation, Horned Serpent attacked People, and the Great Spirit sent Thunder to help them. In the battle that ensued, Thunder threw the greatest lightning bolt ever seen. The mountains shook, and the stars broke loose from the skies. One landed right on top of Horned Serpent."

Towa continued, "Yes. This pendant chronicles that sacred story."

Koracoo stared at the gorget that rested like a shining beacon on Towa's cape. The carving was exceptional. The stars shooting around the head of Horned Serpent seemed to be coming right at her.

"Why have you kept it hidden from us?" Gonda asked.

"Because it's none of your concern! It's not a thing for ordinary eyes, especially not Standing Stone eyes. It's ancient. Can't you feel its Power?"

"I can," Sindak said, and backed away. "It gives me a stomachache."

A stray breath of wind stirred Koracoo's hair, and she jumped as if at the touch of a hand. "Why would the dead girl have had an identical pendant?"

"It couldn't have been identical," Towa said. "It must have been a fake, a copy."

Gonda shook his head. "I don't think so. It was exactly like the one you're wearing."

Towa shook his head vehemently. "It can't be."

"Why?"

"Because the other belongs to the human False Face who will don a cape of white clouds and ride the winds of destruction across the face of the world. Obviously a dead girl can't do that." Towa stuffed the magnificent gorget back into his shirt. "It was a fake."

Gonda's gaze flitted to where his pack rested, as though he longed to go get it, but he didn't.

Koracoo waited for a time longer, then said, "The end of the world will, I suspect, take care of itself. In the meantime, you suggested that the Hills warrior with the sandals might be following us. Why?"

Gonda's brow furrowed. "He may just be tracking the children like we are, and so his path necessarily intersects ours."

Koracoo said, "Towa? Sindak? Your thoughts?"

Towa scanned the darkness. "He is a Hills man, that's certain, but—"

"Unless he stole the sandals." Sindak folded his arms across his chest. "He could have taken them during an attack on a Hills village—which means he could be a Flint warrior, or Landing warrior, or anything else. Even a Standing Stone warrior."

Koracoo gently smoothed her fingers over Corpse-Eye while she considered his words. The polished wood felt like silk. He was right. The sandals told them nothing certain about the man—if it was the same man. But . . . if he had followed them, there was a reason. Was he a spy for Atotarho? Keeping track of them? If so, the man would have been dispatched with several other warriors—runners he could send home to keep the chief informed of their progress, or lack thereof. If he was not one of Atotarho's spies, Gonda could be correct that he was just a desperate family member trying to track down his own captured children, and his path happened to coincide with theirs. In that case, he might be an ally, at least in this pursuit.

It was the last possibility that made her hands clench tightly around CorpseEye. The sandaled man could be a scout sent out by Gannajero to monitor her back trail to see if she was being followed. If so, right now, he could be running ahead to tell the old witch about them.

"It's getting late. Let's all think about this, and we'll discuss it more tomorrow. Gonda, I will wake you at midnight."

He nodded.

Koracoo walked out into the starlight and took up her guard position beneath a towering oak tree. In the dark rain-scented gloom, three deer trotted by, their pale antlers swaying in the ashen gleam. She watched them until they caught her scent and disappeared into the trees like silent ghosts.

The three men beneath the ramada stretched out and pulled their capes around them for warmth. It took less than a few hundred heartbeats for Sindak to start snoring softly. Gonda, lying close beside him, seemed to be staring up at the ramada roof. Towa had his back turned to both of them.

After a time, Koracoo's thoughts returned to the gorget.

If the pendants were not identical, they were very nearly so. The only way an artist could have accomplished such a feat was if he'd been holding Atotarho's pendant in his hand when he'd carved the second one.

And that led her to some wild speculation. What if—

Movement caught her eye. She straightened suddenly. It resembled a black spider, far out in the darkness, silently floating between the trees, paralleling the trail that headed north. Now and then starlight reflected from its body, revealing long legs and perhaps flashing eyes.

It's probably just another deer.

But tomorrow at dawn she would check for tracks to make certain. It kept her alert and watching every wind-touched limb that swayed . . . while she contemplated the possibility that the sandaled man had given the dead girl the pendant to take with her to the afterlife. Even if it was a superlative fake, it would have been a rare, precious gift. Why? Had she been a relative? Or was he trying to buy her goodwill? Perhaps to help him when he reached the bridge to the afterlife?

On the other hand, maybe he'd given it to her so that she could take it to the human False Face in the Sky World and set him on his journey, fulfilling prophecy.

Koracoo knelt at the base of the oak and wondered.

Thirty-two

Dim bluish light filtered through gaps in the ramada's roof and landed like a finely woven scarf across Gonda's face. He rolled uncomfortably to his side and struggled to get back to sleep. Sometime during the night, Sindak and Towa had rolled closer to him, pinning him in. He could barely stretch his legs out. Worse, the constant low drone of the wind slashed through his dreams, becoming Tawi's voice every time he drifted off.

After an eternity of restless shifting, he finally rolled to his hands and knees and crawled over near the tree trunk, where he stretched out in the soft sweet-smelling birch leaves and closed his eyes again.

Sweat drenched his face; it rolled down his neck to soak the collar of his hide shirt. He wiped his forehead on his sleeve and stared blankly at the patchwork patterns of light that decorated his closed eyelids. Weariness clung to his shoulders like a granite cape.

Gonda! Tawi screamed.

"Stop it," he whispered. "Stop dreaming. You can't change it."

Moments later, he felt himself sinking deeper into sleep. His breathing melted into soothing rhythms. The sounds of the wind faded. Darkness smothered the light. . . .

And the snow fell around him in huge wet flakes. "Where, Tawi?"

"Over there!" Her voice wavered in the icy gusts that lanced Yellowtail Village. Tawi pointed. "Near the giant oaks!"

Tawi looked so much like her sister, Koracoo, that sometimes it stopped Gonda in his tracks. She was beautiful, with an oval face and large dark eyes. Though tonight, fear twisted her features.

Gonda ran along the palisade catwalk, confidently slapping warriors on the shoulders as he passed, trying to get closer to the place Tawi swore she had seen movement in the forest. She ran behind him, her moccasins patting softly on the wood.

Warriors had been coming to him for over a hand of time, whispering that they'd seen movement out in the trees, reporting vast numbers of enemy warriors sneaking through the darkness. But there'd been no attack. No warriors had materialized. Everyone was so terrified, he wasn't sure who or what to believe.

"When will Koracoo be back?" Tawi asked as they continued along the catwalk. "I thought she was supposed to be here before dusk."

"She was. I'm worried about her."

Gonda was more than worried. He was terrified that something had happened. Had she met the full force of the enemy out there? Was she even now fighting a desperate retreating action, trying to get back to the safety of Yellowtail Village? Or worse? He longed to dispatch a war party to go look for her, but she had ordered him to keep all of his three hundred warriors inside the palisade until she returned. It seemed foolish. If he could just send out five or six scouts, they might be able to bring him enough information about the enemy's strength that he could prepare for the attack he felt sure was coming.

But he would not disobey her orders. He never had.

Besides, she'd dispatched two scouts at dawn. Neither had returned.

Tawi grabbed his shoulder hard. "Right there. See?"

She pointed, and Gonda stared out into the darkness.

"There, Gonda! In the center of the oaks."

Gonda pulled an arrow from his quiver and nocked his bow while he scanned the trees. "Tawi, all I see is falling snow and branches blowing in the wind. What did you think you saw?"

"It wasn't just me, Gonda. Four of us were standing here when we saw flashes in the oaks."

"Flashes?"

"Yes, like chert arrow points winking. Or maybe shell beads."

Gonda squinted at the oaks again. On occasion, as a limb flailed, the old autumn leaves flashed silver in the starlight that penetrated the clouds.

"There's something out there, Gonda! I swear it."

"I believe you, Tawi. I just don't see it." He turned and looked out at Yellowtail Village. Three longhouses encircled the plaza, one for each clan: Turtle, Bear, and

Wolf. Unlike the Hills or Flint Peoples, they had small longhouses, barely two hundred hands long, but each stood over thirty hands tall. The elm-bark walls looked shaggy in the snow. The plaza was dark and empty, but the firelight seeping between gaps in the longhouse walls cast a pale amber glow over the forty-hand-tall palisade of upright pine poles. There was only one way into the village—the massive front gates. He'd stationed fifty warriors inside to guard the gates. The rest of his warriors were on the catwalk, staring out at the darkness. He could hear them hissing to each other, and the fear in their voices made his stomach muscles knot. "Is the village prepared?"

"Yes, all of the children are in bed being watched by elders."

"Good. I—"

"Gonda!" a woman shouted.

He spun and saw young Kiya, fifteen summers old, waving her bow at him. "Two runners! Coming from the west!"

Gonda sprinted toward Kiya and gazed out over the chest-high palisade wall. They'd just stepped out of the forest. One man was supporting the other. Both looked wounded. "It's Coter and Hagnon. Quickly, climb down. Tell our men to open the gates."

As Kiya ran to obey, Gonda tucked his arrow in his quiver, slung his bow, and trotted down the palisade repeating, "We're going to open the gates. Prepare to be stormed. Keep your bows focused on the area just in front of the gates! . . . We're going to open the gates.

Get your bows up! Be ready! . . . This could be a ruse to get us to open the gates! Don't be fooled!"

As he raced for a ladder and began to scramble down, his nerves were strung as tight as a rawhide drum. He hit the ground running.

Just before he arrived, two warriors pulled the gates open barely the width of four hands, and the scouts slid through. "Close the gate!" he shouted. "Get the planks down!"

Men dropped the locking planks back into position, securing the gates.

Inside the village, noise rose, people asking questions, running along the palisade to look down at the wounded scouts, arrows clattering in quivers.

But outside . . . outside . . . Gonda heard nothing.

He lunged for Hagnon, who had Coter's arm draped over his shoulder. "Marten? Take Coter to one of the medicine elders. See that he's taken care of, then get right back here!"

"Yes, Gonda."

Marten pulled Coter's arm over his own shoulders and started dragging him toward the closest longhouse.

Hagnon looked like he was about to collapse. Streaks of blood covered his square-jawed face and splotched his war shirt. "Gonda, G-Gonda, I—"

"Hagnon, what happened?"

With terror-bright eyes, Hagnon grabbed Gonda by the shoulders and leaned forward to hiss, "They let us through, Gonda. They thought it was a big joke."

"Who did?"

Hagnon shook his head. "Most are Mountain People warriors, but there may be Hills or Landing warriors out there, too. There are so many, I didn't—"

Gonda grabbed his arms and shook him. "How many? Quickly!"

Hagnon swallowed hard and glanced at the nearby warriors. Softly he replied, "There must be, I—I don't know, maybe over one thousand, Gonda. Or . . . more. I—I didn't get a good look. They are spread out through the forest, aligned for waves of attacks."

Gonda felt like he'd been kicked in the belly. He released Hagnon's arms, stiffened his spine, and praised, "You are worth your weight in copper, my friend. Your bravery will be rewarded. Now get to the Wolf Clan longhouse and tell the matrons what we're facing."

"Yes, Gonda." Hagnon tried to trot away, but ended up staggering.

When Gonda looked back he found himself surrounded by warriors. All eyes fixed on him, waiting for the bad news. In the faint firelight cast by the houses, their faces looked pale and drawn.

Gonda held out his hands and made a calming motion. "Now, remember, no one has ever breached these walls. So long as you each do your duty, we'll make it through this. Do you understand? Just do your duty."

"But, Gonda . . ." Kiya wet her lips and stared at him with huge eyes. "Did he say thousands?"

"Hagnon couldn't see very well, Kiya. He was wounded, scared, trying to protect his friend; he probably saw far more warriors than there were. I'm sure I would have."

A small round of nervous laughter went through the crowd.

Gonda smiled and raised his voice for all to hear: "And it doesn't matter how many there are! You are well trained. I've seen to it myself. I know you can fight off any attack. You're the finest warriors in the land! Now, get to your posts!"

Warriors scattered.

Before Gonda had taken two steps, war cries tore the air and the people on the catwalk started shouting and running. The enemy hit the palisade like a hurricane, shaking the ground at his feet. . . .

Gonda woke. He glimpsed branches above him, heard rain falling. The colors melted together as images collided and spun wildly, carrying him back to . . .

The plaza throbbed with a sourceless pounding of sobs and angry shouts. Women moved among the wounded who had been dragged against the southern palisade wall behind the Wolf longhouse. They yelled to each other to make themselves heard over the roar of battle. Orphaned children huddled together between the longhouses, crying and reaching pleadingly for anyone who passed by, calling the names of family members who would never answer again. Scents of urine mixed nauseatingly with the coppery odor of blood.

"Blessed gods," Hagnon murmured darkly. "How many have we lost?"

"Too many," Gonda answered. "I need to know what the matrons think. Has Chief Yellowtail given any orders?"

"I can tell you what the matrons think; they say we must keep fighting. And Chief Yellowtail is too injured to say anything. I'm not sure he's going to make it through this. Is there any hope that the surrounding Standing Stone villages may be sending warriors to our aid?"

"None. That's why our enemies attacked at night. No one will see the smoke from the fires until dawn."

"Gonda, everyone is asking the same question." Hagnon lifted his arms. "Where's Koracoo and her war party?"

A sinking feeling invaded Gonda's belly. He balanced on a knife's edge, waiting for the moment when he would know all was lost, and he had to give the order to run. "I don't know, Hagnon. I—I don't know."

He couldn't let himself think about her, or he'd crumble into a thousand pieces. At least their children were safe in the Bear Clan longhouse, warm in their hides, being watched over by Koracoo's mother.

He ran a hand through his drenched black hair. What was going on out there? It was like the enemy was holding back, waiting for something. They kept attacking in short bursts, shooting arrows at the warriors on the catwalk while others ran up to the palisade with pots of oil and tossed them on the walls. The last wave would line up outside the trees and shoot flaming arrows into the oil and over the walls into the longhouses—or anyone who happened to be standing in the open.

"So far, we've been lucky," Hagnon said. "We've been able to put out all the fires they've started."

"The snow has helped. Things are too wet to burn easily."

Those with the worst injuries had been laid out side by side in the middle of the plaza. There was no hope for them. If they happened to be struck by an arrow, it would be a quick way to die. Moans penetrated the melee. Gonda followed a winding path that led around them and looked upon the wounds with a horrified feeling of despair. Many had belly wounds. Others had heads or chests bandaged with blood-soaked rags. Most were dying, dying swiftly, their strength too drained by the loss of blood to survive.

Gonda trotted down the length of the house, past the five fires, to where the clan matrons huddled together. Standing beside the gray-haired elders was the Speaker for the Women, Yanesh, who announced the matrons' decisions.

When Yanesh saw him, she rushed to meet him. Tall and thin, with long graying black hair, she had a dignity about her.

"Yanesh, have they heard my reports? Have they met in council? What are they saying?"

She took him by the arm and led him away. "They met with the council less than a half-hand of time ago. They say we must keep fighting. They say Koracoo is coming."

Gonda rubbed a hand over his numb face. It felt like an act of betrayal to say it, but he whispered, "I'm not sure she is, Yanesh. Something's wrong, or she would have been here by now. The time is coming, soon, when they will have to decide what to do if the enemy breaches the palisade."

"They have already decided, Gonda. We will keep fighting."

A weary fury seared Gonda's veins. "No. No, they don't understand. We should plan some kind of diversion that will allow the women and children to escape. Maybe if we can lure the enemy out into the forest—"

"We will keep fighting, Gonda. We will fight until Koracoo arrives. Elder Wida had a vision that Koracoo will arrive at the last instant and save us."

Gonda stared at her. Though he believed that unseen Spirits walked the land, and that souls traveled the Road of Light in the sky to reach the afterlife, he'd never put much faith in visions. "Yanesh, please. Tell them what I said. *Make them understand!*"

Yanesh put a comforting hand on his shoulder. "I will Gonda. Now, you'd better return—"

Screams rose outside, and a series of thuds sounded on the longhouse roof. Within moments, flames burst to life.

"Bring the ladders and water pots!" Yanesh shouted.

As people scurried to obey, Gonda sprinted outside. Hundreds of flaming arrows arched through the night sky overhead, leaving smoky trails. He ran hard for the ladders that led up to the catwalk and climbed swiftly to look out over the palisade. As he unslung his bow and pulled an arrow from his quiver, a strange hush settled over the enemy.

Gonda frowned. He was standing next to Kiya. "What are they doing?"

"I don't know," she said. "After they fired the flaming arrows, they all retreated into the trees and went silent."

"Silent? Why?"

"Maybe"—she wet her lips—"maybe they're leaving. Maybe they've decided the cost is too high. We've killed hundreds of their warriors."

Gonda surveyed the dead bodies that scattered the area between the gates and trees. He guessed the number at around two hundred—not nearly enough to make them quit, though many had also been wounded and dragged off.

His gaze lifted to the trees. As though a monster had awakened, thousands of eyes suddenly sparkled in the light of the fires. They were on the move. Winding through the trees. Their grotesque shadows wavered against the stark fire-dyed forest.

"They . . . they're moving their forces up." He spun around and shouted, "They're coming! Get ready!"

Though he heard a few whimpers eddy down the line, his warriors stood tall, their nocked bows aimed at the tree line.

When the enemy finally emerged from the trees, Gonda stood stunned.

They'd been reinforced. They'd kept him busy while they'd assembled the necessary forces for one massive final assault against the palisade.

The enemy war chief, a tall man wearing a wolfhide headdress with the ears pricked and the long bushy tail hanging down his back, strode out front and raised both hands high into the air, as though daring anyone to shoot him.

"Blessed Spirits, that's Yenda." Gonda's belly muscles clenched tight. The last time they'd fought, it had been a chance meeting of two war parties in the forest. Gonda and Koracoo had barely escaped with their lives. The man was the most powerful and revered Mountain People war chief in the land. He was also a filthy murderer. Gonda pulled his bowstring back and held it taut.

"Yenda? Are you sure?" Kiya asked.

"I'm sure."

"Gonda!" Yenda roared like an enraged bear and spread his muscular arms wider. "You see I brought friends this time. Prepare to die!"

Gonda shouted back, "After you, Yenda!" and loosed his arrow. The white chert point glittered as it sailed down. Yenda spun just in time. Gonda's arrow lanced through his cape.

"Attack!" Yenda shouted, and waved his warriors forward.

They burst from the trees like ants swarming from a kicked anthill, and hundreds of arrows streaked through the starlight.

"Fire!" Gonda shouted, and spun to . . .

He jerked awake, panting, his heart hammering his ribs.

Koracoo turned from where she stood beneath the oak watching the trails. His eyes locked on her, and he thanked the Spirits that she was alive. *She's alive. Everything is all right.*

But as the memories of the final outcome flooded back, he weakly rolled to his side and gazed out across the rolling starlit hills.

The entire world seemed to be dying around him, and he didn't know how to stop it.

Thirty-three

Odion

To the east, a turquoise band stretches across the horizon, but the arching dome of Brother Sky still glitters with the largest campfires of the dead. The leafless hickory trees to the north resemble a gray haze, spotted here and there with evergreens. Soft voices carry. Gannajero and her men stand around talking. They have already packed up. We'll be going soon.

We children sit in a circle, waiting for orders. Zateri has her arm over Wrass, who lies curled on his side. He's been throwing up all morning. His face is a mass of swollen purple bruises. If I didn't know it was Wrass, I'm not sure I'd recognize him.

Tutelo and Baji kneel to my left. Baji's gaze keeps searching the clearing, as though she expects to see her relatives appear at any moment. Or perhaps, like me, there's a war party woven into the fabric of her souls. Right behind her eyes. A war party erupting from the trees with bows aimed, killing Gannajero and her men.

Soon . . . please, Spirits . . .

This morning hope is like a wild starving beast in my heart, eating me alive.

The short burly warrior, Waswan, tramps away from Gannajero and calls, "Here, you brats. Biscuits!"

When he gets closer, he tosses us each an acorn-meal biscuit.

With a sense of panic, I watch mine arc through the air. It takes forever to fall into my hand. By the time I catch it, my stomach is twisting and squealing. I immediately bite into it. It tastes stale, but wonderful. In no time, it's gone. I lick the crumbs from my hands and stare down painfully at the tiny bits that remain. Leaving anything for the hungry birds and mice is becoming almost impossible.

I hesitate. I can't seem to force myself to brush the bits onto the ground. Grandmother always said if you took care of the animals, they would take care of you. Our People believe that animals allow themselves to be killed. They see a human's hunger and willingly sacrifice themselves so that the One Great Life of all might continue. Every time I brush the crumbs from my hands, I am, in a small way, sacrificing for them.

The other children are breathlessly watching me. They seem to be waiting to see what I do.

I clamp my jaws. My hands are shaking when I brush the last bits of biscuit onto the ground.

They do the same.

Zateri has the harder problem. She is holding Wrass' uneaten biscuit.

"Wrass?" she says softly. "You should try to eat."

"No, I—I can't. Please save the biscuit for me." He keeps his eyes closed, as though the pale beams of dawn light slanting through the trees are stilettos puncturing his brain.

I'm not sure, if I'd been holding the biscuit, that I could have saved it for him. But Zateri is braver than I. She tucks it into the top of Wrass' legging and says, "It's there when you want it, Wrass."

"Thank you," he answers weakly. "I know th-that wasn't easy." He slits open one eye and smiles gratefully at her.

Zateri's face brightens. She strokes his hair gently. "Try to sleep for as long as you can."

Tenshu and Waswan stand talking five paces away. Tenshu is thin, with a deeply lined face and sunken cheeks. Waswan is glaring at him. His square jaw moves with grinding yellow teeth. He's knotted his greasy black hair at the base of his skull and secured it with a shell comb. He wears a new cape today, made of finely smoked elk hide. Across the bottom, there are white images of wolves chasing each other. He must have won it in the last game.

They both turn to watch Gannajero and Kotin. The old woman's gravelly voice is too low to hear, but she's waving her arms, and I wonder what has upset her.

Tenshu says, "Gods, what's wrong with her? We're headed to our biggest game ever. She should be leaping with joy."

Waswan's moonish face twitches. "All morning long she's been ranting about the Child."

Tenshu shakes his head. "There was no child. Hanu and Galan both searched the fire cherries. She's lost her soul, Waswan. Maybe we should get out of here before she kills us."

"One more game; then we'll go."

Tenshu massages the back of his neck. "All right. I just

wish she'd let us travel the rivers. It would be so much faster. I hate these steep mountain trails."

"And she hates the waterways. There are too many people. Rivers are crowded with towns, people fishing, and other canoes. She's afraid someone might recognize her."

"Well, it slows us down."

Zateri glances at the guards, then leans forward to whisper to me. "Tonight. We have to do it tonight."

I jerk a nod and mouth the words: *All right. Tonight.*

Kotin steps away from Gannajero and calls, "Waswan? We'll meet at the Quill River camp north of Bog Willow Village. Don't be late! We're expecting hundreds. Get going."

The short burly warrior says, "Yes, Kotin," and turns to me. "You, boy. You're coming with me today."

I stand up. "But, please, what about my friend, Wrass? He's too sick to walk all day."

Waswan says, "He'll either walk, or he'll die on the trail with his head split open. Now, move. This morning, we're starting off in the trees. Go to the hickories."

I turn to wave good-bye to Tutelo, who watches me walk away with wide frightened eyes.

Tenshu walks up to the rest of the group and says, "You two girls are coming with me." He points his war club at Tutelo and Baji.

They both stand.

I lose sight of them as I march out into the forest with Ugly. Wrass and Zateri must both be going with Kotin, because Gannajero always travels alone. Once we part at dawn, none of us see her again until dusk.

"That one." Waswan aims his war club at the high

spreading branches of the largest hickory. In the sky above, Cloud People drift, their bellies glowing pale gold. "Climb up."

I grab hold of a low limb, brace my moccasin on the hickory trunk, and pull myself up.

Waswan climbs behind me. When I reach the first large limb, I take a moment to grind my heel into the bark, then lift my nose to smell the air. A frightening scent rides the wind. I twist around on the limb to scan the brightening horizon. There is a black splotch. . . .

"Hurry up, boy! You're slow today."

"Do you smell that?" I sniff the east wind.

"I told you to climb. Do it!" He pulls a stiletto from his belt and stabs the bottom of my moccasin. The sharp tip goes straight through the hide and punctures my heel.

"I'm going!" I say. Tears burn my eyes as I climb higher. I finally step out onto the thick limb that leads to the next tree and begin working my way across it. I pretend I'm balancing on a log bridge across a creek.

Father's voice echoes in my ears: *Just watch your feet. Don't look down.*

Halfway across, I grab hold of a branch that sticks up, and turn back to look at Waswan. He has stopped.

He's standing on the limb with his hands propped on his hips, staring out at the narrow valley that cuts through the mountains. A black cloud of smoke trails across the sky. The acrid scent of burning longhouses grows stronger as we climb.

"What village is that?" I ask in a trembling voice. The burning village lies where the valley runs down to a wide river, perhaps a half-day's walk away.

Waswan's head doesn't move, but his gaze lowers to me, and hatred gleams in his eyes. I do not know why he hates me, but he does. Perhaps because I am a Standing Stone boy.

"That's Bog Willow Village. It's one of the filthy villages of the Dawnland People. By now, they're all dead or run off."

"Who attacked them?"

"Men you will meet tonight."

"How do you know? D-did your people attack the village?"

He stares straight through me as though I'm not really here. "Keep moving, boy. We have a long way to go." A cruel smile twists his mouth. "And tonight is your night. Many victorious warriors will be there."

I'm shaking as I edge out onto the limb and hurry across it. *Don't think about it. Don't imagine . . . don't.*

Runners often come to speak with Gannajero in the middle of the night. They wake me, but they never stay for long, and they always leave with a bag of riches. I have wondered what they tell her. Perhaps they are warriors about to attack a village? Does that mean there will be new children tonight?

I climb onto the giant limb of the next tree and head for the trunk. When I get there, I wrap my arms around it and rest my cheek against the cold bark while I grind my heel again. My whole body suddenly feels like it's roasting. I can't think straight.

Waswan crosses behind me and orders, "Climb down. We'll walk through the rocks for a time; then we'll climb up again."

I place my feet on the branches like a ladder's rungs. Just before I jump to the ground, a squirrel chitters and leaps away through the tree. While I'm watching, Waswan nocks an arrow and shoots it through the heart. The squirrel falls as lightly as a feather. It makes a soft thud when it strikes the earth.

I jump to the ground, and Waswan climbs down beside me. Without a word, he walks over, pulls his arrow from the squirrel, and tucks the small animal into his belt. Its bushy tail glints reddish in the light.

"Walk," Waswan orders. "Straight toward Bog Willow Village."

"But it's burning. Why would we go there?"

He gestures toward the rock outcrop ahead. "Stop talking, boy. Walk."

Thirty-four

As Sindak led the way back to the place where he'd hidden the night before, icy leaves crunched beneath his moccasins. He felt vaguely numb. He hadn't gotten much sleep in the last three nights, and that, along with the fact that they hadn't been eating well, was taking a toll on his strength. He veered off the trail and headed out into the glistening grass. Frost coated everything this morning, shining like a thick layer of crushed shells in the tawny halo of morning light that lanced through the trees. The brittle mustiness of late autumn filled the air.

"Where are we going?" Koracoo called from behind.

Sindak pointed with his bow. "Over there. See that huge hickory tree? That's where I hid from the warriors last night."

Towa's distinctive steps were close behind him. Koracoo was slightly farther back, and Gonda's footsteps came from far in the rear. Sindak turned halfway around to look back. Gonda was trudging along with his head down, as though totally defeated. His war club was almost dragging the ground, and he didn't even seem to notice.

Towa caught his gaze, turned to look back at Gonda, and trotted forward to catch up with Sindak. In a low voice, he said, "I think he's becoming a liability to us."

"He is. But until Koracoo figures that out and orders him to go home, there's nothing we can do."

Towa's buckskin cape fluttered around his long legs as he walked at Sindak's side. "Even if Koracoo ordered him to leave, I doubt he'd do it."

"I suspect you're right. He's going to stick to us like boiled pine pitch until he gets us all killed."

Sindak followed his own tracks across the frozen mud toward the leafless hickory. "Did Gonda keep you awake half the night with his moaning and thrashing?"

"Yes. I was deeply grateful when Koracoo woke him to take his watch. That's when I finally got to sleep."

Sindak sighed. "Me, too."

As they approached the hickory, the cold indigo shadows of the massive limbs began to enfold them. Sindak tugged his cape more tightly around him, and circled to the left. His own tracks were unmistakable. Last night's mud had squished up around his moccasins, leaving clear prints that, this morning, were crusted with frost.

Sindak stopped and waited for Koracoo, and eventually Gonda, to arrive.

Sunlight tipped Koracoo's lashes with gold as she looked at him. Even exhausted, trail-worn, and filthy, she was still a beautiful woman. Her large dark eyes resembled black moons, and the dawn light blushed color into her small nose and full lips.

In an irritated voice, Gonda said, "Did you plan on showing us something, Sindak?"

"What? Oh . . . yes." He turned, embarrassed. Had he been staring at Koracoo? "This is where I hid last night to allow the warriors to pass by."

"And where were the warriors?"

Sindak gestured out toward the trail that forked thirty paces away. Towering pines scalloped the edges of the path. "The warriors came up the trail and took the fork that heads off to the west."

Gonda shoved black hair out of his eyes before he stalked over to examine the trail.

Koracoo said, "Where did you leave the children's tracks?"

Sindak swung around. "Right back there, War Chief. In that grove of chestnuts."

Koracoo's gaze traveled up the trunk of the closest tree and into the branches that stretched almost two hundred hands in the air. On one of the largest limbs, a squirrel sat chewing a chestnut. Discarded bits of the nut fell from its jaws and floated down like brown snowflakes to litter the ground at the base of the tree.

"Koracoo?" Gonda called. He was kneeling in the frosty trail, outlining something with his fingers.

She turned and frowned. "What did you find?"

Gonda waved her over. "Come and see for yourself."

"He must have found the trail of the warriors who chased me last night," Sindak said, and trotted toward Gonda.

Sindak and Towa arrived a few steps ahead of Koracoo

and the three of them bent over Gonda, trying to see what he'd discovered.

Gonda tipped his chin up to look at Sindak. "I thought you said there were three warriors? I only see the tracks of one man."

Sindak's bushy brows pulled together over his hooked nose. "I heard the footsteps of three people," he insisted. "At least for a time. Then two vanished, and only one remained." He straightened and looked behind him, to the south. A mixture of pines and birches gleamed in the sunlight. "Perhaps the other two veered off back there somewhere."

Gonda grumbled under his breath, and Koracoo said, "Gonda? See if you can find any other tracks in that direction."

Gonda rose to his feet and started walking back along the trail, searching. Sindak turned to go with him, but Koracoo said, "No, stay here, Sindak. Help me follow out these prints. Towa, why don't you go and help Gonda."

Towa's mouth pursed distastefully, but he said, "Yes, War Chief," and trotted away.

Koracoo watched him go with narrowed eyes. When he was out of earshot, Koracoo looked at Sindak. "What do you see down there in that track, Sindak?"

Sindak knelt to examine it more carefully. In places the frost had created a strange pattern of tiny intersecting bars. It almost looked . . . "Blessed Spirits," he whispered. "That's a herringbone design! You don't think—"

"I'm not sure what to think." Koracoo swung Corpse-

Eye up and propped the club on her left shoulder. The breeze blew her chopped-off hair around her face. "I wanted to get your impression before I brought it up with the others. Did he sound like a big man when he passed you last night?"

Sindak thought about it. "It was raining, War Chief. The wind was blowing through the trees. There was a lot of noise. I can't say for certain."

She watched him through hard, unblinking eyes. "What else did you notice?"

He flapped his arms against his sides. "Not much. As I said, for a time I thought I heard three people's steps, then two vanished . . . and at one point I would have sworn I smelled rotting flesh."

Koracoo cocked her head. "Rotting flesh?"

"Yes, the tang reminded me of a two- or three-day-old battlefield."

Koracoo rubbed her thumb over CorpseEye. "Anything else?"

He thought about it. "I heard a rattle, like branches clattering together in the breeze. And, off and on, I heard the man speaking to someone. I couldn't make out any of his words, but he sounded sad. At one point, I thought he called—"

"*Koracoo?*" Gonda leaped to his feet and trotted back toward them carrying something.

"What is it?"

Gonda lifted the scrap of cloth into the air, holding it high enough for her to see. "It's a fragment of a girl's dress, I think."

Koracoo's face suddenly turned to stone, and Sindak

wondered if she feared it might be from her daughter's dress, as the copper circlet had been.

Koracoo wet her lips, seemed to gird herself, and walked out to meet Gonda. "Let me see it." She held out her hand.

Gonda draped the soft doehide over her palm. Red-and-yellow quillwork decorated the lower half. "It isn't from Tutelo's dress; don't worry about that," Gonda said, alleviating her fear immediately.

As relief shot through her, she seemed to deflate like an air-filled bladder. The hide in her hand quaked softly before she clenched her fist around it. "The quill-work is exquisite," she remarked; then she lifted the fragment and smelled it. "Is this what you smelled last night, Sindak?" She held it out.

Sindak leaned close enough to get a good whiff of the putrid odor. "Yes. But the taint on this fragment is faint. I could not have smelled this from thirty paces away behind the hickory tree."

"No," Koracoo replied softly, and turned the fragment of dress in her hand to study the quillwork. As though something horrifying had occurred to her, she suddenly seemed to go rigid. Softly, she said, "No, I suspect our friend with the herringbone sandals was carrying another dead body."

Gonda's head jerked up. Panic tensed his round face. "Herringbone sandals? You found something. Where?"

With her eyes still on the quill pattern, Koracoo instructed, "Show him, Sindak."

"Yes, War Chief." They stepped two paces away and knelt.

Towa stopped beside Koracoo. His long braid had come loose from its rabbit-bone skewer and hung over his cape like a black glistening rope. He squinted at Sindak and Gonda. "What are they looking for?"

"Another piece in a great mystery," she said. "Towa? The sandal tracks you found yesterday—did you see any evidence that the man was carrying something?"

Towa's handsome face went blank for several moments while he thought about it. "It's possible. There were several tracks where he'd slipped in the mud and had to regain his balance. He might have been struggling to balance something heavy."

Sindak and Gonda stood and returned.

Gonda said, "I swear those are the same sandal tracks we saw at the midden and the cornhusk doll meadow."

Koracoo nodded. For days now, she'd had the uneasy feeling that it was they who were being hunted. She'd dreamed last night that she was a snowshoe hare, running with a bursting heart, trying to reach a burrow before the wolves caught her. Were the Spirits trying to tell her something?

"Towa, you're a thinker. Think this through for me. If these tracks, and the tracks you found yesterday, as well as the tracks Gonda and I found at the shell midden and the meadow, were all made by the same man . . . what is he up to?"

Towa shrugged, but his eyes began darting over the sky and trees as he tried to figure it out. When he seemed to be having trouble, Sindak said, "Give Towa time; he'll figure it out. He really is a genius when it comes to analyzing information."

Towa gave Sindak a *for the sake of the Spirits, don't tell them that* look, and Sindak added, "Watch this. Towa, which of these things doesn't fit? A wolf, a fox, a dog, and a pile of shit in the middle of the plaza?"

Towa immediately answered, "The dog."

"The dog?" Gonda growled. "That's idiotic. Why?"

"Because dogs are the product of generations of careful breeding. Wolves, foxes, and the person who shit in the plaza, obviously are not."

Gonda and Koracoo stared at them.

Finally, Gonda said, "You know, these warrior things seem awfully complicated for you two. Maybe you should just trot along home and let us unravel the intrigue necessary for finding the children."

"You didn't think Towa was brilliant?" Sindak asked in genuine disbelief.

Gonda propped his hands on his hips. "Promise me something, will you? If you see somebody behind me with a bow, do *not* try to analyze the situation. Just yell. I'd rather learn about it through an incoherent cry than by choking on my own blood." He stalked away, back to kneel beside the sandal prints.

While Sindak and Towa muttered to each other, Koracoo concentrated on the sounds of the day. A riot of birdsong filled the trees, and the wind sawed lazily through the ice-crusted branches. Far in the distance, through a weave of trunks, Koracoo saw movement. She kept watching. The way they swayed, the bob of their heads, told her they were men.

"Find cover!" she ordered. "Now! Run for the trees!"

Gonda leaped up instantly and dashed away, his long

legs stretching out, heading for the forest shadows. He was accustomed to such abrupt orders, but Sindak and Towa stared at her as though too stunned to move.

Koracoo growled, "I ordered you to run! *Run!*"

Both men seemed confused, but they charged after Gonda, disappearing into the trees.

Koracoo raced in the opposite direction, pounding along, and stamping out, the tracks they'd made this morning when they'd left the ramada. She ran up and back, confusing as much of the sign as she could in the time she had. It wouldn't help much, but it might force the enemy to stop long enough that she could kill them.

When she spied a pile of deadfall in a copse of sour-gum trees, she dove behind it. The scent of damp, rotting wood filled her nostrils. A few scarlet leaves still clung to the branches and rattled in the breeze. From here, she could watch the trails in both directions and see across the clearing to where Gonda was hiding. And he, in turn, would be watching her.

Thirty-five

It didn't take long.

Less than one thousand heartbeats later, two men trotted up the trail, coming from the east. They had their heads down, tracking. They would have passed the ramada where Koracoo's party had made camp last night. The enemy warriors knew their prey was close.

Koracoo studied their plain buckskin capes and rabbit-fur leggings. They bore no clan symbols and had no distinctive designs that she could clearly identify as coming from any of the five Peoples south of Skanodario Lake. An old knife scar cut a white ridge across the tall man's ugly face. He was big, with meaty shoulders, and would be a formidable opponent if she had to face him. The other man, shorter and skinny to the point of looking starved, would be easier.

When they trotted to the place where she'd tried to obscure the trail, they stopped. They were less than twenty paces away.

The big man said, "The tracks go in both directions here."

"Yes, someone started running back and forth, as though panicked."

Skinny's gaze moved around the clearing, searching for hidden threats. He had a strangely narrow face, as though the bones had been pressed between boards when he'd been a baby. "Do you think these were made by people from Hawk Moth Village? Or is the old witch right and we're being followed?"

Hot blood surged through Koracoo's veins. The old witch? She clutched CorpseEye in a hard fist.

"I don't like this, Galan. If it weren't so lucrative, I'd say we just sell all the children and run home to our families."

Galan nodded. "Well, go, if you want to. But I'm staying. This war is making me rich. In another moon, I'll have enough goods to provide for my wife and children for the rest of my life." His gaze scanned the pile of deadfall where Koracoo hid. He seemed to sense something amiss in the shapes and colors. "Not only that, I can do whatever I want to, and my clan can never find out. How often does a man have such freedom?"

"Don't you worry that someday you'll meet one of the children, and she'll be able to identify you? I do." Hanu tapped the scar on his face. "Even twenty summers from now, I'll still have this."

Galan laughed. "Gannajero never sells children without a guarantee that they'll be bashed in the head when the buyers are finished with them. By the time she lets them go, they've seen too much to be allowed to live. Just make sure you do what you want with them before she sells them."

The desire to kill consumed Koracoo's flesh at the same time that grief drowned her heart.

These men were scouts. They must have been dispatched to search out Gannajero's back trail. That meant the children were not far ahead of them. Her odds of rescuing them would substantially improve if Gannajero had two fewer warriors.

All I have to do is follow their tracks right back to her lair. . . .

Probably. But they'd lost the trails many times before. Which meant she couldn't just kill them. A pity.

She was shaking with rage when she laid CorpseEye aside and nocked an arrow. Shifting slightly, she aimed at the big man's chest, and let fly. Before it had even struck his heart, she'd grabbed CorpseEye, leaped the log, and was pounding toward Galan.

The man saw her, cried, "No!" and raised his war club. His feet kicked frost into the air as he charged her, screaming.

Koracoo lifted CorpseEye just as the man swung at her head. When their clubs met it sounded like lightning cracking. He shoved her away, and Koracoo ducked, spun, and bashed him in the kidney.

"You bitch in heat!" he cried, and swung his war club blindly. "I'm going to kill you!"

Koracoo ducked the blow intended to crush her skull, and danced back. As she lifted CorpseEye again, the man shrieked a war cry and charged. She spun in low, cracking him across the kneecap. He staggered. Koracoo twirled and broke his right arm. Galan's war club dropped to the ground, but he didn't give up.

He shouted, "Gannajero will avenge my death!" and lunged for her, one hand shooting for her throat.

She didn't dodge fast enough. He body-slammed her to the ground and got his hand around her windpipe. As he squeezed, he said, "Does she have your children, bitch?"

Gasping for breath, Koracoo dropped CorpseEye, pulled a stiletto from her belt, and stabbed him repeatedly in the side and back. All the while, he howled and kept the pressure on her throat, strangling her.

Sindak and Towa raced toward her. Sindak cried, "Make sure the big man is dead! I'll take care of the other one."

Sindak clubbed Galan in the head and pulled him off Koracoo.

Koracoo sat up, rubbing her injured throat.

Blood poured from Galan's head wound, but he managed to smile at Sindak. Sindak lifted his war club to kill him.

"No!" Koracoo shouted hoarsely. "Don't kill him, Sindak!"

Sindak whirled to stare at her in confusion, and she said, "They were . . . Gannajero's scouts. . . . Make him . . . tell you . . . the meeting place."

Sindak's eyes flared. "Where are you supposed to meet Gannajero tonight, you piece of filth?"

Gonda ran by her, heading straight for the dying warrior, and fell to the ground at his side. He shouted in Galan's face, "Tell us! You have nothing to lose now! Tell me and I'll make sure your family knows where your body is!"

Blood poured down Galan's face. He stared up at Gonda as though he couldn't quite see him. "Too late," he said. "You're . . . too late."

"Too late for what?"

Galan chuckled. "Children . . . all dead."

Gonda seemed to go weak. He straightened for a few instants; then he balled his fist and slammed it into Galan's face, shouting, "Liar! You're lying! Tell me you're lying!" Gonda kept hitting him.

Sindak didn't seem to know what to do. He stepped away, then glanced uneasily at Towa and Koracoo.

Koracoo got to her feet and, holding her throat, staggered toward Gonda. The dead warrior's face was bloody pulp, and Gonda was still slamming his fists into his face. She put a hand on Gonda's shoulder. "Stop. Gonda . . . stop! If we hurry, we should b-be able to track them right back to her camp."

Gonda swung around to look at her; then his gaze shifted to the clear tracks they'd left in the frost. "Blessed Spirits. Sindak? Towa? Take their weapons and their packs. We're leaving immediately!"

Sindak and Towa obeyed, ripping the men's packs from their shoulders and emptying their quivers.

Koracoo mustered her strength and walked over to pick up CorpseEye. After she tied the club to her belt, she wiped her sweating face on her cape. Her throat ached.

"Sindak," she ordered, "take the lead. If the trail forks, Gonda and I will follow one path; you and Towa will follow the other."

"Yes, Koracoo."

Sindak took off at a slow lope with Towa behind him.

She started to follow, but Gonda said, "Koracoo?" She turned.

"Forgive me." He unthinkingly threw his arms around her in a hard embrace, as he'd done a hundred times. "I'm sorry," he said. "I was almost too late."

Somewhere deep inside her she heard Odion cry out, *"Mother!"* and she went rigid in Gonda's arms. He seemed to understand. Slowly, reluctantly, he released her and moved back.

They stared at each other. In Gonda's eyes, she saw barely endurable pain, and enough guilt to smother a nation. From the excruciating expression on his face, he must see in her eyes exactly what she was feeling: *nothing.* There was only emptiness in her heart. It wasn't natural. It was monstrous, and he did not understand it.

"Koracoo?" he said barely above a whisper. "Are you all right?"

"The frost is melting quickly, Gonda." She held a hand out to the trail. "Please, hurry."

Thirty-six

Odion

Ash from the burning longhouses floats through the air like black snowflakes.

I shove food into my mouth as fast as I can. We sit on the shore of a river lined by white cedars and scrubby bladdernut trees. I've heard the warriors call it Quill River. The water is covered with ash and reflects the lurid light of dozens of campfires. There must be three or four hundred men here. For the first time ever, Gannajero gave us each a wooden bowl heaped with food: roasted dog meat, freshwater clams and mussels, boiled corn gruel, squash, and dried plums. She must have Traded for it. Every warrior here swaggers around with a stuffed pack, smiling. More than a dozen games are in progress. Shouts and jeers fill the night. And there are many new children. Too many to count. Gannajero walks through them, selecting the ones she will keep. I try not to look. To feel.

The old woman ordered us not to say her name, told us she'd slit our throats if we did. For tonight, she is "Lupan." A man. I study her bloodstained war shirt and ratty buckskin cape. Her toothless mouth is sunken in over her gums, but she frequently utters throaty laughs—just like the warriors. Her disguise includes a headdress made of long black hair and decorated with bright feathers. If I didn't know better, I'd be certain she was a man.

Wrass sits beside me, picking at his food. He places a single mussel in his mouth and chews slowly, as though it hurts to move his swollen jaw. His face looks even worse tonight than it did at dawn. The bruises have turned black. In the flickering firelight, his face almost seems to be covered with short-tailed weasel fur.

I say, "Bog Willow Village must have had plenty of food stored for winter."

He answers, "They won't need it any longer. Eat as much as you can hold."

I shove an entire handful of roast venison into my mouth and chew. The meat is rich and tangy. My shrunken belly knots around it.

Tutelo leans her head against my shoulder and sighs as she sucks roast squash from her fingers.

Baji and Zateri have been sitting with their heads together, eating while they whisper. Zateri has removed her bag of Spirit plants and tucked it beneath her leg. She keeps scanning the many cooking pots around the campfires. When she sees me looking at her, she silently picks up the bag and crawls over. "Hehaka is out serving the warriors. Maybe if I can get this bag to him, he can—"

"No," Wrass whispers. "We can't trust him. He's been here too long. He may think some of them are his friends."

I nod. "Wrass is right. One of us has to do it."

"Which one? How do we g-get close?" Zateri stutters, and her two front teeth seem to stick out farther.

I look around our small circle. All of us are terrified. No one wants to volunteer. Least of all me.

Wrass puts a hand to his head and closes his eyes as he weakly says, "Whoever does it will probably be killed. All of you need to understand. Tomorrow morning, they will start asking who was close to the pot. They'll figure it out, and they'll come looking for the person responsible."

"But Wrass," I say, "there are so many warriors here. There must be a thousand blood feuds between them. Why would they suspect us? I don't—"

"They will, Odion." Wrass slits his eyes and looks at me. "They will. Just accept it." He takes a breath and lets it out slowly. "The poison will only be in Gannajero's pot. They . . . they'll come after us first."

I doubt this, thinking she must have too many enemies to count, but I do not say it—because suddenly, clearly, I understand why Wrass insists the person who does it will die. That is the price. Whoever volunteers must be willing to sacrifice his or her life for the rest of us.

I shrink into myself. My shoulders hunch forward, and I stare at the ground. *Not me, gods. Please, not me.*

From my left, Tutelo rises. I jerk around to stare at her. She is standing tall, with her chin up and her tiny fists clenched at her sides. Half the copper ornaments are now gone from the sleeves and hem of her tan dress. Frayed threads hang loose. "I'll do it," she says. "I'm little. No one will be afraid of me."

I start to object, but Wrass cuts me off. "Tutelo, you are very brave. But I don't think—"

"Wrass, I'm just young, I'm not stupid. I can do it. But . . . but will you promise me something?"

"What, Tutelo?"

A strange glow lights her dark eyes. "I don't care what

happens to me, but I want Odion to be safe. And Baji and Zateri. When the bad men start getting sick, can you get them away?"

"You would give yourself up? For them?" He has one eye closed, and slits the other.

Tears glisten on her lashes. "Yes, if you promise me you'll get them away. And get yourself away, too."

Wrass sucks in a deep breath and lets it out slowly. As of tonight, he is our undisputed leader. Whatever he says, we will do. But he is very sick. He can barely hold his head up. "Why would you do that, Tutelo? You have only seen eight summers. Why would you give up the rest of your life for us?"

She squares her thin shoulders. "My mother is a war chief. She would give up her life for any of her warriors. I always wanted to be like her, to be a war chief someday." She looks around the circle. "I can do it, Wrass. I want to do it."

My heart aches. But I do not say a word. Fear is gnawing its way through my belly.

Zateri tucks the bag of Spirit plants into her legging, edges forward, and puts a hand on my sister's arm. "Tutelo is brave, Wrass, but . . . I'm the one. I know how many Spirit plants to add, and I may be able to poison more than one pot. If I can do that, they won't automatically suspect us." She gazes out at the laughing warriors, and a mixture of fear and hatred tense her face. "The more of these men we can kill the better. Maybe some of the new children can escape. And maybe all of you can escape."

Wrass asks, "Do you know what they'll do to you if they catch you?"

She lowers her eyes, and her face flushes. "I'm not going to lie to you. I'm scared to death of what they'll do . . . mostly scared of what they'll do before they kill me. But I can stand it, Wrass. If I know you're all safe, I can stand anything."

A faint smile touches Wrass' lips. "What if one of us gets injured escaping? He will need you and your Healing knowledge. I think you're the only one of us who is not expendable, Zateri."

Zateri's mouth quivers. "But I—"

"You're too valuable. Not you, Zateri."

He does not look my way, but I feel Wrass thinking about me. Waiting for me to speak.

Baji sits up straighter, girding herself, and smooths long black hair away from her face. She knows from firsthand experience what the warriors will do to her before they kill her. How can she volunteer?

Baji says, "Me. I'm the one, Wrass. I'll do it."

"You?" I say. "Why—"

Wrass grasps my arm to stop me from continuing. He nods at Baji. "Baji may be the only one of us who can get close enough."

"Why do you think that?" I demand to know.

With tears in her eyes, Baji answers, "Because, silly boy, I'm beautiful. I can make the men want me enough that they'll carry me right into their camp and sit me down by the stew pot. No matter what happens, by the end of the night, I *will* have dumped the Spirit plants in that pot." Her eyes are stony, resolved to do what must be done.

Wrass studies her for a long time before he asks, "Are you sure about this, Baji?"

"Yes, it's . . . it's for my sisters. If I die, you'll carry my bones home, won't you? So I can travel to the afterlife to be with them?"

Wrass' eyes glitter. "If I have breath in my body, I will find and carry your bones back to your people. I give you my oath."

A trembling smile comes to Baji's lips. She holds out her hand. "Give me the Spirit plants, Zateri."

Zateri pulls the bag from her legging and hesitantly hands it over. "Baji, if you can, only use half the bag in Gannaje-ro's pot, then—"

"No." Baji shakes her head. "I want her dead. I'm going to dump it all in. I can't wait to see her writhing on the ground clutching at her throat and vomiting her guts out."

Zateri swallows hard. "All right."

Wrass' head doesn't move, but his gaze shifts. He looks at me with haunted eyes.

Pain constricts my heart like strips of wet rawhide drying in the heat of Elder Brother Sun. He's already chosen Baji, hasn't he? What could it hurt to tell him I'll go? He wouldn't pick me. He's already said that she's the only one who can get close enough. He wouldn't pick me . . . would he?

I sit as though made of ice.

Wrass lowers his gaze and looks away. The firelight casts the long shadow of his hooked nose across his cheek. "All right, Baji. You're the one. But you can't do it until later. After the warriors have been drinking corn brew and fighting for half the night, their guards will be down. I'll tell you when. Agreed?"

Baji nods. "Yes."

Wrass hangs his injured head. "Let's all finish eating and get as much rest as we—"

Kotin appears out of the crowd and walks toward us with two men. All are swaying on their feet, laughing and shoving each other. Having a good time.

When he stops before us, Kotin bares his broken yellow teeth and says, "You, Chipmunk Teeth, go with Pestis. He'll take good care of you."

Zateri starts shaking.

Pestis staggers forward. He is short and squat. His eyes are rolling in his head, as though he can't keep them still. "Come here, girl!"

Zateri seems to have petrified. She just stares at him with her jaw clenched.

Kotin lunges for her, grabs her arm, and hauls her to her feet. "I said go with Pestis!" He shoves her into Pestis' arms.

Her legs are trembling when Pestis drags her out into the forest, far away from the camp.

Not even victorious warriors would couple with a child. Gannajero must have sent out advance scouts to move through the war party and find the men with dangerous appetites. Or, perhaps these men do not know Zateri and Baji are still girls? Has Gannajero told them they are women? Baji could be mistaken for a woman, but Zateri . . .

"You, Standing Stone boy," Kotin says, and I jerk around to stare at him. "Go with War Chief Manidos."

The muscular giant squints at me and says, "He's a skeleton. Don't you ever feed them? I don't want him. What about the other boy? At least he has some muscles on his body."

Kotin eyes Wrass. Wrass glares defiantly at him and braces his hands on the ground to stand.

Kotin says, "You only think you want him. We beat him half to death last night. He'll throw up all over you."

"Oh, well . . ." The giant's lips pucker. "All right, I'll take the skeleton."

I do not move.

"Get up, boy," Kotin orders.

"No!" Tutelo cries and runs forward. She throws herself at Kotin, slamming her fists into his legs. "Leave my brother alone! Leave him alone!"

"You little wildcat." Kotin puts a hand on her head and shoves her hard to the ground.

Tutelo starts wailing in a high-pitched voice I've never heard before.

"Tutelo!" I cry and leap to my feet to run to her.

But Kotin catches me by the back of the shirt and swings me around and right into the giant's arms. Kotin smiles. "We've been saving him for you, Manidos. He's fresh. You'll like him. If you don't, I'll refund half the price."

Manidos crushes my hand in his and drags me away into the forest. My heart is thundering. He's in a hurry, walking fast, trying to get far away from the camp. I can't keep up and keep tripping over rocks and roots. Each time, he hauls me to my feet without a word.

Thirty-seven

Gonda trotted in the lead. Ahead, black smoke billowed into the night sky, creating what appeared to be a massive thunderhead that blotted out the campfires of the dead.

The People of the Dawnland called their country Ndakinna, meaning "our land," and it was a beautiful place, filled with towering tree-covered mountains and rushing rivers. Despite the stench of smoke, red cedars, firs, and black spruces scented the air with sweetness.

He slowed down to trot beside Koracoo. Her short black hair clung to her cheeks, matted by sweat. They'd been running most of the day. "The war party may still be there."

She nodded. "They will certainly be close by. Be especially careful. We are all so tired we're shaky and vulnerable."

Gonda forced his wobbly legs to climb the steep trail and trotted through thick pines. When he reached the crest of the hill, he saw the burning village. The sight was stunning. There had to be over one hundred houses. The pole frames had collapsed into heaps, and flames leaped fifty hands into the air above them. Koracoo stopped beside him. In the firelight, her flushed face looked like pure gold. She didn't say a word. She just looked out over the horrifying vista.

"Blessed gods," Gonda said. "I had no idea Bog Willow Village was so big."

Koracoo took a deep breath and coughed, then rubbed her throat. "A Trader once told me over one thousand people lived here."

By Standing Stone standards, the Dawnland People had a crude, backward culture. Their houses were partially subterranean pit dwellings made by digging a hole in the ground twenty-five hands long and around twenty wide, then erecting a pole frame over the top and covering the oval structure with bark. They lived in their pit dwellings from fall through spring, but abandoned them in the summer to fish the many lakes and streams and gather plant resources.

"The attack was brutal," he said softly, and scanned the hundreds of bodies that littered the ground. Crushed baskets, broken pots, and other belongings were strewn everywhere, probably kicked by racing feet.

"To make matters more complicated," Koracoo said, "there will be survivors roaming the forest, waiting for a chance to kill any enemy warrior they find."

"Which means us."

Sindak and Towa stopped beside them, breathing hard, and stared out at the devastation. Sindak's sharp gaze moved across the village, then out to the blackened spruces that fringed the plaza, and finally westward to the endless blue mountains. "Who attacked them?"

Koracoo answered, "Flint People, probably. They've never gotten along with the Dawnland People. Let's continue on."

She broke into a trot again, taking the lead.

As they moved closer, the gaudy orange halo swelled to fill the entire sky, and ash fell like black snowflakes, coating their hair and capes.

Gonda said, "This happened just a few hands of time ago."

They veered wide around the burning houses, passing them from less than fifty paces, close enough to see that most of the bodies lay sprawled facedown, as though they'd been shot in the backs as they'd fled. The coppery tang of blood and torn intestines was redolent on the wind.

Gonda trotted by the last burning house and out onto the main trail that led south. He'd gone no more than two hundred paces when he saw a new orange gleam in the distance.

He slowed down and lifted his arm to point. "If that's a warriors' camp, it's huge."

Sindak frowned. "Are you sure it's not another village?"

Koracoo said, "It's a warriors' camp."

Towa shook sweat-soaked hair out of dark eyes and said, "We lost the children's trail two hands of time ago when it was obliterated by thousands of footprints, but it was heading right for this village. Do you think Gannajero was bringing the children here to meet the victorious warriors?"

Gonda's knees trembled. *Don't think about it.* He

stiffened his muscles to still them and replied, "Victorious warriors always have plunder in their packs. That's why Traders follow war parties. If I—"

Koracoo interrupted him. "Let's stop talking and find out."

She loped toward the orange gleam. Gonda, Sindak, and Towa fell into line behind her.

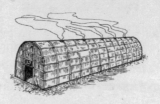

Thirty-eight

In the middle of the night, Wrass lifted his head and looked around. There was only one guard, Tenshu. The warrior had his back to Wrass, watching Gannajero and Kotin. The old woman stood thirty paces from her fire. In her ratty buckskin cape and long black wig, she looked so much like a toothless old man, it astonished him. She was haggling with an ugly little Flint Trader and gesturing to the new children. She'd selected five. They sat in a group, roped together, crying. Gannajero kept shouting and shaking her head. Kotin, who stood at her side, held his war club in a tight grip. No one was sitting around her fire. The pot stood unwatched.

Wrass studied Tenshu from the corner of his eye. Gannajero must have figured that Hehaka, two girls, and an injured boy wouldn't be a problem for one trained warrior. He glanced at Hehaka, Tutelo, and Baji. Despite the noise and shouts, they slept soundly eight hands away. His gaze moved over Hehaka, to the girls. They were pretty. Especially Baji. She was lying on her back. A dark halo of long black hair spread around her face. In another time and place, he might have asked his grandmother if he could . . .

Grandmother's dead.

Tenshu chuckled softly, apparently amused by Gannajero's contorted face and waving sticklike arms.

Wrass slid over and pulled the bag from Baji's legging. She was so tired, she didn't even move. He tucked it into his moccasin and rolled onto his hands and knees. The pain in his head almost flattened him. He closed his eyes for several moments and concentrated on breathing in the cold night air. It took all his strength to stifle the urge to vomit. When he felt a little better, he reached for a rock twice the size of his fist and clutched it in his hand as he rose to his feet.

As quiet as morning mist, he sneaked up behind Tenshu, who was laughing out loud now . . . and slammed the rock into the back of his skull. The warrior let out a surprised grunt. When he whirled, Wrass hit him in the temple as hard as he could. Tenshu staggered, trying to swing his war club at Wrass, but his arms had no strength. Wrass slammed the rock right into Tenshu's forehead.

Tenshu staggered backward, then dropped to his knees. Wrass hit him over and over, until he heard the man's skull crack. Wrass stopped only when Tenshu collapsed facefirst to the ground and his limbs started violently twitching and jerking.

Baji, Hehaka, and Tutelo scrambled up and were staring at Wrass with wide eyes. Tutelo started to cry, or scream, but Baji clamped a hard hand over her mouth and hissed, "Quiet, Tutelo! Be quiet."

Hehaka was watching with wide luminous eyes, as though he couldn't believe that anyone could kill one of Gannajero's men.

Wrass tossed the rock aside and wiped his bloody hand on his cape. When he'd managed to stiffen his legs and stand up straight, he said to Baji, "Run."

"What?" she said in confusion.

"Run. Now. All of you. Don't stop. By dawn there will be so many tracks leading out of here, they'll never be able to track you."

"But I—" Baji reached for the bag in her legging. "Where's my bag? I'm the one—"

"I'll do it. Now, for the sake of the gods, go."

Baji grabbed Tutelo's hand and lunged to her feet.

Hehaka rose unsteadily beside them. "But . . . where will we go? Who will feed us?"

Wrass' eyes narrowed. Was the boy totally unable to care for himself? "Baji will help you."

Tutelo struggled against Baji's grip, crying, "But where's Odion? I can't leave without Odion! Where's my brother?"

"I'll wait for Odion. You have to go, Tutelo," Wrass said. "Hurry. I'll take care of Gannajero and her men, kill them all, right down to the last breath in my body. But you have to save yourselves or it will mean nothing. Do you understand? My life for yours. That's the Trade. Now, please, get out of here before I lose my nerve."

Baji looked at Wrass with so much admiration in her dark eyes it made him a little dizzy. She tightened her hold on Tutelo's hand and vowed, "I'm coming back for you, Wrass. And I'm bringing a war party with me. Come on, Tutelo. Hehaka? Move!"

Tutelo opened her mouth to cry, but no sounds came

out. Finally, she whimpered, "Tell Odion I love him. Tell him!"

Wrass nodded. "I'll tell him."

Baji dragged Tutelo out into the trees and trotted away. Hehaka ran after her, but he kept looking back at the camp, probably searching for Gannajero. The darkness swallowed them.

Wrass staggered. The pain was almost too much to bear. He longed to lie down and weep. Worse, he was having trouble seeing. The campfires were blurs amid a sea of moving bodies and drifting smoke.

He forced his shaking legs to carry him over to Tenshu. After he tugged the warrior's club from his dead hand, he had to lean against a tree trunk to keep standing.

"I can do this," he hissed to himself. "I just need . . . to breathe . . . for a moment."

He thought about his father, whom he'd watched die at Yellowtail Village. The arrow had struck Father in the leg, slicing through the big artery. It hadn't taken long for him to bleed to death . . . but it had seemed like it.

Wrass hefted the war club, testing its weight. It was almost too heavy for him to wield effectively. Sucking in one last fortifying breath, he looked up at the campfires of the dead and whispered, "Please, meet me at the bridge, Father."

Then he slipped back into the trees and staggered through the shadows, heading for Gannajero's campfire.

Thirty-nine

Sindak looked across at Towa, then past him to Gonda and Koracoo. All four of them had flattened out on their bellies on the rocky hilltop overlooking the enormous warriors' camp that stretched along the western bank of the Quill River. Over one hundred fires burned, and each was encircled by a rowdy group of triumphant warriors talking, eating, shoving each other playfully. A group of captive children, roped together, huddled to the west, near the tree line, and on the northern outskirts of the camp, four fistfights raged. He also spotted three men coupling with captive women while their friends laughed.

Sindak slid sideways across the frozen grass toward Towa and remarked, "This is worse than the Wolf Clan longhouse at midnight."

Towa kept his gaze on the camp. "You're just jealous because my clan is the largest and the oldest."

"Yes, well, the person who said that being really old was a virtue had seen sixteen summers. Large, however—that could have been any male."

Towa ignored him. "From this distance, I can't see very clearly. How many warriors are down there?"

"I'd guess around four hundred, maybe five."

"Are they all Flint People?"

"Most are. But I see Mountain and Landing warriors, too."

Towa turned to stare Sindak in the eyes. "So, if we walk in there and try to grab a few children, we'll be dead in less than ten heartbeats."

"I'd say five."

Towa's mouth quirked. "Do you have any helpful ideas?"

"No. How about you?"

Towa rubbed the back of his neck as though the muscles had knotted up. "Well, if I run hard for ten or twelve days, I should be home."

Sindak nodded. "When you get there, put in a good word for me, will you? My clan matron, Tila, thinks I'm a coward."

"Sindak, I doubt that even your glorious death will be enough to convince—"

"*Towa,*" Gonda whispered, as though to shut them up.

They both turned to watch him sliding toward them on his belly. Ash had settled on Gonda's heavy brow, filling in the lines of his forehead like black paint. His chopped-off black hair stuck to his wide cheekbones. "We're moving closer. Nock your bows."

"Closer?" Sindak said. "Why? So they can see the whites of our eyes when they kill us?"

Gonda scowled at him. "We're not going to get that close, imbecile. There's enough firelight that if we spot the children, we may be able to shoot their guards and sneak in and rescue them before anyone knows it."

Towa glanced uneasily at the camp. "Forgive me, but even if our children are there, they're surrounded by hundreds of warriors. We'll never—"

"Look at me, Towa." Gonda glowered. "Try to forget your own hide. We're going to circle around the western edge of the camp, then work our way north through the trees, staying about ten paces apart. Do you understand?"

Towa's brows knitted over his straight nose. "Of course."

Koracoo ordered, "Nock your bows. We're leaving."

She slid backward down the hill and trotted for the cover of the spruces. Gonda gave them one last hostile glance before he rose to follow her.

Sindak pulled an arrow from his quiver and pointed it suggestively at Towa's chest. "Concentrate and you may actually get lucky and hit what you're aiming at."

Towa smiled and turned to the camp again. Warriors' faces gleamed with a rose-amber hue, and the echoes of laughter and songs rang through the night—but the whimpers of children and screams of the wounded thrummed beneath the revelry.

As Towa nocked his bow, he said, "It's a good day to die. But I don't plan on it."

Forty

Odion

I sit with my teeth chattering. Manidos lies flat on his back, snoring, two paces away. I can't seem to keep my head still. It keeps jerking, as though my backbone is injured. I saw a deer do this once. Father's bow shot had gone high, slicing the buck just below the spine. When the animal fell, its antlered head continued to jerk and thrash until it died. Father said his arrow must have damaged the deer's backbone. I reach around to touch my lower back. I can't tell. Everything hurts.

I glance around like a stunned owl. I should run. . . . I . . . should. But I only have the strength to pull Manidos' blanket close below my jerking chin. Manidos gave me the blanket. He said it was a present because I'd been a good boy. The blanket is made from strips of moosehide, and it's warm. The strips have been dyed red, yellow, and white and woven into beautiful geometric designs. It's very valuable. I can't believe he just gave it to me. I . . .

Horrifying images struggle to rise behind my eyes. I shake my head hard, trying to make them go away. "No."

He makes me lie down on my stomach. . . . His body is heavy, forcing the air from my lungs. . . .

"No, no, no," I whisper. "D-don't."

I try to stand up, but shake so hard my legs collapse beneath me. I hit the ground like an unfeeling lump of clay. It takes three tries before I manage to stand up again.

My gaze searches the camp. A few hundred warriors stagger about and laugh. The sounds of drums and flutes fill the air. Perhaps another one hundred warriors sit before fires, eating bowls of food. I smell the rich scents of roasted duck and sacred tobacco smoke on the night wind. My gaze lingers on their capes. Every color in the rainbow shines in the firelight. I see pure white doehide capes, and pure black capes decorated with seashells. Porcupine quill-work glimmers, and polished copper ornaments blaze. And their jewelry! Every throat is encircled with strings of beads, etched copper and human skull gorgets, and a wealth of bear claw and elk ivory necklaces.

Who are these men? Where did they get this wealth?

Something tugs at my memory, and I lift my nose and sniff the air. Despite the thick blue smoke that hangs in the air above the camp, I know the odor of burning long-houses. It is a scent engraved on my heart. A village is burning somewhere close by. They must have stolen the capes and jewelry. They . . . I—I remember.

My jaws ache. . . . He's holding my head in granite hands. . . .

A scream rises and strikes the backs of my clenched teeth. I do not let it out, but the effort makes me stagger and collapse to the ground.

My gaze moves haltingly over the camp, as though my eyes can only jerk from one place to another . . . and I see Wrass. He is standing with his cold hands extended to Gannajero's fire, warming them. His face is swollen and bruised.

One of his eyes is half-closed. A war club is tucked into his belt. . . . Why is he free? Did Gannajero release him?

A sudden cold wave flushes my body. *Where's Tutelo?*

I struggle to my feet just as Wrass starts walking back toward our place in the forest, and I stumble toward him, through the trees, paralleling his path. He doesn't see me for a long time. Then he whirls and stares into the trees as though he knows someone is there.

I call, "Wrass? It . . . it's me."

"Odion?"

I stagger into the open, and relief slackens Wrass' hideous face. He says, "Thank the gods," and runs to me.

He hugs me hard, and I start to cry against his shoulder, terrible wrenching tears that make me feel as though I'm suffocating. "Wr-Wrass, I—I'm hurt."

"I know, Odion. But you're alive." He strokes my hair and in a strong voice, says, "Listen to me. We have to run. This is our chance. Can you do it?"

He backs away and stares down into my eyes. It's as if the strength in his body is flowing into me through his gaze. I can feel it. My heart starts to beat harder. Hot blood surges through my veins.

I swallow hard and say, "Why haven't you already run? You should be gone!"

"I couldn't leave you here by yourself, Odion. Now, let's—"

Frantically, I grab his arm and say, "Where's Tutelo? Is she—"

"Right after I killed Tenshu, I told Baji to take her and run. She said to tell you she loves you. She should be far away by now, which is where you and I need to be."

I stare dumbly at him. "But where . . ."

Over Wrass' shoulder, I see Kotin suddenly look toward the clearing where we'd been sitting. Confusion lines his face. He says something to Gannajero, who waves him away and continues haggling for the new children while Kotin stalks toward the clearing.

"Wrass?" I hiss. "Kotin . . . he's . . ."

Wrass swings around to follow my gaze, sees Kotin, and orders, "Odion, move! Start walking; don't run."

"You lead. You—you lead, Wrass, please?"

Wrass moves past me and heads out into the dark trees, following a deer trail. I try to stay no more than one pace behind him, but his legs are longer than mine. I have to half-run to keep up. Wrass is breathing hard, and he's put one hand to his head, as though he's sick, but he moves swiftly along the trail, winding between enormous chestnuts and pines that seem to pierce the smoky belly of Brother Sky.

Behind us, I hear Kotin let out a sharp cry; then he shouts, "Tenshu's dead! The children have escaped! Waswan? Gather four of our new men and get over here!"

Neither of us turns around. Wrass walks until we're out of sight of the camp; then he starts running. We lunge down the trail, panting, scrambling through a thicket of nanny-berry shrubs, running with all the strength in our bodies. Ahead of us, a scrubby grove of prickly ash trees stands out like a cluster of spikes. Old autumn leaves have blown around the bases of the trees and created a pile ten hands deep and forty hands across.

Within moments, feet pound behind us, the heavy steps like a staccato of arrows thumping a longhouse wall, coming up the deer trail.

Wrass casts a glance over his shoulder and stops dead in the trail.

"What are you doing?" I cry in terror. "Keep running!"

Wrass grabs my hand, places the war club in it, then hisses in my face, "Hide in those leaves, Odion. If they find you, swing the club as hard as you can, and don't stop swinging. No matter what you hear or see, keep swinging. Do you hear me? I'm going to lead them away. I'll meet you at the fire cherry camp at dawn."

"But Wrass, I'm scared. I want to go with you! Let me—"

He growls, "I told you to hide. Now do it!" Wrass shoves me hard in the direction of the prickly ashes, and he breaks into a run.

I careen forward, stumble into the spiky trunks, and bury myself in the deep leaves.

I hear shouts. Men calling to each other.

The pungent scent of the moldering leaves surrounds me. I try not to breathe, or move. I see nothing. Pitch darkness. The leaves rustle softly when I blink my eyes. I should close them . . . but I can't. I must keep watch, even if only on the blackness.

"*The filthy brats!*" Kotin snarls. His feet bang against the trail. As he approaches my hiding place, I feel his steps in my bones. I tighten my grip on the war club. Another man runs behind him. His steps are lighter, more like a dancer's. "I wager it was that older boy, the one with the hawk face. I knew he was going to be a problem."

"He killed one of your best warriors, Kotin. He's no longer a boy. He's a man," Waswan says.

"In just a few moments, he's going to be a *dead* man."

"He's Gannajero's property. I'd think hard about that."

"Well, come on!" Kotin growls. "He's injured. He can't be that far ahead of us. Gannajero will flay our skin from our bodies if we don't catch them."

"She'll really miss the two girls. You'd better hope that new group of Mountain warriors finds them."

Their steps pound away up the trail, heading in the same direction as Wrass.

Relief makes me weak. Breath escapes my lungs in a rush, and the leaves crackle and resettle over my face.

Please, gods, let Tutelo and Baji get away! Let Wrass escape!

Painful, horrifying images of Yellowtail Village, burning, flash behind my eyes: people running . . . screams . . . flaming arrows arcing through the sky as I clutch Tutelo's hand and duck through the hole in the palisade wall to emerge in a big group of children and elders . . . then the mad rush into the forest, tripping, falling, Tutelo shrieks . . . warriors all around . . . nowhere to—

Odion?

I go rigid.

The voice is inhuman, the haunting song of wolves on a blood trail.

Odion. Are you coming?

Sobs choke me. My eyes squeeze closed in terror. How does he know my name?

Follow me, Odion.

As though my body is moving without my souls willing it, I brace one hand on the ground and I'm rising up, leaves cascading away from me. I sit amid the prickly ash saplings, holding the war club across my lap. After the blackness, the firelit forest seems almost bright.

"Where are you?" I call.

I'm here.

I see him. Shago-niyoh . . . the Child. Leaning against the trunk of a chestnut. A dark hooded figure. Is it a man? Or a Forest Spirit? He's tall, broad shouldered. Inside his hood there is only midnight.

Follow me, Odion, he says again, and turns in a sable whirl of cape and heads away through the forest, his steps soundless.

I look around. There is no other choice. I could try to find Wrass, but the warriors will be right behind him now. He may already be dead.

I stand on shaking legs and clench the war club to will courage into my terrified souls. Then I rise and stumble after him through leaf-covered rocks, and over slippery piles of deadfall. Shago-niyoh stays twenty or thirty paces ahead of me, close enough that I can keep following, but never close enough that I can really see him.

When I lurch through a tangle of old vines, I stumble and lose him. The snow-tipped black pine needles reflect the firelight, giving the forest a strange unearthly shimmer.

"Shago-niyoh?" The forest seems to be closing in around me, the trees bending down to stare at me.

A footfall rustles; a sandal crunches in leaves. *Warriors!*

I spin around on the verge of screaming . . . but I see only a faintly darker splotch in the night forest. Does he have a hump on his back? Is he an old man? As he moves away, on down the trail, he seems to walk hunched over, and there may be a walking stick in his hand. Clicks accompany his steps, like a stick tapping the ground—or claws on rocks.

I rush after him.

In less than two hundred heartbeats, he's far ahead of me. Very far. I can barely see him. I run, trying to catch up.

Silent as a shadow, he slides through the nightmare of dark trees, and I swear he's flying now, sailing between the trunks like an owl on a hunt. Wings whisper . . . but is the sound coming from him, or somewhere else in the canopy?

Tears trace warm lines down my cheeks. I batter my way through brush, fighting to keep sight of him . . . and my heart goes cold and dead in my chest.

Ahead, on the deer trail, are four warriors. Coming my way. He's led me right to a group of warriors. They are marching two girls in front of them, and I recognize Tutelo's walk. Her head is down. Baji walks beside her, holding her hand. Then I see Hehaka to Baji's left.

I spin around to look for Shago-niyoh. Where is he? Why did he bring me here? Why doesn't he do something? Tutelo is his friend, isn't she?

My gaze flits through the forest, stopping on every shadow, searching for him. Trees sway in the cold wind. Brush rattles.

He has abandoned me.

As the warriors get closer, I hear Tutelo crying . . . and Hehaka laughing.

Forty-one

Veils of smoke blew around Koracoo's tall body, drifting past Sindak, who walked ten paces behind her. He cast a glance over his shoulder and saw Gonda and Towa appear and disappear amid the trees. The tempting smells of roasting meat and frying cornmeal balls pervaded the air.

Despite the raucous voices, the clattering of pots, and banging of horn spoons against wooden bowls, there was a strange silence in the wavering firelit shadows of the forest. Wind Mother had stilled to a barely discernible breath, quieting the branches. No owls or night herons called. Sindak's steps upon the pine needles were ghostly, almost not there.

They had cut across two main game trails as they'd wound around the western side of the camp, and now approached a third. Koracoo took a moment to look down; then she aimed her nocked bow at the trail, telling Sindak to look when he passed, and she continued on.

Sindak slowly made his way to the trail. No wonder she'd wanted him to see. Small footprints covered the mud. Even in the dim firelight, he could tell the children had been running. His gaze followed the deer trail as it curved out into the trees, and his pulse sped up. Reflected firelight danced like leaping giants in the tamarack boughs. He swiveled to look back at the camp, where around thirty children sat—five huddled in a knot, roped together. The braided hide ropes around their necks and hands shone—then his gaze shifted back to the deer trail. Had the running children escaped?

He heard Gonda's steps closing in behind him, no more than five paces away, and Koracoo had gotten twenty paces ahead. Sindak aimed his bow at the trail, telling Gonda to look, and continued on. He had to hurry if he was going to—

Koracoo stopped. It was as though she'd suddenly turned to stone. She was so still her black hair caught the light and held it like a polished copper mirror. Deer did that—froze suddenly at the sight or sound of a predator.

Sindak held his breath, waiting to see or hear what had alarmed Koracoo.

In less than five heartbeats, four warriors carelessly walked up the deer trail. They were still fifty paces away. He glimpsed them as they weaved between the dark trunks of the trees. The men were joking with each other, chuckling as they herded two girls and a boy before them. One kept reaching forward to fondle the older girl's small breasts, while the little boy laughed.

Sindak saw Koracoo subtly pull back her bowstring and aim in the men's direction. He did the same. Behind him, Towa and Gonda had gone silent.

Just as the warriors rounded a bend in the game trail, a bloodcurdling childish shriek tore the air.

Sindak jerked, trying to see where it had come from, but he—

Thirty paces ahead, a thin little boy ran out of the trees, onto the trail, and launched himself at the lead warrior, swinging a war club that was much too heavy for him. He was off balance, struggling, but he surprised the lead warrior and landed a solid blow across the man's left wrist. Sindak could hear it snap from where he stood. The warrior bawled, "He broke my wrist!"

The three other warriors lunged forward, but the boy didn't run. He swung the war club with wild fury and cried, "Tutelo! Baji! Run! Run!"

From behind Sindak, Gonda shouted, "Odion? *Odion!*" and the name rang with a familiarity that shocked Sindak.

The warrior who chased me . . . !

The taller girl grabbed the other's hand and fled into the forest as the attacking boy ducked a blow aimed at his head, brought his war club around, and cracked it across his attacker's left hip. The enraged warrior let out a roar as he staggered sideways and bellowed, "You're dead, boy!" He lifted his club over his head and swung it down, but the boy parried the blow, though it knocked him flat on his back on the ground.

Gonda shoved past Sindak with his war club in his fist, rushing to get into the fight.

Koracoo shouted, "Gonda, no! Use your bow!"

Gonda ignored her. From the expression on his face, he wanted to kill these men with his own hands.

Sindak leveled his bow, but before he could let fly Koracoo's and Towa's arrows flashed through the air in front of him. Towa's missed and splintered against a tree. Koracoo's lanced through the shoulder of the man with the broken wrist, thrust him backward into his friend, and threw the second man right into Sindak's line of fire. He loosed his arrow, and it struck the man in the left lung. As he staggered, clutching at the shaft in his chest, Gonda leaped in front of him and bashed in his rib cage; then he whirled and landed a deadly blow to the throat of the man with the broken wrist. He yelled, "Odion, get out of the way!"

The boy parried another blow that drove his war club into his chest and, as though in disbelief, cried, "*Father?*"

The boy's attacker lifted his club for the death blow, and Koracoo rushed forward, twisting, leaping, swinging her legendary war club so fast that her movements became a supernatural dance. She spun and crushed the spine of Odion's opponent, then kicked his feet out from under him and brought CorpseEye down across the bridge of his nose with a shattering *whump*.

The last warrior pulled a stiletto from his belt and leaped upon Gonda, knocking his war club from his hand. Both men landed hard on the ground, rolling, kicking, trying to gain leverage over the other.

The boy, Odion, staggered to his feet and stared at Koracoo. He looked stunned, like a clubbed animal. Koracoo ran past him to help Gonda.

Gonda's opponent managed to get on top and was trying to gouge out Gonda's eyes when Sindak calmly nocked another arrow and shot Gonda's opponent through the head just as Koracoo swung CorpseEye to kill him. The man dropped on top of Gonda like a rock. CorpseEye sliced through thin air above him.

Panting, Gonda shoved the dead man away and clambered to his feet. He pivoted to look at Sindak, who still had his bow up, and gave him a grateful nod.

"Father?" The boy blinked at Gonda. "M-Mother?"

Gonda staggered to the boy, dropped to his knees, and embraced him hard enough to drive the air from his young lungs, saying, "Odion. Odion, I told you I'd find you."

From behind a tree trunk, the other little boy stepped out and stood gaping at them. He had a starved face, with dark eyes and a flat nose. "You killed them!" he said. "Who are you?"

In the camp, men had started to stand up. They must have heard the commotion and suspected it was more than an ordinary fistfight. A few warriors started drifting in their direction.

Koracoo ordered, "Towa, Sindak, help Gonda get the children to safety. I'm going after Tutelo and the other girl. I'll meet you at the overlook hill." She ran past Gonda and her son and lunged onto the trail with her feet flying.

Contrary to orders, Sindak was right behind her, pounding into the trees.

Forty-two

A sudden cold tingling sensation made Gannajero turn away from the man she was negotiating with and stare out at the clearing where Hehaka and the children who were not working should be sleeping. The wind had come up. Branches swayed and glimmered in the firelight. She did not see Tenshu standing guard.

"Ojib? Where's Tenshu?"

He turned toward the clearing. Ojib was of medium height, but wide across the shoulders, built like a buffalo bull. His nose had been broken one too many times and spread across his flat face like a squashed plum. "Kotin went to check on him. He's supposed to be guarding the—"

"Go find him."

"Yes, Lupan." Ojib broke into a trot just as several men on the western edge of camp rose to their feet and started heading in that direction.

The short, ugly little Flint Trader she'd been negotiating with, Tagohsah, said, "Throw in another five shell gorgets and they are yours." The sides of his head had been shaved, leaving the characteristic single ridge of hair down the middle of his skull. He'd decorated the roach with white shell beads.

"Five?" Gannajero scoffed. She glared at the roped children, who looked up at her with tear-filled eyes. They were *beautiful*. Worth a fortune to the men who craved them. "I'll give you three," she said.

"Done." Tagohsah gleefully rubbed his hands together. His anxious gaze flicked to her pack where it rested by her feet.

Gannajero knelt to retrieve the payment. As she pulled out the gorgets and tossed them onto the pile, she saw Kotin. He was walking in from the southern edge of the camp with Waswan, shoving the beaten hawk-faced boy before him. The boy had his jaw clenched. His hands were tied behind him.

Tagohsah chuckled. "It's a pleasure selling to you, Lupan. You have a good eye for child slaves. These are top quality." He knelt and began scooping the pile of wealth into his own pack.

Gannajero rose to her feet, and locks of long black hair swung around her wrinkled face.

Ojib had reached the clearing, along with two other men, and shouts rang out. Ojib bent down, as though examining something on the ground, then rose to his feet, looked at her, and ran back. The other two men remained standing over whatever lay upon the ground.

When Ojib arrived, he said, "Tenshu is dead. The children are gone."

"That's impossible!" she exclaimed. Rage flooded

her veins. She pointed to her pack. "Pick that up; then find Chipmunk Teeth, rope her with the others, and meet me at our camp."

"Yes, Lupan."

She tramped across the camp to meet Kotin and Waswan. The hawk-faced boy glared at her as she approached. Kotin flashed broken yellow teeth and called, "We caught him! Are the others back yet?"

"What others?"

Kotin's grin faded. He'd been with her for moons and could probably tell his life was teetering in the balance. "The Mountain warriors you hired this afternoon. They went after the girls and Hehaka."

The rage in her body burned like fire. "Hehaka is gone, too? I told you he was the *one* child that would cost you your life if he ever escaped!"

Kotin threw up his hands and cried, "I'll find him, Ga—Lupan! I thought he'd already be back. Just give me—"

Her attention shifted to the northern hill that sloped down to the river. Tilted slabs of rock jutted up between the spruces, ashes, and white walnut trees. She hated Dawnland country; it was little more than densely clustered mountain ranges cut by an endless number of rivers, streams, and creeks. It was exhausting to traverse.

She squinted. Something moved there—a glimmer. She scanned the hill carefully. In the sky beyond the hilltop, the campfires of the dead blazed and vanished through the drifting smoke.

Gannajero started to look back at Kotin—but she

had seen a glimmer. A cold shiver passed through her when it appeared again.

The blue sparkle moved among the spruces, disappeared, then flashed again farther east, as though walking down toward the dozens of canoes bunched at the river landing.

"Kotin? Do you see that?" She pointed.

"See what?"

"On the hilltop, you fool. Look!"

The sparkle flashed again in the branches of a mountain ash tree. "There! See?"

Kotin shrugged and shook his head. "I don't see anything."

Breathing hard, she clenched her jaw. She couldn't take her gaze from the scrubby ashes. Then, for a brief instant, the glimmer became two fiery eyes, and the hair on her arms stood on end. She could *feel* him turn to look at her. He seemed to materialize out of nothingness—a shape, blacker than the background sky, tall, wearing a long cape. His hood buffeted in the wind.

Then he was gone.

Gannajero lifted a hand to clutch her constricted throat. "We're heading south immediately, Kotin. Gather the slaves. Collect our payments."

"South?" Kotin said. "Into the lands of the People Who Separated? But we've never—"

"That's why we're going there! No one knows us. Find a Trader. Buy us two canoes, and let's be on our way."

Kotin shrank back from her anger. "Shall I hunt for the missing girls and Hehaka first, or—"

"I said we're heading south *now*. Forget them!"

"All right. I understand. I'll get things organized. But none of us have eaten, Lupan. We've been so busy trading—"

"That's true." Waswan nodded. He was sapling thin and looked half-starved. He held Hawk-Face's sleeve. "I'm hungry."

"The stew pot at our campfire is full. Feed the men quickly!"

Kotin backed away from her with his hands up. "Right away, Lupan. Come on, Waswan. You can help me collect our last payments; then we'll eat, and leave."

They trotted into the center of the camp, calling orders, assembling the new men she'd hired. Most trotted for the pot to eat, while Kotin and Waswan worked through the camp, collecting payments, dragging Hawk-Face with them. The boy was a nuisance. He kept tripping, sliding his feet, falling on the ground—anything to slow them down. Waswan ended up clubbing the boy in the head to make him stop.

Gannajero stared at the northern hill again, and an unearthly fear gripped her. She couldn't seem to get her feet to move. In the dark spaces between her souls, she heard him laugh.

"Don't witch me, Child!" she snarled through gritted teeth. "That's why I left you for the wolves. I did everything I could for you, and you betrayed me!"

The faint laughter continued, rising up from the darkness that lived and breathed deep inside her.

Her slitted gaze tracked across the camp, staring at the firelit faces of hundreds of warriors. Then she trudged to her own campfire and began arranging her packs.

Four of her newly hired men were gobbling down spoonfuls of stew as fast as they could, joking between bites. Two others were digging in their packs for their cups. Three of the men were Flint warriors; two were Mountain people—including War Chief Manidos, who was a real catch; and one was a young warrior from Atotarho Village. All were slit-eyed thieves with no honor at all, loyal only to themselves and the acquisition of wealth. *Perfect.*

Gannajero knelt to tie three packs together and saw Kotin and Waswan shouldering through the camp, dragging the roped children behind them. Whimpers and coughs filtered down the line. The last child, Hawk-Face, kept stumbling to the side to vomit. How hard had Waswan hit him? She wasn't sure he was going to survive the night—and if he did, tomorrow he'd wish he hadn't. The boy staggered along with his head down and his eyes narrowed in pain. Chipmunk Teeth—just ahead of him in line—kept speaking softly to him, but Hawk-Face never replied. He looked sick to death.

Kotin stopped in front of her. "We bought two canoes. They'll be waiting for us at the river landing."

"Good." Gannajero rose to her feet and growled, "Fill your bellies and let's go. We're done here."

"Yes, Lupan. We should—" Kotin halted abruptly and stared at the men.

She followed his gaze. Two warriors stood over the stew pot with their empty cups in their hands. Obviously they'd been just about to fill them when their gazes had been drawn to War Chief Manidos.

Manidos grimaced suddenly, then grabbed for his

belly. "I don't feel . . . very . . ." He walked unsteadily to the side and started retching violently.

"What's the matter with him?" Kotin asked.

"I don't know. Maybe he—"

Another warrior stepped away from the fire, bent double, and vomited.

In less than three hundred heartbeats, all of the men who'd eaten from the pot were on their knees or writhing on the ground. Manidos had both hands around his throat, clutching it as though to strangle himself. His face had gone blue.

Gannajero swallowed hard and backed away. Kotin and Waswan retreated with her, dragging the children behind them.

Softly, Gannajero ordered, "Tear their packs off their backs. Get everything loaded in the canoes, along with the children."

"But what about the men? They're sick. Shouldn't we try to—"

"Bring only the men who didn't eat from the pot. Leave the others."

She tramped away across the camp, shouldering between laughing warriors, heading for the canoes, wondering who'd done it. A rival Trader in the camp? Or one of her own men? A traitor who wanted everything for himself? It wouldn't be the first time she'd been betrayed by one of her own.

Gannajero's gaze involuntarily slid to the northern hill. "Isn't that right, Brother?"

She had to clench her fists to keep from shaking as she hurried for the landing.

Forty-three

Koracoo clutched CorpseEye in both hands and chased after Tutelo and the other girl, Baji. Baji was leading Tutelo at a dead run through the towering pines, sticking to paths choked with brush and no wider than the span of her own girlish shoulders, which made it tough for adults to follow her. The girl thought like a warrior.

Koracoo kept catching glimpses of their dresses, and thrashed after them. She battered her way through a thicket of nannybushes and charged ahead. Behind her, she heard Sindak curse as he followed.

"Tutelo?" she called loud enough her daughter might hear her, but not so loud the warriors in camp would. "Wait!"

As she ran, Koracoo shoved aside the fact that Sindak had disobeyed her order to stay behind. Between the weave of trunks, she saw warriors moving, heading for the clearing where Gonda and the others had been. They would, of course, be gone by now, headed for the overlook hill to wait for her arrival. But the warriors would go crazy when they found their dead friends. The hunt would be on. And there were so many of them.

A horrifying cry rent the night. Koracoo jerked to look.

At the western edge of camp, a boy had broken free and was making a run for it. Two warriors chased him, cursing at the tops of their lungs. In less than twenty paces, the lead warrior tackled him and knocked him to the ground. The enraged scream split the darkness. He fought wildly, biting and kicking until the big warrior clubbed him senseless. The man dragged the boy to his feet and hauled him, stumbling drunkenly, back to the other children, where he roped him to the line.

When the boy lifted his head, Koracoo saw his face. . . . Wrass. At least she thought it was Wrass. He'd been beaten so badly it was impossible to tell for—

"Koracoo, there! To the right," Sindak said.

She tugged her gaze back to the forest and glimpsed flashes of copper slipping behind the bare branches of an elderberry shrub forty paces ahead.

"Tutelo! Stop running!"

There was a moment of shocked silence; then her daughter called, "Mother? . . . *Mother!* Baji stop! Let me go! That's my mother!"

"It's a trick, Tutelo. We can't stop!" Baji shouted.

Koracoo leaped a fallen log, rounded the edge of the elderberries, and ran flat-out for the girls. They were now ten paces ahead. Baji was still dragging Tutelo by the hand, trying to get away, while Tutelo tugged as hard as she could to make her stop.

"Baji, let me go! Please, that's my mother!"

Koracoo called, "Tutelo, I'm here. I'm right here! Baji, please stop!"

Baji finally whirled around to look, saw Koracoo, and her eyes narrowed uncertainly. Tutelo dropped to the ground and started wrenching to get her hand free of Baji's grip. "That's my mother! It really is!"

Baji released Tutelo. As Tutelo struggled to her feet, Koracoo ran forward, grabbed Tutelo, and hugged her hard. "It's all right. I've got you."

Tutelo wept, "Oh, Mother, Mother," and buried her face in the hollow of Koracoo's throat. "Odion said you were coming. He knew you'd come for us!"

"Of course, Tutelo."

When Koracoo looked up, she saw Baji eyeing Sindak with murderous intent. The girl looked like she was on the verge of running away again.

Baji said, "You're not Standing Stone. You're Hills. You're the sworn enemy of the Standing Stone People."

"Yes, I am," Sindak replied. He slowly spread his arms as though in surrender. "But not today. My name is Sindak. I'm a friend to Tutelo's parents."

Koracoo rose to her feet, holding CorpseEye in one hand and Tutelo's fingers in the other. "Gannajero's warriors are on their way, Baji. We have to—"

Sindak glimpsed the man silently running toward them, his body flashing between the trees, but before he realized it was not Gonda or . . . a crazed Dawnland warrior rushed out of the trees with his war club raised, crying, "You Standing Stone filth! I'm going to kill you!" and charged.

Sindak shouted, "Koracoo, get down!"

She dove for both girls, dragged them to the ground, and covered them with her own body as Sindak raced by her to block the blow meant for Koracoo's spine. The crack of their war clubs sounded thunderous.

The enemy warrior roared, shoved Sindak away, and swung with all his might. Sindak ducked under the whirring war club, skipped sideways, and with all his strength brought his own club around to bash the man in the back of the head. The warrior reeled forward, weeping and mumbling. Sindak hit him again, and he collapsed to the ground.

"Come on," he said. "Let's get out of here! There's no telling how many more survivors there are out here who want to kill us."

Koracoo leaped to her feet, hauled both girls up, and ordered, "We have to run hard."

Forty-four

There hands of time later, they crouched around a tiny fire in the dark depths of a narrow valley that cleft the long mountainous ridge. Thick plums and sumacs surrounded their camp on the northern slope and kept them hidden from prying eyes. High above, the campfires of the dead wavered through a smoky haze.

Sindak sipped his spruce needle tea and scanned the dense branches of the staghorn sumacs. Scrub trees that grew four or five times the height of a man, they had dark smooth bark that reflected the multiple shadows cast by the flames. Beyond the sumacs, a thicket of thorny plums spread fifty paces in every direction. The sweet tang of rotting fruit filled the air. Most of the sharp-toothed leaves had, thankfully, been blown into the branches, leaving their small clearing almost bare.

Gonda kept feeding twigs to the blaze to keep the children and the tea warm. Despite their desperate situation, the muscles of his round face had relaxed. It made him look ten summers younger.

Sindak glanced at Koracoo. She stood five paces to the east, watching the game trail they'd followed to get here, while Towa watched the trail as it left the clearing and headed west.

None of them seemed inclined to talk, least of all, Towa. He'd been brooding over something, but they hadn't had a chance to discuss it yet.

Hehaka, Baji, Odion, and Tutelo huddled together on the opposite side of the fire from Sindak. From their expressions, Sindak suspected three of them would be standing shoulder to shoulder for the rest of their lives. All of them except Hehaka. The other children acted as if they had to watch what they said around him.

That intrigued Sindak.

He could tell that Baji was from the Flint People, and even if he hadn't known, he would have guessed Tutelo and Odion were Standing Stone—but he hadn't been able to place Hehaka's People. And the boy was . . . odd. His starved face resembled a trapped bat's, all ears and flat nose, with small dark eyes. The boy kept lifting his chin to sniff the air, as if scenting them to identify whether they were predator or prey.

Odion shifted, as though he'd come to a decision, and called, "Father?"

Gonda looked up. "What is it, my son?"

"Tomorrow. We have to go to fire cherry camp."

Gonda tossed another twig on the flames. "I don't know where that is, Odion."

"It's less than a day's walk away." Odion blinked and stared up at the night sky. After five or six heartbeats, he wet his lips, then pointed slightly southwest. "It's there . . . I think. I'll find it."

Gonda exchanged a curious glance with Koracoo,

who had turned to listen to the conversation. Gonda said, "I'm not sure it's safe to head west, Odion. What's at this fire cherry camp?"

Odion stiffened his spine as though to bolster his courage. "Wrass is going to meet us there. He told me. He'll be there waiting for us at dawn. He—"

"Odion?" Koracoo called, then hesitated. She turned and walked back into the clearing. Her red cape looked orange in the firelight. She knelt beside her son, and he looked at her with his whole heart in his eyes.

"Yes, Mother?"

Koracoo petted his dark hair. "Odion, forgive me. I was going to tell you tomorrow, after you'd eaten and slept, but . . . Wrass won't be there. He was captured by Gannajero. I watched—"

"No!" The high-pitched scream rang through the forest.

Sindak instinctively clutched his war club.

Odion leaped to his feet and stared at Koracoo as though she were a complete stranger; then he charged up the dark eastern trail like a man running for his life.

"Odion?" Gonda lunged to his feet and chased after him, calling, "Odion? Odion, no! We'll find him, but not tonight!"

Chaos erupted among the children. Baji and Tutelo stood up and started talking at once. Hehaka bent forward and put his hands over his ears, as though he couldn't bear to hear any of this.

When Gonda caught up with Odion, he grabbed the back of his shirt and shouted, "Odion, stop! We'll find Wrass. Just not tonight. Not tonight!"

Odion burst into tears and fought against Gonda's iron grip. "Let me go, Father! I have to find him *now*. You don't know. Y-You don't know what they'll d-do to him! I know. Ask Tutelo. Ask Baji and Hehaka!"

Gonda dropped to his knees and forcibly pulled Odion into his arms. Odion slammed his fists into his father's face and shoulders. "Let me go! Father, I have to find him!"

Gonda lifted his son off the ground and carried him back toward the fire.

Odion writhed and kicked, shouting, "Wrass needs me! Let me go!"

"Stop it. Odion, stop!"

Three paces from the fire, Gonda set Odion on the ground, grabbed his son's frantic fists, and held them against his chest. "Listen to me. We can't just charge into a camp filled with hundreds of warriors. None of us, including Wrass, will live through it. We need to think about it, to plan. You're a warrior now. Think! We'll go after Wrass in the morning."

Odion wailed, "You're lying! You're going to take us far away!"

"I am not lying! Tell me when I've ever lied to you?"

Odion's thin body was trembling. He swallowed hard and whispered, ". . . Never."

Gonda ripped open his cape and tucked his hand into his shirt over his heart. "I give you my oath as a Standing Stone warrior that I will never, *never* abandon another Standing Stone warrior being held in an enemy camp. I will find him and bring him home, even at the cost of my own life."

Sindak's gaze shifted to Koracoo. Her eyes had narrowed at Gonda's words, as though she disagreed.

Sobs shook Odion. In a choking voice, he said, "Oh, Father. Wrass saved me. If they find out what he d-did, they'll kill him!"

Gonda gripped his son by the shoulders and held him at arm's length. He solemnly stared into Odion's brimming eyes. "Then his name will be counted among the bravest warriors of our People, and I will honor him for the rest of my life. But I am not going to risk all of our lives foolishly. Do you think I should?"

Odion squeezed his eyes closed for several agonizing moments, then said, "No."

Gonda hugged the boy tightly. "We just need time, Odion. Time to consider how to—"

"Father, I—I understand, and I won't endanger anyone else, but I'm going after Wrass and the other children at first light."

Gonda shoved back to look into Odion's brimming eyes. "Alone?"

"Yes."

The bold confident tone of the boy's voice filled Sindak with awe. He had no idea what the child had been through, but it could not have been pleasant, and yet Odion was willing to charge back into the mouth of the beast to rescue his friend.

Gonda's eyes narrowed with pride. He softly said, "Sometime while I was away, you became a man, my son."

Baji stood up. "You're not going alone, Odion. I'm going with you."

"Me, too." Tutelo shot up beside Baji and clenched her jaw as though daring anyone to tell her she couldn't go.

Hehaka just hung his head and stared at the ground.

Gonda turned to Koracoo. "What do you say, War Chief?"

Koracoo's gaze lingered on the determined young faces around the fire. "There are many things we must discuss first. Both of you, come and sit down."

Gonda held Odion's hand and led him back to crouch before the flames. Odion waited with wide eyes for his mother's next words.

Koracoo gently smoothed her hand over CorpseEye and said, "Sindak? Towa? I was going to wait to make plans until tomorrow when we were rested, but apparently we need to do it tonight. You must have many questions for the children. Why don't you start?"

Towa marched forward, as though he'd been eager for this moment. "Thank you, War Chief."

Towa knelt beside Sindak, and his long black braid fell over his right shoulder. He studied the children one by one and said, "We're looking for a girl who was captured in a raid fifteen days ago. Was there another little girl among you? She has seen ten summers, and has long black hair that hangs to her waist." The children frowned at each other and shook their heads. Towa continued, "Her front teeth stick out like a squir—"

"Zateri!" Tutelo cried, and Odion and Baji nodded.

"Yes, Zateri." The elation in his voice was obvious. "So she was with you?"

"Yes," Baji said. "But her hair is not long. It's cut

short in mourning." She drew a line across her own hair to show how short, just below her chin.

Sindak leaned forward. "Is she all right?"

"She was alive the last time we saw her."

Towa bowed his head and exhaled in relief. He put a hand over the sacred pendant beneath his cape. "Then we must continue on, War Chief, though we will understand if you want to take these children to safety first."

Odion whirled to stare at Koracoo. "I'm going with them, Mother."

Koracoo stood for several moments, staring out into the darkness, before she heaved a sigh and said, "It's too dangerous to take the children with us. Dangerous for them as well as for us. They'll distract us and slow us down. I am inclined to send them back—"

"No, Mother!" Odion cried.

"I agree," Towa interrupted. "Someone must get these children to safety, while the rest of us continue on the trail."

"Towa's right," Sindak said. "If we aren't on Gannajero's trail at dawn, we may lose it forever. I suggest that you, War Chief, and Gonda take the children home, while Towa and I go after Zateri."

Tears silently ran down Odion's cheeks. "Zateri isn't the only one. You have to free *all* of the children. *All of them!* How are you going to do that? You need us. We know Gannajero's meeting places, and how she hides her trails. We know how she thinks, and what her men look like. You don't know any of these things!"

Sindak's brows lowered. The boy was right. Having that kind of knowledge might make the difference between life and death. "If you can describe her men to us, we—"

"No." Odion shook his head. "You have to take me with you."

"You have to take *us* with you," Baji said.

Sindak frowned. That little girl had a gaze that could lance right through a man's vitals. She was a born clan matron or warrior. He'd hate to have to stand before her in a council meeting ten summers from now. On the other hand, looking into those eyes across a bow wasn't going to be a pretty sight either.

"My inclination," Koracoo said, "is to send the children to Atotarho Village with Sindak, while we continue searching for the other children."

Shocked, Sindak objected, "But you need me the most, War Chief. I'm the best tracker, and I—"

Gonda said, "If any of us has to go, it's you. You bring out the worst in people."

"I bring out the worst in *you*. Let's look at facts: I'm not the one who's spent the past half-moon staring at his feet with his war club dragging the ground. And despite your woeful conduct, I've been nice!"

"That's what you call being nice? You obviously don't grasp the problem."

Sindak scowled and said, "War Chief, Gonda is the expendable member of this party. He should take the children to the closest Standing Stone village, and remain there until we come for him."

All of the children had started to whimper and

sniffle. Koracoo glanced around the fire. "Towa? You've been quiet."

Towa looked up from where he'd been glaring at his hands. "This entire discussion is irrelevant to me."

Koracoo's brows arched. "Why?"

"Well, you're not going to like this, Koracoo, but our chief ordered us to obey all of your orders—except one."

Koracoo's chin lifted. "Which one?"

"He said that if you ever ordered us to stop searching for his daughter, we were to go on without you." Towa watched her hands tighten around CorpseEye and added, "I'm sorry, but neither Sindak nor I have the luxury of retreating with the children. We must find our chief's daughter and bring her home."

Her gaze slid to Gonda, probably considering Sindak's proposal, and Gonda suddenly straightened. "Koracoo, think about this. You're asking one man to sneak through a war-torn country with three children and miraculously get them to safety. With two of us, it might be possible. But not one man."

Towa said, "He may be right. There are thousands of warriors on the trails."

Gonda added, "It's regrettable, but the children are probably safer traveling with us—"

"—right into the jaws of death," Sindak finished for him. "Really, War Chief, this is silly. None of us is safe if we're stumbling over children while we're trying to draw back our bows. Send Gonda away with the children."

Gonda leaned forward and gave Sindak a smile.

Sindak waited for him to speak, and when he didn't, asked, "Why are you looking at me like that?"

"I was imagining your head in a stew pot."

Sindak could suddenly see his own boiled eyes staring up at him. *Scary.*

"Well, then, there's another reason. If he's planning on murdering me, I'd rather not have him here."

Gonda laughed softly. "Of course not. Without me to keep watch on you, you'd be free to spend all of your time excitedly following your minuscule erection from one pipe stem to another—"

"Enough." Koracoo's eyes narrowed. She glanced back and forth between them for a time before she said, "I've made my decision."

They all fell silent.

She squared her shoulders. "We're taking the children with us, and leaving long before dawn. I want to be at the river landing just before sunrise."

"Very well." Towa nodded.

Sindak had assumed the children would cheer. They did not.

The silence stretched. The children glanced at each other, but there wasn't even a smile—just a sober realization that tomorrow would carry them right back into Gannajero's lair.

Only Hehaka reacted. He said, "You're taking me home?"

Wrenching sadness filled Koracoo's eyes. "Finish your cups of tea and get to sleep. We must all be well rested."

The children drained their cups and curled up around the fire without another word.

Koracoo added, "Gonda, take Towa's guard position.

Sindak, I'll wake you in three hands of time to take my watch."

"Yes, War Chief."

Gonda and Koracoo trotted in opposite directions and took up their positions guarding the trail.

Forty-five

Sindak threw another handful of twigs onto the low flames and glanced at Towa. His black eyes and straight nose had a pinched look. He fiddled with the hem of his buckskin cape, creasing it between his fingers.

"You've been brooding since we left the warriors' camp. What's wrong?"

Towa tilted his head uncertainly. "I'm not sure about this, so don't fall down and kick your heels in a fit."

Sindak sat back. "What?"

Towa spread his hands, palms up. "When Gonda and I were lying on the overlook hill waiting for you and Koracoo, I thought I saw . . . someone . . . maybe two people . . . down in that camp."

"Two people?" The expression on Towa's face made Sindak go still. "People you knew?"

Towa rested his hands on his knees. "I'm sure I'm mistaken, all right?"

"You've already said that. Who were they?"

Towa grimaced. "Well, the one I really saw looked like Akio. He was—"

"Don't be ridiculous." Sindak laughed. "He's too fat to have waddled this far."

Towa jerked a nod and let out a breath. "I'm sure I'm wrong."

"Why would he be here? After Atotarho made the deal with Koracoo, the elders decided not to send out the war party, so there's no reason—"

A hot tide swelled in Sindak's veins and rushed through his body. The logical conclusion struck him with the force of a war club to his head. "No," he said. "I don't believe it."

Towa ran a hand through his black hair. "I don't either. But why else would he be here?"

"Akio?" Sindak hissed incredulously. "The traitor?"

Towa didn't say anything. He just tossed another clump of twigs onto the tiny blaze to keep it burning. A bed of red coals had built up. It would continue to warm them for a couple of hands of time.

Sindak said, "You said there were two people you recognized. Who was the other?"

Towa ground his teeth for a long moment. His jaw moved beneath his tanned cheek. "He was an old man with gray hair, being carried on a litter by men I did not know. I never saw him step off the litter, but he wore a black cape with white ornaments—maybe circlets of human skull."

Sindak blinked. "Could you see his face?"

"No, I was too far away."

"Well, that's not much evidence then. Many people have black capes with white ornaments." But Towa had seen Atotarho's cape many times. He probably would not mistake it, even at a distance. It was a frightening possibility. In the back of Sindak's thoughts, Gonda's voice hissed: *You actually believe Atotarho sent you along with us to help rescue his daughter.* "And even if it's true, there's nothing we can do about it tonight."

"You're right."

Towa rose and went to his pack by the tree to pull out his blanket. He threw it over his shoulder and walked back to the fire. After wrapping up in it, he stretched out on his back, but didn't close his eyes. He stared up at the dark night sky.

Sindak ground his teeth for a time, then whispered, "Don't go to sleep yet. There's something I want to discuss with you."

"What?"

Sindak glanced at the children; then he swiveled around and, barely audible, said, "I almost fainted when I first heard Gonda call his son's name."

Towa's bushy brows drew together. "Why?"

"Do you remember the night I was late getting to the fork in the trail?"

"The night you were chased by the warriors?"

Sindak nodded. "I swear the man wearing the herringbone sandals was calling a name: *Odion.*"

Towa shrugged. "That doesn't mean anything. There are probably dozens of Standing Stone boys named that."

"But why would a warrior chasing *me* call that name?"

Towa braced himself up on one elbow. "Are you suggesting that he wasn't chasing you? He was chasing Koracoo's son?"

"I don't know what I'm suggesting. Maybe he was.

Or maybe he was trying to tell me that Odion was close, and I should follow him. I don't know, but—"

The pretty little girl, Tutelo, sat up and peered at them with large dark eyes. A halo of black tangles framed her face. She hissed, "It was Shago-niyoh. The Child. He's been calling Odion for days."

"You have ears like a bat," Sindak said. "Go back to sleep."

"It was Shago-niyoh," she repeated.

"Who's Shago-niyoh?" Towa asked.

Tutelo eased away from the other exhausted children and crawled toward them. She got on her knees beside Towa and whispered, "He's a human False Face."

Towa suppressed a smile. "Is he? Did you see him with your own eyes?"

"Yes," she answered firmly. "He's tall and has a crooked nose and a long black cape."

Teasing, Towa asked, "He doesn't wear herringbone-weave sandals, does he? That would answer a lot of our questions."

In a deadly earnest voice, Tutelo replied, "He wears sandals, but I've never seen the weave."

A chill tingled Sindak's spine. The little girl was utterly serious. He glanced at Towa. His friend had a skeptical expression on his face. Sindak shifted to prepare himself, and asked, "So . . . this Shago-niyoh has spoken to you?"

"Oh, yes, he came to visit us many times when we were slaves. He was trying to help us escape."

As though half-amused, but a little worried, too, Towa said, "Does he wear one of these?" He reached into his cape and pulled out the gorget. It was so big it rested like a magnificent shell platter on his chest.

Tutelo moved closer and reached out to touch it. "No, but . . . this is beautiful. Look at the shooting stars! Who made it?"

"Well, our legends say that two of these were created during the Beginning Time. The human False Face who is to come will . . ." His voice dwindled to nothing. He was staring over Sindak's shoulder.

Sindak jerked around expecting to see a war party rushing them.

Instead, Hehaka was sitting up. His mouth opened and closed, as though he couldn't speak. Finally his finger snaked from beneath his cape, and he croaked, "What—what is that?"

"It's a sacred gorget," Towa explained. "It chronicles the story of the death of Horned Serpent. There's no reason to be afraid. It's just a carved shell."

Hehaka shivered. "My father had one like that . . . I think."

"Your father?"

Hehaka nodded his head. "Yes, I think that's who the man was. I'm not sure. I remember almost nothing about my family or village. But I remember that. It used to swing above my eyes when the man bent over to kiss me at night." He hugged himself as though the memory hurt. "The last time I saw it, I was four summers. That's when I became Gannajero's slave."

As though disparate puzzle pieces were being pulled together from across vast distances, Sindak's heart thundered. "What's your nation? Are you from the Hills People?"

Hehaka lifted his nose and sniffed the air, as though scenting them again. "I don't know. Why?"

Towa started to answer, but Sindak cut him off. "No reason," he said. "Go back to sleep, both of you. We're going to run your legs off tomorrow."

Hehaka reluctantly curled up on his side, and Tutelo crawled back beside her brother. But instead of closing her eyes, she kept staring at them.

Sindak positioned himself so that his back was to her and his body blocked Towa from her view, then whispered, "It's not possible, is it?"

Towa gestured lamely with his hand. "It was seven summers ago. Why not?" Towa gave him a knowing look, stretched out on the ground, and pulled his blanket up to his chin. "Sleep, Sindak. You're going to need it."

Sindak exhaled hard and got to his feet. "Later," he said.

He walked up the trail to the east. Only Koracoo's head moved when she saw him coming. Her black eyes fixed questioningly on him.

Sindak stopped a pace away and folded his arms tightly over his chest. "War Chief, there's something I need to discuss with you."

Forty-six

Gonda's gaze shifted between watching the western trail and watching Sindak and Koracoo. They spoke in low ominous voices twenty paces away. Talking about what? Sindak was supposed to be asleep. Everyone else was dreaming by the fire. Though Towa kept flopping and twitching, the children looked innocent and peaceful.

Gonda checked the western trail again. The wind had blown a thick cloud of smoke over the top of them. There was no light except for that cast by the tiny blaze, and it flickered weakly, on the verge of going out. He couldn't see more than thirty paces up the trail. If he was going to stop any intruders, he'd have to hear them, not see them. He tried to concentrate on the sounds of the night. Wind sighed through the plum trees, and the few shriveled fruits that clung to the branches rattled. Limbs creaked. Old leaves rustled as they whipped around the forest.

And Koracoo's soft steps patted the trail behind him.

He turned. Short black hair blew around her cheeks, and he could see the tightness around her dark eyes.

Sindak walked back to the fire and rolled up in his blanket near Towa.

Before Koracoo stopped, he said, "What's wrong?"

She swung CorpseEye up and rested the club on her shoulder. After she'd ground her teeth for several moments, she said, "Towa thought he saw Atotarho in the warriors' camp tonight."

"Impossible. He was mistaken." Gonda examined her face. "But . . . you don't think so, do you?"

"Hehaka told Sindak that his long-lost father owned a gorget like the one Towa wears."

Gonda shook his head lightly, trying to figure out where she was going. "Who's his father?"

Koracoo's gaze lanced straight through him. "The boy is eleven. He was captured when he was four."

"So, seven summers ago . . ." He regripped his war club. "What?"

"Sindak told me that's when Atotarho's only son was captured in a raid."

Gonda felt suddenly as though he were floating. "Are you saying . . . wait . . . I don't understand. Are you suggesting that Gannajero is targeting his family? First his son? Now his daughter? Why would she do that?"

"I don't know, but I have an idea." She turned toward where Sindak lay rolled in his blanket by the fire. "Let's go ask some questions."

Sindak heard them coming and sat up with his blanket still draped over his shoulders. He rubbed his eyes. "I'm listening."

Koracoo knelt in front of him. "When we were in your village Atotarho told us a story. He said that when he was a child, his older brother and sister were captured in a raid. Do you know anything about that?"

Sindak shook his head. "No. However, everyone in our village knows that when he was twenty summers, his younger brother and sister, twins, were captured in a raid."

Gonda glanced at Koracoo. Her eyes had started to blaze. "He lied to us. Koracoo . . . he lied. What's he hiding?"

"Sindak, how old were the twins?" Koracoo asked.

Sindak blinked his tired eyes. "Eight summers, I think. It was devastating for his clan. If she'd lived, his sister would have become the most powerful clan matron in our village."

"What would have happened to Atotarho?" Gonda asked.

"As is customary, he would have married and moved to his wife's village."

"And," Gonda said softly, "the gorget that Towa now wears would have passed to his sister when she became clan matron."

Sindak's gaze suddenly darted between Koracoo and Gonda. "Are you suggesting that maybe she did not die?"

Towa had wakened and lay on his back, listening with his dark eyes narrowed. He said, "If she's alive, why hasn't she returned home to claim her rightful position among our people?"

Koracoo's face suddenly went slack, as though a horrifying thought had occurred to her. She slowly rose to her feet and stared down at Sindak. "Maybe that's why Towa has that gorget. He's supposed to deliver it to her."

Gonda, Sindak, and Towa gazed at her in silence.

Across the fire, Odion sat up. He didn't say a word. He just stared at them as though he finally understood something.

Forty-seven

Green water had been rippling by all night, scalloped here and there with starlit foam that spun off the paddle strokes of the warriors. Gannajero sat in the bow of the lead canoe, snarling at anyone who dared to speak to her.

Wrass, and three children he did not know, rode in the second canoe. Four warriors dipped their paddles and drove their canoe forward. They were moving swiftly, heading south into the lands of the People Who Separated, a group of rebels who'd broken away from the People of the Dawnland many summers before. The banks were thick with dark green holly. Just beyond them, leafless birches and elms grew. They cast cool, wavering shadows across the leaden river.

Wrass repositioned his hot cheek on the gunwale. His headache caused tears to constantly leak from his eyes and silently fall into the river. Before Gannajero had separated them, Zateri had thrust strips of birch bark into his hands and told him to chew them. They'd helped a little. When he could keep them down long enough. He'd thrown up so often his throat was raw and swollen. And he kept having blackouts—long periods where he couldn't remember anything.

A warrior waddled down the canoe, making it rock from side to side. Water sloshed, and whitecaps bobbed away. The man knelt beside Wrass. "You let them catch you, didn't you?" he hissed. "To distract them from hunting the other children? You're a stupid boy. You could be halfway home by now."

It took a gigantic amount of strength to lift his eyes to the man. "Who are you?"

The stars' gleam cast a pewter glow over the warrior's pudgy, florid face. He'd taken off every ornament and piece of clothing that would have identified his clan or People, and wore a plain elkhide cape and black leggings. Wrass tried to focus on him, but he was blurry, his face striped with the dark shadows of the passing trees.

"Gannajero says if you're not better by the time we make camp tonight, I have to kill you." He sounded unhappy about it.

A smile touched Wrass' lips. "That must be hard . . . for a coward like you."

The warrior brutally punched Wrass in the belly, and he scrambled forward to hold his head over the gunwale and vomit into the river. Nothing came up, but he couldn't stop gagging.

"Just wait, boy. If you think it's bad now, when I tell Gann—"

"Akio!" Kotin called. "You lazy fool, what are you doing? Get back to your paddle."

The fat warrior glanced at Kotin, then leaned over

Wrass and growled, "I know you were the one who poisoned the stew, boy. I saw you by the pot. I've just been waiting to tell Gannajero." He tramped away and picked up his paddle again.

The wrenching convulsions continued until the edges of his vision started to go gray and fluttery . . . and Wrass . . . he . . . he was . . .

Vaguely, he felt his body sink into the canoe, and knew his head rested on soft packs.

Forty-eight

Later that night, just before Koracoo was supposed to wake Sindak to take over her sentry position, Gonda filled his lungs with the damp smoky air and walked in her direction.

As frost settled over the clearing, the fallen plums resembled a field of small white river rocks. He tiptoed around the fire, which had burned down to a glistening bed of coals, trying not to wake anyone. Koracoo watched his approach with worried eyes. Every twig on the bare branches behind her was tipped in silver.

Gonda stopped a pace away and gripped his war club in both hands, holding it in front of him like the locking plank of a door that should never be opened.

"What is it, Gonda?"

His hands hardened to fists. "Please, just listen. Don't say anything."

She spread her feet, preparing herself.

When he began, his voice was low and deep. "You'd sent Coter and Hagnon out to scout that morning. They came back at dusk. Coter was wounded. Hagnon dragged him through the front gate and told me that the attacking warriors had let him through. They thought it was all a big joke . . . because it didn't matter what they told me." Her eyes narrowed, and he looked away. He couldn't bear to see the cold, impenetrable wall go up. He plunged on. "Hagnon told me he suspected there were at least one thousand warriors—"

She shifted to reposition her feet.

"—spread out through the forest, aligned for waves of attacks. I kept going to our elders, begging them to let me create some kind of diversion that would allow a few of our old people and children to escape, but they refused. They told me to keep fighting."

He expelled a breath. He dared not look at her now—not until he'd finished. "Two hands of time later the palisade was on fire in fifty places, riddled with holes; enemy warriors were crawling in, swarming all over like rats in a corn bin. I ran through the longhouses, gathered all the children and elders who were still able to run, and led them outside with one hundred warriors at my back. We—we fought hard, Koracoo." His voice was shaking. "Gods, it was terrible. But . . . some . . . a few . . . escaped."

She didn't say a word.

Gonda girded himself, and lifted his eyes to look at her quiet, tormented face.

"Gonda," she whispered with difficulty. "I should never have split our forces and gone out that morning." A sob spasmed her chest. She forced it down. "If I'd kept all six hundred of our warriors in the village, not even one thousand could have breached our walls. We could have saved . . . so many."

She turned away, and her shoulders shook as though there was an earthquake inside her.

For a moment, he just stood there. Afraid. Then he said, "Blessed gods. Forgive me, Koracoo. If I hadn't been drowning in my own guilt, I would have seen that you . . ."

He stepped forward and pulled her against him. How long had it been since she'd let him hold her? For a few blessed moments, he enjoyed the sensation of her body against his. "Don't look back," he said. "If we start looking back, it's all we'll be able to do."

Slowly, Koracoo's arms went around his back, and she clutched him so hard her arms shuddered.

"You lied to me, didn't you?" he asked.

"About what?"

"You told me your greatest fear was the same as mine, that you'd fail to protect your family . . . but that's not true, is it?"

She hesitated. "No."

"No," he softly repeated. "Of course not. You are war chief. Your greatest duty is to keep your village safe."

He could see it all so clearly now. The fear that tied her soul to her body was that she would fail to protect her People. In her heart, she must be swimming toward a shore she couldn't even see.

Gonda kissed her hair, and it was as if a gentle, cool hand were stealing over his wounded souls. He could feel the quiet hush of the autumn evening in the mountains and smell the pleasant fragrance of burning plum branches. The peaceful faces of the children reflected the fluttering firelight. They would never be able to go home. They no longer had a home to go to.

He hugged Koracoo tighter. He didn't want to think of that now. All he wanted was a place where they could lick their wounds, a quiet place to heal, and try to imagine a future.

Against his shoulder, Koracoo said, "Tomorrow, we'll find the rest of the children."

He took a deep breath.

"Yes," he answered. "We will."

Forty-nine

Stand up, Odion. It's time.

Sky Messenger lowered the trembling hands that covered his face and fought to blot out the images. He was jerking and twitching, still hurting, just as his child's body had the night of Manidos' assault. He filled his lungs with air and let it out slowly, then lifted his blurry gaze to look up at Sonon. The creature's quartz-crystal eyes shimmered in the black frame of his hood. "Now? Already?"

Yes.

Sky Messenger picked up his walking stick and used it to brace himself as he staggered to his feet. To the east, he saw the trail he'd walked to get here. It was long and twisting. It slithered through the vast forests like a dark serpent, scaled impossible cliffs, and fought its way across wide, rushing rivers. Had it been so difficult?

Yes, perhaps it had. He remembered how, at the age of eleven summers, the mysteries had been physically painful. He'd been sick with dread, wondering what had happened to Agres' baby sister, and trying to decipher the mystery of the two gorgets. The most powerful mystery of all, of course, had been the identity of the strange bone-carrying creature that pursued him. If any of them had known at the time that one of those little boys was destined to don a cape of white clouds and ride the winds of destruction across the face of the land, or that the strange creature would . . .

Let's walk together, Odion.

He bowed his head and nodded. "I'm ready. Take me."

Sonon turned westward. Elder Brother Sun's shining face had torched the evening horizon. The Cloud People blazed as though burning, and a swath of crimson blanketed the sky just above the bridge. Birdsong filled the fragrant air.

For a few blessed moments, Sky Messenger watched the flocks of wrens and finches fluttering over the bridge. Some of the birds perched upon the planks with their feathers fluffed out. The white-tailed doe stood a short distance away, grazing serenely. And the young wolf sat on his haunches in front of the bridge, his tail wagging, guarding the path, as he had always done.

. . . *Gitchi*—yes, his name is Gitchi, which meant "great." The wolf had earned that name a thousand times over.

Sky Messenger propped his walking stick and started toward the bridge.

He'd taken less than ten steps when he realized that Sonon was not following him, and looked back. The Spirit stood tall in the middle of the trail, his black cape gently blowing around him.

"Are you coming?"

The Spirit did not answer. His quartz-crystal eyes had gone dark. Only a smoky gray haze filled his hood.

A strange chill prickled Sky Messenger's wrinkled skin. He shivered. "What's wrong?"

Something was wrong; he could feel it.

Sky Messenger walked back. Just before he reached Sonon, he saw something on the ground, and stopped.

The bones of a human hand thrust up through the soil, the fingers extended as though they'd clawed their way up through the earth just to reach out to him.

"What's this?"

The Spirit remained quiet.

Sky Messenger scanned the leaf-strewn soil. Other bones lay exposed, scattered along an irregular line—a line beyond which Sonon did not seem able to pass.

Sky Messenger looked up into Sonon's dark hood. The shining eyes were no longer blazing quartz, but filled with tears.

"Did you want me to find this, old friend? Is that why I'm here?"

Sonon's hood buffeted in the wind as he walked back up the twisting trail into towering sycamores.

Sky Messenger watched him until he vanished. . . . Then he gazed back at the bridge. Gitchi stood up and whimpered, calling to him. All the birds that had been perched on the planks took wing and circled, waiting.

"I'm such an old fool. Why did it take me so long to understand?"

He held onto his walking stick as he lowered himself to his knees and spread his cape like a blanket before him.

One by one, he picked up the bones and placed them on his cape, then moved on down the line and picked up more. They were old, fragile. Some crumbled in his hands. He soon found his cape covered with bone slivers. When he'd collected every fragment he could find, he folded the hem of his cape to create a basket for the bones, and grunted to his feet.

"I'll make sure you reach the Land of the Dead," he whispered. "Your work here is done, old friend."

Sky Messenger swung around to face the bridge. The planks had picked up the fading rays of sunlight and gleamed as though sheathed with liquid amber. He steeled himself, and started forward.

Gitchi barked and leaped. His ears were pricked, and his tail ferociously sliced the air.

"Yes, boy, I'm finally coming."

Authors' Note

The next four books are going to be a little different than what you're used to in the People series. *People of the Longhouse* and *The Dawn Country* will be a duology focusing on the early lives of two of the most important, and least known, heroes in world history: Dekanawida and Hiyawento.

The second duology, *The Broken Land* and *The Black Sun*, will chronicle their later lives, along with telling the story of Jigonsaseh, who can justifiably be called "The Mother of American Democracy."

Without these three people and their struggle for peace in fifteenth-century North America, it's doubtful that any of the ideals we cherish as free people would exist today.

Selected Bibliography

Bruchac, Joseph.
   Iroquois Stories: Heroes and Heroines, Monsters and Magic. Freedom, Calif.: The Crossing Press, 1985.
Calloway, Colin G.
   The Western Abenakis of Vermont, 1600–1800. Norman: University of Oklahoma Press, 1990.
Custer, Jay F.
   Delaware Prehistoric Archaeology: An Ecological Approach. Cranberry, N.J.: Associated University Presses, 1984.
Dye, David H.
   War Paths, Peace Paths: An Archaeology of Cooperation and Conflict in Native Eastern North America. Lanham, Md.: AltaMira Press, 2009.
Ellis, Chris J., and Neal Ferris, eds.
   The Archaeology of Southern Ontario to A.D. 1650. London, Ontario, Canada: Occasional Papers of the London Chapter, OAS Number 5, 1990.
Elm, Demus, and Harvey Antone.
   The Oneida Creation Story. Lincoln: University of Nebraska, 2000.
Englebrecht, William.
   Iroquoia: The Development of a Native World. Syracuse: Syracuse University Press, 2003.
Fagan, Brian M.
   Ancient North America. The Archaeology of a Continent. 4th ed. London: Thames and Hudson Press, 2005.

Fenton, William N.
   The False Faces of the Iroquois. Norman: University of
   Oklahoma Press, 1987.

———.

   *The Iroquois Eagle Dance. An Offshoot of the Calumet
   Dance.* Syracuse: Syracuse University Press, 1991.

Foster, Steven, and James A. Duke.
   Eastern/Central Medicinal Plants. The Peterson Guides
   Series. Boston: Houghton Mifflin Company, 1990.

Hart, John P., and Christina B. Rieth.
   *Northeast Subsistence-Settlement Change: A.D. 700–
   1300.* Bulletin 496. Albany: New York State Museum,
   2002.

Herrick, James W.
   Iroquois Medical Botany. Syracuse: Syracuse University
   Press, 1995.

Jennings, Francis.
   The Ambiguous Iroquois Empire. New York: W.W. Norton, 1984.

Jennings, Francis, ed.
   The History and Culture of Iroquois Diplomacy. Syracuse: Syracuse University Press, 1995.

Kurath, Gertrude P.
   *Iroquois Music and Dance: Ceremonial Arts of Two
   Seneca Longhouses.* Smithsonian Institution, Bureau of
   American Ethnology, Bulletin 187. Washington, D.C.:
   U.S. Government Printing Office, 1964.

Levine, Mary Ann, Kenneth E. Sassaman, and Michael S.
Nassaney, eds.
   The Archaeological Northeast. Westport, Conn.: Bergin
   and Garvey, 1999.

Mann, Barbara A., and Jerry L. Fields.

"A Sign in the Sky: Dating the League of the Haudenosaunee." http://www.wampumchronicles.com/signinthesky.html.

Martin, Calvin.

Keepers of the Game. Indian-Animal Relationships and the Fur Trade. Berkeley: University of California Press, 1978.

Miroff, Laurie E., and Timothy D. Knapp.

Iroquoian Archaeology and Analytic Scale. Knoxville: University of Tennessee Press, 2009.

Morgan, Lewis Henry.

League of the Iroquois. New York: Corinth Books, 1962.

Mullen, Grant J., and Robert D. Hoppa.

"Rogers Ossuary (AgHb-131): An Early Ontario Iroquois Burial Feature from Brantford Township." *The Canadian Journal of Archaeology/Journal Canadien d'Archeologie* 16 (1992).

Parker, A. C.

Iroquois Uses of Maize and Other Food Plants. Bulletin 144. Albany: New York State Museum, 1910.

Parker, Arthur C.

Seneca Myths and Folk Tales. Lincoln: University of Nebraska, 1989.

Richter, Daniel.

The Ordeal of the Longhouse: The People of the Iroquois League in the Era of European Colonization. Chapel Hill: University of North Carolina Press, 1992.

Snow, Dean.

The Archaeology of New England. New York: Academic Press, 1980.

————.

   The Iroquois. Oxford: Blackwell, 1996.

Spittal, W. G.

   Iroquois Women: An Anthology. Ontario, Canada: Iro-
   qrafts, 1990.

Talbot, Francis Xavier.

   Saint Among the Hurons: The Life of Jean De Brébeuf.
   New York: Harper and Brothers, 1949.

Trigger, Bruce.

   *The Children of Aataentsic: A History of the Huron People
   to 1660.* Montreal: McGill-Queen's University Press, 1987.

Trigger, Bruce, ed.

   Handbook of North American Indians, Vol. 15: Northeast.
   Washington, D.C.: Smithsonian Institution Press, 1978.

Tuck, James A.

   *Onondaga Iroquois Prehistory: A Study in Settlement Ar-
   chaeology.* New York: Syracuse University Press, 1971.

Wallace, Anthony F. C.

   The Death and Rebirth of the Seneca. New York: Vintage
   Books, 1972.

Walthall, John A., and Thomas E. Emerson, eds.

   *Calumet and Fleur-de-Lys: Archaeology of the Indian
   and French Contact in the Midcontinent.* Washington,
   D.C.: Smithsonian Institution Press, 1992.

Whitehead, Ruth Holmes.

   Stories from the Six Worlds: Micmac Legends. Halifax:
   Nimbus Publishing, 1988.

Williamson, Ronald F., and Susan Pfeiffer.

   *Bones of the Ancestors: The Archaeology and Osteobiogra-
   phy of the Moatfield Ossuary.* Gatineau, Quebec: Canadian
   Museum of Civilization, 2003.

For those interested in a good general overview of Iroquoian prehistory, we recommend chapter 21 of Brian Fagan's excellent book *Ancient North America*. This book is often updated, so you'll want to make certain you get the latest edition.

Also, those who want to know more about how American democracy came from the League of the Iroquois, please read the foreword and afterword in *People of the Masks*. There are references in the bibliography that will help, as well, particularly Bruce Johansen's book *Forgotten Founders*.

Thanks for caring about our nation's rich past.